Nevi'im

Nevi'im

Post-Self book III

Madison Scott-Clary

Also by Madison Scott-Clary

Arcana — A Tarot Anthology, ed.

Rum and Coke — Three Short Stories from a Furry Convention

Eigengrau — Poems 2015-2020

ally

Post-Self
I. *Qoheleth*
II. *Toledot*
III. *Nevi'im*
IV. *Mitzvot*

Sawtooth
Restless Town
A Wildness of the Heart

Learn more at *makyo.ink/publications*

ISBN: 978-1-948743-25-9

Nevi'im

Cover © Iris Jay, 2022 — irisjay.net

First Edition, 2022. All rights reserved.

This book uses the fonts Gentium Book Basic, Gotu and Linux Biolinum O and was typeset with X${}_{\exists}$L^{A}T${}_{E}$X.

If you race only with foot-runners and they exhaust you, how then can you compete with horses? If you are secure only in a tranquil land, how will you fare in the jungle of the Jordan?

— Jeremiah 12:5

Prologue

Upon looking at the sky, many saw the stars and supposed that they must be the campfires of others. How far away they must be, to be such small points of light! Mere pinpricks in the black fabric of the night. They looked up, saw the campfires, and considered that they themselves might be just as the others were, looking out into the night and considering their own fire with dreaming minds.

From *An Expanded Mythology of Our World* by
May Then My Name Die With Me of the Ode clade

RJ Brewster — 2114

There was some draw, some appeal to Dr. Ramirez. At first, RJ suspected that it was the quiet intensity of her confidence, the way she moved through the world with a hunger for knowledge that was at all times colored by the light of the desire to do right by the world as a whole. Then, ey thought that it might simply be that she was a good person. She was the one who believed hard enough and strong enough to follow up on the lost. She was the one who had actually tried, had actually moved forward at a pace that meant progress on the case. Recently, ey had been thinking that it was something more abstract than that.

Concrete? Abstract? The line had long since blurred to meaninglessness.

Ey had been lost for something beyond an eternity, for 'eternity' implied the existence of time, or at least a form of time that actually meant something. Ey had been lost for a day longer than forever, and had ey been lost for only hours, as Sasha had, it would have been longer still. Even then, the word 'longer' held far too much savor. It burned in the sinuses and left eir eyes stinging with tears.

She had been the first one in more than forever that ey had seen. She had been the one who broke through the wall of eir solipsistic existence and encouraged em to reengage with the world. As the orbits of eir life grew smaller and smaller, they had collapsed into a wandering figure-eight around Sasha, the one who made em complete, and Carter, the one who tied em to reality.

And so it was that, even beyond the meetings and interviews, beyond the panels and studies, ey found emself staying in touch with her. Once a week or two, ey would make the long walk from eir flat down to the cluster of UCL buildings and wait until she was free for lunch or dinner, or, had ey yet again forgotten the meaning of time, wait for her to arrive at work early in the morning so that they could get coffee together.

She had not questioned it at all. Even that first time, after ey had hunted down her office in the UCL directory and arrived, unannounced, outside of it to wait awkwardly until she pulled back from her rig. She had simply smiled, shaken eir hand, and they had gone out for an afternoon cup of coffee with no further discussion. It had simply become the thing that they did every now and then.

Perhaps that was why ey liked her? Maybe.

Today, at lunch, ey joined Carter and two of her coworkers, Prakash Das and Avery Wilkins. Vietnamese had been the order of the day, and each of them had consoled em in turn about the loss of eir dear Priscilla, the cat who had been the only other grounding factor in eir life these last two years. A sudden loss of appetite, and then a sudden loss of life, and now ey needed the comfort of friends—or whatever it was that Carter had become—and some noise other than quiet jazz and London streets.

To their condolences, ey had simply raised eir cup of tea and nodded to them, saying, "To deny the end is to deny all beginnings."

"Delphic, as ever," Prakash said, though his smile and the lift of his own glass took any sting out of the words.

Ey smiled too, though ey could feel exhaustion tugging at eir cheeks. Ey had slept, ey knew, but did not remember when. "Oh, trust me, there is plenty more where that came from."

"Where *does* it come from?" Avery asked.

"I am not sure." Ey sipped at eir tea, still too hot to drink comfortably. "Whatever wellspring that was unstoppered in...in there."

"Seems like it stuck around."

Ey nodded.

"Think you'll ever turn it into something?" Avery grinned to em. "You know, write a book. Something like that."

"I had not thought of that. I do not know that I could make a plot out of what feels like millions of words in a rock tumbler. Perhaps a poem."

"Even infinite monkeys," Carter said, as she always did whenever the topic came up. She, of all of them, knew best. She had been in there with em for a few minutes or a few eternities. Another reason to like her. "Either way, you look thrashed, RJ. You sleeping okay?"

"No. Maybe. I do not know."

Perhaps sensing some emotion deeper than exhaustion laying beneath the equivocation, the table fell silent, and ey once again looked out the window into the greying afternoon, thumb-tip tapping rhythmically along each of the contacts on the middle joints of eir fingers.

Once the food arrived, the mood loosened up, and ey was able to smile and laugh and take part in the conversation, and even managed to apologize for being a damper on lunch only twice.

Spring rolls and phở occupied their attention for a while, then, and they ate in silence except for the occasional 'good soup' and other such nothing compliments.

The time neared one o'clock, whatever that meant, and they settled up the bill and took the remainder of their conversation outside, hands stuffed in pockets while clouds of steam preceded them.

More laughter, more companionship. More warmth, despite the cold.

Perhaps this is why, ey thought. *Perhaps Carter and all of those she has introduced to me can add at least a little bit of warmth into the winter of my life.*

No, no, must not think such things. Ey had made eir decision, had ey not?

At the door to the building where the three worked, they all exchanged hugs, another bright spark of warmth in the cold afternoon, enough to carry em back home. Empty home, where ey could listen to more jazz and the distinct lack of purring. Empty home where ey could stare at eir rig and dare emself to delve in, if only to see if Sasha was about after work. Before work? What time was it for her? Time had left em; ey had only words.

Perhaps sleep.

Ey made it a block away before ey heard the sound of jogging behind em, and stepped over closer to the wall to let the jogger pass. The sound slowed, however, and ey was greeted once more by Prakash.

"Hey RJ, mind if I walk with you for a bit?"

"Sure." Ey frowned. "Do you not have work?"

He shrugged. "I do, but I'm getting sick of being cooped up. Begged an additional hour off to just get out for a bit."

"Alright."

A silence stretched for a few minutes before Prakash said, "Nice day, isn't it?"

"No," ey said, laughing. "It is cold and gray. My cat is dead, my job is gone, and my two friends are someone I can only meet in a place I am terrified to go and a researcher of something that is no longer a problem." *Memory is a mirror of hammered silver,* the litany continued within as always. Ey hoped silently. *A weapon against the waking world.* "Dreams are the plate-glass atop memory: a clarifying agent against the- Sorry."

Prakash nodded, as though this was part of a normal conversation. "You're okay, RJ. No luck on the job front? Are you doing alright for cash?"

Ey rubbed away unwelcome tears and nodded. "Enough for another six months here, and then I need to either find a new job or move back to America. My parents have said–"

"Would you be interested in a job offer?"

"From the university?"

He shook his head. "No."

"Where then? I did not know you worked anywhere else."

"Work is probably the wrong word, here," Prakash said, grinning. "But, I mean, if you don't mind heading out of the WF for a while, I might have something for you."

Part of RJ stopped up short—though not, ey noted dispassionately, eir body—and ey blinked rapidly down towards the ground. This was a new, strangely shaped bit of information. There was no opening within eir mind that would fit it perfectly, so ey carefully set it aside. *The waking world fogs the view and time makes prey of remembering.* "And what would this job that you do not work at entail? I am wary of sims."

"Of course. Minimal work on the 'net." He seemed to consider for a moment, then shrugged. "Well, no work on the 'net, actually, but minimal work in-sim."

Ey nodded, waited for Prakash to continue.

"Carter was kind enough to provide us with some extra information. Michelle's core dump from when she got lost, yours from the theater sim that the techs were careless enough to leave around. Some people I'm...not working with at my non-job with have been digging through those and, in combination with the testimonies of the lost, come up with some interesting hypothes–"

"A way back?"

The intensity with which ey replied startled the researcher, who held up his hands defensively. "Sorry, RJ. If I overstepped–"

"No, sorry," ey said. "I did not mean to shout. If it is a way back, I will say yes. If it is a way to 'fix' whatever I have become, I will say no and do not wish to waste your time."

Prakash relaxed and shook his head. "I see. You've mentioned not wanting to lose what you have. I wouldn't have offered if that was on the table. They're not really thinking of a way back, no, but maybe a way forward. Use what you taught us to find—or make—somewhere new."

At this, ey really did stop up short. "What do you mean, 'somewhere new'?"

"Arms races have fallen out of style. It's not really considered fashionable to stockpile weapons or anything anymore."

RJ blinked, nonplussed.

"Technology, however, brings with it a status of its own." Prakash smiled, neither pityingly nor happily. Dreamily. "So if, as you say, dreams are the plate-glass atop memory, and if, as you've said in the past, getting lost put you in a mirrored cage, then these are bits of information related to technology. If one could set aside the cage metaphor and set up a mirrored *world*, well, that would be quite the status symbol."

RJ stood a while in thought, searching Prakash's face until the man averted his eyes. "What would be required of me?"

"Nothing, for now. Just to stay in touch. Eventually, though, we'll get you somewhere we can dig into research and after that, you'll be one of the founders of something big. Really big."

The words came in a torrent, then, and with such an intensity that ey staggered and had to clutch at Prakash's arm for support. "The flow of prophecy climbs up through the years, winter upon winter upon winter, and compels the future to do its bidding. The prophet is only a pipe that sounds when the past...shit. I am sorry. All of that to say 'yes'. I am sorry."

Once the shock of the onrush of words wore off, Prakash nodded, smiling cautiously. "It's okay, RJ. Like I said, nothing needs to be done right now. And I trust that you know not to mention this to anyone. Someone else will talk to Michelle about it. Talk to each of the lost, I mean. No need to bring it up with them. When things are lined up, we can go for another walk after coffee or something. Sound good?"

Ey swallowed dryly, nodded. "Thank you. I will hold on until then."

They started walking again, the researcher explaining that he really did need the air, since all that waited for him was an office sim.

RJ did not mind. What sadness that dug at em from Prisca's passing had been blunted, softened by the prospect of something new. Something ahead of em. Something to look forward to that did not bring with it more exhaustion, more words.

"You know," Prakash said thoughtfully. "I know the things you say sometimes aren't really intentional or anything, but you're not wrong."

"Mm?"

"About prophecy, I mean. Just over two years since you got back and here you are, being invited to compel the future to do your bidding using what you learned."

Ey laughed, earnest and true. "I suppose so. I was going to say, 'the prophet is only a pipe that sounds when the past demands it', and given that I cannot seem to live in this world anymore, that demand is getting to be overwhelming."

Part I

Anticipation

They dreamt and thought and considered, and then many of those who knew the ways to navigate the seas argued that reaching one of those campfires would be a way to quell the loneliness that they felt as a hole in their hearts. "Perhaps they will fill us with joy! And even if they fight against us or sow strife, is that not a form of companionship?"

Others were more cautious about the venture, however. "Is a danger not a danger?" they said. "Is a risk not a risk? We must also consider that we might ourselves be overcome by their might. Is it worth stoking that fire?"

Still others spoke thoughtfully, "It is a danger here, as well. There are wild animals in the dark, and there are those who might fight against us here. Perhaps the goal of exploration is also to ensure the security of ourselves! Could we not also use this as a chance to ensure that we live on?"

From *An Expanded Mythology of Our World* by
May Then My Name Die With Me of the Ode clade

Tycho Brahe — 2346

Convergence T-minus 22 days, 13 hours, 35 minutes

It took Tycho Brahe what felt like an age to remember Codrin Bălan, and then it took him a panicked age longer to remember that, yes, sensorium messages were a thing, had been a thing for more than two centuries, and a third age still to remember how to send one.

There was some unknown urgency within him, and even though he supposed that there was no need to hurry, he nonetheless did not fork, deeming it not worth the time to remember how in his rush. Instead, he simply queued up a message to the historian beginning with a jolt of adrenaline, and began talking.

"Codrin, uh, Mx. Bălan, I really, really need to talk with you. Like, right now. I need to talk with you right now. Can we meet? It's incredibly urgent, I'm sorry. I know it's late. Can we meet?"

As soon as he finished, he began pacing once more and waited for a response, doing his level best not to send another sensorium ping immediately to wake Codrin up, just in case.

Instead, he walked around the small hill in the center of the clearing, muttering now down to the grass, shouting now up to the sky. Half words, half sentences, anything to vent the pressure he felt building inside him, but there was nothing to be done.

When the response finally came, he realized he'd only made it halfway around that hill. Less than a minute must have passed. Time seemed to have stretched itself out long. The response was a mumbled, sleepy-sounding address.

Tycho left before his next footfall hit the ground.

Low clouds hung above the low house on the shortgrass prairie. He forced himself to walk, not run, up to the house, where he could already see a light turning on, vague shapes moving behind the glass. The soft chime that announced his arrival led those two shapes, one human, one not, to look up, and before he even made it to the house's door, Codrin was already there, much as he remembered, though much more tired.

"Tycho Brahe, yes?" ey asked. "Is everything okay?"

He tore his eyes away from the figure beside the historian, what looked to be some large-eared vulpine standing on two legs, looking just as tired as Codrin.

"Uh, yes," he stammered. "No? I don't think so, at least. I'm sorry for waking you. I don't think things are okay, though."

Codrin nodded and stepped aside, gesturing to welcome the astronomer in and guiding him to a seat at the table.

"I will make tea," the fox said. "Though I think perhaps one without caffeine."

"Who...?"

"That's my partner. Dear, Also, The Tree That Was Felled."

Gears crunched to a halt in his mind, thoughts stalling and whatever words he had prepared scattering. "An...an Odist?"

"Yes. Why do you ask?"

Tycho knit his brow. "Well, I mean, the *History*..."

"I know. Not all of them came out in the best light," ey said, smiling tiredly. "But it's a good one, I promise. Now, can you tell me what's happening?"

He forced himself to remain seated at the table, not giving in to the overwhelming urge to pace. "But...I mean, do you remember our conversation years ago? The one about the Dreamer Module?"

Codrin nodded warily. "That some of the Odists were against it, yes."

"Then certainly you can see my concern!" Tycho hissed, leaning toward Codrin.

The historian startled back. "I'm afraid I don't follow, Dr. Brahe, I–"

"Can we at least step outside?"

"If you would like me to be elsewhere, Dr. Brahe, I can be," Dear said, standing at the entryway to the kitchen, three mugs in its paws. *"But I do hope that you will trust me."*

Tycho stared at the fox.

It stepped forward, set the three mugs down on the table, each smelling of chamomile. *"You must forgive me for eavesdropping, but I did hear you mention the Dreamer Module. I can assure you that I share little in common with the elements of the clade that were against its inclusion. It is not something that I particularly care about, but it is fine, I am sure."*

"I can vouch for it," Codrin said, reaching for eir mug but simply holding it in eir hands rather than sipping. "If we absolutely must step outside, you understand that, as it's my partner, I'll likely tell it about our conversation anyway, yes?"

After a pause, Tycho's shoulders slumped as he let out the tension pent up within them. "Alright, alright. Besides, it doesn't sound like there's much use in trying to hide anything from them."

Dear rolled its eyes, but sat at the table anyway. *"You could hide whatever you like from me, Dr. Brahe, I will not look. As you guess, though, the same is not true of some of my cocladists."*

One of them, perhaps Codrin, willed a cone of silence into being.

"I read the *History*, Codrin," he said at last. "So I know you know what's on the Module."

Codrin froze, mug halfway lifted. Dear's ears stood erect, and all sleepiness fled from its features.

"You understand why I'm concerned, then, right?"

The historian set eir mug back down on the table without taking a sip, saying, "Tell me all that you can."

So he recounted the events of the previous hour. The sudden interruption of an impersonal message, a simple note from the perisystem architecture informing him, the astronomer on duty, of the signal received.

"What signal was it? Were the primes echoed back to us?" Dear asked.

He shook his head and recited from memory, "We hear you. We see you. We are 3 light-hours, 4 light-minutes, 2.043 light-seconds out at time of message send. Closing at 0.003c relative velocity. Closest intercept 5 light-minutes, 3.002 light-seconds in 972 hours, 8 minutes, 0.333 seconds. We understand the mechanism by which we may meet. We have similar. Instructions to follow."

There was a long moment of silence around the table as the words sank in.

"The mechanism," Codrin said, finally breaking the silence. Ey sounded hoarse, unprepared. "The Ansible? The instructions for creating a signal that it'll recognize?"

Tycho stared down into the pale yellow tea. "Yes."

"Did you respond?" Ey furrowed eir brow quizzically. "Is that even possible? I never thought to ask."

The silence fell again, and he could feel the expressions of the other two deepen into frowns as he kept his eyes on his tea.

"Tycho," Dear said, and he couldn't understand how the fox could keep its voice so level. *"Did you respond?"*

"Awaiting consent," he mumbled. "That was the last bit of message. Awaiting consent."

"You responded." A statement. One spoken with no small amount of awe. *"You did, did you not?"*

"Yes."

"What did you send?" Codrin said.

"Consent granted."

With the repetition of those words, he pushed the untouched mug of tea further away from him, folded his arms on the table, and rested his forehead on them.

The longest silence yet followed as both Dear and Codrin appeared to take this information in and he, poor, stupid Tycho Brahe, he soaked in his own guilt. It seeped through his clothes, squished in his shoes, matted his hair and pushed against his face. Tycho Brahe, indeed! He should have chosen the name of some far less competent man, all those years ago when he'd first met Codrin.

It was the historian who spoke first, voice sounding calm, somewhere between professional and empathetic. An interviewer's voice. "Have you told anyone else?"

"No," he said, lifting his head, though still not meeting their gazes. "I don't know who I'd tell."

"Are there no other astronomers working with you?"

"There are. Of course there are. I'm sure they've even read the message by now, and doubtless my response." He shrugged, realized that he'd started crying. "But what would I tell them? Extraterrestrials contacted us, asked to board, and I just said 'yes'? Didn't ask anyone, didn't wait to have a conversation, just up and said yes?"

"Well, okay," Codrin said. "Why me, then? We've not spoken in twenty years."

"Instinct?" he said, voice choked with half laughter, half tears. "I have no idea, Mx. Bălan. You listened to my story back then, and I read your *History*, and you seemed nice, and I guess you're just always at the center of things."

The fox across the table giggled—there was no better way to put it—and there was a tink of ceramic as it bumped its mug to Codrin's. *"You, my dear, are so caught in stardom that even astronomers know your name."*

None of that amusement showed in eir expression as ey said, "I am, at that, aren't I? Well, Tycho, what are the next steps?"

"I don't know," he said, finally looking up to the pair, to Dear's grin and Codrin's frown. "I was hoping you'd know."

Ey sighed, leaned over and patted him on the shoulder. "Well, since I'm sure as hell not sleeping anymore, I guess coffee's next. Coffee, and figuring out what to do with our wayward astronomer and upcoming guests."

Codrin Bălan — 2346

Tycho stayed until they could talk him down from the plateau of anxiety he had seemed determined to hold onto for as long as he could. They fed him tea, then ice water, then leftovers, anything they could do to help. They talked to him about how to prepare for the inevitable discussions that would be coming from the other astronomers aboard as well as for the inevitable contact that would come from the Odists or Jonases, seeking answers to why he had done the things that he'd done.

And, once he was able to talk without the volume of his voice continually rising, once he was able to smile again, they sent him on his way, off to go get some sleep, even though the sun was beginning to color the eastern sides of the house in salmon and orange.

"It's alright," he had said, laughing tiredly. "It's always night in the field. It's always night outside, isn't it?"

This left Codrin and Dear to sit in silence for a few minutes. After making coffee, they moved out to the patio despite the chill of the morning.

"What do you think, my dear?" the fox asked, cradling its mug close to its chest.

"Mm? I don't know that I'm thinking anything. I think my brain's too full with new information packed in around sleepiness that I can't actually process anything."

"I would suggest drinking your coffee to wake up, but if it is the same feeling that I have had, that will simply replace the sleepiness with caffeine, and you will be no more easily able to process."

Codrin grinned, nodded, and sipped eir coffee. "I'm a little disappointed I didn't fork to get up so that at least some part of me could keep sleeping and just deal with it in the morning."

Dear laughed. *"You jumped out of bed so fast I thought that we were under attack. I do not think you would have been able to get back to sleep even if you had tried."*

"Probably not."

They sat in silence, drinking their coffee, and watching the sun creep up until the horizon reluctantly let it free. When they realized that they were squinting and shading their eyes too much to actually see anything, they went back inside to claim the couch, huddling under a throw to warm themselves up while Dear's partner puttered sleepily around the kitchen.

This led, of course, to second cups of coffee and warm sweet rolls, and a long hour of Codrin and the fox catching their partner up to date.

"Well," they said. "How do you feel?"

"That is a very Codrin question."

"Yeah, I guess it is. I feel..." Ey paused, looking down into eir coffee. "I feel overwhelmed. I guess that's not a complete emotion, though."

"You want help teasing it apart?"

Codrin slouched down into the couch further, resting the coffee mug on eir stomach. Tiredness clung to em in a thin, sticky film. "I guess. I mean, I think a lot of it is due to exhaustion."

"Seconded," Dear mumbled. *"I am surprised you slept through that, my love."*

"I'm one of the lucky ones who can sleep through anything," their partner said, grinning. "But Codrin dear, first, how do you feel about being woken up so early?"

"I don't think that really entered into my mind. That's how I met Dear, after all. A jolt of adrenaline and then a sensorium message."

"I do hope that mine was not so panicked. From what you said, Tycho was a bit shouty."

Ey laughed. "He was, at that. I hope we sent him home a little calmer. But that made me anxious. Given that I was still fighting my way out of a dream, it felt rather like waking up into a nightmare, rather than out of one."

"Alright," they said. "And how do you feel about meeting him?"

"That's a little tougher. Equally anxious, I guess. Frustrated as well, given how poorly he reacted to Dear. I think he's very much a tasker and hasn't experienced individuation before."

Both Dear and its partner nodded. *"I am not Michelle, and I am certainly not True Name, which is who I am sure he was imagining."*

"I suppose, yeah. So it was frustrating hearing that his first reaction was—or that anybody's first reaction—to one of my partners could be one of, I don't know, distrust? Disgust?"

Dear's ears flinched back, but it nodded all the same. Codrin suspected it had had more than its fill of dealing with the rest of the Odists by now.

"So," their partner said. "Anxious, frustrated, maybe a bit defensive?"

Ey nodded.

"And what about the topic of the conversation? How did that make you feel?"

"I think that's where I'm struggling the most. I've worked on so many projects through the years, and this has the potential of being far and away the biggest of them all."

"Have you accepted it as a project, my dear?" Dear said, grinning slightly.

Codrin hesitated, taking a sip to gain a bit more time to mull that over in eir mind. "I think I have, though I don't know what shape that'll take yet."

"So, how do you feel about that?"

"If we consider the scope of the *History* as ten times that of *Perils*, and if we give this one a cautious estimate of ten times that of the *History*–"

"Ten times?" Dear's partner frowned. "A hundred times the size of *On the Perils of Memory*?"

"Size maybe isn't the best descriptor. Intensity, perhaps?" Ey shrugged. "Working on the Qoheleth project never had me screaming into the void or shouting at the sky. The *History* was longer, but while I can see this one being perhaps shorter, the intensity is going through the roof. I'm not sure how much of that is just being exhausted, though."

"That is about the work, though. How do you feel about the topic? Aliens sending us copies of Douglas? Or perhaps us sending aliens copies of...well, whoever we decide?"

"Frightened? Excited? Anxious? It feels too big to think about, in a way."

"Agreed," both of their partners said at the same time, then laughed.

"But also, to tie those two together, I think my first reaction—the very first thing I thought as soon as I connected Tycho's mood with the topic at hand—was 'God damnit, not again'."

Dear frowned. *"Do you feel obligated to take on the project, rather than actually wanting to?"*

Codrin shrugged. "I don't know what else to say other than that. Obligated, then worried about scope, as though I'd already accepted the burden, such as it were."

"Do you need a vacation, my dear?"

"Good Lord, no," ey said, laughing. "I don't go as nuts as you, fox, but sitting around idly is decidedly uncomfortable. It's not quite an 'I hate my job' feeling, either. It's just more of a 'Why is it always me? Why do I always wind up at the center of these enormous happenings?' feeling."

As though on cue, both Codrin and eir partner looked over at the fox, who burst into giggles. Ey felt so loopy from exhaustion that ey was soon joining Dear in the fit.

"I will accept a portion of that responsibility," it said when it could speak again. *"But the rest falls on my cocladists. I may be one of them, but I am no metonym."*

"I'll accept that," Codrin said.

"We're not wrong, though, you know. Even if True Name and her stanza nudged you towards Dear, you wound up here. You wound up so influenced by the project that you almost resented Ioan when you needed to merge back for the project. I know there were a few tense discussions between you two when it came time to decide who would write *Perils.*"

Ey waggled a hand. "Tense is maybe too strong a word. We were both excited, and it came down to whether it was me because my memories weren't muddied with what ey'd experienced in the interim, or whether those memories would help add to the, uh...damn, what'd you call it, Dear?"

"Umwelt? One's worldview combined with one's experience of the world? I know that I have overloaded the term somewhat, and I am not sorry."

"That's the one. If Ioan's combined knowledge of what I experienced via my memories as well as eir own experiences during the project would provide a better worldview as a canvas for the project. We decided that I'd write and ey'd consult."

"I left you with a tainted soul," Dear said, still sounding loopy.

"So dramatic," ey said, rolling eir eyes. "But you changed me enough that I became a Codrin rather than a Ioan, while Ioan remained one."

"Then May Then My Name tainted em in turn."

"I miss them," Dear's partner said. "I can't imagine seeing them together would be anything but adorable."

"Saccharine, even."

"Don't be a jerk, fox."

"I am not! I am simply stating the fact that my teeth might rot from just how adorable that must be."

"Do you think True Name is pissed?" Codrin asked.

"That May Then My Name settled down with someone? Refused to fork for her, then even to talk with her? That she has taught herself how to hate specifically to hate her own down-tree instance? Of course she is pissed. It is her own stanza rebelling against her."

"From what we've seen, it sounds like their—True Name's and Jonas's—attempts to control the outcome worked as expected, but also that True Name hasn't been seen around the Lagrange System nearly as much in the last few years. Sounds more hurt than pissed, I guess." Ey shrugged. "I imagine having your own clade that upset at you tempers your devotion to a cause."

"Much of the liberal side of the clade distanced themselves from the conservatives when the History *came out, yes. The definition of 'Odist' is quite diluted now. I do not believe that True Name lost much in the way of tools, such as it were; I think she just had to write many of us off, or think of us simply as safe places to store other tools, as she did with you, my dear. She has likely replaced them with yet more finely tuned versions of herself or Jonas."*

"That's a rather horrifying way of looking at it. It sounds so sterile."

"Do not misconstrue me. I am not so far removed from them that I do not feel empathy. True Name is still a fully realized person. She is not a truly sterile being, I do not mean to imply that. She does still have emotions, they simply come from a place that we cannot access."

Codrin finished eir coffee and set the mug on the table, sitting up straighter and rubbing at eir face. "I'll grant you that, though it's still going to take some work to internalize."

"There is no rush, my dear."

"Isn't there?" their partner asked. "Can you imagine True Name not getting involved in this? I'd honestly be surprised if she wasn't already stringing Tycho up by his toes for what he did. If Codrin's to wind up working with her again, maybe ey does need that empathy."

The fox only frowned.

"Either way," Codrin said. "I probably ought to send those two a message. Dear, you're welcome to chime in as well, but I want to share my thoughts on this with Ioan. How long's the transmission time, these days?"

"I think about thirty days? Somewhere around there. Tycho would know, but I don't think asking him right now is a great idea."

Codrin nodded. "Well, nothing for it. I'll write to Ioan and May Then My Name, then get ready for the shitshow that's doubtless coming down on us."

"If I may make a suggestion, my dear," Dear said slowly. *"Hold off until you have a better idea of your feelings on the matter."*

"Why?"

"This is something enormous, as you say. Let it marinate for a day. You will be able to better construct your message with some rest."

"Right, yeah." Ey slumped down in the chair. "Not like they'll be able to do anything, anyway."

Tycho Brahe — 2346

Convergence T-minus 22 days, 8 hours, 23 minutes

Tycho returned to that field beneath the stars after the conversation with Codrin and Dear to find someone already waiting for him.

They'd discussed this potential. There were two branching paths that they had ruled most likely, which was that he'd meet another of the astronomers or a politician. Were the former the case, he was to calmly explain the situation, exploring the ramifications of the messages both received and sent.

If, however, it was someone more aligned with the politics of the System—Codrin had left him with a short list of names—then the conversation would take several different forms based on what they already knew. For instance, if they knew that a message had been received but not what its contents were, he was to explain it calmly and plainly, beginning with the intent of speaking to a lay person. If they knew the contents, he was to explain the import behind him.

If they knew that he had responded, however, the chances were that they were there specifically to interrogate, berate, or potentially cut his access to the perisystem architecture that dealt with the Dreamer Module. Hell, at that point, they might as well cut everyone's access to that bit of the architecture and completely run the show.

The person who met him, however, immediately made his throat seize up.

"If it is True Name," Dear had said after providing a description and forking into a skunk to provide a visual aid. *"Then there is absolutely nothing you can do but go along with what she says."*

"That bad?" he had asked.

"Oh, do not worry, it will all go quite well for you if she herself is there. The outcome might not be what you wanted when you met her, but you will leave feeling as though a great deal has been accomplished. It is difficult to describe or get across in words, as you likely have a very dramatic view of her from reading the History.*"*

And there, sitting on the mound in the center of the field, was the precise skunk that he'd been warned about. Long, thick tail. Short, cookie-shaped ears. Tapered snout pointed up to the sky as she leaned back on her paws.

Well, he thought. *Nothing for it.*

He walked over toward that small rise and, once the rustling of his steps became audible, True Name turned her head toward the sound. It was too dark to see her expression, so his mind flashed through several. Were her teeth bared in anger? Was she smiling kindly? Was she secretly joyous about the news?

"Dr. Tycho Brahe, yes?"

Tycho pulled out his red-filtered flashlight and the spare he kept with him, turning them both on as he made his way up the hill. "Yes. You must be True Name."

"My name precedes me, I see." She laughed. It didn't sound like a mean or wicked one, just earnest, pleased. She accepted the red-filtered light from him and then patted the grass beside her with a paw. "Come, sit with me. This place is absolutely fascinating! I had no idea that such a thing was possible here."

Tycho sat on the mossy ground beside the skunk. "I used to keep it as a place for work or just unwinding, but some years back, I moved in and have just set up camp over in the trees."

"It is delightful," she said, and he could hear the awe in her voice. "How does it work? I thought that there was no way for images to make their way into the System."

He leaned back on his hands beside her to look up into the night sky. "It takes in all of the information from the fish-eye telescope—or any of the telescopes, really—and converts it into data that one can read, and then reconstructs it in here. When it's just stars, just little points of light like this, it's simple enough to display. Color temperature, relative intensity, estimated distance, and so on. When we get close to something, as we did with the Jupiter slingshot, there was too much data, as there would be from any video feed, and the sim just quit displaying anything."

True Name had set the flashlight against her thigh, pointed vaguely up toward her so that he could see her in more detail. Her face was kind, open, and clearly excited. Something about the bristle of her whiskers, the angle of her ears, and the relaxed state of her cheeks worked with her smile to give the impression of wonder and delight, though if pressed, he would've had a hard time defining why.

"Beautiful."

They sat in silence for a while, simply looking up at the stars, both with their red lights pointed toward them to light themselves up. Because it was beautiful, he knew. The night sky, one as pure as this, demanded a reverence, an acknowledgement.

"Which ones do you suppose they came from?" she asked.

"It could be any, at this point," he said. "We have no idea how old their vehicle is. We can know their speed and position with some accuracy, but who knows how much that has changed since they launched."

"Do you mean they might have, ah...attitude jets, I believe they are called?"

"Almost certainly, but more than that, any time they get too close to any system with any appreciable gravity, it'll influence their course."

She nodded in the dim, red light. "Much as they are doing now, perhaps."

"Yes." He thought for a moment, querying the perisystem for information, then shrugged. "They're coming up over the plane of the ecliptic, so there's a good chance that they just used our sun as a gravity assist. A slingshot."

"Picking up a bit of extra speed, then?"

"Yep, it's free energy."

She rested her cheek on her shoulder to look over at him, grinning. "Or perhaps simply to hide where they came from. Maybe they are using the possibility of that assist to obscure their trail!" She laughed, waving a paw up at the stars. "Or they are spying on us, investigating us, Earth, Lagrange. But listen to me, here I am speaking like this is some grand space opera. I have read too much science fiction over the years."

He nodded, grinning as well. "Their speed and the laws of physics make all of those very unlikely. The only reason they may have even bothered to contact us is because we have a chance at some sort of contact that won't immediately fade into light-days."

"They did say that they were moving fast, did they not? I suppose that helps alleviate some of those old space-opera-fueled fears." She returned her gaze up to the sky. "Though, you know, it got me thinking. How many things like this LV might be zooming around the galaxy at incredible speeds? We can be sure now that there are at least three, yes? Our dear home, Castor, then Pollux way on the other side of the sun, and now this new one."

"True. Maybe everyone's just figured out that this is the safest and easiest way to travel."

"You took the words from my mouth," she said with a chuckle. "It makes one wonder, perhaps this is the Great Filter. Perhaps Kardashev was wrong all along, and we should not be looking at the energy usage of a civilization but on the scale from Earthbound, spaceflight, and then uploading, and it is only civilizations that reach that third state that might pass through that filter."

"I'd not thought of it that way."

"There was, of course, no need for you to rush back, but that is what I have been thinking about while waiting for you. Thank you for the light, by the way."

The sudden departure from the topic of the sky above to the here and now shocked Tycho into the realization that he'd fallen in such easy conversation with the skunk. They'd talked like friends, like those who had known each other well but perhaps had just met in person for the first time.

He saw now what Dear had meant, and he was helpless before it.

"Well, thank you for stopping by," he said, keeping this new anxiety out of his voice as best he could. "I'm assuming you wanted to talk about the message and response?"

True Name sat up, dusted her paws off on her thighs, and then turned to face him, switching to a kneeling position. The friendliness was still there in her face, but was now tempered by a down-to-business professionalism "Of course. Can you tell me more about the ramifications of this? I can understand the mechanics of it well enough, but I want to hear from you what the next steps are."

This had not been the question he was expecting, so he took the act of sitting to face True Name, cross-legged, to think about his response. "Well, I suppose they'll send over something uploadable which will drop it in the DMZ. I don't imagine they'll start that for a while yet, given the distances between us. They'll probably want to talk more before doing so, and if they're sending us instructions on how to make an exchange of personalities, that'll give us time to work on that."

"If we want to," the skunk said, nodding. "And, as you were out and we are now gating messages from the Dreamer Module through us, we will keep an eye out for such. We will do our best to keep you in the loop, of course."

He blinked. 'Gating'? Perhaps that meant that they'd cut his access and would be sharing only what they chose with him. "I didn't mean to...I mean, I hope that my response was not too far out of line."

She smiled to him, and while her expression remained friendly, there was the smallest note of pity in that smile. "Do not worry, Tycho Brahe, you are not in trouble. We have been running simulations on the various possible outcomes ever since this portion of the Dreamer Module was okayed. This possibility was on our list and is well within our parameters. We know what it is that we will be doing going forward, and that does not include reprimanding you in any way."

"I'm sorry," he said, before he could even stop himself. "I probably should've asked."

The skunk waved a paw as though the comment was simply irrelevant. "You will even keep access to the Dreamer Module; I meant what I said when you will still be kept in the loop. We will simply have *first* access."

He nodded, hoping that there was still enough red light shining on him that she could see the gesture.

"In fact, that was the primary purpose of my visit. It was nice to get your view of the ramifications, of course, but I wanted to ensure that you would be willing to work with us on this. You keep access to the Dreamer Module, we learn all we can from you. A mutual arrangement wherein you do what you love and we help you out in that, and in exchange you teach us all you can in the process." She held out her paw, grinning lopsidedly. "I know that the concept is rather outdated on the System, but what I am really here to do is offer you a job."

Once the import of her words had sunk in, he laughed and clasped her paw in his hand. "Oh, of course! If it's all the stuff I love, and also I get to talk about it to someone, that sounds...well, perfect, actually."

She laughed and shook on it. The handshake was picture perfect: the right balance between firm and gentle, the right speed, the right duration, all tuned precisely for him. He could see as though from a meter above himself the precise ways in which he was being played like a fiddle.

"Excellent, excellent. I will also be in touch with your friend Codrin Bălan, as well, as I believe ey will be a good person to document much of this, so please expect further contact from em. You will also be in touch with a few of my cocladists—beyond Dear, that is—who will be working with you in various capacities."

He nodded, frowning. *How did she know that I'd met Codrin and Dear?*

"I know that you consider yourself a tasker and that maintaining multiple forks is not your usual MO," she continued. "But if possible, I would like you to keep at least one additional instance to work with us while you continue to work out here and with Codrin. If you have the bandwidth for others, we may have additional tasks. Please keep that in mind, and consider how open to the prospect you will be should you be asked."

"Oh, uh, okay. I guess I just never fork because it seems like an awful lot of trouble. One mind is a lot to deal with as it is."

True Name grinned, said, "I do not begrudge you that. They are rather a lot. These will be long-running, however, so you need not worry too much about the burden of handling the memories for a while, and if you do not want to deal with that at all, so long as everyone is on the same page with me and my team, you need not accept the memory load."

"Well, alright."

"Can you fork now, please? I will take one of you with me and we can work on arrangements there. You are free to get some sleep, if you need."

Tycho nodded, closed his eyes, and dug back through memories to remember just how to create a new instance, taking a good minute and a half before he managed it.

"Sorry, it's been a long time," the original him said.

"It is quite alright. We have much practice under our belts." She nodded toward the new instance. "Can you tag yourself something memorable so that you can tell yourself apart? I suggest 'Artemis', as that is what we have decided to name the remote vehicle."

Both of him frowned, and after a moment's thought, the new instance was tagged Tycho Brahe#Artemis, all while scanning his memory for the reference. Goddess of the Moon, yes, but of the hunt? Wild animals? Artemis with her bow? There were too many correspondences and not all of them savory.

"Why Artemis?" he asked.

"They are flying like an arrow through the night sky, are they not?" True Name said.

"Does that make the others on the ship, uh...Artemisians or whatever?"

The skunk stood, offered a paw to help Tycho#Artemis in standing. "That or Sea People."

"Sea People?" he asked, accepting her paw. As he stood, he realized that he was more than a head taller than the skunk, a fact which had missed him as they sat there on the hill.

"We had better hope for Artemisians, but we must also be prepared for Sea People. Come, Tycho. #Artemis, we will have a place for you to stay. #Tasker, you may stay here, and expect contact soon." She looked up to the sky one last time, and said. "Do you know the poem about your namesake?"

Tycho#Artemis shook his head while #Tasker stood.

"*Reach me down my Tycho Brahe — I would know him when we meet*," she quoted. "*When I share my later science, sitting humbly at his feet; He may know the law of all things yet be ignorant of how We are working to completion, working on from then till now.*"

"I–"

"You are both, Tycho. We may yet share our later science with them as they may share theirs with us. Perhaps we shall take our turns sitting at each others' feet. But Tycho," she said, smiling. "That is a poem about death. Please understand that there is risk here, as well. Now, come with me."

After True Name and Tycho#Artemis left, he stood there on the top of his hill, in the middle of his field, surrounded by his ring of trees, and looked up into the night sky, thinking on all that it meant to be powerless.

Codrin Bălan — 2346

It took both eir partners to talk Codrin down from eir desire to simply get right to work.

"My dear, if, as he said, Tycho was going to take a nap, perhaps you ought to do the same."

"I know," ey replied, shoulders sagging. "It's hard to get out of that mindset of having to just work."

"I know it's enjoyable," eir other partner said. "But seriously, Codrin, even if you're not going to take a nap, take a thermos out onto the prairie and walk for a bit. Tycho is going to need quite a bit of help, given what you told us of him–"

"And if True Name is already involved."

"That too, yeah. So it's probably best to go into the whole thing well rested and prepared for jittery astronomers and...well, whatever True Name is, these days."

Codrin nodded. "That makes sense, at least. Do we even have a thermos?"

"Probably. I'll go digging. Might as well make a fresh pot, while I'm up."

"You, my love, are a true delight," Dear said, tail flitting this way and that.

They grinned, walked off to the kitchen, and started clattering around in cupboards for a coffee therm.

"Dear, have you talked to True Name recently?" Codrin asked after a polite pause.

It shook its head. *"Not in terms of a conversation, at least. I have received a few messages from her in the intervening years, many of which were sent to several Odists as a group."*

"She does that? What are they? Orders or something?"

It shook its head, ears flapping slightly at the movement. *"No. Or, well, not exactly. They are simply updates, or replies to other, ongoing conversations. Some of us still communicate with each other on a somewhat regular basis, and I have been looped into several of those conversations over the years."*

"Wait, 'not exactly'?"

"You have met her. She does not need to order. Oftentimes, she simply suggests."

Ey frowned. "I sometimes worry that we've been attributing almost magical manipulative abilities to her, honestly."

Dear shrugged. *"Perhaps, but she also has had more than two hundred years of study under her belt to find all of the best ways to interact with people. May Then My Name was something of a let-down for her, I think, even from the very beginning, so she had to learn to take on that mantle herself."*

"Especially over the last few years, you mean? With Ioan?"

"Perhaps, though I think that might be ancillary to the fact that our dear May is not on the LVs at all."

Ey blinked, laughed. "I'd almost forgot."

The fox gave em a strange look. *"You forgot that May Then My Name was not here?"*

Their partner showed up, a cup of coffee in one hand and a (far too large) thermos in the other. "Are you forgetting things again, Codrin?"

"No, no," ey said, accepting the thermos with a frown. "Or, well, kind of. I didn't forget that May Then My Name wasn't here, just the ramifications of that, that True Name might not have her as a tool."

"That is more understandable, yes," the fox said. *"Perhaps the True Name here on Castor has diverged from the one on Lagrange in that respect, perhaps not. I suspect that both are disappointed, in their*

own ways."

Standing, Codrin fiddled with the thermos, ensuring that the lid was a mug when removed—two nested ones, actually— then nodded. "I don't know how many dimensions she's thinking on, but I also wouldn't be surprised if she'd had a cost-benefit analysis on losing her to Ioan."

"I would not be surprised, no, which would mean that she has planned around that eventuality. I am sure that May Then My Name is keeping an eye on that. Do not let us keep you, though, my dear. Go for your walk. Think about something else. Enjoy the cold, build a cairn around your worries, and then return safe."

Ey smiled, leaned down to kiss the fox between the ears, then eir other partner on the cheek. "I didn't know that was possible, but I'll try. Back in a bit."

Ey made it two cairns out before caving to the desire to simply get started, and stepped over to Tycho's field. There was a ping of amusement from Dear, to which ey replied with a guilty apology and an acknowledgement that ey'd return soon, all while waiting for eir eyes to adjust to the sudden darkness.

The next sensorium message was a gentle ping to Tycho— nothing so loaded with anxiety as the one ey'd received this morning, just an acknowledgement, a view of the stars.

A voice came from somewhere behind em. "Codrin?"

Ey whirled around to see a dim cone of red light shining on the ground, illuminating feet in a pair of well-worn boots. "Tycho? Sorry for intruding like this. I hope I'm not waking you or anything."

"No, no. Come in. I haven't been able to sleep since True Name left."

There was a small click and then a ray of further red light spread out from a doorway, showing a small hut nestled within the trees. Ey let emself be guided in the door, finding a sparsely decorated room—a desk, a bed, and a massive cork board nailed to the wall, covered in at least three overlapping layers of notes.

"Thanks for having me," ey said, sitting on the offered chair while Tycho claimed the edge of the bed. Once the door was shut, a switch shifted the red light to a normal, warm desk lamp. "I should've mentioned that I'd be coming over, first."

He waved away the apology. "I knew you'd be here, though I didn't know when."

Codrin paused in the middle of unscrewing the lid to the thermos. "You knew?"

"True Name said you would."

Ey frowned, finishing opening the thermos and offering Tycho one of the two mugs of coffee. "What did she say about me?"

"She didn't talk with you?"

Ey shook eir head. "Did she say she would?"

Tycho sipped at the coffee, winced, and set the mug aside to cool. "No, she just talked as though she had, or at least that she knew you'd be working with me."

"Of course she did," ey murmured. "She knows me too well."

The astronomer ground the heels of his palms against his eyes. "I feel like she knew me too well, too. We had what felt like a wonderful conversation where she offered me a job, asked me to fork to send an instance with her to keep working with her, but then quoted some bit of poetry at me and I couldn't tell if it was a threat or a warning or whatever. I'm still trying to recover from that."

"I'm guessing you said yes to both the job offer and the fork?"

He nodded. "It all just sounded so normal. There didn't seem like anything else to do."

"Can you tell me more about both?"

"Well, she said that she knew good deal about the communications and that she'd like me to come help her with the mechanics of that. She'd help me out with resources and I'd teach her what I learn about Artemis as I learned it."

"Artemis? Is that what they're calling the remote...ship? Vehicle?"

He nodded. "Either, really. It cararies people. She said

they're calling it Artemis, that I should tag my fork #Artemis, and that those on the ship were either Artemisians or Sea People, which I didn't get."

"Sea People might be a reference to something from the *Mythology*," Codrin leaned back in the seat, thinking. "Or it could be a reference to a theory about a marauding group of seafarers during the Bronze Age collapse. One that had sacked much of the ancient near east and northern Africa, leading to the prolongation of the collapse."

Tycho's eyes grew wide. "Do you think that's what she's getting at with the reference? That these are going to be some marauders coming to mess with the LV?"

Ey shrugged. "Who knows? Probably both, honestly. Maybe there's even some reference that we're missing. She's True Name, there really is no way of telling."

Nodding, Tycho scooted back on the bed until his back was to the wall, then brought his knees up to his chest. Despite his height, he looked small to Codrin, somehow diminished after the events of the last...goodness, had it only been a day? Diminished, yes, and younger, though he'd always looked as though he was not yet out of his forties in his well-groomed salt-and-pepper hair and well-kept beard.

They sat in silence for a while. Codrin could not guess what the astronomer was thinking about, though ey could see his eyes occasionally darting this way and that, as though connecting one idea to another in the air as well as in his head.

For eir part, ey began structuring the project. There would have to be the journalistic aspect of it, much closer to that of *On the Perils of Memory* than *An Expanded History of Our World*, but if the conservative Odists were also involved, there'd likely also be far more observing than researching.

"Tycho," ey said, startling him out of a reverie. "Do you know what an amanuensis is?"

"Like a recorder? A stenographer? Someone who takes notes?"

"Well, in part, but also someone who thinks about what they're recording," ey said, tapping at eir temple. "They aren't a scribe or a court recorder, but someone there to witness and digest a conversation."

"Like a clerk?" He grinned. "We used to have one of those for our club who would take minutes of the meetings and such."

Ey nodded. "Certainly closer to that than a recorder, yeah. I bring this up because that will be my job in all of this, but I think it'll also be yours. Things like the History are all well and good, and I loved putting the work into the writing, but I also really enjoy doing this. I may wish that the things I get caught up in weren't always so dramatic, but I'll take what I can get."

"What do you mean, it'll be my job too?" he asked.

"Just that you will also be witnessing and thinking about this project, and then coming up with ideas related to it to be compiled into a coherent understanding. That's why we'll be working together, I think. I'm trained to do this work in particular, but I'll need your help in making sense of the science part of it. I'll experience it with you as much as I'm allowed, but you'll have to ensure that I actually understand what's going on."

Tycho laughed. "Well, I'll do my best, but it's not like I have much experience working with Artemisians, either. I'll help with the technical aspects as best I can, though."

"Excellent," Codrin said. "Thank you for that. I'll be managing most of this part, so you won't have to worry too much about the minutiae, but I figured it'd give you a better idea of what to expect when we work together."

He nodded.

"On that note, let's come up with a basic idea of what's next for us. We mostly talked about immediate next steps earlier, but it might be a good idea to start thinking on a larger timescale."

"I guess. I'm assuming it'll be pretty loose, given that we can't guess the particulars?" He waited for Codrin to nod, then continued. "Then we have a month or so before they reach their closest approach as long as we both stay on our own heading."

"Does that mean a month before they upload?"

He shrugged. "Not necessarily. They can upload whenever they want, so long as our Ansible is on and the DMZ is ready. I don't think it's on yet, though. There's probably an effective range beyond which the Ansible won't work well."

"Alright. Have we received any further communications from them? Their message said that they had a similar mechanism in place. Is that something we'll be able to use? Or want to use, even?"

"No further communications that I know of," he said. "But True Name said that all communications will be gated through her, and I don't know if that means that I'll be getting them or just Tycho#Artemis. Hopefully both, if you and I are to be working on this as well."

Codrin frowned. "Well, okay."

"As for us using their mechanism, I guess it depends on if it's something we can reconfigure our Ansible to use, or if we will need to construct something new. If we'll need to construct something new, then we might not be able to do so in time. Our manufactories are meant for repairs rather than construction. Theoretically they could be used for such, but I don't know how long that'd take without someone phys-side to help."

"And would we want to?"

"That feels like a question for True Name, not me," he said after a long pause.

Ey finished eir coffee and replaced the cup on the cap of the thermos. "One of us will have to work up the courage to ask her, sometime. But for now, is it something you would want to do?"

"What? Upload to Artemis?" He looked startled by the question.

"Yes. If it's possible, I mean. I figure it would just be an instance rather than completely investing. I'd also be curious to hear your opinions on that as well."

Tycho tilted his head back until it hit the wall of the hut, staring up toward the ceiling. He sat like that for a good five minutes, during which Codrin remained silent, before leaning forward to pour emself another cup of coffee. "Yes. I don't know about investing completely, but yes, I think I would. Would you?"

Ey smiled, though ey felt just how tired ey was as ey did so. "Perhaps. I have attachments here, though. So the Codrin who uploaded—if ey remains a Codrin—would be severed completely from those ey loves. As romantic as the idea of sailing away on some alien spacecraft might be, it'd be painful to leave, even knowing that a Codrin remained."

"And if your partners uploaded with you?"

The idea caught em up short, and several trains of thought crunched to a halt within em. "If they..." Ey laughed, shaking eir head. "You know, I hadn't considered that, yet. I wonder why? But yes, if they chose to do so, then yes, I'll go with them."

The conversation wound on from there, teasing apart a few possible next steps that lay ahead of them, but throughout it all, at least one thread of eir mind was dedicated to picking at that question.

Why had ey not considered whether or not eir partners would want to upload? It wasn't as though ey didn't attribute the agency to do so to them, ey knew just how independent and intelligent they were on their own. Nor was it that ey hadn't made any guesses as to whether or not they would—ey suspected that Dear would jump at the opportunity.

The root of the issue lay within emself, ey knew. Why was ey not able to make that decision without them doing so first? Was ey really such a follower? Was ey really so stuck living five minutes behind them that ey couldn't imagine making the decision in the face of the possibility of simply reacting to it? Would ey be able to say yes or no to that question if they asked?

Conversely, would ey be able to argue one way or the other, to convince them to come with em or not?

Tycho Brahe#Artemis 2346

Convergence T-minus 22 days, 3 hours, 49 minutes

Tycho#Artemis was unsure if what he was seeing was a flurry of chaotic activity or some tightly choreographed dance. Part of this assessment, he guessed, was due to the relatively small number of individuals for the number of instances moving around. There were probably a dozen instances of True Name that he could see, and then at least that many of a gentleman who looked to be in his well-preserved forties, slender without being lanky, tall without being looming.

And that was it. Well over twenty instances of two individuals milling around what appeared to be a farm of cubicles, each walled with glass, the upper half of which was frosted.

Ringing this bank of cubicles were walls of frosted glass, broken at regular intervals with doors which ey supposed must be offices. Between those doors were couches, looking pleasantly soft in his exhaustion, and an array of padded stools or chairs with interrupted backs which he supposed must be perfect for those endowed with tails, given the occasional skunk or man—Jonas, perhaps?—relaxing in them, chatting amiably during what must be either breaks or informal meetings.

And yet, for all that activity, it was incredibly quiet. There must be dozens of cones of silence set up, spanning cube walls, covering banks of couches, even hovering over those walking the aisles.

"What is this?" he asked the skunk standing beside him.

"Headquarters." She gestured him to a couch already containing a woman, picking at her nails. Short, curly black hair framing a round face. "Though that makes it sound far more formal than it really is. It is a place for Jonas and I to work together in our various instances."

He sank down into the couch beside the woman. "That sounds pretty formal to me. What are you working on that requires cubicles?"

True Name laughed, claiming a stool facing the couch where she sat, straight-backed. "The informal aspect of it is that we are working on essentially whatever we want. Co-working space, perhaps? It is a space where we can have conversations, write, think. If there are a dozen of us, there are three dozen projects."

"And the message from Artemis is one of them?"

"It is several of them, yes. It has spun off a few projects of its own. Ah! Jonas. Which are you?" she said when one of the men blipped into existence, already seated in one of the chairs.

He grinned, crossing his legs in front of him at the ankles. "Di5." He nodded toward Tycho. "Just call me Jonas, though. True Name is just being a snot."

The skunk kicked out at one of his ankles.

"Deserved that," he said. "You must be Dr. Brahe, yeah? Nice to meet you."

He nodded, said, "Just Tycho is fine."

Jonas nodded absently. Without any visible signal a cone of silence fell over the area, dimming what noise remained outside of it to the barest murmur.

"I am Why Ask Questions When The Answers Will Not Help," the woman said in a tone that seemed to sit just shy of laughter. "Answers Will Not Help will do."

"Answers, in a rush," Jonas said, to which she replied with an ankle kick of her own.

"If you call me Answers, I will beat the shit out of you," she said though that near-laugh took most of the sting out of the words.

"To business, then." True Name gestured towards Tycho. "Tycho, here, is the one that answered the message, as you all know, so I have encouraged him to fork and join us. Tycho#Artemis will be working here, and Tycho#Tasker will be working with–"

"Codrin?" Jonas asked, grin turning sly.

"Of course."

"Well, if you're the one to thank for kicking this whole thing off, perhaps you can enlighten us as to why?"

Tycho felt anxiety tighten within his chest. "I uh...I don't know. I guess I was the first one to read the message, and I didn't know what to do with that, so I just replied without really thinking, I guess."

"You were not the first to read the message," True Name said, smiling almost pityingly at him. "And you need not be anxious. As I have already said, we have been wargaming this possibility since we were forced to concede that aspect of the Module."

He frowned. "Well, if you read it first, why'd you let it through so that I could see it?"

"We are not the astronomers," Answers Will Not Help said, shrugging. "That is your job, is it not?"

"Don't you want to control the situation or something, though?"

True Name shook her head. "It is not our job to control."

"But the *History*–"

"Do you remember the motto of the Council of Eight, Tycho?"

He frowned. " 'To guide but not to govern', right?"

True Name nodded. "We are not controlling anything. We are guiding. Of what use would control be in a place such as this? People can do whatever they want."

"Was the *History* wrong then? That you didn't control Secession and Launch?"

"We guided them both," Jonas said, waving his hand. "Just as we guided the *History*. Even the Bălan clade knows this."

"Why, though?" Tycho asked.

"Social engineering," True Name said, then nodded toward Jonas. "We should not get too sidetracked, though. Jonas, you had more questions?"

"I did, yeah. First off, can you give me an overall breakdown of the time frame involved here?"

"Well...wait, can you tell me how long it's been since the message arrived? I haven't slept in I don't know how long."

"A little less than a day."

"Well, then we have a little less than forty days until their closest approach, at which point they'll start moving away from us again."

"And what does that approach mean for us?"

Tycho rubbed at the back of his neck, searching for the best way to explain it. "All it means is that that is the point when the transmission times between our two vehicles will be the shortest, then it'll start getting longer again."

Jonas nodded. "And that approach isn't all that close, is it?"

"Oh God no. Five light-minutes is, uh...ninety million kilometers? Something like that."

"Good, thanks for confirming. I'm going to ungate the next set of messages. Ready?"

Jonas did not actually wait for confirmation before Tycho was given access. Or, rather, access was forced upon him. Like a sensorium message, the text from the perisystem architecture wedged itself into his mind.

If possible, in 400 hours orient down 0.3142 radians relative to your sun reference point source of this transmission to align courses. If possible, accelerate 0.00029c to approach matched velocity. Confirm actions taken.

Instructions for matching consciousness-bearing system transfer mechanism to follow. Confirm actions taken upon receipt.

Prepare airgapped area with locked-down edit permissions dimensions 20m by 20m height 5m and two sandbox areas for rest for us and you dimensions 20m by 20m height 5m. Confirm actions taken.

Prepare party of five consciousness-bearing systems containing one element of leadership, one to record in any capacity, one scientist, two representatives of own choice. Duplicate, prepare to send one set to us, and send other set to above location. Prepare to receive five in turn, similar roles. Expect four categories of consciousness-bearing systems. Confirm actions taken.

We welcome you.

Turun Ka of firstrace, leadership
Turun Ko of firstrace, recorder
Stolon of thirdrace, scientist
Iska of secondrace, representative
Artante Diria of fourthrace, representative

A long silence stretched over the group while the others waited for Tycho to digest the sudden onslaught of information.

"This is," he said, took a slow breath in, then continued, "A lot."

"Talk us through your thoughts," True Name said. "That will help you process, and you may catch something that we have not. This is your role here, Tycho Brahe."

He nodded. "Okay. So, from the top. They suggest we make some course alterations to, I suppose, get us traveling parallel with them, and then accelerate to get closer to their velocity. Does that sound right?"

Jonas nodded. "We've talked with the parasystem engineers who work with the attitude thrusters and propulsion. They say that they can accommodate the maneuver. We can accelerate a little bit if we use half our fuel, but we're beyond the point where the solar sail is doing us much good, the HE engines are too slow, and we want to preserve some of that fuel."

"How much acceleration? I mean, I don't have any training in the physics of spaceflight–"

"We've got that covered."

"Oh. Well, how much acceleration, then?"

"About a third of what they asked. It'll extend the period of time that we're in useful Ansible range by a week or two, giving us about five weeks total."

"If you say so." he shrugged. "I guess this is to help extend the duration that we can transfer back and forth?"

"Yeah, basically," Jonas said. "Do you have thoughts on that?"

Tycho frowned. He wasn't sure why they kept asking him questions about his sentiments on things far outside his area of expertise. Of what use were his thoughts on the matter? "I mean, it makes sense, as far as any of this has."

"How much astronomy you hope to learn from the Artemisians will rely on how long we stay in contact." Answers Will Not Help grinned at him. "Does that bit make sense, at least?"

He sat up straighter. "Oh, uh...you mean someone will be gathering all that information? Will we be able to request it via radio?"

True Name smiled, and this time there *was* pity in the expression. "I know that you said starting from the top, but Tycho, you must understand that you are ideally situated to be the scientist among our party of five. You were the one to answer their call, were you not?"

He couldn't tell what expression or expressions crossed his face, but it must've been amusing, as Answers Will Not Help laughed and slapped him on the knee. "You will be fine, Tycho."

"Why me, though?" he stammered. "There have to be smarter people on board! People who would love to meet aliens and know just what to ask them."

The skunk across from him waved her hand to dismiss the comment. "You will be the scientist. We do not want someone who is smarter than you. We do not want someone who knows just what to ask them. We want you because you are the type of person who grants consent to join us without consulting anyone first. That and a few other factors that we have taken into account leave our decision clear."

"Besides," the woman beside him said, still giggling. "You will get to ask four spacefaring races astronomy questions. Does that not excite you?"

"I...four?" His head was swimming, not aided by the stilted way these Odists seemed to talk.

"Four categories of consciousness-bearing systems. Firstrace through fourthrace. Seems pretty obvious what they are saying to me."

He swallowed dryly.

"You will be the scientist," True Name said. "I will be acting in a leadership capacity, having lost the coin-toss with Jonas. Codrin Bălan will be our recorder. One of my uptree instances, Why Ask Questions, Here At The End Of All Things will be one of the other representatives, and we are searching for the second."

"Two of you?"

"Sending two members of the same clade who look different will give us an idea of how they view forking." Jonas nodded toward the two Odists. "That's why I cheated to win the coin-toss, at least. I want to see what they do with one skunk Odist and one human Odist, as Why Ask Questions is."

"And I will run interference here," Answers Will Not Help added. "I will be learning much the same as Why Ask Questions so that I can interpret messages from the DMZ and Artemis. She is better at working crowds."

Tycho nodded. He felt slow, somehow. Stupid. It wasn't even that they were speaking about things he didn't understand because he hadn't learned them yet so much as they were speaking as though their actions took place on some higher plane of existence, some place completely inaccessible to him.

"Apologies for sidetracking your top-to-bottom reading. Please continue," True Name said.

"Uh, alright." He shook his head to try and clear it. It did not work. "Instructions for transferring a consciousness-bearing system...I'm assuming that's their version of the Ansible?"

"Yes. We received the specifications for that immediately after this message. I will not bore you with their contents, but the sys-side Ansible techs assure us that it works much the same as ours and will require only software changes, nothing physical. That will be ready within a few weeks, if not sooner."

He hesitated, then, seeing no possible reply that wouldn't make him sound like an idiot, continued. "Alright. Then they want us to prepare a space for them. I don't know what air-gapped means, though."

"We're assuming they mean as in a DMZ. Something completely separate from the rest of our System, which is what we were planning, anyway. It's a tech term which means that there is no physical connection between two devices, so they can't possibly communicate unless one plugs in a cable. Maybe that's what they meant?" Jonas grinned lopsidedly. "We'll just have to hope we get it right."

"So, a secure place to meet, which we were planning on anyway. Do you think they're worried we'll attack them or something?"

True Name and Jonas exchanged a quick glance, and the skunk, suddenly more serious than she'd been since he'd met her, said, "Expand on that." Not a question. A command.

He mastered the urge to shy away from her. "I just mean

that, if we can't promise them that we're universally on board with having them visit us, that puts the talks at risk, right?"

She leaned back on her stool, frowning, as two more instances of her forked off and dashed down the aisles to a cubicle. "This is why we are talking with you, Tycho. Thank you for proving your worth so quickly."

"This wasn't part of your calculations or whatever?"

"It was," Jonas said. "But the fact that you thought of it so quickly was not."

He shook his head. "I still don't understand why me, though."

"You are in absolutely no way special, my dear." Answers Will Not Help bumped his shoulder with hers, her voice once more full of smiles. "You are in absolutely all ways average. This allows us to use you as a barometer for how we can expect the rest of the System to react."

"I mean, I guess I'm average, but that doesn't seem like much data. Aren't you asking more people?"

She was back to laughing. "How many people do you imagine know about this, Tycho?"

He sighed, slouching further down into the couch. "Right. Okay. Twenty by twenty by five meters for the conference room and their rest area. Uh...maybe that says how big they are?"

"And maybe just the size of their DMZ so that we can meet on equal grounds on both sides," Jonas said. "We won't know until it happens. It does show us that they rest, though, or at least expect to take breaks from the talks. That they say two means that they think we will as well."

Rest, he thought. *Rest sounds good.*

Aloud, he said, "And I guess the next bit we've already talked about some. Maybe four races. They say 'consciousness-bearing systems' and don't name their races, so maybe it's complicated. If they've picked up three other races before meeting us, maybe very, very complicated."

"I have been thinking," Answers Will Not Help said. "Perhaps some of them were not biological races. They did not say people or species."

"AIs, you mean?"

She shrugged. "Or something. It might also be a caste thing. You will notice that there are two firstrace emissaries, one of which is the leader, and then secondrace and fourthrace only get representatives, no titles. There are many possibilities."

After a pause, he asked, "And is that 'We welcome you' an invitation to join them?"

"Maybe," Jonas said. "We don't know yet. We're going to keep talking to them and try and get a better feel for it. If it means 'You're welcome to join us', that's certainly better than 'We welcome you because you have no other choice'. We're working on it."

Tycho rubbed his face tiredly. "Way above my pay grade."

True Name laughed. "It is, yes."

"Any thoughts on the names?" Jonas asked.

"Well, I guess it's interesting that the two firstrace peo-ple...individuals...er, consciousness-bearing systems share a name. Maybe they're a clade, like...I mean..."

"Like me?" Jonas said, smirking. "Don't worry, Jonases Ka and Ko already had their laugh over it. But no, we don't know that one way or another."

He felt heat rise to his cheeks, but nodded all the same. "The rest, I don't know. They all sound different, I guess. The fourthrace one is the only other one with two names."

"We cannot make any real guesses, ourselves," True Name said. "We have been told that a stolon is a botanical term, but that is likely only a coincidence."

"Well, only other thing I can think of is that they ask for confirmation on all actions taken. What are you going to say to those?"

True Name's eyes grew distant as, he imagined, she accessed an exo with the response text prepared. "To the first, 'We will orient as described and accelerate 0.00014c'. To the second, 'Instructions received, integration commencing immediately, estimated time to completion 428 hours'. To the third, 'Areas prepared'. To the fourth, 'Preparing party, we will duplicate and be ready to send on an agreed upon time'."

"Anything for the 'We welcome you' or the list of names?"

"We will repeat the 'We welcome you' message, and it will be signed with your name," Answers Will Not Help said.

He stood up so quickly it made him dizzy. "What?"

The other three laughed, True Name eventually continuing, "It will be signed 'The Only Time I Know My True Name Is When I Dream of the Ode clade, leadership'. We will send them the complete list of names when it is confirmed. You need not worry, Tycho. Answers Will Not Help was just being a snot, as Jonas so eloquently put it."

He remained standing, swaying slightly and trying to blink away dancing black spots. "I think...I think I need to lay down."

The skunk nodded, stood, and took him by the elbow. "You likely do. You have been awake for almost forty-five hours. We have a room prepared for you."

Jonas stood as well, dusting off his slacks, and shook Tycho's hand. "Welcome aboard. And hey, congrats on first contact."

Codrin Balan — 2346

Codrin found emself in possession of a blissful day of peace after that sudden pile-on of news. Ey acknowledged a request from True Name to act as amanuensis with a faintness of heart that ey hoped the skunk did not notice, worked on a letter to Ioan, and then went back to spending the rest of eir day napping, catching up on a writing project ey had been poking at, shoving Dear around for fun, and watching the fox rehearse its next performance with their partner. This one was to be a ballroom dance where everyone invited would dance with instances of Dear, which would begin disappearing one by one while the rest grew steadily more anxious, as though worrying that they would be next.

It was all very Dear, and Codrin enjoyed the idea immensely.

It was comforting, in a way, to sit on the couch and watch eir partners dance, stumble, laugh, start dancing again, all while this big project loomed outside. It was there, ey knew. It was hovering outside like a storm rolling inexorably over the prairie, ready to lash the sides of the house with bands of rain and rattle the glass with peals of thunder.

But for now, ey was safe inside, laying in supplies, even if they were simply emotional and intellectual reserves for what ey knew would be a taxing endeavor.

The only conversation ey'd allowed about the entire affair came at night, when the three of them had piled into bed, each in their familiar order but pressed now up against each other, perhaps drawing comfort against the onrushing storm.

"How's it going to feel working alongside True Name instead of against her?" their partner asked, voice muffled by a pillow as the fox kneaded on their shoulders.

Codrin replied, voice equally muffled against the back of Dear's neck, "I don't know if I was working against her, necessarily. It felt like it at the time, but now it just feels like we were both doing our jobs."

"You just hated hers."

Ey laughed against Dear's neck, which got a giggle out of the fox in turn. "I guess. It's hard to hate too much because good things came of it, but also you can't say for sure that the same thing would've happened if she hadn't been there. Her, Jonas, the lot of them, they were all helpful in bringing about Secession and Launch how they happened, but who knows? Maybe they would've happened regardless, just with different people at the helm."

There was a long moment of silence, broken only but the occasional noise of contentment from Dear's partner as the fox continued in its back-rub. Codrin spent the time plastering those thoughts over with better ones. Ey thought about how the fox smelled, how its fur felt against eir face. Ey thought about how, once, ey'd wound up between eir two partners in much the same position and it had led to an overwhelming wave of anxiety, a sense that things were wrong, a feeling that ey needed to escape, and how they'd comforted em and then simply fallen back into the habit of laying like this, instead. The fox seemed to draw a sense of security, sandwiched between them, just as Codrin did by having no one at eir back.

"Did you hate her?" Dear said, breaking the silence and eir rumination. It had stopped in its massage and settled for a simple hug instead. *"Do you still?"*

Ey hooked eir chin over the fox's shoulder, humming thoughtfully. "Maybe, in a way. I thought I did at the time. I thought I hated that she was part of the hidden level of control that everyone suspects but no one can prove. All she needed was a black suit, black sunglasses, and an earpiece."

Both of eir partners laughed.

"Now, though, I think resentment is a more accurate word than hate. I resent the feeling of being controlled with no recourse. She may have the brainpower and manpower and analytical skills to read everyone as thoroughly as she did, but I resent how cold she was in actually doing so; intentionally making me angry to make the result seem sensational? There's a lot of cynicism bound up in that." Ey shrugged. "There's no point in hating her. I don't dislike the System as it stands after her and Jonas's manipulation, but I resent the cynicism it took to get here. I don't resent being here, but I do resent the phys-side manipulations that led to me being here."

After yawning, Dear's partner asked, "Think you'll be alright working beside her while you resent her?"

"If it was just me, no," ey said. "If that cynicism is directed at the Artemisians and Tycho and whoever else, rather than just at me, It'll be fine, I think."

"Besides," Dear said. *"You will still get to see great things, my dear. You may be tired, yes, but out of however many billion people on board, you will get to see great things."*

The conversation trailed off from there, and the three slept well that night, each dreaming their dreams of cynicism or skunks or aliens or astronomers or love.

The reprieve lasted until morning when, upon waking, Codrin discovered a note on the floor, written in the Odists' distinctive handwriting:

Mx. Bălan,

It has been requested that we pull together a team of five to act as emissaries to exchange with a team of similar composition from the Artemisians. They have left specific instructions for the roles that should be involved: someone in a position of leadership, a scientist, a recorder, and two representatives. We have the following:

- Leadership: myself, True Name
- Scientist: Dr. Tycho Brahe
- Recorder: you
- Representative 1: Why Ask Questions, Here At The End Of All Things of the Ode clade

However, we will need one more representative. It would be vanishingly easy for me or Jonas to pick someone who would be fitting for our enterprises, but why do that when it would potentially be much more interesting to let you pick? It ought to be someone outside the Ode clade or your polycule, but beyond that, I find myself fascinated by the idea that you—you, who have your feet on the ground and head in the clouds—might pick someone about whom I know nothing. With two Odists on the team already, one of whom is one of my uptree instances, I am sure you can see that we will have the situation under control from our end.

Please make your choice today, and I will look forward to seeing the two of you at systime 1700 for a candlelit dinner in Tycho's delightful sim. If they are interested in joining, your partners are also welcome.

Cordially,

The Only Time I Know My True Name Is When I Dream of the Ode clade

Attached was the full text of both messages received so far.

After reading the note, ey placed it face down on the table and headed to the kitchen to make coffee. Ey needed at least some mood-altering substance before engaging with that, and it was far too early in the morning to reach for wine.

When Dear read the note, the fox made a sour face. *"I am not sure whether she is trying to be funny, strategically honest, or simply a brat."*

Ey slouched in eir chair at the table, focusing on the coffee, doing eir best to pick out and name different notes in the flavor. Something fruity. And caramel, perhaps. "I didn't know she was capable of humor."

"Everyone is capable of humor, my dear. Whether or not they intend it is the question."

"Want to come to a dinner party with me, then?"

There was a long pause during which several emotions played out on the fox's face before it replied. *"I will have an answer for you by systime 1500. I cannot decide right now."*

"Dinner party?" Dear's partner stumbled from the bedroom, creases from a pillow still evident on their cheek. "How many do I have to cook for?"

"None, thankfully," Codrin grinned. "Or perhaps just Dear and I. We've been invited to one."

They stopped at the end of the table, leaning down onto their hands. "Well, Dear is frowning, so I'm assuming it's complicated?"

"True Name would like me to join her and the rest of the emissaries to the Artemisians for dinner, and she's invited you two as well."

"No," they said flatly. "And now, it's time for coffee."

A warning glance from Dear kept Codrin from asking further after that. Instead, ey said, "I have an unrelated question for you once you're caffeinated."

They waved their hand noncommittally as they stumbled into the kitchen where a mug sat waiting for them already.

Once everyone was awake enough for conversation, ey

asked eir question. "Either of you know someone who would be a good choice to balance out this diplomatic party? Someone less likely to try and shape the whole venture to their will, but not as passive as an amanuensis?"

Dear shrugged. *"I can get you in touch with plenty of artists. How opposite of an Odist viewpoint are you looking for?"*

"I'm not sure that's quite the goal, so much as someone who can be engaged and can contribute without being as cynical as anyone from True Name's stanza or as singularly focused as Tycho. I think what might be good is just someone ordinary. Someone normal. Boring."

Dear's partner raised their eyebrows. "If you want someone who would be interested, is pleasant to be around, and is able to engage in a conversation without going down a rabbit hole or starting a fight, I think I know someone."

"Slander. I can engage in conversations and I do not go down rabbit holes or start fights."

"Yeah, but absolutely no one would call you boring, Dear."

It preened.

"Sounds promising," Codrin said, flipping the note over and studying the list. "What do they have that would counterbalance this, beyond being ordinary?"

"She's earnest about everything. It's really endearing, actually. She's likeable without being manipulative or cynical. She's interested in people, too, and tries to see the good in them like it's her job." They paused, grinned, and shrugged. "I mean, she was my therapist before I uploaded, so I may be a little biased."

"A therapist? That's a really good idea, come to think of it." Ey leaned forward onto eir elbows. "Someone who can understand humans and just be a normal human is what I was thinking of. What's her name?"

"Sarah Genet. Want me to see if she's free? She's a tracker, I'm sure she'd be willing to send a fork for something like this."

"Why not? She sounds like a nice enough person to meet either way."

Dear nodded enthusiastically. *"I am always curious to meet friends of others from before they uploaded! You are not exempt from this, my love."*

They smirked, looked up at the ceiling for a minute or two, then nodded. "She's getting ready, and will be over at noon or so."

Codrin had never seen a therapist either before or after uploading. Before, it had been a luxury that eir family couldn't afford, and after, ey had been so busy—first with getting used to uploaded life, then with study, then with work—to have considered it much.

Ey had, however, seen a counselor in school as mandated by the school itself. Mr. Nicolescu had been a kindly old gentleman, but one who seemed perpetually on the brink of collapsing from exhaustion. It made sense, given the size of the school, the requirement to meet with every student once a year, and the lack of any other counselors. Ey had been a good student and a quiet kid, and seeing him any context other than the required visit was often a sign that something had gone wrong.

Sarah Genet immediately reminded em of Mr. Nicolescu in many ways. The way she walked, the way she held herself, her smile, the way she listened with her whole attention on whatever someone had to say.

Ey liked her immediately, a feeling which ey'd questioned ever since composing the *History*.

"So, all I was told coming into this was that I was needed for a project that might interest me," she said, once she'd been offered coffee, snacks, and a seat at the table. "If you're going to go all mysterious on me, I'm probably already going to say yes, but make your pitch."

"Quick pitch?" Codrin said. "Aliens found our Dreamer Module signal and are going to upload a diplomatic party in a few weeks, and you were suggested as a good candidate for the talks."

A few long seconds of quiet followed before Dear's partner

laughed. "Sorry Sarah. You see why I wanted you over here to have this conversation in person?"

"You're telling me, good Lord." She shook her head, folded her hands on the table, and smiled. "Alright, now give me the longer pitch."

"Alright. The Dreamer Module broadcast, in short, contained instructions on how to build a message that would work with our Ansible, allowing anyone who found it to upload to the LVs. A few nights ago, someone picked that up and answered."

Ey slid the note from True Name across the table and waited for her to read.

When she had finished, Sarah said, "Whew, alright. That's a lot. So in however many hours, we should expect a team of five of them, and we'll send a team of five in turn. Any idea what we'll be talking about?"

"No clue. Clearly science of some sort, given their request for a scientist. Probably coming to an agreement, if they're asking for a recorder of some sort, though that's just a guess on my part. The "We welcome you" bit sounds promising, at least."

She read through the note once more, set it down, and sipped at her coffee. "Well, you already know that I'm in, but I'm happy to say that this doesn't change my decision. Why me, though?"

Dear's partner answered, "Have you read the Bălans' *History*, yet? *An Expanded History of Our World?* I know I pointed you to it."

"More than pointed," she said, laughing. "You all but forced me to read it, so, yes."

"So you know of True Name, right?"

"The one who tried to guide everything? Yeah, I remember. I didn't miss her name on there, either."

Codrin sighed. "I had the chance to interview her—me and my root instance both did—and she's a lot to deal with. I'm sure it's some calculated gesture that she leaves the last choice up to me, but all the same, I wanted to pick someone who was the opposite of her."

"So you figured a therapist would be good? A psychologist?"

"Yeah, someone who can maybe understand the Artemisians better without doing so specifically to manipulate them."

She held her coffee cup in her hands, tilting her head thoughtfully. "You know, it's a good intuition, but you might also want to be prepared for there to be nothing I can offer. They're clearly similar enough to us that they can learn our language, but that may be where the similarities stop. They may be so alien to us that we might not be able to understand them at all, at least not truly."

Codrin frowned.

"Not that it's hopeless, of course. I'm still happy to help. Honored, even! Just an eventuality you might want to prepare for."

"Well, maybe you can help us understand the Odists better, if nothing else."

Dear kicked at eir shin beneath the table.

Sarah laughed. "Have they sent us anything to teach us their language?"

"One of their languages, perhaps," Dear chimed in. *"There seem to be four different species."*

"One of them, right," she said. "If we only sent them our *lingua franca,* though, maybe they have similar."

"I don't know, actually. Those are the messages I have, but I don't know if they're the only ones," Codrin said. "We'll probably learn more tonight. You alright creating a long-running fork for the project? That's what she made Tycho do."

"Oh, that's fine. It'll be my first time working on a big, organized project like this."

Ey laughed. "Same here. I've worked on big projects and organized projects, but not both at the same time."

"I'll look forward to dinner, then." She looked down, plucked at her blouse, and shrugged. "Think this is good enough for it?"

"If it's at Tycho's, it'll be too dark to tell, but I don't think he owns anything other than flannel shirts and jeans. You should be fine."

"Alright. I'm curious to see what someone who tried to shape large swaths of recent history looks like."

Tycho Brahe#Artemis — 2346

Convergence T-minus 22 days, 5 hours, 2 minutes

Despite the exhaustion that had come down on him like a hammer, Tycho found it difficult to get to sleep. It weighed him down like stones on his chest, even as he lay in bed in the room that True Name led him too. It was a comfortable bed in a nice enough room, and still he lay there in the dark, staring up at the ceiling with eyes that burned.

He did not know how long it took him to actually fall asleep, but when next he woke, ten hours had passed, and dreams of Artemisians clung to him still. They were always just out of sight, and their conversations were just slightly below the level that he could hear them, and yet, he knew it to be them. Knew they were there, just around the corner. Knew that, above all else, he wanted to meet them.

When laying in bed gained him no further insight from the dream himself from the dream, he climbed out, showered in the *en suite*, and, when he was dressed, opened the door to find True Name waiting across the hall, two coffees in hand.

"Do you feel more well-rested, Tycho?"

"I guess, yeah," he said, accepting the offered coffee. "I hope I didn't sleep through too much."

True Name began walking, letting him fall in step behind her. She laughed. "Of course not, my dear. Nothing much that you need to worry about has happened in the last few hours. We have been working on information control and hunting down those willing to help with the effort for setting up the Ansible system to upload to Artemis. That is what you will be working on today, you and a passel of nerds. I think that is the collective term, at least."

So out of place was the humor that it took him several silent steps and a sip of his coffee to relax from the adrenal rush of the statement. "Well, if you say so. No further communications from them?"

"One, but I will not ungate it on you yet, as it is quite large. It is instructions for one of their languages. Secondrace's, apparently. I will ask you to learn some of it, enough to be polite, but both Why Ask Questions and Answers Will Not Help are working on that with more forks."

Tycho quickstepped enough to fall in beside True Name as they made their way back to the central hub of the complex. "That feels somewhat out of place to me."

"How do you mean?"

"Well, if firstrace is there in a leadership capacity, why not send that language?"

The skunk shrugged. "We do not know. They did not include any of that information in the message. It will be something that we can ask, whether prior to or at the conference."

He nodded and looked out at the bustle of the room, as active as it was when he had arrived and when he had gone to sleep. He wondered if the various forks shifted their sleep schedule such that there were always True Names and Jonases at work.

"So, uh...what's on the schedule for today?"

True Name tilted her head momentarily, then nodded. "You will be working with Answers Will Not Help and two others to help spin up the effort to work on getting the upload side of the Ansible working to their specifications."

As if on command, Answers Will Not Help appeared before them, followed shortly by two others. Tycho supposed that the skunk must've sent each a sensorium ping.

The Odist grinned to him, then gestured to each of the new guests in turn. "Sovanna Soun is a sys-side Ansible tech, who will be working on that part, and–"

Tycho was already leaning forward to shake the hand of the other guest, a slight gentleman who looked every one of the seventy years he had been prior to uploading. "Dr. Verda, wonderful to see you again."

"Likewise, likewise."

"You two know each other, then?"

Tycho nodded. "Paolo was one of my professors, yes."

"Well, what do you know," Answers Will Not Help said, laughing. "Right, then. If the three of you will follow me?"

They made their way to a conference room where they sat around a long table, both True Name and Tycho still nursing their coffees. Answers Will Not Help pulled a wheeled whiteboard over and uncapped a marker, beginning to diagram on the board.

"I will be managing the effort," she said, writing 'AWNH' and circling it at the top. Two lines were drawn diagonally down from that. "As mentioned, Ms. Soun will be working on the Ansible software modifications. Dr. Verda will be working on the math side required to have the Ansible track the ship as it moves. It was built to be mobile in case we did need to send or receive anyone from Lagrange in an emergency, but I am told that it was meant to require manual intervention."

Tycho frowned. "Two people working on all of that?"

"Two clades, yes." She continued to diagram on the board. "As discussed, Ms. Soun will begin with a clade of ten to work on the software, and Dr. Verda will begin with a clade of two. Both can expand as needed. We need to ramp this up and complete the changes required within two weeks, so it is important that we be able to move quite quickly."

"And what about me?"

Answers Will Not Help wrote his name next to hers, then

drew connecting lines to all three names already on the board. "You will be acting as Artemis consultant and manager. We will deliver all messages through you and you will pass on any information required bidirectionally. Due to your relative inexperience with forking, your specialized knowledge of our visitors, and a certain bold *je ne sais quoi*, we will be keeping you at one fork for the time being."

Dr. Verda laughed. "Bold? Our Jo– er, Tycho?"

He felt a heat rise to his cheeks as Answers Will Not Help replied, "He is the one who said yes to the Artemisians before we had the chance to do anything about it."

Everyone looked at him.

"Uh, sorry."

"What the fuck, man," Sovanna said, laughing. "So all this is your fault?"

Answers Will Not Help laughed as well, waving her hand. "Do not be too mad at him. Or do, but do not tear into him too much. He has already received the Odist third degree."

"I have?"

"True Name threatened you with death, did she not?"

Tycho froze. "I...what?"

The skunk grinned over the rim of her coffee cup.

"Even the smart and bold may be denser than lead, I suppose."

Sovanna laughed and patted him on the arm. "Don't worry, Tycho. I was just giving you shit. No idea what Answers is talking about."

Answers Will Not Help capped the pen and, with startling speed, threw it at Sovanna. It struck her in the shoulder, getting a yelp from the Ansible tech and making both Tycho and Dr. Verda jump. The grin never left her face as she spoke, but her voice was frigid. "You are not permitted to call me 'Answers', Ms. Soun. Understood?"

Eyes wide and hand holding onto her shoulder where the pen had struck, Sovanna sat, wide-eyed, and nodded.

"Now, if there is no further need for third degrees, shall we begin?" Her voice was back to its normal, joyous self with a surprising adroitness. Something about her seemed decidedly ungrounded.

The three nodded together, silent.

"Excellent. One moment, then."

The three walls of the room that did not contain the door quickly expanded outward, leaving a broad, open room. Fourteen desks sprouted from the floor, divided into a group of ten and two groups of two.

"Cubicle walls?"

When Sovanna shook her head and Dr. Verda nodded, both pods of two sprouted cubicle walls around them, the pod of ten melding into shapely desks. With a final flourish of a bow, Answers Will Not Help welcomed them into the room. Above the pod of ten hung a sign that read 'Ansible', and the two pods were labeled 'Astro' and 'Admin' in turn.

It was all quite skillfully done, but Tycho still felt a slight pang in his chest. It was generally considered a violation of social norms for public sims to violate Euclidean space without warning, but private sims were beholden only to the holders of the ACLs. This room would occupy at least one office on either side, if not more.

Quite unnerving.

Answers Will Not Help spoke as she walked. "Begin by estimating your work. We will meet in one hour. After that, we will meet twice a day, more often as needed. Please feel free to ping me if you need anything. I have granted you all access to cones of silence and music, which you may use at your discretion or when requested. Tycho, dear, with me."

Sovanna forked as she walked, further instances of her blipping into existence beside her, each one walking up to claim a seat. It took Dr. Verda longer to fork, but soon, there were two of him.

Tycho simply followed his new boss to the admin pod. She

gestured him to one of the cubicles while she took the other. Once they sat, the wall between the cubicles lowered itself and he found that their two desks faced each other. At a gesture, a cone of silence fell over them both.

"Alright, Dr. Brahe. I am going to grant you access to the language dump that they sent our way. I would like you to take a look at it over the next hour and see how easily you might be able to pick it up. From what it sounds like, they already have a good grasp on our *lingua franca*, but in order to be polite, we ought to also work on learning one of theirs."

He nodded. He could already feel the presence of that information lingering on the periphery of his memory. "I'll give it a go. I've never learned another language but I guess there's a first time for everything."

"Excellent, thank you. Again, you do not need to gain mastery over it. That will be my job. Why Ask Questions and I have several instances working on it already. If you find yourself in need of assistance, let me know and I will request a merger from them so that I can pick up what they have learned." She waved a hand and a few notepads spooled out of the air between them, along with several pens. "I do not know your preference, but here are some materials for you. You are also welcome to create further copies if you need, and should you require anything more advanced, ping me and I will make it happen."

He collected the notepads into a pile on his desk, setting the pile of pens next to them. Each was unique, probably to give him a variety to choose from.

"Please also be prepared to set aside your work should the others request any further information from you. I believe Dr. Verda would be the most likely, as you are not an Ansible tech, but one never knows, yes?"

"Alright," he said, jotting down on one of the nicer pads with one of the nicer pens a list of what he was to do. "Language, be available. Anything else?"

"Nope, that is it. Your #Tasker instance will be working on

separate items." She waved a hand again and the cone of silence dropped as the cube wall once more raised up between them. Muffled on the other side, he heard, "See you in an hour."

Codrin Bălan — 2346

Convergence T-minus 20 days, 21 hours, 23 minutes

Codrin was not sure what ey expected out of a dinner in the middle of a clearing beneath the stars, but ey found emself quite taken with it. A round table had been set up atop the hill on which ey had interviewed Tycho so many years ago, along with six chairs evenly spaced around it. The whole table was lit by a single candle burning in the center and the starlight from above.

True Name greeted eir party of three with a bow when they entered the sim. "Mx. Bălan, Dear, wonderful to see you two again. Ms. Genet, a pleasure to meet you."

The three bowed politely in turn.

"Nice to meet you too, The Only Time I Know My True Name Is When I Dream," Sarah said.

"Please, just True Name is fine, but welcome all the same. Shall we?"

"Please." Dear sounded its usual self, Codrin was pleased to note. No anxiety or anger colored its tone. While the dark was pleasant, ey wished for at least light enough to see Dear's expression. As far as ey knew, the fox hadn't seen the skunk in two decades, not since their Death Day party, and that amidst a crowd. Certainly not since the *History* had come out.

At the table, introductions were made. Tycho remained as nervous as he'd been before, but ey was happy to see that he had at least gotten some sleep at some point, and none of the exhaustion that had so visibly gnawed at him when last they spoke was evident.

Why Ask Questions looked much as the Odists that resembled Michelle did, though far happier and more ebullient than any Codrin had met. She was, as Codrin#Pollux had described her two decades previous, perilously friendly, comfortably casual, and a shithead. Ey liked her immensely. "Delighted to meet you all. Codrin, nice to meet you face to face on this LV. And Dear, how long has it been?"

The fox grinned, nodded its head to her. *"I believe nigh on sixty years. You are looking well."*

"As are you! Your other partner did not wish to join us?"

In the light of the candle, Codrin watched the fox's grin falter, and ey suspected that it was taking it a good amount of energy to maintain a pleasant façade for dinner. *"They were not able to make it, no, but they send their best."*

They had not.

The discussion veered perilously close to an argument when Dear stated that it would be joining Codrin.

"Dear, you've had nothing positive to say about True Name basically ever. Why the hell are you going to this?" they had asked toward the end.

"Because I want to learn more if I can." It had paused, then added more quietly, *"And because Codrin is going and I want to be by eir side, if only as a fork."*

Their partner had wilted and nodded. "That, at least I can understand. I love you both, is all, and I'm not comfortable with either True Name or her up-tree instance. I want you to be careful, but I suppose you're right. Having the two of you there makes me feel a little better than it being just Codrin, at least."

Ey shook away the lingering rumination and gratefully accepted a glass of wine that Dear offered. The skunk had been pouring one for everyone, and ey supposed that wine might help make the evening flow more smoothly.

Once everyone had received their glass, she raised hers and said, "To Artemis."

They all raised their glasses in a toast, Dear adding, *"To exciting times."*

Why Ask Questions laughed. "How do you imagine user11824 will take all of this?"

"Horribly, of course. When do you plan on releasing the news?"

"Tomorrow," True Name answered. "We will release a priority alert into the perisystem feeds. Answers Will Not Help is working on that now, I believe. I trust that none of you have told anyone else?"

Sarah and Tycho shook their heads.

"Just my partners and Ioan," Codrin said.

True Name frowned and there was a brief pause as, ey assumed, she sent off a sensorium message to another of her instances. "Do you think that Ioan will tell anyone?"

Codrin shrugged. "I didn't tell em to, but I didn't tell em not to, either. I imagine ey'll tell May Then My Name."

The skunk sat silent, looking down to her glass of wine. Ey couldn't quite read the emotions on her face in the flickering of the candlelight, but given eir previous conversation about True Name losing her up-tree instance to hatred, ey could guess that there was at least some anxiety behind that silence.

Eventually, she asked, "When did you send the message? Was it eyes only?"

"It was, yeah. I sent it about noon. Why do you ask?"

"I would like to let my clade back on Lagrange know to either discuss this with em or to prepare for the possibility that ey will tell others. Five hours is not too long, though. As long as ey has not published anything to the perisystem feeds, of course."

Ey frowned. "Should I not have?"

"Oh, no, you were perfectly welcome to, Mx. Bălan. While I do wish that you had informed me before doing so, I understand your reasons." Her expression brightened. "But come, let us not talk about such at table. How are you all feeling about the upcoming adventure?"

"Scared," Tycho said with a nervous laugh. "Excited, but also scared. I worry that I caused a huge problem. I know you promised me that what I did was okay, but all the same, I worry."

True Name nodded. "I understand. I harbor my own fears. We have to rely on the fact that all of the tests of the DMZ passed and that there really is no way for the border to be crossed. May Then My Name tested it quite thoroughly."

"If you say so. From what Tycho#Artemis sent me, it sounds like it'll be a trade, too."

"A trade," Sarah said thoughtfully. "Why, do you think?"

Why Ask Questions laughed. "No clue. My personal guess is that it is a hedge, that they are wanting to meet on both vehicles so that we can see what their lives are like while they see what ours are like, but also it gives them a chance ensure that we still meet on territory that they control, just in case we decide to murder all of them when they arrive."

"Is that something we're worried about, too?" Tycho asked.

"It was Tycho#Artemis that brought it up in the first place," True Name said.

He blinked, then shook his head. "I've only heard from him via sensorium message. He hasn't merged back down yet."

"*I will never understand taskers,*" Dear said, giggling. "*With apologies to present company, of course.*"

Tycho looked nonplussed.

Codrin grinned. "Dear's an instance artist. Its entire existence is built around forking. If it did not fork, I'm sure it'd explode."

"*I would, yes, and you lot would have to clean it up.*"

Everyone around the table laughed.

True Name began to turn her gaze on Sarah, but Tycho interrupted her before she could speak. "How sure are we that this is real?"

Silence, minus a pop from the candle flame in the center of the table. Codrin found emself holding eir breath.

True Name's gaze bore down on Tycho with such intensity that the astronomer shied away from her.

"I...sorry."

"Please expand on that, Dr. Brahe."

"I just mean...how sure are we that this signal is real? How sure are we that it's coming from the Dreamer Module and thus outside of Castor?" He shrugged, still looking cowed. "I've been worried about the whole thing since it showed up, but the more I think about how long we've been going and all the risks involved, what's the probability that it's just us dreaming that there are aliens out there? They learn our language and tech so fast it's hard not to worry."

The silence fell once more, and Codrin imagined True Name and Why Ask Questions both sending off rapid-fire sensorium messages. Ey caught a glint of excitement in Dear's eyes. Ey suspected it'd have plenty to say before long.

"It is not zero," True Name said after nearly a minute. "Low, yes, but it is not zero."

"Does that–"

"There will be time, Dr. Brahe. Please do not worry. The best and brightest are working on this." She raised her glass, and in the meager light, Codrin could see that confident smile return. "Yourself included."

Tycho nodded, lifting his wine glass an inch or so off the table in a token response to the toast.

"How about you, Ms. Genet?" The skunk asked. She had, Codrin realized, read the silence as well as em, finding the perfect moment to guide the conversation back on track. "Assuming that they are indeed real, how do you feel about our guests?"

Sarah set her wine glass down, looking up to the stars. "I don't know if 'curious' is an emotion, but that's at the forefront of my mind. I'm not feeling anxious or scared, and I guess I'm a little excited, but more than that I'm just feeling curious about the whole venture. Will they look like us or will they look like, uh...Douglas, was it? Douglas Hadje? If we're to go visit them on Artemis, too, what will we look like? How will we talk? How will we empathize with each other?"

"You are a psychologist, yes?"

She nodded. "Yes. I think that's why I'm so fixated on trying to learn as much as I can. I'm curious about what makes them *them*."

True Name smiled brightly and nodded. "As am I. I am glad that you decided to join us on this. I think that having the perspective of someone both interested in and experienced with those aspects will prove eminently useful."

"Glad you're having me along."

"And Codrin? How are you feeling about this?"

Ey sat up straighter and thought for a moment. Ey was feeling quite a lot. Ey was feeling jerked around. Ey was feeling all too passive. Ey was excited. Ey was scared. Ey was still trying to process Tycho's question, wondering how ey would reply without thinking only of the implication that the Artemisians might be an artifact of the System going haywire.

Ey was incredibly happy that Dear had decided to join em at dinner.

Not all of those felt like things that ey could share, so ey settled for a safer answer. "I'm feeling excited and nervous both. I'm excited because this is another unprecedented thing that I get the chance to see, and I'm nervous because that very unprecedented nature means that I have no foreknowledge to lean on. I'll be working in the dark as the...what did they call it? Recorder?"

Dear reached over and took one of eir hands in its paw. *"You have lived through several unprecedented events, my dear. How does this one differ?"*

Ey fiddled with eir wine glass in eir free hand as ey thought. "I think because I don't have a frame of reference for what to expect. Launch was exciting and unprecedented, but I also knew that life would continue on in many of the same ways that it had before afterwards. Winding up in a relationship was new and unprecedented, but I can still comprehend my partners as people."

"Fox people."

Ey grinned. "That too, yeah."

True Name raised her glass. "I will drink to that, Mx. Bălan. I will admit to feeling some of the same trepidation around not having a frame of reference. We are limited to a few letters and a language primer as yet. I do not know what to expect, and that is, as I am sure you can imagine, a somewhat frightening idea for one such as myself."

Ey raised eir glass and smiled warily, returning the subtle squeeze that Dear gave eir hand. Ey was thankful for the dim light of the candle, which let em make out the features of the two Odists sitting across from em, but not a whole lot more; ey could only hope that the same was true for them. It was enough to make out True Name's charismatic confidence, if nothing else. Ey could certainly see what the skunk was doing, deftly avoiding the question of reality, keeping the conversation flowing smoothly, guiding and steering.

"And you, Dear?" Why Ask Questions asked. "I know that you are not joining us, but I am interested in your thoughts all the same."

The fox retrieved its paw from Codrin's hand, choosing instead to wave it up at the sky. *"This is the first time that I have been to this sim. It is yours, is it not, Dr. Brahe?"*

The astronomer nodded.

"It is truly a delightful place. I have stars in the sim where my partners and I live, but they are the familiar constellations that we remember from our time on Earth, though certainly more stars than I ever saw in the Central Corridor."

"*We* ever saw," True Name added. "We got the moon, a few planets, and the brighter constellations."

"Yes," Dear said with a hint of a bow. *"This, however, is incred-*

ible. We are seeing the stars as if there were a glass dome over our heads. They do not twinkle. The constellations are not quite as I remember them. They feel older, somehow. We are sitting beneath the universe, it feels, and above us lies eternity.

"You must forgive me for monologuing, it is an old habit, but when I think about what is happening, when I hear about Artemisians and emissaries, I feel every minute of that eternity. I feel every molecule of that universe. You ask how I feel, and I would say that I feel small. Insignificant, even. We have been on our journey for twenty years and have made it only a light-month from Earth. How much of that eternity must they have been traveling?"

A thoughtful silence followed the fox's short speech. It was Sarah who finally broke it, lifting her glass much as True Name had. "To eternity and the weight of the universe."

Dear sat up and clapped its paws, grinning brightly. *"I am pleased that you are going on this excursion, Ms. Genet. What a perfect toast."*

They all laughed once again, raising their glasses toward the single flame in the center of the table.

"I think that is a note to begin dinner on, yes?" True Name said, waving her paw above the table, plates and flatware appearing, along with several dishes of various types.

She must've talked Tycho into giving her some ACLs in his sim, ey thought. *Because of course she did.*

"Please! Eat. Enjoy. I did not make it, but you may pretend I did if you would like to bolster my ego."

The self-deprecating comment was delivered so easily that Codrin found emself laughing even before realizing it.

"No more shop talk until dessert," Why Ask Questions added. "Or I will have Tycho bounce you from the sim. There is lasagna, and I will not have you spoiling that."

Tycho Brahe#Artemis — 2346

Convergence T-minus 19 days, 6 hours, 58 minutes

The dream repeated each night.

As always, the hallway continued however many miles dream-logic determined it must, and as before, he kept walking down it, kept walking and walking and walking, right hand always trailing along the wall. That wall was of smooth stone, something coarser than marble and smoother than concrete, and as he felt it play out beneath his fingers, he heard the voices ahead of him.

There was a room, there ahead of him. He could see the light spilling into the comparatively dim hallway. Sunlight, cool and bright. He could see that the left-hand wall of the hallway continued. A corner, then, the hallway dumping him out into the southeast corner of the room.

Southeast...how did he know that?

There on that wall, shadows played. Shadows of leaves, the arc of a fountain.

And in that room, that soft rush of water only served to muffle the voices of so many others. They had to be the Artemisians. They had to be. But the water was just loud enough, added just enough white noise, that he could pick out no singular detail. There were fricatives. There were plosives. There were sibilants.

And the harder he listened, the more details he almost-but-not-quite heard. First there was the sound of a masculine voice, and then the sound of something more feminine. First there was the careful modulation of some machine-produced voice, then the melodious tones of something undeniably organic.

And he wasn't supposed to be there. He was supposed to be somewhere else. He wasn't allowed. He wasn't permitted. He was supposed to be somewhere different, not creeping along the unending right-hand wall of the hallway, straining to hear yet more detail from a group of incomprehensible others.

And still he crept along. Still he strained to hear, still he stared at that wall, hoping for the barest glimpse of the smallest shadow, hoping to discern the shape of the unknown.

And then a silence fell among the voices.

And then he turned the corner.

And then he was blinded by the sun.

And then he awoke, the lights of the room staring down at him reprovingly.

The dream always seemed determined to cling to him, as it had the day before and the day before that, and even as he showered and dressed, even after True Name once more met him at his door and handed him his coffee, he tried as hard as he could to remember even the smallest detail of those voices.

"You seem distracted today," the skunk observed. "Not just tired. What is on your mind?"

He jolted to awareness and smiled sheepishly to her. "Uh, just a dream sticking with me from last night. Third night in a row I've dreamed about them."

"The Artemisians?"

He nodded. "It's like I can hear them talking, but not any details about them. I can hear *that* they're talking, I guess. I keep trying to learn more and then I wake up."

True Name smiled. "I know the feeling, yes. It is that desire to know more, yet having it kept from you. Are you dreaming in their language or in English?"

"I can't even tell that. Sometimes I think it might be one and then some little phrase sounds like an accented version of the other. I wouldn't be surprised, though. I've been learning as much of that as I can during the day."

"I imagine so, yes. Would you like a small break from language acquisition? If you are having dreams about them, perhaps you can come up with some specific questions and we can send them a message." She patted him on the arm. "Time-boxed, of course, but it may give you a chance to come up with some ideas that we have not."

"Really? You'd let me do that?"

She laughed, nodded. "Of course, Tycho. You are always welcome to ask to do something other than what you are. We would request that you fork to do so. However, since this is not your area of expertise, I am sure that Answers Will Not Help will be willing to give you, say, two hours to work on something else if it will also serve to increase our knowledge of the situation. One moment, please."

There was a moment of silence as True Name stood at the entrance to the central work area, sipping—or, well, lapping at—her coffee. After a moment, Answers Will Not Help showed up before her.

"Morning, dear," she said. "Everything alright?"

"Tycho would like to take a few hours to work on a message to the Artemisians. Are you alright with that?"

Answers Will Not Help laughed and nodded. "Oh, by all means. We will get by without him for a bit. See you at lunch, Dr. Brahe?"

He nodded.

After a minute or two, another woman stepped into the sim, looking almost-but-not-quite identical to Answers Will Not Help. Perhaps a long-lived fork? The ebullience was toned down somewhat. Still the same grin—but kinder. Still the casual dress—but more of a weekend outfit. "Tycho Brahe, yes? True Name says I will be helping you out on writing a letter."

"Oh, uh," he frowned. "I guess so. Answers Will Not Help?"

She waved her hand in a non-answer, instead beckoning him over to another door along the wall. "Come on. Let us get this going. I am excited to hear what you come up with."

True Name raised her coffee cup to him and smiled. "Good luck, Tycho. Do keep in touch."

The office was much smaller than the conference room where he'd initially met Sovanna and Dr. Verda. They sat on opposite sides of a desk, where the Odist swiped two notepads and two pens into existence. "Alright, so I have been told that you had a dream. Tell me about it."

As he did, she jotted down details on her own notepads, occasionally asking him questions—do you remember what the air smelled like? Were there human voices as well? Why were you anxious about being found out?—and though it felt silly at first, he realized that she had teased out greater details of what it was that his dreaming mind was curious about.

"Alright," she said. "Let us come up with five questions out of this. They seem to like the number five."

"If you think that we can do one paragraph per question, perhaps we can ask about whether there are common areas that have a *lingua franca*, too. I think we have *how often do the four races interact?* already."

She shrugged as he wrote down the question. "I do not see why not. We are not limited on bandwidth. I would also like to know if they have similar strategies of forking, if they even have such. As part of that, we can ask about clade structures and naming, given the implications of both Turun Ka and Turun Ko."

He took a moment to write this down, as well as a few other sub-questions she mentioned along the way.

"What else do you think would be helpful?"

"Well, there's lots I want to know, but since we only have so much time before the talks begin, I guess we should keep it relatively short."

She nodded.

"What about when each of the races joined? That would give us an idea of how long they've been traveling."

"Good one." She grinned, tapping her pen against the table. "I knew we kept you around for a reason."

Had she said it in any other tone of voice, had all these Odists not been so good at choosing his responses for him, it could have easily come off as insulting, but it was said with such obvious affection that he laughed. Something about her was ever-so-slightly different from Answers Will Not Help, though he couldn't put his finger on what. She was more earnest, perhaps. More focused on making him feel good rather than only seeming always on the edge of laughter. Perhaps this was the Why Ask Questions who would be among the delegates, the one who had eaten with Tycho#Tasker.

And yet she'd not given her name, and so he was forced to consider the 'long-lived fork' scenario.

This is why I'm a tasker, ey thought. *I'll never understand clades.*

"Should we also ask where they came from?" she continued.

He frowned. "I don't know about that one. It can be a very involved answer, and who knows, maybe even touchy. Perhaps a separate set of questions for science down the line, since those will take them more time to come up with. Maybe we can come up with a list of questions to have them prepare answers for at the conference."

"Oh! Wonderful idea!" She paused, likely sending off a note to one of her cocladists. "We will tackle that at a separate time. I agree with you, though, that keeping this to more cultural and social topics will help. We can offer similar in return. Let us ask about leisure activities, then. What kind of stories do they tell? How do they tell them? Is storytelling limited to certain individuals, or considered a skilled trade? Is there a concept of work to make leisure time important?"

Tycho scribbled the rapid fire questions down on the pad, nodding as he did. Once he was finished, he said, "That got me thinking of another question, but I'm not sure how well it fits, so feel free to poke holes in it. How do you feel about asking if they dream?"

She laughed delightedly and clapped her hands. "Oh, I absolutely love it, my dear. I only have one request of you."

"Yes?"

"That must be the entire question. We can expand on the others with our little sub-questions and a paragraph of why we are asking them, but for this last one, it must be the only three words that they read pertaining to it. 'Do you dream?'"

He blinked, tilting his head. "Are you sure?"

"Of course I fucking am," she said, grinning widely. "I am the politician, you are the nerd. Now, let us hammer out some answers to these questions for ourselves that we can send. Answers to the first four, I mean. We will not answer 'Do you dream?' for ourselves."

Tycho stopped himself from asking why, realizing she would likely answer in the same way. "Alright, then. This is fun, thanks for giving me the chance to work on it."

"Of course, of course." She giggled, leaning across the table to ruffle his graying hair. "You fucking taskers, you need breaks, too."

He laughed, struggling to re-comb his hair with only his fingers, once more surprised at just how comfortable she made him feel. He liked her, whoever she was.

Ioan Bălan — 2346

Convergence T-plus 9 days, 4 hours, 48 minutes
(Castor-Lagrange transmission delay: 30 days, 14 hours, 36 minutes)

"I never wanted this. I never wanted any of this!" the skunk shouted, stamping her foot and jabbing her finger toward em. "You talk about how much I mean to you, how much this place means, and then what? Nothing ever comes of it."

"What the hell *is* supposed to come of it?" Ey stood quickly enough to knock the chair back onto the ground, all but lunging toward her. She stood easily a head shorter than em, but, having decided that this wasn't menacing enough, ey forked two times in quick succession, three of em advancing on her.

Rather than quail under the threat or simply run away, she stood up straighter, arms crossed, her expression proud and defiant. "Really? Are you *really* sure that you need all this to make your point?"

Ey—all three of em—faltered in eir advance as the skunk continued.

"I never, *ever* should have stayed around here," she said, voice suddenly frigid. "And I certainly never should have stayed with an asshole like you."

With the slam of the door still ringing in the air, eir two forks quit as ey stumbled back to the chair, slowly righted it, sat down heavily, and buried eir face in eir hands.

Ioan made sure to stay still even as the lights came down and the applause began, holding eir position all the way until the noise of the audience was muffled by the curtain. Ey finally sat back in the chair, stretching eir arms up and taking a few long breaths.

A pair of soft, fur-covered arms draping over eir shoulders and an equally soft-furred cheek pressing against eir own brought em out of eir reverie, if reverie it was. Ey tilted eir head against her cheek and held her arms to eir front.

"Hey asshole," the skunk said, echoing the epithet from a minute before.

"Hi May." Ey grinned, turning eir head enough to get at least a sidelong glance at her. "Well done on that 'ever'. Thought you were going to punch me in the stomach or something."

She nipped at eir shoulder, letting em feel sharp teeth even through the thick fabric of the costume, before standing up. "That would be out of character, my dear. Both for my character and me. Might be fun sometime, though."

They made their way backstage, letting the hands—several of whom were also them—deal with the scene change. Backstage, then back behind even that to their dressing room, where they were each able to get straightened up in front of the floor-to-ceiling mirror.

As always, when coming face to face with emself in costume, the feeling of being someone else all but disappeared, and ey marveled at the fact that ey'd even let May talk em into this however many years ago. If there was one thing that ey was, it was a historian, right? It was a writer. An investigative journalist, right? Ey was in no way a stage actor, right?

But the Ioan that stared back at em, one skinny almost to the point of gaunt, one with sallow skin and sunken eyes, was proof of the opposite. It had taken em at least a year to really, truly master the art of forking over and over to carefully modify one's appearance. It felt counter to so many instincts, and even still, ey left a Ioan back home, unchanged from the view of emself that felt most at home, just to ensure that there remained some tie to that. May had chided em for this, but ey couldn't let go entirely.

"I do not know why you decided to write a scene where I have to yell at you," the skunk said, bumping her shoulder against eirs. "Love the story, hate the scene."

"Hey, we've had our arguments."

"Well, yes, but I do not like those, either, so that is not a point in its favor." She grinned, poked em in the side with a dull claw. "And never during any of them have I yelled at you or called you an asshole."

Ey laughed and reached up to tug at one of her ears. "Well now's your–"

Ey froze.

The longer ey held still like that, the deeper May's frown grew, the more her tail twitched this way and that in agitation. Still, she let the silence be and didn't touch em, unwilling to interrupt what must be a rather long sensorium message.

Finally, ey sagged, rubbing eir hands over eir face. "Uh, sorry. Can you send a fork back home? I'm going to have to try and push that out of mind for the time being, and I don't want both of us to be in that state."

The skunk nodded and forked off a new May, then stepped from the sim. The remaining instance sighed and slipped her arms around eir middle. "You cannot leave me totally in the dark, my dear, or I will be distracted worrying about something I do not know. Can you at least tell me something so that I do not lose my fucking mind?"

Ioan grinned and returned the hug, resting eir chin atop her head. "Dreamer Module," ey mumbled. "That enough for you?"

Back at the house, the root instance of Ioan was walking circles around the dining room table, 'pacing holes in the rug' as May would say.

Did say, it turned out, when she first entered.

"Sorry." Ey pulled out a chair at the table and sat, but did so very carefully, deliberately trying to avoid simply wanting to get up and pace all the more. "News from Castor."

At that, her ears perked and she pulled out the chair beside em. "Alright, spill it."

"Someone picked up the signal from the Dreamer Module. They say they understand the bit about how to use the Ansible and an astronomer—Tycho Brahe, who Codrin interviewed for the *History*—gave them permission to without thinking."

The skunk frowned, sitting up straighter in her chair. "So aliens are going to upload to Castor?"

"It sounded like they were forty days out from their closest approach. Codrin didn't know when exactly the upload window was." Ey frowned as ey picked apart the remaining bits of message. "Apparently they've named the remote ship Artemis and the aliens Artemisians. That's about all I received, other than Tycho said 'yes' and Codrin will be working with him on it."

"I am assuming more will be coming soon, knowing you and Codrin." She doodled on the surface of the table with a blunt claw. "I am also assuming that other Odists are not far behind in moddling. How long ago did this happen?"

Ioan squinted, then shrugged and just brushed eir hand along the table, a sheet of paper unrolling from nothing with the message itself written on it. Ey unlocked the clade-eyes-only ACLs and handed this to May, who read carefully.

"So, thirty-ish days ago. Nothing we can do but wait for further messages. Anything we send back will be two months too late." She hesitated, set the paper down, and looked at em searchingly. "What do you make of the second half, though?"

"I'm still trying to process that."

"Do you not feel the same?" She reached out a paw to take one of eir hands in her own. "You got into theatre after all, did you not? You are not doing much in the way of history these days, other than the occasional paper. Did you really feel as though you had been sucked into all those projects with no input?"

Ey let her lace her fingers with eirs as ey thought. Words were a long time coming. "A little, I suppose, but this bit about feeling a lack of agency is new to me. I don't know that I ever felt that strongly about being dragged along or anything."

"Perhaps it is Dear."

"How do you mean?"

She squeezed eir fingers between her own. "I think Codrin and Dear settled into a life of their own on Castor, but you know Dear. It is intensely focused on these big dramatic gestures. And before you say it, I am focused on drama, but rarely are my actions in life dramatic. I am happy with the life we have built. I am happy living with you and loving you and pushing you into writing increasingly weird plays."

Ey laughed, lifting her paw to kiss her knuckles. "Well, sure. You got me to settle down, I guess. I don't think Dear is capable of settling down that much, but its patterns are familiar. It will do as it does and drag others with it."

"I hope you do not resent me for that," she said, tapping at eir chin with a finger. "I do not get the impression that you are unhappy, my dear, but I occasionally worry that your life now is not entirely the one that you wished to build."

"I have no idea. I don't think I had any real plans for building a life." Ey sighed. "Which I guess is kind of where ey's coming from. Without direction, any influence feels like getting yanked around. I felt yanked around by True Name shoving you into my life, though I love you dearly now that you're here."

May beamed happily at this, and ey was reminded of eir promise to emself to say that more often.

"Do you think ey will be able to take greater control of eir life?" she asked. "You still occasionally get stuck, but I was surprised when you were the one who asked me how to write a script."

"Well, only because you wouldn't shut up about how bad the one you had was." Ey rolled eir eyes. "Skunks are so annoying. Ow!"

"If you call me annoying again, I will pinch you again. A third time will earn you a bite." She grinned, teeth sharp. "All the same. I am glad that you are happy. I do wish we were closer to Castor, though, so that you and Codrin could have an actual conversation about this. You may not be able to respond much about the Artemisians, but perhaps you could explain some of your thoughts on agency."

Ey nodded. "I'll do that, yeah. Any suggestions?"

"Ey could ask #Pollux," she said thoughtfully. "Perhaps ey could do a grand gesture and surprise Dear. I have loved it every time that you have surprised me. I do not think that Codrin#Castor has learned how to do that yet."

"I'm not sure I know how to teach someone how to do grand gestures."

She tugged at eir fingers. "You have become a playwright and performer, my dear, do not sell yourself short. Besides, to hear Dear tell it, ey is not incapable. The name thing, of course. The surprise dinner a few years back. The forking stuff for its gallery show. Ey is just shy, perhaps."

"It's a Bălan thing," ey said

"And it is our job as Odists to fuck with you until you break out of it. I have faith in em, just as I had faith in you." She slid the paper back across the table to em. "You just need to pass that on."

Codrin Bălan — 2346

It was not at all surprising that dinner at home was far less stressful than dinner with the Odists out in Tycho's observatory. While the conversation throughout the meal had been nothing but pleasant, the food delightful, and the location and single candle a stunning setting for a dinner, a tension had nonetheless hung above the table throughout. While Sarah had appeared relaxed and True Name and Answers Will Not Help seemed to earnestly enjoy the evening, Tycho had been hovering on the edge of terror, Codrin had remained hypervigilant, and Dear had seemed to have put on a mask of pleasantness that involved choosing its words most carefully.

This was confirmed when they returned home and the instance of Dear which had accompanied em to the dinner sagged, exhausted, and then quit. The instance of Dear which had remained behind, when confronted with the onslaught of memories, sighed and simply shook its head. None of the triad seemed at all interested in discussing the dinner.

It was eir other partner who had suggested the smaller party for the next night. While they hadn't explicitly mentioned that it would be a counter to the first party, it was certainly implied. Something to cleanse palates, as well as to give further time for Codrin, Tycho, and Sarah to interact before they were to go on their journey. All three—four, including Dear—had immediately agreed.

So it was that they sat around the table, there in the modern house on the prairie, sharing wine and desserts and pleasant, easy conversation.

"So," Sarah said, leaning back in her chair. "I was thinking about the fact that we seem to have wound up with jobs. Honest-to-goodness go-to-work-for-the-day jobs. What did you do before this? You all know that I was a psychologist before I uploaded. I still am, I guess. Dear, you did theatre, right?"

The fox nodded. *"Michelle was a high-school theatre teacher. I suppose you can see why it is that we are so dramatic."*

She laughed. "Some things carry through even two hundred years later, I guess."

"Nearly two hundred sixty, yes. I would complain about being old, but when one is functionally immortal, bitching loses its savor."

"You bitch plenty, Dear," its partner said.

"Yes, but how often do I bitch about my age?"

Codrin shrugged. "You bitch about immortality a lot. Does that count?"

The fox smiled primly. *"It does not, my love."*

Still laughing, Tycho said, "It's probably no surprise that I was an astronomer on Earth as well."

"How'd that even work?" Sarah asked. "When I was there, we could barely see any stars."

"All space-based stuff. Besides, radio telescopes don't need quite so dark of skies. Amateur astronomers were the hardest hit. They had to drive way the hell up into the mountains, and even then, wait for winter when logging season was over. I taught, too, and a few classes were out there. I volunteered at a dark-sky site."

"That makes your sim make a lot more sense."

He nodded proudly. "The landscape is based off one of those sites."

Eyes turned to Codrin, who shrugged. "I went to school, then a year of a history degree at university before I uploaded at twenty to help my little brother out after my parents died. I never really had a job, just interests that got all the stronger once I got here."

"Had you needed to get a job while down there, what would it have been?" Dear asked. *"I have a guess, but I want to see how close I am."*

Codrin picked up eir glass and leaned back against eir chair, thinking. "I wanted to be a librarian quite badly. History was a secondary interest. I planned on getting a bachelor's in something like history or literature and then a master's degree in library science."

Dear tilted its head. *"I was close on the bachelor's but was not expecting the master's. What drew you to that?"*

"Books."

Eir partners both laughed.

"What other answer could I possibly give?" ey said, grinning. "I like books. I like knowledge. I like having it all collected in one place, even if books were falling out of fashion back when I was phys-side."

"A horrible shame. I do not have the same attraction to them that you do, my dear, but they are still delightful."

"You take it to almost a fetishistic level, Codruț," eir other partner said, the playful, diminutive form of eir name adding another layer of teasing. "For which we love you, of course."

Ey rolled eir eyes. "Domestic abuse, I say. Let me turn it back on you, though, what did you do?"

They heaved a deep sigh. "Line cook at a diner."

"Is that why you're so into cooking?"

"Basically, yeah. I wanted to be a chef, but you kind of need to start at the bottom and work your way up. I just gave up on actually doing that and uploaded instead."

"I had a similar job in school, actually." Tycho said. "Nothing fancy but I–"

He trailed off, staring up into space with a blank expression, then shook his head. "Uh, how willing are you all to talk about the Artemisians?"

Shrugs all around.

"Uh, sorry," he said, pausing a moment longer, and then sat up straighter when a few folded sheets of notebook paper slid down to the table in front of him, neatly missing both wine and half-eaten tiramisu. "Tycho#Artemis sent a list of questions to the Artemisians today. I think they weren't expecting the reply to come for a day or two, but it showed up after only five minutes, minus transit. Weird..."

"What sort of questions are we talking about?"

"Social and cultural, it looks like. Nothing really scientific. Want me to go through them?"

They all nodded.

"Alright. He asked when each of the races joined and the answer sounds complicated. It looks like about a thousand years or so between each."

"So they started about four thousand years ago?"

He looked up to the ceiling as he calculated. "There are specific numbers. They add up to...five thousand, three hundred twelve years ago. Thing is, I'm not sure if that takes relativity into account. From our perspective, that could be a much larger number."

"Holy shit," Dear's partner said. "Think they're batty?"

Dear laughed. *"It depends on how sane they were before they started and how their system is structured. Probably, though."*

"Well, I guess we'll find out soon enough. Let's see...there were a few questions about how the races interact. It sounds like they have several common areas available, but there are still enclaves of the different races that mostly keep to themselves. Apparently most speak a form of secondrace's primary language because firstrace was...uh, hmm. They say electronic. I'm not sure what that means. Maybe they were robots of some sort? AIs? They didn't need to talk with words. All races except firstrace still have several different languages of their own which they speak at home and in their own sims."

Codrin nodded. Ey had summoned a pen and notebook and was already taking notes. "Will they be teaching us any of them?"

"He said he's already learning the secondrace language. Maybe you should, too."

Ey scribbled down a note to emself to ping True Name for access.

Sarah was leaning forward on her elbows, looking particularly interested. "I would like to as well. One can learn an awful lot about a person or group based on the language they speak."

Codrin amended the note to include her name. "I'll have True Name send it our way."

Tycho shrugged. "I'm not going to bother. If #Artemis is able to merge back, I'll pick it up then. I'll make sure he does it before he leaves."

"Good idea, yeah. The more who speak it the better, just to be safe."

"Alright. Next set of questions were about forking."

There were a few blips of other foxes behind Dear, startling Tycho.

"Apologies, Tycho," it said, grinning widely, tail whipping about behind it. *"I may not be joining directly in the endeavor, but I am intensely curious to hear about this."*

"Well, alright. I hate to disappoint, but it sounds like the only times they fork are in an emergency or during a contact like this — 'convergence', they call it. They have to petition some sort of central leadership called, of all things, the Council of Eight, which sounds like two representatives from each race, to create any long-running forks."

The fox flinched back as though slapped, its ears laid flat and its brow furrowed.

"They provided additional information, though. They say that fourthrace had the same concept of forking that we appear to, so they understand our questions around dissolution strategies and clade structures. #Artemis also asked about their naming system, and apparently Turun Ka and Turun Ko are from something akin to a clade that existed before the voyage began. Something from when they were electronic but not on their system.

"Instead of forking, they have individual, fine-grained control over time. This is how they responded so quickly, apparently: they slowed time way down so that they had as much as they wanted to write their response. They ask if this will be accommodated during the talks and there's a note from True Name here saying that, even if it were possible, she's going to answer no. Tycho said she looked upset."

"Unpleasant business," Dear muttered darkly. *"Unpleasant to an extreme."*

"Well, what's the next question, then?" Codrin asked. Whether it was the mention of the Council of Eight or the news about forking, ey couldn't guess, but the fox was clearly upset as well. "Perhaps we can move away from this one."

"Next, they asked about leisure activities. It sounds like they're fairly similar to us in that very few people have actual jobs, but several have what they call 'intensive leisure activities, such as scientist or author'. He asked if they have stories and if so, what kind, and their answer goes on quite extensively."

Codrin scribbled hastily to take down the question. "Can you ensure that I get a copy of the responses, too?"

"Perhaps we all should get a copy," Sarah suggested. "I'm curious about the language bits and this thing about stories."

"As am I. If True Name allows, I will ask for a copy as well."

"Me too," its partner said.

"Can you give us an overview of their answers?" Codrin asked.

"Sure," Tycho said slowly, skimming through the rest of the page and onto the next. "They say that stories are of the utmost importance to all races, that there is no limitation what kind, or who may tell them, but that, quote, 'of the occupations that many hold, that of storyteller is the one held in highest regard'."

Dear brightened considerably. *"I will forgive them their atrocious naming choice for their leadership, then. They do sound interesting aside from that."*

"I'll admit to being mostly confused about it, or at least more focused on the astronomers they have on board, but it's all still interesting." He flipped over to the last page and frowned. He sat silent for several seconds as he stared at the paper, as though willing further meaning to rise from it. "I'll quote the last bit in its entirety. #Artemis asked, 'Do you dream?' There's no further questions or explanation."

Dear rolled its eyes. *"How very us. I bet Why Ask Questions suggested that."*

If Sarah had been interested before, she was nearly staring holes into Tycho now. "What was their answer?"

" 'You have asked the correct question. We are eager to meet you.' Verbatim. That's it."

A silence fell over the table while they digested this, each in their own way.

Codrin sipped eir coffee while ey thought. *The correct question* made it sound as though they had reached some sort of milestone, perhaps, especially when taken with *we are eager to meet you*. It made it sound as though humanity had completed a mission by asking that.

And yet, there wasn't an answer to the question given, if Tycho was right about the message. They didn't say yes or no, they didn't say what about. They simply seemed to be smiling through the page, and ey couldn't tell whether that smile was one of satisfaction, encouragement, or pride.

It was Dear who broke the long silence. *"Is there anything else to the message?"*

Tycho shook his head. "Nothing from the Artemisians, no, but #Artemis has added a note here that he asked that because he's been dreaming about them every night." He paused for a moment before adding, "I have too. The dreams aren't like the ones he describes, but just this feeling that someone is coming and that it will be this momentous thing and we have to be as ready as we can be."

Sarah nodded. "There's no real interpretation to dreams other than they can reflect some of what you were thinking during the day. It sounds like you're both quite focused on it. Anxious, perhaps."

Tycho nodded eagerly in agreement.

"Very much so," Codrin said. "I had a dream about them last night, too. It was just this vague idea that I knew they were coming and that I needed to be observant."

"That makes sense, given your role," she said. "I haven't been remembering my dreams since we got the news. I don't think I've been sleeping very well."

"Even for me, who will not be joining, it very much all feels like a dream," Dear said. *"The whole thing does."*

After their guests had left and the trio sat down on the couch for a bit before bed, Dear dotted its nose against Codrin's cheek. *"My dear, I do not want to talk about it now, but I have something to tell you about this business with time modulation that may prove useful to you."*

Ey nodded, feeling the fox's nose tip still lingering near eir cheek. "I'll look forward to it, Dear. At your own pace."

"It is nothing bad. Just stressful, and I do not yet know how to put it into words. I will say that this will impact all Odists in approximately the same way, though, which is why you should know if there are to be two of them joining you."

Tycho Brahe#Artemis — 2346

The sight of the dissemination of the news of Artemis was beautiful in much the same way that a ballet was. This was, he supposed, largely due to the well-coordinated dance of both messages flying back and forth and countless Odists and Jonases moving back and forth in the largest of the conference rooms he'd seen yet.

He knew that there were sims where one could fly. Flying, after all, fit well within the realm of something that any number of people could consensually imagine together. They held a perennial appeal for a certain type of person, of which he was not. A fear of heights combined with a certain neurotic work ethic led him to stay away from those sims in general. If it was fun and not also productive, he felt little need to engage. It may have been unhealthy, it may not have been, but he had never stuck around anyone long enough to hear either way.

Now, however, he could see the utility.

A whiteboard had sprouted up from the floor, beginning at waist height for the shorter Odists and extending up by now a storey and a half. Panels on it showed the news feeds and commentaries piped in through the perisystem architecture, that foam of conceptual computer-stuff that tied all of the sims together and allowed cross-sim communications.

Even now, as more news flowed into the board, it would pop up from the bottom and the whiteboard would inch ever higher.

And standing before it, whether they were standing on the ground or however many meters above it, Odists and Jonases worked, tagging each of the feeds with arcane symbols, drawing lines from one to the other, conversing in small knots, popping into existence and quitting as needed.

This involved none of the graceful floating that ey had seen before on eir excursions to sims whose owners allowed such. They were not drifting about on the breeze, they were simply standing on something that was not there. If they needed to move to another level, they would simply walk as though on a ramp or step up as though on a ladder. It was productive movement at its very core, and it immediately appealed to him but for the height.

The Odists were not tall. Every time he was near, Tycho felt that he dwarfed them. He could easily have rested his chin atop True Name's head without lifting it at all. "You, who have your head in the clouds and feet on the ground," he remembered her having said about the Balans, and the phrase had stuck with him. His feet were a steel-toed anchor, and though he towered above the others, he could never name the feeling of being that much closer to his beloved stars.

And yet here he was; Tycho Brahe, terrified of heights.

"What am I watching?" he asked Answers Will Not Help beside him.

She nodded toward the board and the quiet, purposeful bustle of activity before it. "We have released the news about the Artemisians out into the feeds. You are watching the observation and shaping process."

He stood up straighter, fixing his posture as though that would quell second-hand vertigo. "How did you do it? How are you doing it?"

She laughed. "Come. I will show you. We will need to go to the top. It is like walking up stairs, do not worry. Just will the step into being."

"Uh, the top?" He furrowed his brow. "What happens if I fall?"

"You will probably die," she said, shrugging.

He stumbled back from her. "What the fuck?"

"I am kidding, Tycho Brahe." She laughed, sounding giddy. "You will fall onto whatever level you are currently on. You are, what, 190 centimeters? 195? That is not too far a fall."

Still frowning, he lifted a foot, imagined there to be a step and set it down, landing about ten centimeters above the floor. He brought the other foot up to join it and then looked down, windmilling his arms for balance. "J-Jesus..."

"Fucking nerd," Answers Will Not Help said, laughing. "Come on, it is not too bad. Try to take bigger steps, too, or it will take forever to reach the top."

She stepped as though she were taking stairs two at a time, and within a handful of bounding steps, had reached the top of the board. She gestured at the five topmost panels.

Deciding that he wasn't brave enough for the leaps and bounds, he simply looked straight ahead and began walking as though up a staircase. It was dizzy-making, and he had to gulp for air a few times to ensure that he was still grounded, such as it were.

"Look to the side, as though you are looking over a banister, perhaps," she called. Several of the Jonases and Odists were watching now, and they laughed at the remark.

Despite the heat burning in his cheeks, Answers Will Not Help's suggestion helped a good deal, and he was able to complete the rest of the journey quickly enough, though by now, the top of the board was easily two storeys up.

"Took you long enough, nerd." She elbowed him in the side, grinning.

"Is that just my name now?"

"Might as fucking well be." She walked over to one of the panels of news feed. This was labeled *Science* beneath, and seemed to head up a column of related material that continued down to the ground. "Let us just start here."

Studiously avoiding looking down, he read the contents of the panel.

> On systime 227+52 at 2328, the Dreamer Module on Castor received a structured message from an external source, alerting scientists and perisystem technicians to a fast-moving artificial construct. The message, which follows, suggested that the entity or entities at the other end of the signal understood the instructions for utilizing the Ansible receiver, provided trajectory information, and asked for consent to upload. Consent was granted two minutes and thirteen seconds later by a member of the astronomical community. Further messages have been exchanged, and talks are underway for an exchange of emissaries.

The message was published by none other than Sovanna Soun.

A *member of the astronomical community* was a much better way to describe him than he suspected the Odists might otherwise.

He walked to the next panel over and read.

> **Credible sources** announce that ALIENS have discovered our LV and are ON THEIR WAY TO GREET US. The *Powers That Be* could not be reached for comment. In order to prepare for an invasion, all sim owners should *lock down* ACLs for their sims and **interrogate** ALL visitors!

He laughed. "Did you write this one?"

"Oh, no. We have some of our pet propagandists write much of them."

The next two feeds seemed to be fairly credible news sources. Boring and straight-forward announcements regurgitating the scientific report in lay terms.

The final panel contained simply the first two messages that had been received followed by `Leaked anonymously ;)`

"That one *was* my doing," Answers Will Not Help admitted, grinning. "I thought it particularly cheeky."

"I guess it is, at that." He rested a hand against the whiteboard—blessedly stable—and looked down carefully. "So what's happening beneath us?"

"We are tracking the dissemination of the news. We follow each of the sources to see where it is being quoted and referenced. There is some delicious perisystem tech going on there that I will not bore you with."

"And you're just watching?"

She gave him a pitying look.

"Right." He sighed. "Can I see?"

She shrugged. "Sure. Step down the same way."

Still leaning against the whiteboard, he stepped down a meter or so to the next row of panels. Below the 'leaked' documents, he read a spray of conspiracy theory rambles. Next to each were long scribbled notes, mostly in a shorthand he couldn't untangle.

"What are the green-tinted ones?"

"Shaping." Answers Will Not Help nodded to one. "That is one that I wrote. When I say that we have been shaping the response, this is what I mean. We have simply been participating. We are not doing anything crazy here."

He leaned closer to read.

Listen, I don't think it's unreasonable to find this all hopeful. Like, seriously? Aliens! How cool is that? We've all had our dreams (or nightmares!) about them over the years, right? By virtue of us being on a hunk of computronium hurtling through space, it's kind of at the forefront of our minds, isn't it?

All I'm saying is that we gotta be at least a little bit careful. There's this DMZ that everyone keeps talking about, but what I don't understand is just how it works. Like, okay, it's a set of sims that one can't get in and out of? How the hell is that supposed to work? They (Artemisians???) can upload there, but what does that even buy them? A way to take up space?

I think I'd feel a whole lot better about this whole thing if there was more clarity, is all. I'm a bit behind because holy shit this is all coming fast, but do we have any Ansible/perisystem nerds on this feed? Help me out! Explain this to me like I'm stupid. It's true enough, after all.

From this panel, several branching replies headed down the board, and alongside each, further notes from the Odists and Jonases. He picked one at random and read that next, though in the time he had taken, the board had continued to creep upward.

I don't think any one person knows how the perisystem works, and the DMZ just adds a layer of complexity on top of that, so don't feel like you're stupid. I've been a perisystem tech for 130 years and it took me three forks just to get caught up on this.

You can think of the DMZ in two ways. One would be to think of it like a separate System. It works exactly like the one we're on. Sims, forking, ACLs, all that. Just like how the LV Systems are like separate Systems from the Lagrange System, though, we all had to upload using an Ansible connection. That is how the border between the LV system and the DMZ works. You basically have to go through something like a software Ansible to get in and out, and just like the real Ansible, there's a bunch of security in place so that there can't be any pirate signals.

The other way to think of it is like the lungs and the whole LV as a body. The DMZ can expand to take in more individuals (can't say people anymore if we're going to be letting Artemisians on board), but it can't expand beyond the capacity of the LV System itself, nor, indeed, beyond some pre-determined limits. In this metaphor, the individuals entering it are the air, and the pre-determined limit is the chest cavity.

This is how we keep the rest of the System from getting 'contaminated', which I've heard brought up before, and those limits are in place to keep the DMZ from driving up the cost of forking on the rest of the System should it expand much further. I had to dig super deep for this—no clue why it was buried—but the DMZ will have its own, separate reputation market to manage this, since it'll be a different size, but just like how currencies phys-side affected each other, with inflation and deflation, we'll probably see some fluctuations in the markets here, but I wouldn't expect anything too bad.

Anyway, hope that helps!

He nodded toward the panel he had just finished reading. "So you injected a question you probably already knew the answer to and some tech answered it to help make everyone feel better?"

"Better is not quite the right word. Calmer, perhaps. There is an appropriate balance between happiness and anxiety that we want to strike."

Tycho frowned. "I never got that about the *History*."

"We do not want people to be too happy because unlimited happiness is a happiness with no defense mechanisms." She poked him sharply in the side with a finger, making him wince and jerk his arm to guard himself better. "A purely happy society would feel that pain as agony and be unable to do anything about it. A society that is just anxious enough can enjoy security but also guard itself from further pain. It can be happy but also wish for more happiness."

Rubbing at his side, he began to step down away from the scrolling wall of information. "If you say so. I don't see why it wouldn't be self-regulating, though."

Answers Will Not Help fell into step beside him. "It might, sure, but there is no guarantee in the face of immortality. We are just the safety mechanism, the limiting factor."

"You just keep it from swinging too far one way or the other, you mean."

"I knew you were a nerd," she said, laughing. "Got it in one."

"How do you decide what the limits are, then?"

"Data analysis." She gestured back to the board. "Predictive models. Countless simulations. We do not steer in any one particular direction, we simply provide the bumpers around the extremes."

He breathed a sigh of relief when his feet touched the ground again—the real, visible ground—then turned around to look at the board stretching upwards. He didn't believe that they didn't steer the system. Even if they didn't do so consciously, there was no guarantee that they weren't imposing their own ideas and ethics on everything around them.

He declined to mention this, however. The last thing he wanted was another poke in the side.

Codrin Bălan — 2346

Convergence T-minus 5 days, 0 hours, 51 minutes

Late spring was for picnics. This was, ey was assured, a universal truth.

Once the rains had calmed down and before the oppressive heat began to drift lazily in, this was the time for those who are in love to drag a thick blanket out onto the prairie, park next to one of Codrin's cairns, and share sandwiches and fizzy drinks. This was the time for parking in the sun, laying back on the blanket, heads together and feet radiating outwards, sharing in small silences and comfortable conversation.

"There is no reason that aliens should interrupt this," Dear had stated plainly and then dragged its partner off to the kitchen to make sandwiches and bottle up gins and tonic to bring out to the prairie.

All the same, this picnic was more muted than usual, and when they settled onto their backs, Dear's ears tickling the tops of their heads, the conversation felt careful, as though all words should veer around the topic that was on everyone's minds.

A bit more than two weeks after first contact, and the entire LV seemed to be talking about nothing else. Dear had even postponed the opening to its new show. News from Tycho was that, from day one, the Odists had been working on and shaping the spread of information.

113

Codrin suspected that this had come when it did in part due to the transmission delay from Lagrange, and, given what ey expected would happen with Ioan and May Then My Name, ey did not doubt that this tight control was for good reason—or at least what True Name considered good reason.

Ey had kept that thought to emself.

Ey expected True Name would be visiting eir down-tree instance and eir partner before long. Ey had suspected she would do as much as soon as ey had read anxiety in her expression at the mention of May Then My Name. She had surely sent a message back to L5 within seconds of em telling her such.

It was the reaction that ey was most worried about. True Name was a touchy topic with Dear, and the cold hatred of one of its cocladists was...well, ey could read melancholy in the fennec's face as easily as any other emotion. Ever since news of May Then My Name's thoughts on her down-tree instance had made their way across the light-days of distance, there had been more of that. There had been days of silence, days of tears, days of walking the prairie for hours at a time. When pressed, it would simply say, *"She is the best of us."*

Ey suspected that it was worried that cracks were showing across the clade. Ioan had admitted to having such concerns as well, and even mentioned that May Then My Name herself seemed to be harboring fears. "If Dear overflows with undirected energy," Ioan had written once, years ago. "Then May overflows with tears. It's the only time she ever asks to be alone, and I will go stay with Douglas. I make a lot of chicken soup for her to have something comforting, though I'm not sure how much it helps. She will spend hours in bed, letting out all of the overwhelming emotion that she needs to in order to become whole again. I love her deeply, but I'm sure you must know the pain of watching someone you love going through something like that."

That had been another thought ey had kept to emself.

The worry lay not in how May Then My Name might react—

though Ioan had always mentioned when ey was laying in supplies for chicken soup—but in how True Name would. May Then My Name may be the best of the clade, or at least the best of that stanza, and even True Name knew that.

So today, they mostly lay in silence. It was not unpleasant, for the sun was on high and the temperature was perfect and ey could simply lay there with those ey loved.

It was Dear, of all of them, who broke the silence.

"I have been thinking about something that Sarah said." It sounded content enough, which Codrin was pleased to hear. *"She said that we should prepared to not be able to understand them for their inhumanity."*

"What about it?" their partner murmured. More than content, they sounded sleepy.

"There is much we can learn about semiotics from them. We have the ability to guess, but vanishingly few chances to check. If they are truly alien from us, we may be able to confirm many hypotheses that we have had for centuries by now about how a different mind can form and hold ideas."

"Different environment, different *Umwelt*, you mean?" ey asked.

"No no, that term applies to those who exist within the same environment. Our environments up until now have not even been connected. We have completely different semiospheres, do we not? We cannot even make assumptions about how they form their ideas, how their semiosis works, at least not at first. It could be that there are key differences in how they are able to take in information and make meaning of it."

"New senses?"

Ey could feel it shrug against the picnic blanket before it said, *"Perhaps. Perhaps they can sense radio waves, or perhaps, as suggested by their letter, they can sense time in some new way if they have fine-tuned control over how they experience it."*

"Don't we have forking and merging?" its partner asked. "Aren't those new senses? Or at least sensations?"

"In a way, I suppose, but we can learn them. They are tied to will, as one wills a fork to exist, and they are tied to memory, as one deals with the merger as though one is remembering the fork's experiences."

Ey could feel the idea click into place. "But we may not even be able to experience that in the same way as them. We may learn it in a fundamentally different way. Maybe we won't even be able to take part in it because we ourselves may be fundamentally different."

Dear sat up quickly, laughing. "Yes, precisely! What an interesting problem. I am excited to see what all we learn."

The other two sat up. Codrin was not at all surprised to see the grin on the fox's face.

"This is, of course, all supposing that they really exist."

Their partner laughed. "Is this in doubt or something?"

"Tycho said something at the first dinner, yeah," Codrin said. "He asked if there was a chance that they weren't real and that we might actually be dreaming the whole thing up."

"Wouldn't that take an awful lot of dreaming to accomplish? Dream the incoming signal, dream our...uh, instruments, I guess, tracking Artemis, dream up this whole thing about races and such?"

Dear shrugged. It looked quite pleased. "Perhaps, but is that not an internally consistent dream? A dreaming mind that starts with the proposition of aliens and enough knowledge of our little world would be able to construct a consistent narrative to get us to where we are. The Dreamer Module, the micro-Ansible, the DMZ, all of it." Its grin widened, the volume of its voice rising. "Or perhaps the System aboard Castor is losing coherency! Perhaps our world is falling down around our ears and we would never know!"

Codrin laughed, watching the fox get more and more animated. "I'm pretty sure we'd know whether Castor is failing or not."

"Do not be so sure about that, my love. We have very little insight into the world outside of the LV."

"I'm pretty sure we have at least some," eir other partner

said. "Even if it's just by way of our communications with La-grange and Pollux."

"Yet even that may be a dream!" Dear giggled. *"You see why this is interesting to me, though, yes? If Artemis is real, then we gain new insights into semiosis. If it is not, I get my beloved natural death."*

Ey rolled eir eyes and shook eir head. "Foxes."

"You love me and you know it."

"Well, I mean, yes, but that was never in doubt." Ey leaned back on eir palms. "Either way, I hope that they're real. That feels like the better scenario to me."

"Boring."

"Hush, you," their partner said, poking at the fox's thigh.

"Both of you. Boring, boring, boring." It laughed. *"But I admit that I hope that they are real, as well. I am more excited about the semiotics of aliens than the idea that Castor is failing. For instance, there is much we can learn about them from their language, I expect. I am no linguist, but how they describe their control over time, should they choose to do so, will provide much insight into the ways something that is not us perceives and interacts with their world around them. They may process signs—signs in the semiotic sense—in a very different way, and we will be able to use that and apply it to the hypotheses that we have formed over the years."*

"Are there problems in that area that need solving?" Codrin asked.

"I do not know. It is something which is interesting to me for its own sake. Perhaps we can learn more about sensoria," it said, shrugging. *"For those who desire children, perhaps there are implications within that which will allow them to experience such."*

"Do you want children, then?"

"Good Lord, no." It laughed. *"I did not wind up with that desire. That is something for other elements of the clade. I am sure that Hammered Silver and her stanza would pounce on the idea."*

Its partner laughed. "I thought not. Besides, can you imagine a synthesis of the three of us? A historian chef that forks like mad."

They all laughed.

"I don't know how much of a historian I am anymore," ey said. "But doubtless they would keep my love for books."

Dear tilted its head. *"Are you not? You have taken on historiographical projects in the years since the* History, *have you not?"*

Ey shrugged. "I have incomplete thoughts on that."

The fox nodded. *"I will not push, but I am eager to hear them at some point."*

Ey nodded. "Of course, Dear."

Their other partner yawned, then let out a contented sigh. "You know, if sunlight had weight, I would use it as a blanket. It's such a nice feeling."

"'If sunlight had weight'?" Codrin laughed. "That sounds like a line of poetry."

They threw a pebble at em. "I need at least the feeling of a blanket over me if I'm going to sleep."

"Going to take a nap? We've got a blanket right here."

"I also need a bed beneath me."

Ey picked the pebble up from where it had landed on eir sarong and tossed it back at them. "Well, go in and take a nap, then. I think it's walking off the sandwiches and gin for me."

They tossed the pebble at Dear in turn. "Back to work with you?"

"Perhaps. I will send a fork with each of you."

As fox and historian walked out into the prairie, Codrin finally worked up the courage to ask Dear the question it had wanted to ever since their conversation on semiotics. "Do you wish you were a part of the emissaries?"

"No." Its response was flat and immediate. *"I have curiosity about the knowledge, but no desire to actually join in the experience."*

"You don't have to answer, but do you know why?"

It thought for a moment, then shrugged. *"My existence relies on understanding and responding to the actions and emotions of others. I will wait until there is a way for us to understand, and then I will experience it if I am able. If I am not, then I will simply revel in the story that you write."*

"I'll bring back as much information as I can. Maybe some of them will stick around and you can give them a performance down the line."

The fox laughed. *"Perhaps, yes."*

They walked in silence for a while longer. Codrin eventually gave up on walking off the gin and simply let sobriety back in.

"One more reason, my love."

"Hmm? Reason for...?"

"For not wanting to be a part of your talks. I do not want to be a part because of this time manipulation business. I remember how it felt to be one of the lost. I remember experiencing centuries or mere seconds in that endless place of no time. I remember wondering if I would die out there after a hundred years had passed by, and I also remember only a few minutes going by before Debarre showed up."

"Wait, *he* was the one who got you out? I would've thought some clinic technician or something."

"Of course, my dear. Why do you think we are so close to each other? Even after all that business in the early days, we are still close." It grinned. *"Please do not tell him this, but I have always been a little in love with him since then. Our tastes in partners differ, so few of the clade have never acted on it, just as Michelle never acted on it. I believe End Waking is the only one who has, and even that is complicated."*

"Ioan seems fond of End Waking."

"Of course ey does," Dear said primly. *"He is much like me if I was in any way serious."*

Codrin grinned. "Crazy, then?"

"A different kind of mad, perhaps. He is highly principled, though, and that along with the seriousness is a draw to Debarre, I think." After a few more steps, the fox added, *"But yes, as mad as any of us. None of us will be comfortable with such an eternity."*

Ey nodded, thinking back to the conversation they had shared so long ago, back when ey was newly Codrin. *Trauma, if trauma this is, forges bonds,* it had said.

"Not keen on more trauma, then?"

It shoved em playfully. *"You are a brat. I was just about to say that."*

Ey laughed.

"I will not go, though," the fox repeated. *"I will await your stories, but I will not go."*

"I'll bring back some good ones, then."

"I know you will. It will be an experience that I am sure many will want to know about. I know that, should you choose to write about it, the three Systems will look forward to it."

Ey nodded. The idea of a project such as this lingered in eir gut like a weight, and the fact that dread tinged the excitement ey had about it only added to eir anxiety. Ey kept these thoughts to emself.

"But, my dear, do be watchful. There will be two Odists on that mission, and they will share in some of my trepidation." It took eir hand in its paw and gave the back of it an affectionate lick. The gesture seemed to be one designed to minimize the anxiety in the statement, but eirs or Dears, ey could not tell. *"They share that same trauma. Be watchful and remember what I said: even True Name has emotions, even she will be affected."*

Ioan Bălan — 2346

Convergence T-plus 10 days, 2 hours, 3 minutes
(Castor–Lagrange transmission delay: 30 days, 14 hours,
36 minutes)

Ioan knew that it would be quite a while yet before eir and May's forks merged back down. Time Is A Finger Pointing At Itself, the director of the play, was quite strict but she also drank like a fish and clung jealously to some remnant of productions she'd remembered from more than two centuries ago, so it had become a comfortable rhythm for Ioan, May, and any other actors who wished to join to follow her to a pub that served strong drinks and greasy food.

Ey had been planning on a simple dinner on eir own, perhaps catching up on some reading, but with this knowledge and the fact that May was now here with em, the plan evolved into something more involved. Staying inside didn't feel right. Something about the news had them in mind of stars, in mind of looking up to the sky, so they wound up grilling burgers out on the patio and talked as they watched the stars come out one by one, sitting there in the house's backyard.

The burgers had long since been finished and the grill long since put away when Ioan felt an automated sensorium ping of someone entering the house, followed shortly by a real-time message from who had just arrived.

She did not give em time to react, nor even to stand. Ey had only managed to turn to look to the door opening out to the patio before the skunk stepped out onto the concrete, lit only by the string of lights tucked beneath the overhanging deck.

"I...what? True Name?"

She bowed quickly before holding her paws up in a disarming gesture. "Ioan, May Then My Name. I apologize for the brusque entry, but I believe we need to talk."

May growled, pushing herself to her feet. "I will leave you to it."

Ey had only ever seen eir partner furious on a scant handful of occasions, but now ey could add one more to the list. Her teeth were bared, tail bristled out, and hiked up, paws bunched up into fists. In the two decades since the research and publication of *On the Origin of Our World*, May's view of her down-tree instances had dropped precipitously, and all but one of those moments of fury had been triggered by her own clade.

"May Then My Name, please," True Name said, clasping her paws before her and bowing once again, lower this time. She sounded contrite, small. "I know that you do not hold me in high regard, but all the same, I would prefer if you stayed, as I am assuming that you have both received the same news."

May hesitated, frowned, and crossed her arms, but did not move to leave.

"Thank you," the other skunk said, straightening up and brushing her paws down her blouse, a nervous gesture ey had never seen on one who always looked so in control. "I will not take up too much of your time, as there is much to be done. Even though there are several of me already at work and this is my only task, my mind is still torn in many directions. May we please step inside where there is more light?"

Ioan looked up to May, who shrugged. She still looked as though she would like to either quit or bounce True Name from the sim entirely.

Once they were seated inside, True Name stared off into

space for a moment, and Ioan imagined her rifling through several exocortices at once, digging out a collection of files and memories.

"Alright," she said, shaking her head to focus. "First of all, may I see the message that you have received from Co-drin#Castor?"

"There was some content that was clade eyes only, but I'll share the first half with you."

"And there is nothing in the second half that pertains to Artemis?"

Ey shook eir head, drawing the first half of the message out from the tabletop as a bit of foolscap which ey handed over. "Co-drin had questions on careers. Nothing pertinent."

The skunk skimmed the message rapidly while Ioan and May looked on. Eir partner still held fury in her eyes. Ey only felt tired.

"Alright, this is much the same information that we received earlier today." True Name folded the slip of paper and slid it into a pocket in her slacks. "I am sure that you can guess why I have arrived in such a rush, but to be clear, True Name#Castor learned that Codrin had sent you this update. Ey was free to do so, but...well, it is our job to consider information security and hygiene, so she sent us an additional message immediately upon learning of this."

"And you are here to shut us up," May said.

True Name lowered her gaze. "I am here only to provide suggestions as to that same security and hygiene."

Ioan marveled at the sight of the skunk. She had always seemed so proud and in control, and now she looked to be on the verge of panic. She looked, of all things, frightened.

"Okay," ey said. "But didn't you and Jonas plan for this? Run simulations?"

"We did, yes. We even ran the fact that it might be you who received the information through our models," she said, nodding to em.

"But you did not count on me," May said.

There was a tight silence that lingered a long few seconds before True Name nodded. "We did not count on you. We did not count on *both* of you. We did not count on..." She took a shaky breath, recomposed herself, and continued. "We did not count on what changes the dynamic between you two would lead to."

"Your models included a historian, you mean," Ioan said. "And now you also have one of your own. You've got two actors, one of whom was purpose-built by you specifically to influence others."

She looked stricken, gaze jumping between em and May. "When one has lived so long with a certain set of expectations, having them subverted is a shock. May Then My Name, I do not begrudge you your feelings toward me. It is not my goal to win you back or anything like that; all I can do is admit my shortcomings and try to do better by you, even if that is, as you have requested, leaving you be. I truly am happy for you—for both of you—as you have accomplished something that I never could, that Michelle struggled with from the beginning. However, I have a job. I have goals to work towards. I have a vision that I would like above all things to uphold."

"You have painted yourself into a corner," May said. Her voice had lost the edge of anger at her down-tree instance's admission and apology.

True Name giggled.

It was a startling sound coming from her. Ioan had seen her laugh, grin, and smile, but they were all tightly controlled. They were all laser-focused cues to guide her interlocutor. The giggle held amusement, yes, but also nervousness. It seemed to be covering a much larger, less grounded emotional outburst. Ey had been considering just how much of this interaction up until this point was a carefully constructed act, how much of her visit could be dismissed with a wink and a grin, but there was something far too real about that giggle.

Ioan and May looked to each other and frowned.

"I'm sorry, True Name," ey said. "I mean this in all compassion, but you sound like you're about to lose it."

The skunk giggled again, sounding even less grounded, then rested her elbows on the table and buried her face in her paws, grinding the heels of her palms against her eyes before straightening the longer fur atop her head. "I am, yes. At least in a way. There are many threads happening at once and, as May Then My Name put it, I have painted myself into a corner with this one."

"Make your pitch, then," May said, voice softer still.

"It is a small ask, I hope," the skunk said, folding her hands on the tabletop once more. "Do not publish any of this information in the feeds or in some new book or play, and do not put it anywhere in the perisystem architecture. Not yet. I ask that you keep it between yourselves, Jonas, me, and other Odists. You may, of course, keep communicating with Castor, but I would ask that you not pass this on to Pollux yet. Codrin and True Name are working together, per the message I received, so I imagine our messages will contain similar content, but should anything interesting come up, I would be much obliged if you shared with me. Are you open to that?"

"Sure," Ioan said.

May shrugged. "I may talk to A Finger Pointing and End Waking about it, but I think you will have the rest of the clade under control before I wind up speaking to any of them again. I will likely also share this with Douglas."

The skunk stiffened in her seat and sat silent for a moment. "May I be there when you do? I would like to impress upon him the gravity of the situation."

"Absolutely not."

True Name winced, wilted, nodded. "I see. Well, if you would pass on my request for information security, I would be very grateful."

"I will," May said. "I will also be telling Debarre."

There was a long silence. Ioan could not read either of the skunks' features, nor guess at the sudden tension in the room.

"We'll also pass on your request," Ioan said at last, earning em sharp a glance from May.

True Name nodded slowly. Standing and once more brushing her blouse flat, she bowed. "Thank you both and apologies for the intrusion."

May stood as well and stepped around the table, taking the other skunk's paws in her own. It was strange to see the gesture of kindness after so tense a discussion, but the expression on May's face as she looked at her down-tree instance showed none of the friendship implied.

Ioan marveled. If the sight of two skunks that shared so much in common and yet differed in such fundamental ways was uncanny, seeing them touch in like this after so much acrimonious history bordered on distressing.

"You wrote to me back in 197," May said. "You pointed me toward Ioan and you told me, 'You are, in many ways, a better version of me, and the completeness that you bring to our stanza ensures that we add up to something that is greater than the sum of its parts.' You told me that you still love me in your own way. Do you remember that?"

The skunk canted her ears back and nodded.

May let go of her paws to hug her arms up around her cocladist's shoulders. "I still believe that."

True Name leaned into the hug. Ey couldn't see her face from where ey sat, but ey could still hear the sharp intake of breath and see the shaking of her shoulders.

After a moment, May leaned back, rested her paws on those shoulders, and said, "But please leave and do not ever, *ever,* come to my house again."

Tycho Brahe#Artemis — 2346

Convergence T-minus 6 days, 1 hour, 2 minutes

"Alright, are you ready?" True Name said.

Tycho nodded, "Ready as I'll ever be."

The transition from System proper to DMZ was as seamless as any, though when he checked systime, he found that nearly twenty seconds had passed. That would be an unimaginably long transit time within the system, where the transit between sims would take place faster than he would have been able to perceive.

"Well, that was not so bad," True Name said, walking out into the cloistered courtyard that had been set up for the meeting. "Now, let us check communication."

He wasn't able to sense anyone other than True Name and Answers Will Not Help. There were no options for a sensorium message with any others. He strained as hard as he could to sense Tycho#Tasker or Codrin or anyone else he could think of. There was simply nothing there. The sim was immutable and the disconnection complete.

True Name stood for several minutes in the shade of a tree, looking thoughtful as she ran through some internal checklist. At one point, he felt a sensorium ping from her, which he returned.

"Fantastic," she said, nodding. "Exos all there, no access to feeds, no transit, nothing. Reputation market looks on track for the DMZ as well."

Tycho checked his reputation, pegged at a minuscule *1000 Ŕ*, and then the costs. Sim creation into the millions, forking well into the tens of millions. No possible way he could afford either. "Will they arrive with the same amount?" he asked.

"Yes. We could not think of a way to decouple reputation entirely from the core functionality of the System," Answers Will Not Help said. "But we could at least make everything prohibitively expensive. This will allow us to make small changes if need be, but forking will be well out of reach."

"Really? Isn't that kind of fundamental to our existence here?"

"Allowing them to fork might prove dangerous, Tycho. We do not know how large their consciousnesses are."

He shrugged. "Well, sure, but if our goal is to provide an accurate representation of ourselves..."

The two Odists frowned at each other before True Name said, "You do make a good point. We will take it under consideration.

He nodded and began prowling through the courtyard. It consisted of a large, square area, a fountain in the center, and a large table beside it—"I will have full ACLs and enough rep to modify this if need be," True Name explained—all surrounded by a ring of trees, and that with a ring of covered walkway.

He paced around the perimeter, watching the way the sunlight shone through the trees and cast dancing shadows on the ground. They had been his idea, a lingering remnant from his dream. At two opposite corners, hallways led off to rest and sleeping areas. He walked down the one that led to the humans' quarters, turned around, and looked back toward the courtyard. The view was much the same as in his dreams, though here, the columns from the covered walk offered regularly spaced shadows along the wall.

He nodded approvingly and made his way back out to the central meeting area.

A copy of Jonas had also made his way into the sim and was poking his way around the table, inspecting pads of paper and pens. As he watched, another Jonas appeared and then quit.

"Alright," the Jonas said. "Transmission across the border works as expected. Memories transfer without loss, and merging is the same as always. No radio, no textual transmission, so you'll have to rely on a fork transiting the border to relay news."

"Wait, so neither party will be able to communicate outside of here?" Tycho asked.

"Nope, all locked down. You'll have to rely on the grapevine; Codrin has volunteered an instance. We can open it up later if we want."

"But if we're using forks and they're not allowed, won't that look strange?"

"You ask a lot of questions for a tasker," Answers Will Not Help said, laughing. "But yes, your point stands. Perhaps we will allow them one fork, maybe limited to their rest area. Thoughts?"

Jonas shrugged.

True Name made a note to herself on one of the pads. "We will talk about it back at headquarters."

"Will leave it up to you," Jonas said. "Still, good job, everyone."

Answers Will Not Help bowed with a flourish. "I am glad that you enjoy, O great political teacher."

He laughed and tossed a pen at her.

"Are you regretting your decision to stay behind?" True Name asked.

"Does it count as regret if I never wanted to go with?" He grinned, shrugged. "But it's a good setup you have. Only one set of cocladists, only one politician. It gives them a wide gamut to experience."

The skunk nodded. "Perhaps we will open it up at the end

and you will get to meet them. Maybe some of them will stay behind and live within the DMZ."

"We'll see." Jonas nodded to Tycho as he joined them around the table. "And here's to our scientist. Thanks for providing us with your dreamscape. It's a nice place to hold a conference. We've got everything from ancient Roman architecture to twenty-second century S-R Bloc conference tables."

Tycho shrugged. "It seemed like a nice place. Glad you like. When is this even going to happen, by the way?"

"Three days from now. They'll be one light-hour out, at that point, which will provide minimal risk during transit while still giving us the most time for the conference. With our burn, it should give us about six weeks together until we reach the point where we're at one light-hour apart again."

"Six weeks sounds like a long conference."

"We do not know how long the conference will last," True Name said. "It could be over in an hour if they prove to be pests. All we will need to do is shut down the Ansible, leave the DMZ, and wipe everything within it."

He frowned. "Wouldn't they be able to leave, too?"

"The border is governed by stronger ACLs than we are used to. One must have entered via the System in order to exit again, which they will not have done." She grinned. "But I do not expect that we will need to do this. With all of the chatter we have done in the last few weeks and with what my cocladists say about the language, they sound like a nice enough group."

"How do you figure?" Tycho asked. He prowled through his memories of the language that he'd learned in the interim. "It feels mostly...uh, normal, to me, if that's the right word. They've got all the same concepts for what we have. Bunch of words about fur, seems like."

True Name grinned all the wider. "Which automatically makes them better."

"That's mostly the point, though," Answers Will Not Help said. "They do not have a superfluity of words for war, weapons, fighting, of course, but they also do not have words for discussion that are so fine-grained that we will be out of our depth. They will talk much like us, which makes them easier to predict."

"Besides," the skunk continued. "You have read all of the messages we have received. They sound excited to meet us. They keep talking about how long it has been since they have had one of these 'convergences'. I *am* picking up the sense of an ulterior motive behind all that they say. Or, well, perhaps not an ulterior motive so much as a deeper version of their explicitly stated motives of having these talks. I think that they might want something out of it that they are not stating outright."

Tycho pulled out one of the chairs at the conference table and sat down, the others following suit shortly after.

"Isn't that kind of shady, though?" he asked.

Both Jonas and True Name shook their heads.

"Political adroitness isn't a bad thing," Jonas said. "It shows that they are a social culture, and that they are willing to at least try and move us in a certain direction. That, in turn, means that we can do the same to them without feeling bad about it."

"One would think that constructing something like this–" Tycho waved his arm at the sim and, by extension, the System that contained it. "–would require some sort of politicking, right?"

"Well, sure, but it could've been an authoritarian regime that press-ganged its population into building their version of the System in the first place."

"What about the other races, though?"

He shrugged. "That wouldn't have proved much. Maybe their System would have remained a totalitarian regime and they subsumed the other races. Still, seeing things like secondrace's language being the *lingua franca* rather than that of firstrace helps. Seeing these little glimpses of individuality are heartening. They sound like a varied culture, which is good for us."

Tycho nodded.

"And before you ask why that does not make it more difficult for us," True Name said. "Them having a varied culture means that there are at least some that might be sympathetic to us."

"Or susceptible to," he said.

He regretted the words as soon as they were out of his mouth. He felt in a precarious position, surrounded as he was by three politicians. Calling them out on their machinations was surely a dangerous move.

Answers Will Not Help giggled. Even True Name and Jonas were grinning. "You continue to amaze and delight, my dear," she said. "But yes, it does make them susceptible to our wicked ways."

He smiled cautiously. "Well, if you say so."

"Come on, let's head back," Jonas said. "We'll reset the sim, grab some dinner, and then we can go back to planning."

It took another forty seconds to transit the DMZ barrier going the opposite direction, and this time he could feel the slight resistance as he transited, as though some process were investigating him from head to foot, from outside in, to ensure that he was who he said he was.

Throughout dinner, he remained quiet, and no matter how hard he tried, he was not able to focus on the food. It was good, of course, as much of the food had been during his stay, but some part of his mind remained elsewhere. It remained back in the sim, back focused on the conversation that he'd had with the politicians of the team.

Since he'd arrived—even before then, even before the message from Artemis—he had felt in over his head. There was something about these people, something about the world that they'd set up that showed how they worked on some higher level than him. Their minds were so fundamentally different that, no matter how much they tried to explain the political ramifications, no matter how much they showed him their work in shaping the response to the news, he just couldn't take it all in.

It had seemed that True Name and Answers Will Not Help had loosened their control over him the longer he stayed with them. They paid less attention to him. They spoke more in commands than guiding questions. They smiled less and focused harder on the tasks at hand. Even Why Ask Questions, who he'd found himself liking quite a bit after working with her on the letter, had grown busier and busier.

He felt as though he had been purchased as a tool and then simply set in his drawer until it was time for him to be used.

How much input would he even have in these meetings? Was he to be, as Codrin had said, merely an amanuensis? Was his job simply to be there, observe, and pick up on the science aspect? Would he be allowed to take part in the conversations? Would he get to know the Artemisians?

There were far more questions than there were answers and, apropos to the situation, none of the answers were helping, so the cynical part of him kept thinking *why bother asking?*

It was almost too much, sitting there at dinner, trying to chat amiably, trying to enjoy the food, while all these questions and so many more circled around inside his head, hunting for some release, but there was no way that he could hope to ask anyone at the table that night, none of the True Names, none of the Answers Will Not Helps or Why Ask Questionses, and certainly none of the Jonases. Perhaps he could ask Sovanna or Dr. Verda—on hold until there was further astronomical data to process—but they were busy enough with their own worries that didn't surround acting as emissary to an alien race to bother with the social engineering going on around them.

After dinner, he begged the evening alone to rest in his quarters and paced, composing his message in his head.

"#Tasker," he said at last, beginning the sensorium message. "Can you talk to Codrin some about just what it is to be an amanuensis? I know ey talked to you about that and all, but I'm really not sure what it is that I should be doing, or what I even can do. I know I'm supposed to listen and record along with em, and I know I'm supposed to ask all the fancy science questions, but I'm starting to feel like that'd be better served by writing down a list of questions for one of the Odists to ask.

"Hell, I'm starting to feel like *they* wish that's all I'd do. They're nice enough, and they seem confident in their decision to use me as the science representative, so it's not like I'm off the team, I just don't know that I'll have any say in any of this, and I guess...I guess I'm just feeling lost.

"I'm sending this to you rather than em so that you're up to date. I feel like you ought to know some of my thoughts since you're...well, you're me. If I were any more confident in my ability to fork and merge just for this, I'd just do that, but even that feels way outside my realm of expertise. But also...even Codrin feels clicks above me. I don't want to make em explain every little detail to me just because I'm so socially dense.

"Get back to me if you can, but if not, at least let Codrin know so, that when ey arrives tomorrow for orientation, ey's got this knowledge, too.

"Anyway, uh...thanks, me. I'll merge down before we take off. I hope you're sleeping better than I am."

Part II

Experience

And so they sat around their campfire and talked and discussed and argued and strove and fought and laughed and wept. They sat around the campfire and raised their hands in vote, and it was decided that an ark was to be created and sent to explore, and any who wanted to go to see those campfires would have the chance. Those who dreamed of the opportunity chose universally to travel. Those who saw the risk as overwhelming did not. Those who knew that this might be an opportunity for themselves and for those who might consider them ancestors decided as they would: to go or to not.

From *An Expanded Mythology of Our World* by
May Then My Name Die With Me of the Ode clade

Codrin Bălan#Castor — 2346

Convergence T-minus 3 days, 7 hours, 44 minutes

The pattern-matching portion of eir mind could not stop making comparisons between this and previous projects ey had been involved in with the Odists. *On the Perils of Memory* had been a fairly disorganized affair, begun hastily and over far too soon, leaving the conclusion feeling outsized for the duration of the events at hand. *An Expanded History of Our World* (or *On the Origin of Our World* when taken with May Then My Name's *An Expanded Mythology of Our World*) had been a vast, sprawling affair that was fairly well organized throughout, though transmission times toward the end had begun to hinder coordination.

This, then, lay somewhere in between. While the news had been sudden and the pace nearly frenetic, it had been nothing if not organized. What had begun as a simple message had turned into a flurry of activity, where dozens of forks from four clades coordinated to plan around eventualities, discuss linguistic profiles, and work with Sarah Genet in her role as psychologist to find weak spots in the team and areas where they could shore each other up during the talks.

And through it all, hundreds of Odists and Jonases worked behind the scenes to ensure that every potential possibility was summarized and provided to the team through meeting after

137

meeting, presentation after presentation, quiz and question-naire.

Every time Codrin thought *hey, this is almost like-*, ey was brought up short by all of the ways it wasn't. It was organized and guided, but without the careful precision that ey now knew to be the case for the *History*. It was hectic and *ad hoc* but without the spur-of-the-moment surprises that came with *Perils*.

Consequently, ey kept finding emself stumbling when presented with a pattern that fit one project and then failed to fit completely.

At last, though, they had dotted all of the 'i's they could find and crossed all the 't's that they could think of and gathered to begin the final preparations.

The five of them trickled into the boardroom. They'd been told to dress 'nice, but comfortable', which didn't change anything for True Name. Why Ask Questions had dressed in a matching outfit. Tycho had swapped out a plaid flannel shirt for a plain white one, but remained in his jeans. Sarah had opted for a blouse and slacks that fit well with her middle-aged, mid-career psychologist aesthetic.

It left Codrin feeling somewhat overdressed for the occasion, but ey shook it off as best ey could. A few years prior, ey'd written a short paper on traditional clothing styles that had been ported into the System, many of which had seen a resurgence, up where cost was no longer a barrier. Ever since, when nicer dress was required, ey'd taken to dressing in various levels of traditional Romanian garb from the nineteenth and twentieth centuries. For this project, that meant an embroidered, wide-sleeved blouse and a simple, ankle-length wrap-around skirt, over which was layered *fotele*, an over-skirt rather like an apron, in rich, embroidered red, with a simpler panel of fabric hanging from the back.

Ey had even braided eir hair. Ah well.

"Alright," a Jonas said. He held a clipboard with a checklist he appeared to be reading from. "Greetings. True Name?"

They proceeded down the line, each reciting their version of the Artemisian greeting while an instance of Answers Will Not Help judged and corrected them. Ey recited eir greeting when eir turn came, but only from the most automatic portion of emself remaining. The rest was spent thinking about how much ey'd miss eir partners. How much ey'd miss home.

Jonas ticked a box on his clipboard. "Fork and tag your new instances #Castor. Codrin, we'll need another instance from you tagged #Assist."

Codrin and the two Odists forked immediately. Sarah took a few seconds, and Tycho apologized profusely thirty seconds later when he was finally able to manage the feat.

"I'm still not used to it, sorry."

Jonas waved away the comment. "You're fine, Tycho. Not everyone is True Name."

Both instances of the skunk made a rude gesture at him.

"Yeah, well, fuck you too." He laughed. "Alright. The rest of the tasks will be specific to each group, so–" He forked, and the new instance continued, "–#Artemises, with me to Artemis Staging#553a49c. The rest to Castor Staging#ad89ae3."

Ey lingered for a few seconds and thought. One thing this project had that none of the others had had was the feeling of stepping away from home and leaving it behind completely. There would be no coming home for dinner after a day of interviewing or researching. There would be no returning to the tightly controlled chaos that had become the comfortable dynamic among eir little family. Ey stood, watching the others step away, including the other versions of emself, and soaked in the sensation of longing.

When ey stepped through to the DMZ staging sim, ey was greeted by a nearly identical boardroom to the one ey had just left. There were, ey noted, far more whiteboards lining the walls, not to mention far more Odists and Jonases at work just beyond.

"We have an hour," Jonas said. "So let's finalize our plans for information gathering."

Codrin pulled out a chair at the table and sat between Tycho and Sarah. "Will this be mostly on Tycho?"

The astronomer shrugged. "We're the science side, yeah, but we can exchange all the math we'd like without meeting like this. I think it'd be better to say that we'll be talking about the differences in how we learn and proceed through science. It'll be good to learn what we can, and I plan on asking a ton of questions, but it's almost more Sarah's arena." He grinned, added, "Don't get me wrong, though. I'll still be more in my element than Tycho#Artemis."

"Correct," True Name said. "Tycho will be asking questions on math, physics, and astronomy, Why Ask Questions on biology and linguistics, and Sarah psychology, sociology, and health, but her other duty will be to observe how they answer and glean the different ways in which they learn and communicate to see how they tick and where our common ground lies."

"And I observe."

She nodded. "As always, yes, though I do not believe you will need to remain silent. Feel free to ask your own questions."

"What will you do?"

The skunk smiled and lifted her shoulders in a shrug. "What I do best, my dear. I will guide the questioning, perform risk analysis, and assess lines of control and weakness."

Ey had been prepared to make a mental note to pull apart her answer to come up with a way to divine her true intentions, but so honest was her answer that ey was wrong-footed into silence.

They talked through a few more plans, though there was nothing that they had not already covered on the docket. Another short language quiz. First questions they'd ask. A quick run-down of what textual descriptions of their races they had sent. The Artemisians had been startled by the Castor's inability to receive anything but text, so the descriptions had seemed hasty.

Something to ask about, Codrin thought.

All five of the party sat up with a start from a sensorium message, a little thrill of adrenaline, alerting them to the time.

Codrin was caught off guard at the lack of fanfare that their departure received. The Jonas who had been running the debriefing waved, and none of the others in the room did more than look over their shoulders as they were shunted over to the DMZ and ey was left blinking in the dappled sunlight of the meeting area.

Codrin Bălan#Artemis — 2346

Arrival.

Arrival and light and noise and a slick, slippery feeling to the air about em.

Codrin stole a few long seconds with eir eyes squinted shut. The light itself was loud, the noise bright. Everything was just slightly off, just slightly wrong.

And then, those seconds passed, and the noise was less blinding, and when ey opened eir eyes, ey no longer felt deafened, and ey was able to take in the world around em. The ground, the dome above, the colonnaded walls, the greenery beyond. Tight-fitting stone, slick and polished.

Before em stood what ey supposed must be the Artemisian delegation.

Turun Ka and Turun Ko, judging by their identical appearance, stood half again as tall as em. Their flesh, what might have otherwise been skin, was made of what looked to be a supple, rubbery material in gunmetal grey. Powerful thighs supported a stocky torso, and the fact that they were leaned slightly forward was counterbalanced with a thick, lizard-like tail behind them. Their shoulders were sloped and narrow, and ey could see now why they had described themselves as equally comfortable

143

on both two and four legs: their hands were clawed and padded with five fingers and an opposable thumb, but so were their feet.

Atop a long neck rising from their shoulders sat heads with a distinctly canine bent. They were shaped, in fact, not too dissimilar from Dear's, though the ears were less outrageously large.

It was the faces, though, that captivated eir attention. They did not have visible mouths or noses, their 'muzzles' instead being covered with a somewhat lighter grey version of that same supple coating. *Porous, perhaps?* ey thought. *To let them smell? I don't suppose they need to eat. Maybe for speech?*

Rather than eyes, there was a mirrored panel of black, looking more mercury than plastic or glass. No visible eyes, no visible expressions.

Well, this will be interesting.

To their right, a being of similar shape stood on two legs, though they were far smaller, coming up only to Codrin's chin. The longer ey looked, however, the more those similarities began to fall away. Yes, they stood on two powerful legs; yes, their body was canted forward and kept on balance with a thick tail; yes, they had an elongated snout.

However, rather than that supple plastic, they were coated in a scaly hide, washed in oil-sheen colors. Where the firstrace representatives had little in the way of facial features, though, Stolon almost seemed to have a surfeit. Their eyes were bright and curious, their mouth seemingly ready to a smile—or some other expression, ey reminded emself, as what appeared to be a smile to humans may not be so to thirdrace. They did not have hair, as made sense for what looked to be a type of lizard, but they did have a crest of what appeared to be feathers of a sort, or perhaps massively elongated scales.

Beside Stolon and standing a head shorter than even them was a creature that reminded em so much of Debarre that ey was caught off-guard. The resemblance was uncanny: a svelte coat of brown fur with a creamier white starting beneath the chin and heading down over their front—or at least, ey assumed it continued beneath the thin, blue tunic they were wearing—and a black-tipped tail behind. Plenty of whiskers, dark eyes.

The last of the Artemisians, Artante Diria, looked almost-but-not-quite human. Her features seemed far smoother, with a nose that melted into her face and earlobes that ramped smoothly down into her neck below. Beyond that, however, the differences were negligible. She could easily get lost in a crowd of humans with no problem whatsoever, another face of Asian descent, perhaps. She even wore a blue tunic and sarong of nearly identical cut to what ey wore so often.

All five stood still, expectant.

No, not still. Frozen. They stood frozen before the party of emissaries, unmoving. Nothing was moving. The air was still, the light seemed frozen, and it was eerily silent.

Frowning, ey looked beside em at eir own cohort, and much the same held true. There, at least, there was a hint of movement: Sarah was turning slowly to face a noise to her left, over towards where Why Ask Questions was standing. The movement, however, was more than just slow. It was syrupy. It was thick. It was out of phase with em.

All of it was out of phase with em. Everything. The world as a whole.

"The hell...?"

Ey stepped forward enough to look down the line to either side of emself.

Tycho: frozen, confused, blanched.

True Name: eyes held open defiantly, a grimace on her muzzle showing some internal strain.

Sarah: shocked, startled, curious.

Why Ask Questions: mid-shout, a splash of black fur creeping up over her cheek, a ghost of a muzzle before her face.

"What the hell?" ey repeated.

"You are recorder Codrin Bălan, *anem?*"

Startled, ey whirled to face the party of Artemisians. One of the firstrace members had stepped forward. Assuming the lineup was similar to their own, ey supposed it must be Turun Ko, the recorder, with Turun Ka as leader on the end. Its voice was surprisingly mellifluous for a being that seemed to be an artificial construct.

"Y-yes," ey said, shaking er head. "What...is this...I mean, is this time?"

Turun Ko tilted its chin up in a gesture ey could not understand. "Yes. You have skewed-departed-slid-away from common time. It is normal-not-unusual for the recorder consciousness-bearing system to detach-accelerate from common time at first. Those such as you and I are primed-eager to observe over time."

Codrin gripped eir notebook and pen closer to eir chest. "Common...so, the other emissaries are moving at the same time, I'm just moving slower?"

"Faster. You are existing-in-time faster, thus the other emissaries appear-seem to be moving slower."

"How do I get back?"

The firstrace...member? Firstracer? The firstracer dipped its snout with a twist to the side that gave em the sense of a shrug. "There is no hurry-rush. We exist in synchrony. I will teach-instruct you to find common time. I must ask: you are four individuals in five forms in two phenotypes. Are you still five consciousness-bearing systems?"

It took em a moments work to disentangle the question before ey realized that Turun Ko was asking about True Name and Why Ask Questions. They were, ey supposed, still closer to being one individual than any two non-cladists.

"Yes. The Only Time I Know My True Name—or just True Name—and Why Ask Questions Here At..." Ey trailed off, looking at the woman who still appeared to be in mid-shout. The splash of skunk-fur appeared to have crept further up her cheek, though so out-of-phase was she with eir local time that it was hard to say for sure. More, though, something seemed...off about her. She seemed not quite as ey remembered.

"Recorder Codrin Bălan, please continue."

"Uh, right, sorry. True Name and Why Ask Questions Here At The End Of All Things are cocladists, forks of the same root instance. Why Ask Questions is actually a fork of True Name, who is, in turn, a fork of the root instance, Michelle Hadje. They have individuated. They are...separate consciousness-bearing entities."

Turun Ko lifted its chin once more. "Representative Why Ask Questions is in pain."

"Pain?"

"Pain-of-existence. Pain-of-state-of-being. She is un-whole. This is why we must ask."

Ey nodded. "She looks scared. Frightened, or something."

"Frightened, *anem*, the correct word. Both representative Why Ask Questions and leader True Name are frightened. They are un-whole. They are in pain. Leader True Name is hiding-obscuring it better. Why?"

Something about this discursive, almost lazy form of questioning made Codrin feel as though ey would be late. Ey wanted to urge Turun Ko to get them back to common time. *That's silly, though,* ey thought. *We have all the time we need, if hardly any is passing out there. If 'out there' is even the right term.*

Ey said, "I only have a guess as explained by one of their cocladists, that–"

"Cocladists is multiple forms of one individual, *anem?*"

"Yes...uh, *anem,* correct. One of their cocladists suggested that they might react poorly to the..." Ey trailed off, hunting for the best phrasing. "To the malleability of time. They underwent some experiences in the past regarding time, so I think they're afraid."

"Will they remain afraid-in-pain? Will they cohere?"

Codrin was silent for a long moment as ey thought about this. The part of em that wanted to say 'yes, of course' argued against the part of em that was intensely focused on that wave of skunk fur creeping its way up over Why Ask Questions's cheek.

"I don't know," ey said at last. Ey pointed carefully toward that trim of fur. "How long did it take for this to appear?"

"0.16 seconds common time from your arrival-constitution." Turun Ko stepped closer, bowing its head to investigate the fur. "She is existing-in-time slower. She appears-seems frozen because she is in slow-time. She skewed-departed-slid-away from common time 0.18 seconds after arrival by a skew of -2.6. Think-remember, recorder Codrin Bălan, and you will know these things."

Ey tilted eir head and then, considering how it felt to have a merge available to remember, tried to remember the 'skew' factor by which eir experience of time differed from common time. The concepts were hazily defined to em—ey didn't know what common time was, where the point of reference lay—and yet all the same, ey knew that eir time-skew factor was +2.18.

On a spark of intuition, ey tried to 'remember' being at a skew of one, and sure enough, the world stumbled into movement again, though everything was moving half as fast as ey expected. Sound came through slowly, and ey could hear words beginning—words from Sarah, from Tycho, from Turun Ka. It was unnerving to hear that they had been time-stretched without having their pitch modulated, but ey supposed that would be helpful in time-skewed conversations.

Ey felt the briefest twinge to eir sensorium and frowned. "What was that?"

"I have tied-attached-synchronized my time skew to yours. If you require help with skew manipulation, I will assist. Think-remember common time, recorder Codrin Bălan."

Ey nodded and slowly allowed Turun Ko and emself to slip back into common time. There was the faintest sensorium *click*, as though a pin had slid into a shallow notch, informing em that this was the shared moment.

"–My True Name Is When I Dream of the Ode clade will accompany," Turun Ka was saying. "Representative Artante Diria will show you to your rest area. We will conduct formal greetings in one hour common time."

True Name wavered, reaching out a hand to grip at Codrin's sleeve. She remained stubbornly skunk, clinging to that appearance of being in control. "Thank you, leader Turun Ka," she said, words coming out slowly, spoken through clenched teeth. "Our apologies."

The firstracer bowed, tucking its chin close to its chest. "There is no need to apologize. Allowances are granted to those who arrive from new worlds. Representative Iska will accompany you to discuss further accommodations." It turned to face the rest of the emissaries. "You all may rest and acclimatize in the rest area we have provided for you. We welcome you."

Artante Diria bowed at the waist, a gesture so easy and recognizable that the four representatives all reciprocated more out of habit.

"Welcome. You may call me representative Artante Diria. This way, please," she said, gesturing with a hand.

Codrin hesitated, watching as something happened to bring Why Ask Questions back into sync with common time. Her shout completed and then turned into a low moan as she crumpled to the ground, retching. For the first time since ey'd met Michelle nearly four decades ago, ey watched the dueling identities of a mind split. Skunk and human battled for primacy even as True Name moved to help her cocladist to her feet.

"Where are they taking them?" ey asked once ey'd caught up with Artante and the other emissaries.

"There are several unison rooms available in the compound. They will be given one as quarters."

"I'm guessing those are rooms where time can't move?" Tycho asked.

She smiled, nodding her head in assent. "Move is the wrong word, but skew is locked in unison for all of the inhabitants, though that of the room may still diverge from common time. Your rest area will not be a unison room, but if this proves uncomfortable, we will accommodate you. Through here, you will find your beds and desks. Should you need anything in addition, please ring the bell by the door, and someone will be by to assist. I will come for you in one hour common time for the formal greeting."

They bowed once again and each walked to a bed, picking at random. They seemed comfortable enough. The desks, while plain, were a touch that Codrin appreciated, and ey set eir notebook and pen down so that ey could prowl around the room.

The far wall held window seats that looked out over a garden of strange, colorful vegetation.

As ey sat on one of these, playing with eir new-found ability to modulate time, Tycho approached. Ey enjoyed a secret moment of amusement, making the astronomer walk first slowly, now quickly, before settling back into common time once more.

"Codrin," he said, sitting down beside em. "I want to get your opinion on something before I say anything stupid."

"I am no stranger to saying stupid things, but I will do my best."

The astronomer's smile was weak as he leaned in closer, whispering, "Just between us for now, promise?"

Ey frowned, nodded. "Can you move to fast time? Same as hopping sims or creating things: have the intention of being at a time skew of +2."

Tycho blinked, looked nonplussed for a moment, then seemed to Codrin to start breathing incredibly rapidly. Ey followed him into fast time.

"This is...strange. Very strange," he said, looking around, back over to where Sarah appeared frozen in the act of sitting on the edge of her bed.

"It really is. Still, this will give you enough privacy to speak freely, I believe."

He looked back toward the door, worry painted on his face, and nodded. "I'm not totally sure how I know, but I don't think that was Why Ask Questions. That was Answers Will Not Help."

Ioan Bălan — 2346

Convergence T-plus 28 days, 13 hours, 35 minutes
(Castor–Lagrange transmission delay: 30 days, 14 hours, 36 minutes)

Ioan knew what was coming, so ey was able to brace emself well enough when May came barrelling out of the default entry point on the dandelion-ridden field that ey was not totally bowled over, managing at least a somewhat graceful descent to the ground. The skunk had already looped her arms around eir middle and tucked her head up under eir chin before ey was even able to sit up straight enough to get eir arms around her.

"You nut." Ey laughed, reaching up to tug at one of her ears affectionately. "Good to see you, too."

"Ioan, I am in no way sorry for knocking you over," she said, voice muffled, her grip around eir middle tightening. "Though I am dreadfully sorry that this happened again. I missed you."

Giving up on the prospect of sitting up straight, ey leaned back onto one hand, propping emself up. "No need to apologize, May. I'm just happy to see you again."

The skunk leaned away from em enough to dot her nose against eirs. Her eyes were quite red and ey could see tear-tracks in the fur of her cheeks. She looked a mess. "Do not take my apology away from me. I have been saving that one up."

"Alright, alright," ey said, pressing eir nose a little more firmly to hers for a moment before leaning back again. "Apology accepted. Are you feeling better?"

She sat upright rather than leaning against eir front and nodded. "Yes. I was able to get a lot out that I think has been pent up for a while. Thank you for giving me the space. I promise I did not fuck with your pen collection."

"Good. I had it all perfectly organized." Ey plucked a dandelion from the field and tucked it behind her ear. "Now, do you want to talk about it? Or should we do that later? That was longer than the last few times."

"Later, please. I want to say hi to Douglas and wash my face and just be normal for a bit."

Douglas Hadje met them on the stoop of his house and, as had become their ritual over the years, hugged the skunk, lifted, and twirled her around. Her bushy tail streamed along behind her.

"Hey May," he said, setting her back down again and kissing her cheek. "Glad you made it through."

"Of course I made it through. You still have at least seventy nine years of me haunting you before I can do something else." She grinned. "And even then, the contract is renewable."

"Ornery as ever." He laughed. "Well, want to come in?"

"For a bit, and then I want to come back out here and lay in the grass and bake in the sun."

After May had cleaned up and Ioan had helped Douglas prepare coffee and some sandwiches, they sat around the table to catch up.

"So, what news of the aliens?" Douglas asked.

The skunk squinted at him. "Has Ioan not been keeping you up to date?"

"A little. Ey said ey wanted to wait until you got here, though."

"Whatever." She rolled her eyes. "Well, out with it, then."

"I've gotten several messages from Codrin over the last few days. Ey said they would be heading out to start the talks later that day."

"So they have been into them for a while, now." She looked thoughtfully up to the ceiling. "A few weeks, perhaps?"

"Or maybe they're already over," Douglas said.

"A gloomy thought. I would like to hope that they are going quite well. Codrin is there being a Bălan, Tycho is there being a nerd, this Sarah Genet is there being a whatever a Sarah Genet is like, Why Ask Questions is there being a shithead." She wrinkled her nose. "And True Name is doing her best to control the whole thing."

Ioan was pleased to see the mildness of the skunk's expression. It really did seem like many of those overwhelming emotions had burned themselves out over the last few days.

"It's weird," Douglas said. "Every now and then, I'll hear about something from one of the LVs that's anchored to a certain time and I'll remember, 'Oh shit, yeah, they're billions of kilometers away by now', and then I have to spend some time trying to conceptualize that distance."

Ioan nodded. "The transmission delay throws a wrench in things, doesn't it? I was just thinking about that on Secession day. We were celebrating and it sounds like they were, too, but we didn't learn about their party until a week later."

"The thing that always catches me off guard is that our days do not seem to line up any longer," May said around a bite of sandwich. "I mean, they do, but when the delay is off by half a day, we start getting messages at shit o'clock in the morning. It is a strange feeling."

"Exactly."

"I hope they're still in the talks, too. Codrin sounded hopeful, at least. The messages that they'd been getting from the Artemisians were interesting, especially the language snippets. I'm guessing the powers that be made em promise not to send the full message text yet, but what they have learned is fascinating. Four races on one ship must be a hell of an experience. The DMZ sim sounds pleasant, though, and all of the work they've done to prepare is really kind of impressive." Ey sipped eir coffee to buy a moment's time to think before saying, "There was a bunch of stuff in there for you, too, May. We can go over that later, though."

The skunk frowned, finished the last of her sandwich, and then settled back in the chair with her coffee. "You cannot leave me hanging, my dear. May I at least have a preview?"

"Well, Codrin's worried about you. As is Dear."

"The memory thing?" Douglas asked.

Ey nodded.

May averted her gaze, looking out the window to the rolling field beyond. "I am worried, too. You know that."

"I know. Reading between the lines, though, I think ey's worried about the whole clade. Ey's worried about you and Dear, and ey's worried about how True Name and Why Ask Questions are going to act through this. Dear reacted poorly to the whole time-modification thing."

She nodded and sat in silence for a minute before setting her cup down. "We are not doing as well as many of us would like, no. I have news as well, but I would like to share it outside where I can sit in the sun and feel the grass. Is that okay?"

Ioan and Douglas collected plates and coffee cups, then the three of them trooped out into the field while May spoke.

"We have lost May One Day Death Itself Not Die and I Do Not Know, I Do Not Know. Death Itself stopped talking, and then she stopped moving. In Dreams visited for a while there, and a few days ago asked me to come visit as well. That is why this spell seemed to last longer than usual. Evening hit, she smiled at us, shrugged, and then quit."

May's voice was thick as she continued. "They all lived in the same house, did you know that? All ten of that stanza. Many of them did not even talk with each other, and none of them ever forked. They were always quite unstable. The next morning, I Do Not Know was gone, and Names Of The Dead said that she had quit shortly before sunrise."

Ioan and Douglas remained quiet as they walked. The skunk

didn't seem to be quite done saying the things that she needed to.

She continued after a few minutes of mastering emotions, voice clear once more. "In Dreams and I talked quite a bit. She said that there have been fewer instances of instability in older clades than expected, given *On the Perils of Memory*. Fewer uploads are susceptible to the long-term effects of unceasing memory than expected, I guess. I was pleased to see that Debarre seems to be doing well."

"That's heartening," Douglas said. "At least in a way."

The skunk nodded. "I am pleased that the System is more stable than feared, but I am unhappy that we seem so strongly affected. In Dreams said that she is going to do some research and see if there are ways that we can at least improve on the way we deal with the effects. I do not know that there is a way to get rid of them entirely, at least not without further individuation, but the least we can do is help keep ourselves sane for longer."

Ioan took her paw in eir hand and lifted it to kiss the back. "Please, yeah. If you lose it, I'll be furious."

She laughed and gave em a pitying look. "Mx. Ioan Bălan, you are pretty good at acting furious on stage, but I do not believe for a second that you could actually feel that way. Even Codrin was able to have a normal meeting with True Name after she did as she does with em."

Ey did not laugh. Neither, ey noted, did Douglas.

"I am sorry," she murmured, ears laid flat.

"'Furious' is the wrong word, May. I'd lose my damn mind." Ey took a shaky breath and rubbed at eir face. "I can't tell you you're not allowed to or anything, since I know it's not really up to you, but please at least try to stick around."

"I'm not going to pile on or anything," Douglas said. "But I will say I'd be pretty upset, too, so if there's anything I can do to help, I will."

May dragged them both to a stop in the field. Her expression started out angry, then screwed up into sadness, and finally settled on tired. "I love you both and I promise I will do what I can to stay here, stay grounded. I cannot speak for the rest of the clade, and certainly not for Dear to soothe Codrin's fears, but I will do what I can."

It was not uncommon for these reunions to be tearful, Ioan knew, but it was a different sort of pang that settled in eir chest with the news, and it was a few minutes before ey was able to speak again. "Sorry, you two."

The skunk stuck her tongue out at em. "I will allow you this one apology, but do not make a habit of it. You are allowed to cry at sad shit."

Ey rolled eir eyes and shoved at her.

"Well, I was promised laying in the grass and baking in the sun," Douglas said. "So come on, we can at least enjoy the rest of the afternoon."

Codrin Bălan#Castor — 2346

Codrin was pleased to see that some magic wrought by the Ansible engineers both here on Castor and their counterparts over on Artemis allowed the Artemisians to assume what must be their natural forms and that they weren't greeted by a gaggle of Douglases. Ey'd never seen Douglas, but it would have been unnerving and difficult to differentiate them. They'd even come wearing clothes—those who wore them, at least, this Iska and Artante Diria—which ey supposed they would appreciate. One of those benefits of System-to-System Ansibles that they'd enjoyed on their transit from Lagrange to LVs, as well.

So it was that they found themselves lined up opposite their counterparts across the table from each other, exchanging their formal greetings.

"*Rehasiër munachla achles eslosam. Tapotevier les unachadev itek The-Only-Time-I-Know-My-True-Name-Is-When-I-Dream-am, True-Name itet.*" The skunk bowed formally, deep and at the waist.

The firstracer before her bowed its head, a movement that took place solely in the neck rather than the waist. "Greetings, and thank you for letting us join you. I am the leader, and my name is Turun Ka."

Ey watched the exchange of greetings curiously, making note of what gestures were made, before bowing emself and saying, "*Rehasiër munachla echles eslosam. Tapotevier les unechrenum Codrin-Bălanam.*"

Turun Ko, opposite em, responded with a similar motion of raised head. "Greetings-hello, thank-you-and-gratitude for allowing our delegation-emissaries. I act as observer-recorder and am called-named Turun Ko."

Ey tilted eir head, noting the confusion on eir side of the table at the choppy, synonym-ridden greeting, filing away a question to ask of the recorder later.

The greetings continued down the line. Tycho and Stolon greeted each other as scientists. Iska, who startled em in their resemblance to Debarre, and Why Ask Questions greeted each other, followed last of all by Artante Diria and Sarah.

There was a small shuffle as the delegates from both craft sat at the table, Iska politely requesting that their chair be raised and the surface area made smaller so that they could more effectively reach the table, which True Name accomplished with a gesture. Both Turun Ka and Turun Ko set their chairs aside and squatted down on their haunches before the table instead.

"Thank you once again, and welcome to this convergence," Turun Ka said. Its voice was pleasantly musical. "It is a pleasure to meet those who are new and different from us, and we are always grateful when luck and chance allow us to do so."

True Name nodded, a hint of a bow from where she sat. "Thank you for joining us, and welcome to the Launch Vehicle Castor. We are honored to have you aboard. If you need anything at all, please do not hesitate to ask me, as I bear full ACLs for the sim. You will find your rest area down there—" She gestured with a paw toward one of the hallways. "—where you will have limited ACLs that will allow you to modify many of the objects there and will allow you to fork once."

The reactions around the table were mixed. Turun Ka and Turun Ko remained impassive—they seemed to move only with intent, and when not required, they were as stationary as statues. Stolon tilted their head in a quizzical manner. Iska's expression was hard to read, but were ey pressed to put a name to it, ey would have called it unnerved, or perhaps startled. Given the similarities of her features to the humans around the table, Artante looked quite pleased.

"There will be no time skew?" Iska asked, voice high pitched, each word dipping in tone.

"We were not able to accommodate that, no."

"You appear-seem displeased or uncomfortable," Turun Ko said, head pointing down the table toward Why Ask Questions. "Can you explain if able or comfortable?"

She looked over to True Name, who gave a small nod of permission.

"Some of us here on the System do not feel comfortable with unbounded time," she said. "We will discuss more as the meeting continues."

"*Aën*," it said. *Okay.*

After a moment's silence, the skunk continued. "Per our agreement, this meeting here on Castor will be focused on knowledge-share surrounding the topics of linguistics and science, with particular attention to astronomy and spaceflight, while those aboard Artemis will focus on society, politics, and psychology. I would like to open with a round of free questioning, if you are amenable, in order to find a few examples for which directions to take the meeting in moving forward. Do you agree?"

"Yes," Turun Ka said. "One question per delegate should be an appropriate way to begin. I invite you to ask first, leader True Name."

The response was quick in coming. "We have divided civilizations up into a range of classes depending on their energy usage: planet scale, planetary system scale, and galaxy scale. At what stage were each of your races, and, if you have ran across any additional races, at what scale did they work?"

"Our race lived at the scale of planetary system," it replied. "We appear the way we do in our post-biological state in or-der to survive in a variety of environments beyond those of our world-of-origin."

"*Lu*," Stolon said, speaking slowly. "Planetary scale for us. For other three races."

True Name glanced to Codrin, ensuring that ey was taking notes. "Thank you. Would you like to go next, leader Turun Ka?"

"Yes. By what means do you collect the materials needed for your civilization, whether for the embodied world or this one?"

"Mining on our planet and our planet's moon," the skunk said after a moment's thought. "As well as limited mining of as-teroids at stationary points of orbit."

"You call Lagrange point, *ka*?" Stolon asked.

She nodded. "Correct."

"We saw...*lu*..." They chattered their teeth for a moment, then looked to Iska. "*Baenå' luta' 'esbrohakadåt'?*"

"Space-constructs," they said, filling in. "We saw constructs of various size at your planet-moon and planet-star Lagrange points."

True Name stiffened, but any response she might have had was preempted by Tycho. The astronomer, who had appeared largely overwhelmed by the meeting to date had steadily grown more excited during the questioning phase. "You did? How? Ra-dio? When did you see them? During gravity assist? How–"

"Tycho, hold up," Sarah said, laughing. "There will be time."

Stolon, meanwhile, was clacking claw-tipped fingers against the table and bobbing their head. "*Za lutatier! Za, za,*" they said quickly. "Will say, will say. Excited also, scientist Tycho."

Codrin grinned, scribbling further notes in eir notebook. Ey was pleased to see that there was also excitement around the table, rather than simply anxiety.

"Scientist Stolon, please answer scientist Tycho's question regarding how," Turun Ka said, voice bouncing through tones.

Amusement, perhaps? Codrin thought. The atmosphere certainly seemed to have lightened.

"Radio emanations, *anem.* Too far for visible light, useless light."

Tycho grinned, nodded. "Apologies, that will be my question, then."

"I ask," Stolon said. "How launched vehicle? We see also another, we learn language from."

"A station—a construct, as you say—rotating with the Castor and Pollux launch vehicles at the end of long launch arms, released us at tangential velocity, then photon sails, Hall Effect engines, and gravity assists on our way out of the system."

"You move not so fast, *ka?* Conserve fuel?" They chattered their teeth again. "Sorry sorry, will ask again soon."

"I am pleased to see the scientists excited," Turun Ka said. "Recorder Codrin Bălan? Recorder Turun Ko?"

When Turun Ko did not speak, Codrin asked, "Does your system allow you to forget?"

"Memories degrade-rot," the other recorder said. "Saves-preserves storage. Garbage collection process trims-prunes old-unaccessed memories."

Both True Name and Sarah reached for their pens to make note of the answer.

Codrin smiled and nodded eir thanks.

"Recorder Codrin Bălan, do your bodies-physical-forms continue to live after embedding-uploading of consciousness?"

Ey shook eir head. Realizing that the gesture may not translate, ey said, "No, they are destroyed in the process of uploading. Or embedding, as you say."

Both Iska and Artante Diria took notes of this answer.

"I have a question," Sarah said, when the silence drew out. "Do you have the concept of mental illness? Depression, disordered thinking, disconnect from reality?"

"Yes," Artante Diria said. "We have not discovered a means of removing such after embedding. I will ask next. I infer that you have not either. What treatments do you have for mental illness?"

"Talk therapy, mostly. If one is careful, one can reduce the effects by forking with intent to change, though this can have complex effects on other parts of the personality. It's come up in the past with the–"

Why Ask Questions rested a hand gently on Sarah's forearm. Both she and True Name were frowning.

"We will discuss later, perhaps."

"Yes, in time," the Odist said. "For my question, I would like to know how you manage linguistic drift."

Iska straightened up. "Our common tongue began primarily that of secondrace, of my race, but has incorporated many aspects of other languages. Languages within each race, including for pure *Nanon*, the basis of our common tongue, are uncontrolled, but common tongue is managed via central authority."

"Thank you, representative Iska."

"I will ask the final question," they said. "You say that we will have the ability to fork. Is there not risk of divergence?"

True Name answered, "There is. Why Ask Questions is a fork from me, and I am in turn a fork from the root instance, Michelle Hadje. We have individuated in the last two hundred twenty-odd years."

That unnerved, anxious expression returned to the secondracer's face, but they bowed their head all the same. "*Aët.* Thank you."

Standing, True Name bowed deeply once more. "Thank you once again for joining us. Let us retire to our rest areas to compare notes and strategize, then reconvene in one hour's time to begin in earnest."

Both delegations stood and returned their acknowledging gestures, whatever they might be, and each walked toward their respective rest areas.

"What do you think?" Why Ask Questions asked. "Real or dream?"

Tycho frowned. "It's too early to–"

True Name elbowed him in the side and laughed. "She is being a brat. Do not fall for her trap."

"Yeah, yeah, fuck you too," the other Odist said, grinning. "Do keep an eye out, though, my dear. We must act as though they are real for now, and we must not lose focus on the talks, but the answer may well be relevant later."

"Do not confuse our scientist, please," the skunk said mildly, then winked to Tycho.

If the comment had been meant to reassure Tycho, it fell flat. The astronomer's look of confusion only deepened.

Codrin let the three pass em, catching Sarah's eye to walk slower. Once Tycho had wandered toward the coffee setup and the Odists were several paces ahead, heads together and talking quietly, ey asked, "What do you make of it?"

She shrugged. "I'm not sure yet. The questions were all reasonable, but I wasn't really able to figure out if there was a direction to them. The question about mental health seemed to be earnest, as though they were looking for an actual solution to the problem, while Stolon's question about launching was very to the point. Hard facts, that sort of thing."

Ey nodded.

"Weird that they'd ask about our bodies living on after uploading, though," Tycho said, coffee in hand. "What could they possibly want with that knowledge?"

"Not sure," she said. "Maybe trying to figure out incentives for uploading? I really don't know."

"I'm feeling kind of lost after all that." Codrin sighed, hunting down the partitioned 'room' ey'd claimed as eir own and stopping outside the door. "It's overwhelming. I have no idea what avenues to go down from here. I want to ask why Turun Ko speaks the way it does, I want to ask about their opinions on forking, I want to ask all these questions, but I'm not sure how welcome that'll be in my role."

"I don't know about that either, as representative. I hope

I get to ask more. Though, well..." Sarah glanced over to where True Name and Why Ask Questions had sat at a table, still talking earnestly within a cone of silence. "I don't know what's more interesting. The emissaries or the Odists."

Tycho Brahe#Artemis — 2346

Convergence T-minus 3 days, 4 hours, 12 minutes

Tycho found himself focusing most on True Name after the long spate of introductions.

A small part of him wondered at this. All four races of Artemisians sitting around the table with them were fascinating in their own way. Part of him wanted to get lost in exploring the intricacies of Turun Ka and Turun Ko. Another desperately wanted to learn as much as he could from Stolon despite the stated goal of focusing on social interactions and history for this instance of the meeting.

And yet it was all so overwhelming. So much was happening all at once. So many things demanded his attention that the part of himself tasked with observing all but shut down, and instead he focused on True Name.

Why Ask Questions—or perhaps Answers Will Not Help—had calmed down, at least to the point where she was able to sit still and look down at the table. Her introduction had been stammered and, after that, she had remained quiet and withdrawn. It seemed as though she was spending every joule of energy she had on remaining still, remaining herself. Even then, a wave of skunk would occasionally wash over her form and she would clench her eyes shut

Codrin bore eir usual curious, attentive expression. Something about em seemed to suggest that, when working, ey became a camera of sorts, taking in all light, all sound, all sensation and storing it away for future reference. Even when the façade of work dropped, ey seemed built to witness.

Sarah, too, wore a look of calm curiosity. He figured she would be, in her own way, working the hardest of the group. She was the one tasked with watching the ways in which the Artemisians acted, trying to deduce some clear picture of them as individuals and as a society.

Tycho wished for that same sense of calm, of stability.

And so, with the other emissaries well known and the Artemisians perhaps too interesting to look at, he focused on True Name.

The skunk appeared to have an internal struggle of her own, not dissimilar from Why Ask Questions's/Answers Will Not Help's, but, as far as he could tell, she was better able to hold it at a distance, wrap it all up and set it down, observe rather than fight. Only twice that he had seen since they had gathered around the table had there been a wave of that human form of Michelle Hadje spreading across her features, but that was quickly mastered.

How much must be going on beneath the surface? he wondered. *She seems like she's a hundred percent here, and yet there's still something deeper going on.*

She caught him looking and gave him a wan smile, before addressing the table. "I think that it would be beneficial if we were to know the specialties that everyone holds, as that might help us better understand the ways in which we speak."

"By specialties," Artante said. "You mean our primary areas of interest?"

True Name nodded. "Yes."

There was a brief blur around the Artemisians as, Tycho guessed, they shifted to fast time to discuss this.

When they dropped back down to common time, Turun Ka

tilted its snout up. "We are amenable to this. By role, then, I act as leader for this delegation as well as a member of the Council of Eight, which serves in a leadership role for the collected societies here on what you call Artemis. My specialization is on interspecies communication."

The skunk's ears flitted briefly as it spoke. "Thank you, leader Turun Ka. For my part, I act as leader for this delegation. There is no central leadership for our System, but I am a member of a group of individuals and clades keenly interested in the stability and continuity of our society." She smiled, strain showing around her eyes. "This was not always the case, as the System was originally guided by a group of individuals also known as the Council of Eight. This was disbanded two hundred years ago once the society reached equilibrium, but I was a member from start to end."

The firstracer rocked its head from side to side in a gesture that Tycho supposed must be amusement of a sort. "We share a commonality."

True Name nodded.

"I serve as recorder here," Codrin said when no one else spoke up. "I am a historian and writer, and have often found myself taking part in large-scale events as an amanuensis so that I might witness and then write a coherent story after."

"We are similar-alike, recorder Codrin Bălan," Turun Ko said. "I serve and have served as observer-recorder since creation and launch of our vehicle-system. I specialize in creating stories-accounts-retellings of events so that others may listen-learn-understand. I am pleased to meet you."

Codrin nodded to it, smiling. "As am I."

"I am named Stolon of thirdrace, of–" The lizard made a sort of hissing, chittering noise. Their name for their own race, perhaps? "I am specializing in astronomy and spaceflight. I dream of stars."

Tycho sat up straight. Another astronomer! He couldn't have asked for better luck. "Really? I'm an astronomer, too," he said, unable to keep the excitement out of his voice. "That's the whole reason I came along on these launches in the first place. I wanted to see the stars. Where do you come from? How did you wind up out here?"

True Name frowned. "One set of questions at a time, Dr. Brahe. There will be a time for asking such as these."

He sat back, chastened, but a glance at Stolon shared a similar sort of jittery excitement. They kept tapping and drumming their claws on the tabletop, forcing themself to stop, and then doing so again. He made a mental note to steal some time with the thirdracer.

They continued around the table.

"I am Iska of secondrace. I specialize in time skew artistry. I tell stories through the ways in which we move through time. I serve as representative for my race, but also as an artist who may come away with a story."

Codrin laughed. "How delightful."

Iska cocked their head in a familiar gesture of confusion.

"One of my partners—romantic partners, that is—is an instance artist. It performs art through the creative use of forking. It'll be pleased to hear that there is something analogous here."

The secondracer bowed, their short ears canted back. "We will have to share knowledge on this during our talks."

Sarah spoke up next. "I am a psychologist and therapist. I study the way people think and help them by listening. I have a particular interest in being here to see the ways in which we are similar or different in how we learn, solve problems, approach the world, and so on."

Artante smiled. "I serve a similar role, representative Sarah Genet. I listen and I talk and I help. That is my role here, as well. Iska will bring back the story, and I will aid in understanding."

The two smiled at each other, both looking pleased. Tycho imagined they were feeling some of the same excitement that he was on learning that Stolon was a fellow astronomer.

All eyes turned towards Why Ask Questions/Answers Will Not Help, who gave a weak shrug. "You must forgive my state at the moment. I cannot speak without great effort. My focus is on politics."

"The offer to hold further talks in a unison room remains available," Iska said.

Why Ask Questions shook her head, though whether at the suggestion or out of the inability to speak, Tycho couldn't tell.

They bowed their head. "It will remain available. Please ask if you require. Time skew is a part of our existence, here, and has been since the first convergence. It is how we have managed to learn your language and prepare for your arrival. We work at a high positive skew."

"We had wondered about that," Codrin said. "Your reply to our letters was almost instantaneous. Even when we had several instances of a single individual working on a problem, we were slower."

"Some problems are more difficult to work on in parallel than others," Artante said.

"I suppose responding to a letter is one of those, yeah, unless it's responding to otherwise unconnected points in a letter."

The fourthracer nodded. "We were like you before we arrived. We had the concept of forking but not of time skew."

Tycho kept waiting for True Name to interrupt, for her to tell them that they needed to stay on topic, but the skunk seemed interested enough in the topic to let it continue.

"I would like to know more, representative Artante Diria." The skunk sat up straighter, quelling a wave of human form before continuing. "When we fork, our new instances can quit and we are presented with their memories so that we may have the experiences of both instances should we choose. Is that how your system worked?"

"Similar, yes, though only if the fork was created from the current instant."

True Name tilted her head, gestured for the representative to explain.

Artante looked thoughtful as she continued, more slowly now. "I could fork from who I am now and then be able to accept the memories of that instance without issue. If I were to fork from who I was five minutes ago, accepting those memories would be very difficult. Forking from more than a day in the past made accepting memories all but impossible."

Stunned silence from the emissaries greeted this explanation.

"Is there a portion of this that needs clarification?" Artante asked, frowning.

"We can only fork from the present. From the current instant, as you say," Codrin said. "That's a fascinating idea, though. Do you know how it worked? If Dear—my instance artist partner, that is—could do that, it would open up worlds of possibilities to it."

She bowed apologetically. "It has been nearly a millennium since I have been able to fork, recorder Codrin Bălan, and even then, I was not very adept at it. In one of your letters, you discussed dissolution strategies; I was what you would call a tasker. I will ask another of my race for details after the conference."

Codrin grinned and elbowed Tycho in the side. The astronomer rolled his eyes.

"As am I," he said. "Never got the hang of it, never really felt the need to."

Artante laughed, nodded. He was pleased at the familiarity of her expressions. It made at least one of the Artemisians he could read.

"How did you adapt to time skew?"

All heads turned toward Why Ask Questions. The question had been mumbled and quiet, but surprising coming from one who had been otherwise silent.

"Many of us did not," Artante said. "During our convergence, it was primarily those who would be labeled taskers who took part."

"Did others have trouble like me?"

There was another brief blur from the Artemisians as they discussed among themselves. Tycho saw Codrin frown and make a note.

That they needed to do that is probably telling, he thought.

"Not in the same fashion, but some experienced difficulties, yes." Artante hesitated, glanced at Turun Ka, and then continued. "We have decided that it would be best to revisit this topic later on in our meeting, however, as we do not want to distract from other topics we must cover during our time together."

Why Ask Questions/Answers Will Not Help nodded. "Would appreciate that," she said, the words coming out slurred and elongated as she veered into and out of slow time. She seemed to be having an increasingly hard time remaining in common time, not to mention remaining in one form. "Can we take a break for a few minutes?"

Turun Ka stood from where it had crouched. "Yes. Please feel free to return to your rest area or a unison room for the next fifteen minutes common time, and then we shall reconvene."

"Can we do so in a unison room?"

"Yes. Representative Iska will see to the arrangements. One of us will fetch the other emissaries to guide you back to the new meeting location."

The soft-furred secondracer stood still for a moment, squinted. "You should be locked to common time for the time being. It is very difficult to synchronize skew with you, though. I don't know why. I will contact a system technician during our break."

"If I walk backward, time moves forward. If I walk forward, time rushes on," she gasped out, then laughed hoarsely. "If I stand still, the world moves around me!"

True Name jolted at the brief recitation, standing quickly and taking her cocladist by the elbow. "Come, my dear. Let us get to the room."

Tycho looked to Codrin, who only frowned.

Something had happened, just then. Something of import. He had no clue as to what it had been, though. Neither did he understand how he knew, he realized, but he knew that it was something distressing. Something wrong.

Ioan Bălan — 2346

Convergence T-plus 28 days, 19 hours, 29 minutes
(Castor-Lagrange transmission delay: 7 days, 5 hours, 31 minutes)

May made it through dinner—Ioan was heartened to see that she'd actually eaten all of the chicken soup ey'd made—before padding off to a beanbag to curl up. She kept up a dozy conversation for a few minutes while Ioan cleaned, but even that tapered off to silence. When next ey looked back, the skunk was asleep.

Every time ey'd left her to sleep out on the beanbag in the past, though, she'd spent the next day disoriented and moody—ey suspected this is what she'd meant when she said she slept better next to someone all those years ago—so once ey finished the (unnecessary but meditative) task of cleaning, ey knelt beside the beanbag, wormed eir arms beneath her, and scooped her up.

She made a sort of drowsy chirping noise as ey lifted her, hugging her arms around eir shoulders for the short journey to the bedroom. Long as her tail was, ey had to be careful not to step on any of her fur with it hanging limply, almost to the ground.

Once there, ey helped her out of her clothes, unsteady as she was, and then tucked her into bed, leaning down to put a kiss on her cheek.

"Ioan?"

"Yes?"

"Can you stay?"

Ey nodded, forking off a copy to finish cleaning up and taking notes. After a few minutes of eir own bedtime routine, ey slipped into bed with her. Ey was certainly tired enough, ey realized.

And so now, back at home, back in their own bed, alone together, May and Ioan had the conversation ey felt they truly needed. They talked quietly, almost *sotto voce*, now that it was dark and comfortable and they were no longer surrounded by the loud, raucous colors of Douglas's field. They shared their kisses, their small touches. They reaffirmed, in so many small, unspoken ways, their love for each other, and they talked.

"What do you think they are learning?" May murmured, nose-tip poking up against Ioan's chin.

Ey had to speak carefully to respond, lest ey bump her snout. "Who can say? Perhaps they are learning, perhaps they are teaching."

"Poetic.

"There are Odists involved, it's going to be poetic through and through."

She laughed and poked em in the belly with a claw. "Jerk."

"That's me, yeah," ey said, grinning and nudging her muzzle this way and that with eir chin. "The Odists are learning how to manipulate new species. Tycho's learning about the stars. I can't speak to Sarah, but Codrin is along for the ride."

"Did ey have much more to say about eir doubts?"

"A little. Ey's still feeling more caught up in the events than an actual participant, but I think ey's also starting to look for ways out of the cycle. I don't know if ey has picked up any specific ideas on how to take charge, but that ey has decided to do something in the first place is change enough."

The skunk nodded. "You are a careful lot, but it is nice to see when you do become more assertive."

"We lack your flair," ey said, ruffling up some of her fur.

"I also enjoy that, do not get me wrong. Not everything needs flair." She perked up, dotted her nose against eir chin, and asked, "You said something about time modification earlier, but I was distracted and did not think to ask about it. What does that mean?"

"Oh, right. It sounds like the Artemisians don't fork, and instead rely on the ability to change how fast they experience time. Individuals or groups can speed up their perception so that the world around them seems to slow down, that sort of thing."

There was a long moment's silence, and were it not for the shallowness of her breathing, ey might have thought May had fallen asleep. Eventually, she whispered, "I do not like that."

Ioan dipped eir chin enough to bump eir nose against hers. "Codrin said Dear got quite upset about it, too. It warned em that there would be two Odists among the emissaries and that ey should watch out."

She remained still, no reciprocating press of nose to nose. She continued in her whisper. "Once, when I was in school, I performed in a play that used the works of Emily Dickinson throughout. I still remember it. *Time feels so vast that were if not For an Eternity— I fear me this Circumference Engross my Finity—*"

Ey remained quiet as ey mulled over the words. The archaic language felt opaque to em, but, as ey prowled through synonyms, ey began to piece together meaning. "You've mentioned eternity before in the context of getting lost. This sounds almost relieved, though, that eternity exists, lest everything get too overwhelming."

"There was no eternity in there, Ioan. Time was beyond vast. I *was* engrossed. There was no me left. When we were pulled out, we were finally confronted with eternity again."

" 'We'?"

May took a while to respond. "Michelle and the author of the Ode."

Ey nodded, letting the comment about the Name slip by, asking instead, "And being stuck in a place with malleable time would bring back a lot of that?"

"Yes. Codrin is right to be careful. The clade struggles enough with stability as it is." She broke the tension of the moment by licking eir chin. "On a happier note, In Dreams mentioned a hypothesis about the struggles we've had with memory."

"Oh?"

"Well, happier for the System, if not for us. I guess she has hunted down some other clades that have been having problems. She says there are uniting factors, such as a weaker boundary between subconscious and conscious, a greater sense of the numinous, and so on. I am too sleepy to remember the details, but she is looking into it." The skunk giggled. "She says we should get therapy."

"Oh, you definitely should," ey teased. "Maybe this Sarah Genet is still on Lagrange. That's what she does."

"She is a therapist?"

Ey nodded.

A moment's hesitation, and then May nodded. "I let In Dreams know."

"Good. The more minds working on this, the better."

"Are you really that worried, my dear?"

Ey frowned, shrugged. "That's part of it. More, I just feel helpless. I'm not worried about you going sideways any time soon, honestly, and certainly hope you don't at all, but should that happen, watching helplessly would be...well, it's a big fear of mine."

May hugged herself closer to em, snout once again ducking beneath eir chin. "I understand. I am stuck with the related fear of losing control. I do not like the feeling of not being in control of my emotions, even for these brief periods, but if that were to just become my life..."

After she trailed off, ey tightened eir arms around her, brushing fingertips through fur.

They lay like that in the quiet and the dark. Eir fork apparently finished up with eir notes and quit, but given the topics of conversation and lack of any insistence on behalf of the instance, ey declined to accept the merge. Ey did not want to be distracted from the simple task of petting May, of enjoying the feeling of having her back.

"May?"

The skunk poked her nose against eir collarbone. "Mm?" She sounded half asleep.

"I really can't lose you. You know that right?" Ey felt her tense in eir arms, but continued, "I said ages ago that I'm not built for a life with death in it. That's why I'm here. That's why I uploaded in the first place, to get away from that."

"Ioan," she said, voice hoarse. "I already–"

"I know, you already promised. I believe you. I'm not trying to berate you, I'm trying to say I love you."

"Ioan Bălan, if you make me cry again, I will smother you in your sleep."

Ey laughed. "It sounds like it's already too late."

"Thin fucking ice, buddy." May sniffled and squirmed around until she could tuck back against eir front. "I love you too, my dear, top to bottom and front to back."

As ey settled in for sleep, kissing the backs of the skunk's ears, ey marveled that ey could only *remember* the Ioan who never thought to form attachments, who could never remember to ask May if they were in a relationship, who continually wondered how she wound up in eir life, could only remember em as some other person. Ey could only remember em as though from a distance. That Ioan was gone. Ey had slipped away into the past while the Ioan ey was now wasn't looking, and had never come back. Ey wished em luck, this younger version of emself. Ey wished em happiness and fulfillment. And, should that Ioan ever find emself struck by the wonder of love, ey wished em courage in the face of it.

This Ioan, the one ey was now, understood the value in attachments, and yet ey could still marvel, twenty years on, at just how much more complete ey was with May in eir life.

Codrin Bălan#Artemis — 2346

Codrin#Artemis,

I am finding myself overwhelmed by the strangeness of the goings on during this whole venture. I know that you have it worse, given the fact that you are having to deal with meeting four alien races as well as experiencing an entirely new system, complete with an entirely new take on reality.

Still, this remains strange for me. I'm curious to hear what sort of information you are getting from the social and political side of the talks, as I think it will help me form a more coherent picture of the Artemisians so that I may ask better questions when I'm so very, very out of my league, here on the science side. I asked True Name about this, and she just shrugged and said, "So long as you do not forget what we are here for in the DMZ, I see no reason to prevent knowledge sharing."

First, here is what we are finding, seen through the eyes of the scientifically inept:

- Iska is quite upset about the lack of "time skew", as they call it, and has stated that they refuse the single fork they're permitted in their rest area. They have not elaborated on this, but I find it interesting that skew, this scientific feat that they have accomplished, is so thoroughly engrained in their society (secondrace has been

179

on Artemis for nigh on four millennia by now) that dissolution seems alien or even abhorrent to them. I know that forking is integral to our society, but it does make me wonder if it has reached that point yet. Dear would be furious without it, of course, but would that sentiment be universal after only 231 years? Are you missing it? Are the Odists?

- Stolon and Tycho are so happy to have met each other that both parties have had to shush them on several occasions. I would prefer to let them have at it, but I do also understand the desire to talk about sciences *other* than astronomy and spaceflight. Why Ask Questions is our biologist and linguist here, and she has been the other primary participant, speaking mostly with Iska and Turun Ka.
- Artante and Sarah are almost as perfectly aligned as Tycho and Stolon; they are both psychologists, though it sounds like the Artemisians' approach to such bears some striking differences. Notably, there are some time-related disorders that have largely gone over my head (something about "lacking a feel for common time" and "unison rooms"? Perhaps you can enlighten me), and there are some approaches that Sarah has found interesting, including forms of proactive therapy using, you guessed it, time. Something about practicing through skew, making time to take time.
- It is almost impossible to get a read on the firstracers. It's not just that they do not have facial expressions, so much as their penchant for absolute stillness unless a gesture is required (I've begun cataloguing these: uplifted head = nod; head tilt = shrug; chin tilted far down, exposed neck = bow; turning head far to the side = frustration, maybe?). This has led to some frustration, primarily on True Name's part. Ioan's mentioned in the past that May Then My Name calls the root of her skill a sort of 'registering', as though she's gotten very good at figuring out

what her 'target' needs in order to be convinced. Sounds like she's struggling to use that to her full abilities, here.

- Turun Ko and I have been getting on quite well. I asked it about its speaking style (which, in case the same is not true over there, includes lots of synonyms strung together throughout its speech). At first, I thought this was a way to find a more exact wording for a concept, but the more I listened, the less I thought that was the case. Why Ask Questions suggested that it might be trying to fit the ambiguities of their *lingua franca* to ours. When asked, though, it said that it was a deliberate effort on its part to remain in the mindset of an Artemisian (they've adopted that word quite readily) in order to better record from an Artemisian point of view. I don't think we'll be struggling with this much, as we haven't learned their language well enough to think like them. It says that it will complete the learning process after the convergence "depending-relying on outcomes", on which it would not elaborate.
- I've read that it was speculated that most cases involving contact from an extraterrestrial species would take part on the visiting culture's terms, given that anyone who has made it far enough in their social and technological development to reach us will be beyond what we have accomplished, so at least we've confirmed that.
- On that note, everyone seems to have learned our common tongue quite well *except* Stolon. Don't tell Tycho, but I think the similarities between them run quite deep. Neither of them seem particularly interested in language except inasmuch as it allows them to better talk about astronomy.
- What do you think, are we just dreaming this all up?

Now, for my questions:

- Given Dear's reaction, how are TN/WAQ taking to this "time skew"? Not well, I imagine. Dear sounded worried for us (which I suppose is its job); are you or any of the other emissaries in danger? TN says she has received a message from her counterpart already, but gave no indication as to its content.
- Tycho is in his element here, but Iska seems relatively out of theirs. I imagine Iska is doing better on their home turf, but is Stolon put out by the relative paucity of scientific conversation, as Tycho said he would be?
- How are you all taking to time skew? I'd like to know more specifics of the mechanics and social implications so that I can understand Iska's reticence better.
- The Artemisians ask for regular breaks, where they always retreat back to their rest area. Probably five minutes every half hour. When asked, Turun Ko said, "Consensus synchronization, planning-strategizing responses," by which I infer that they are used to being able to step aside for conversations to ensure they are all on the same page. Does that hold true there? TN is currently instructing them on the use of cones of silence to see if that helps.
- How are you liking it? Other than the inability to fork, I'm taken by the relatively prosaic nature of the talks, incomprehensibility aside. Do you like it there?

Codrin#Assist, pass on my love back home.
— Codrin#Castor

Codrin#Castor

When I first got your note, I was worried that I'd not have time to squeeze in a response, until I remembered the tools at my disposal. This keeps happening over here. I'll find myself feeling rushed to complete something, then remember "oh, wait, I'll just move to fast-time, and then I can do whatever I want." I even got some writing done during our rests. As such, you'll probably get this seconds after you sent your letter, modulo transmission time.

Talks are going somewhat slower here than I think anyone expected. The Artemisians are incredibly patient with all of us, though, for which we're grateful.

The reasons for this are almost entirely up to the Odists. True Name and Why Ask Questions are both struggling with the time skew, WAQ more so than TN. Michelle quit forty years ago, and since then, I've not seen the shifting of form that she struggled with.

WAQ, however, immediately fell back into that. She's hardly spoken at all, and looks to be continually on the verge of getting sick or losing control completely. She seems to be able to either speak *or* maintain her form but not both, and even then, it comes at a dear price. When outside unison rooms (see below), she has a very hard time remaining in common time. Often, the best she can manage is to stay within ±1 of it.

TN is also struggling, though to a lesser extent. She is striving to remain as in control as she can, but there will still be the occasional silence as she is overcome, as was Michelle. During these, she will clench her fists or grit her teeth, and there will be the occasional glimmer of Michelle in there. As such, this has put a damper on our discussion, though, to Dear's worries, no, we don't seem to be in any danger.

To that end, we've moved the talks to a unison room. These rooms ensure that everyone within them remains synchronized to the same time skew, though the room itself can skew faster or slower than common time (which, I'm assured, is the same as ours, based on similar constants; managing time skew feels much like most System interactions such as forking or traveling, and common time feels like a pin in a lock clicking into place as you skew faster or slower). To that end, the unison room (or wing, perhaps) has become TN/WAQ's rest area while the other three of us have our original room. I don't know what to call it. Phasic room? They haven't been able to provide an answer because it's just "the rest of the world" to them.

As you mention, Iska is somewhat out of their element because of this. They're a skew artist, analogous to Dear's instance artistry. They seem uncomfortable in a unison room, though they remain very polite about it.

To your question about breaks, you're right that they are used to stepping away to talk about something before providing an answer. Before our shift to the unison room, they would readily shift up to fast time to discuss topics. After about a relative skew of ±1 (moving twice as fast/slow as common time), sound does not transmit to others, so it acts as a cone of silence, in that sense. Tangentially, I've found that touch also does not transmit well after skew ±0.5, probably to prevent injuries.

Tycho and Stolon are, as you suspected, quite frustrated with the lack of scientific discussion going on. Several times during breaks, they've shifted to fast time to get as much chatting in as they can. Tycho honestly seems quite fascinated by Stolon, and I suspect he's found a kindred spirit, though he has expressed some frustration about their lack of mastery over our common tongue. He said that they're both studying during their breaks in order to better converse.

All in all, though, I quite like it here. It is very different, and I find myself missing my family (and the food!) quite a bit, but honestly? I am also finding that I truly enjoy time skew. Codrin#Assist, don't tell Dear this.

In terms of knowledge share, you're spot on in much of what you bring up. The firstracers are hard to read, as you say, though you can add 'rocking head side to side = amusement' to your list. You don't mention much about Iska, but they're really quite nice after one gets past the clipped nature of their speech. I like them plenty.

Artante is curious. Her mannerisms are incredibly familiar, which I originally chalked up to the similarity in species, but it's come to light during discussions that she has picked up an obsession with the media that was embedded in the Dreamer Module broadcast. She's watched all of the videos several times over (more than seventy hours worth!) and listened to all of the audio enough to know how things sound (Iska's speech is clipped, I've mentioned, and occasionally misses intonation around questions/commas *qua* pauses/etc., and the firstracers' melodious speech often sounds more like singing than speaking). She and Sarah have had much to talk about, though both leaders nudge them often back to sociology and psychology as it relates to political systems, rather than therapeutic applications of forking or whatever. We'll have to ask them how she got that video within a system after this is over. 230+ years and you'd think they would've figured that out on our end by now. Ah well, engineers and their priorities.

TN here struggles with the 1racers lack of expression, though I had been chalking much of that up to her struggles with skew until you mentioned it. There have been a few misses in the conversation, where the two leaders will wind down a conversational blind alley and have to back up to the point where they turned the wrong corner. So patient is Turun Ka that this has been all the more frustrating for us, as it's difficult to tear down the assumptions that we've built up in the interim. Now that I say that, though, perhaps it is also frustrating for it, too, we just can't tell.

Are we dreaming it? Given how dreadfully immediate everything has felt, if we are, it is closer to a nightmare than a dream. Given what is happening with the Odists, I'll stick with TN's original assessment: the chance isn't zero, but it is small.

Anyway, I should head back to common time and catch up with Sarah before we head back to it. I want to make sure we talk more about the reasons why they picked 'recorder' as a required profession for this meeting. If it's about telling stories,

I'm all for it.

BĂLAN CLADE-EYES-ONLY MATERIAL

Codrin#Assist, pass on my love. Can you also check my work with Dear? I think I remember that Why Ask Questions Here At The End Of All Things was initially forked to shape sentiment sys-side during Secession, and that Why Ask Questions When The Answers Will Not Help was forked to shape sentiment outside the System. Is this correct? I've only met the two of them recently, so I'm unsure how that plays out in their social interactions.

END BĂLAN CLADE-EYES-ONLY MATERIAL

Thanks for acting as go-between for us. It'd be nice to be able to send a message directly to #Castor, but alas, DMZ.

Tycho Brahe#Castor — 2346

Convergence T-2 days, 19 hours, 3 minutes

"Do you eat?" Why Ask Questions asked. "We should probably wrap up shortly for rest, but if you feel the need to eat, we can ensure that you are able to do so."

Turun Ko tilted its head to the side. "Is eating required-necessary for proper function?"

She shook her head. "Not at all, no, but it is a comforting thing for us, so the ability to do so is present."

The two firstracers turned their heads to the side in a negative. Artante bowed. "I would appreciate the ability to do so."

"The same, *ka*," Stolon added.

Why Ask Questions nodded and stood. "I will provide a short primer if you need. Otherwise, shall we reconvene in nine hours? This will allow us time to recuperate."

"Ten hours would be preferable," Iska said.

"Can arrange sleeping area?" Stolon appeared concerned, adding, "Require additional warmth."

The rest of the table got to their feet while True Name said, "Of course. We will endeavor to make your stay pleasant. Why Ask Questions and I hold ACLs to this sim, including for your rest area. If you will permit us to enter, we will make any changes required."

Tycho watched as the Odists and Artemisians disappeared around the corner—and for several seconds after. It felt as though his eyes had been locked into place there, no matter how much he wanted to turn around and hunt down a chair more comfortable than those around the table.

"Tycho? Coming?"

He jolted, forced himself to look away, and smiled to Sarah, abashed. "Yeah, sorry. Guess I'm kind of beat." He rubbed his hands over his face, ground the heels of his palms against his eyes. "Lead the way, I guess."

They trudged off to the room, stepping around the corner in time to catch a second Codrin handing Codrin#Castor a few sheets of paper. Ey waved.

"Any news you'd like me to forward on to your #Artemis instances?"

"Oh, uh." Tycho frowned. "Not really, I guess. If you're sending notes. I guess just wish them well. I hope Tycho#Artemis is getting a chance to talk with Stolon. They seem neat."

Ey grinned, nodded. "Lots of time, from the sound of it. Ey'll tell you more," ey said, gesturing toward Codrin#Castor. "I'm just the messenger, though. I only get a few minutes here at a time."

"I won't keep you," Sarah said. "But if you could send the other me a note asking about the overall mood and sentiment over there, I'd be grateful."

Codrin#Assist hesitated, a look Tycho couldn't puzzle out crossing eir face. Finally, ey nodded. "I will, but you will find much of interest in Codrin's letter. I'll leave it up to #Castor's discretion to share, though."

Codrin#Castor frowned, flipping through the pages of the letter ey'd received. "We'll find some time to talk, yeah. Thank you, #Assist. I'll have another letter for you in the morning."

Ey bowed and disappeared back through the DMZ barrier.

"Complicated stuff happening over there?" Tycho asked.

"Very, but...well, let me digest this a bit before sharing. Should eat, too."

He nodded and headed over to the buffet table lining one wall, poking around through the dishes on offer. He settled on a simple sandwich, and the three of them sat at the dining table to eat in a bit of blessed silence.

Once they were finished, Sarah asked, "It's only fair that I ask you as well as the emissaries. How are you feeling about things so far?"

When Codrin didn't respond, Tycho shrugged. "Overwhelmed, still. I really like Stolon, and kind of wish I could just talk with them for a while instead of working through this whole process."

"Maybe we can figure out how to do break-out meetings or something."

"I guess, yeah. See if we can beg time and space for our one fork each. Still, I understand the reason for things working the way they do. We're not having an astronomy conference."

Sarah laughed. "That might be easier, yes. Certainly easier to connect on sciences than the social side."

"You seem to be connecting quite well with Artante," Codrin said once ey'd finished the salad ey'd settled on. "And it sounds like the same is true on Artemis."

"Oh? Does it sound like much the same dynamic over there?"

"Well, for us three, yes. For the Odists, no. It seems like–" Ey cut emself off, averting eir gaze from the entry as True Name and Why Ask Questions came in.

Neither looked happy. They paused their rather heated discussion and served themselves dinner before making their way over to True Name's partitioned-off rest area. Before sliding the screen shut, the skunk nodded to Codrin. "You may share, Mx. Bălan. If you already know, then there is no harm in the others knowing, too. Perhaps Ms. Genet will have some insight, as well."

With that, the screen slid shut and the room went silent, the two Odists apparently having set up a cone of silence.

"Well..." Ey shrugged. "I guess I'll just read you the pertinent parts. There's some clade-eyes-only stuff, so I'd prefer not to just hand it over."

Once ey had finished explaining what Michelle went through and describing the situation aboard Artemis, the three sat in silence.

"Well, I guess that explains their sour mood," Sarah said at last. "That rather changes things, doesn't it?"

"How?" Tycho asked. "Or, well, how do you mean? The mechanics have changed over there, but I'm guessing you mean something more subtle."

She nodded. "It's no longer an even playing ground on Artemis. Our leadership role is acting in reduced capacity and it sounds like one of our representatives has been all but taken out by the time skew."

He sat back in his chair, feeling marginally more human now that he'd eaten. He tried to picture how this must look given the spotty descriptions provided in the letter and the few details Codrin had seemed willing to fill in.

None of that seemed to jive with his experience with any of the Odists he'd met until now. Dear was weird, sure, but even it seemed to be completely in control of itself—more so than most anyone he'd met, at that. To think of True Name as being barely able to hold it together and Why Ask Questions all but non-functional beggared the imagination.

"It's weird," he said, looking up to the ceiling. "I almost wish I was over there. I mean, don't get me wrong, I feel sorry for True Name and Why Ask Questions, but the ability to literally steal some time to have a conversation sounds completely up my alley. Way more than forking, honestly."

"Well, when Tycho#Artemis returns, you'll at least get to remember that."

He laughed. "I guess, yeah. I'm eager to hear what all they've been learning. It's been interesting hearing what I can. I don't have the eye for learning styles that either of you two do, so

I'm missing out on that aspect, but even just hearing information about their gravity assist and how much they were able to learn about us as they zipped through our system was surprising. They ignored Lagrange and Earth entirely, and didn't bother with Pollux, since it was easier to align with us, anyway. It makes them seem like past masters at this, even if it's only the fourth time they've done it. Makes sense, though. Earth wouldn't hold much interest for an LV that can't even access it, and they're not going to stop to deal with the Lagrange System if they have access to us. Who knows, maybe they've gone past way more civilizations than those on Artemis, we just happened to meet the criteria. True Name mentioned that maybe rather than energy usage, a better measure of how advanced a civilization is would be whether or not they've discovered uploading."

Codrin had started jotting down notes part way through, nodding. "These are good questions to be asking. We'll have to find a way to work them in. I'll send them over to Artemis in the morning, too, so that the other Codrin can ask, as well."

He nodded.

"You mention that some portions of life on Artemis are appealing to you," Sarah said after a healthy pause. "Is that more positive than you were feeling about them before?"

"I guess," he hazarded. "I was more afraid of them, perhaps, but in that way that one is afraid of the unknown at one's doorstep. Afraid of the dark rather than afraid of monsters."

Codrin grinned. "Well put."

"But now, well...I know I'm not supposed to anthropomorphize them, but having met them, they're a lot less scary because there are still similarities between us. They breathe. They sleep. They get frustrated. That, combined with the appeal of time skew over forking, has me feeling much more curious than anxious."

"It's almost impossible not to anthropomorphize to at least some extent," Sarah said, nodding. "It's just how our minds work. I'll agree with you on that, though; even though they are still worlds different from us, it's not like we totally lack commonalities. Most of the differences seem to be surface ones, actually. Gestures and body language are foreign, but the number of truly fundamental differences in how we think has been pretty low so far, and mostly restricted to the two firstracers."

"They do seem to be operating on a different level," Codrin said. "I think if they had expressive faces, True Name would like them immensely."

She nodded, then asked, "Has your opinion of them changed?"

Ey shrugged. "Not particularly. I am curious about this time skew thing, but not nearly to the extent that Tycho is. I think it's tempered by being in a relationship with an Odist. It'd be fascinating, but Dear will never be able to experience it, or at least never agree to. I still bear a lot of the same anxieties, but I'm getting more comfortable with the process, because this role is familiar to me, at least."

"Doing a job you know how to do?"

Ey nodded. "It's my job to observe, to take in information and form it into something coherent."

"Which is fascinating to me," she said, sounding excited. "It's got me thinking about how I approach this, too."

Eir smile was weak. "I enjoy it when I'm in the middle of it, but it's hard not to feel like I lack agency, sometimes. After more than a hundred years, that part is starting to get old."

"Looking forward to something new after this?" Tycho asked.

Ey shrugged noncommittally.

"Well, I'll learn from you while I can," Sarah said. "And if you need any help or anything, or want me to spell you for a bit, I'll do what I can."

"Thanks, yeah." Ey sighed. "My thoughts on it are incomplete as yet. I'll figure it out over time, I'm sure."

"I'm glad to have you about either way," Tycho said, surprising himself with the earnestness in his voice. "You're really...I don't know. Grounding, perhaps?"

Ey laughed. "What does that mean?"

"Like you're here to witness it, and so everything that happens will have to have at least some basis in reality."

"It's quite important to feel witnessed," Sarah added. "Not just for ensuring that an experience is real, but for personal validation."

"Right. You being here makes me think I'm not crazy, that maybe I really am a part of something big."

Codrin crossed eir arms and leaned back in eir chair, expression thoughtful. "Thank you both, I'd not thought of it that way. *That's* a role I feel more comfortable with."

He nodded, then stifled a yawn. "Weird times. Weird, but interesting. I'm at least feeling better about just inviting aliens over without consulting anyone first. For now, though, I'm going to try and sleep, and see if I can snag some extra time with Stolon in the morning."

Tycho Brahe#Artemis — 2346

Convergence T-minus 2 days, 17 hours, 6 minutes

"We would like to ask you about the history of your species."

There was a brief pause as the Artemisians once more blurred into discussion. Iska had set up the sim such that the Artemisians remained in skew while the emissaries sat in a unison room, the table spanning an entrance arch. It had certainly helped with the True Name and, as he was now convinced, Answers Will Not Help. Neither seemed particularly back to baseline, and Answers Will Not Help continued to fluctuate between forms unless she focused on one at a time, but neither looked as though that took quite as much effort as it had originally.

"Are you able to narrow the scope of your question?"

The skunk frowned, tilted her head, and thought for a few long seconds. "I would like to learn about how it is that each of your species arrived at the point where you uploaded. I would also like to know if this is how a convergence has occurred in the past."

Yet another blur.

Tycho watched Codrin add a tick mark to a growing list on his notebook then dash off a few marks next to it in some sort of shorthand. "Keeping track of private discussions?"

The recorder nodded. "And what the general topic was that spurred it."

After a few seconds, the Artemisians slid back out of fast time, and Turun Ka spoke once more. "To your second request, yes, this fits the pattern as established after the first convergence. When we approached a star for a gravity assist, we confirmed radio transmissions following a familiar pattern and halted our planned maneuver to orbit the second planet from the star. There, we found a planet-bound civilization of approximately two billion biological individuals. We analyzed the language well enough to learn it within a day common time, and were able to initiate contact. I will allow representative Iska to describe from here."

The secondracer sat up straight. "We approached the communication with caution until we were able to ascertain that the object appeared to be a solid cylinder with few moving parts. After establishing a line of communication, we were able to understand that they were like those that we had called embedded. After approximately..." They trailed off, blurred into fast-time, then returned. "Approximately fifteen months, we were able to modify both of our systems to accept uploads from the other. Our talks were not as structured as this convergence, and we became secondrace without much discussion. Eight billion of our estimated forty billion embedded individuals joined this ship and–"

Turun Ka and Iska blurred into fast time. Codrin added another tick mark.

"–And eighteen thousand consciousness bearing entities from firstrace remained in our system."

"Over the next seventy-eight years," Turun Ka continued. "We resumed our voyage, utilizing the star and outer planets for further gravity assists to achieve an acceptable velocity. For third- and fourthraces, we approached the convergences much as we approach this one, and in both cases, we were able to do so with a similar vehicle moving out-system."

"And in each case, the decision to join was mutual?" True Name asked.

"Yes."

"Will you allow us to join you should we ask?"

Silence greeted the question. Codrin frowned and scribbled an extensive note.

"An answer is not necessary," the skunk said. "Though am I correct in inferring that this question is more complex than a simple yes-or-no answer?"

"*Anem.* Correct."

The skunk leaned back in her chair briefly. She looked to be covering an expression of exhaustion, as though she desperately wanted to rub her face with her paws in an attempt to wake herself up, but dare not at the moment.

Finally, she said, "Are you able to address my first request?"

"That is another complex question. It is not yet time to have that conversation."

She nodded. "To make sure that I am understanding correctly, you are not comfortable explaining how it is that each race went from a biological form to an uploaded form at this point. *Anem?*"

"*Ato esles,*" Turun Ko said. *Except us.* "Would be better to describe-explain us as post-biological. Physical form to uploaded-embedded form."

"Is the knowledge itself uncomfortable, or the act of sharing it with us as emissaries?"

Another silence, another note from Codrin.

"Would it be uncomfortable for us to explain how we as a species moved from physical to embedded?"

"Now is not the time for the exchange of that information," Turun Ka said. "There will be time for this discussion once prerequisite discussions are held. To explain this to us now is confusing."

"Can you expand on 'confusing'?"

"We do not know why you would tell us such a thing at this moment," Artante said. "This is not the time to discuss this."

True Name sat back as she digested this.

"Without explaining how we came to be as we are," Answers Will Not Help said, voice shifting between registers as her species shifted in turn. "May we explain why we are interested in an exchange of this knowledge?"

A blurred discussion, another tick mark.

"You are proud of having achieved this, *anem?*" Turun Ka said. "A separate embedded society from the physical society you have left behind on Earth?"

She nodded. "We are, yes, and it could be that we might learn some information that might make it easier on us during the embedding procedure."

"And easier on you?" Artante asked.

Both Odists bridled at this, but Codrin preempted any arguments by leaning forward and saying, "There are several core improvements that could be made to our systems that affect all inhabitants."

"But also you specifically," she confirmed. "I mean no disrespect by suggesting such. One is of the utmost importance to oneself, and this is admirable in its own right."

After a long pause, True Name nodded. "If there is a way that the Ode clade might benefit, then we would be interested. The issues that affect us are, to our knowledge, unique to our clade."

"You see, then, why this conversation is complicated."

The skunk may have masked her frustration, but that only let her exhaustion shine through all the more. "I think it is appropriate to table this question for now."

Artante nodded and Turun Ka lifted its snout in assent.

"You have lived with each other for millennia now," Sarah said. "Do you continue to have topics such as this which are uncomfortable to discuss with each other?"

Another fast-time conversation.

Iska answered for the group. "As our core society, no. There are aspects of each others' societies that do not mesh, however, so there are times when we remain separate as species, but there is nothing that is uncomfortable among the Council of Eight or common areas. Individually, we bear our own discomforts and taboos."

Tycho wound up tuning much of the meeting out after that. The day felt long already, and though he couldn't tell what time it was, he just wanted to stand up and walk around.

The mood around the table was not tense, *per se,* but he could tell that the Odists were frustrated by just how much of their questions were missing the mark, how many conversations it was not yet time to have. He couldn't read any of the Artemisians well enough to see any of the same on them, though he suspected that Stolon's apparent antsiness was borne of the same boredom he felt.

When they were finally able to take a break, he was eager to stand and stretch, then disappointed when Stolon ran off with the other delegates. He would have to catch up with the thirdracer another time.

Instead, he followed Codrin and Sarah out into the central colonnaded plaza where they could walk around and enjoy the sight of sunlight on alien plant life.

"Why does everyone seem stressed?" he said, once they'd made a lap around the plaza. "We have as much time as we want up here, basically. Shouldn't we just go slower and accept that it might take a while."

Codrin yawned, rubbing a hand over eir face. "I don't know if it's a time thing. I think True Name is stressed because we haven't figured out how to have conversations correctly. It's a sort of mutual misunderstanding. We don't know why they won't answer *x* while they have no clue why we'd even ask it in the first place, and then the script gets flipped for the next question."

"Didn't we know that going in, though?"

Ey shrugged. "Knowing and experiencing are not the same thing. Also, I think we were lulled into a false sense of security by how easily the first conversations went. It felt like there was more mutual understanding there than there really was."

Tycho laughed, brushing fingertips against one of the columns as they walked past. "On one hand, I feel incredibly out of place with all that we're talking about, since I'm just the scientist. On the other, though, I guess I feel lucky that I'm not faced with the same problems."

"I imagine that Tycho#Castor is having a bit of an easier time of it," Codrin said. "Still enjoying yourself here, at least?"

"I guess. Or, rather, I'm not sure if 'enjoying' is the right word. I'm still fascinated by everything, and there's so much I want to do and ask. I just feel like everyone else is working on another level from me. True Name and Turun Ka are clicks above me in terms of how subtly they interact. Even you seem to operate on a different wavelength from me."

Codrin shrugged. "Too much time around Odists, perhaps."

Tycho grinned and shook his head. "Maybe, but I was thinking more that you are here to witness and be an amanuensis. You told me that I'd be doing the same weeks ago, and I still feel like that's way out of my league."

Ey looked thoughtful at this as they made their way back to the meeting room. "I was going to say 'all you need to do is watch', but that's not totally accurate. I'm trained in this, and there's a way of thinking that goes along with that training."

He nodded.

"Either way, don't worry about it, Tycho. You'll get time to talk about the things you want, I'm sure of it. Just make some, even. Catch Stolon to talk about nerdy stuff in fast time."

Ioan Bălan — 2346

Convergence T-plus 29 days, 22 hours, 15 minutes
(Castor-Lagrange transmission delay: 30 days, 14 hours, 36 minutes)

The dinner that Do I Know God After The End Waking had prepared for them was...rustic. That was the first term that ey had
come up with to describe it, and no matter how else Ioan tried
to refine it, ey was left with little else that fit.

It was a venison stew with parsnips and onions, thickened
with tack and stretched with some barleycorns. 'Woodsy' was
not quite the right word, and neither was 'simple', for the skunk
had spent the better part of an hour doting over the cast-iron
pot he'd hung over a low fire, adding salt in what Ioan felt were
miserly pinches, as well as pepper and nutmeg as though they
were the most precious items in the world to him.

When asked where he got the spices, barley, and tack in a
forest, the skunk had laughed, shaken his head, and said, "I am
not a fucking ascetic, Ioan," then gone back to cooking.

So, rustic stew it was.

Very, *very* good rustic stew. End Waking had explained that,
as he had no way to store leftovers, they would need to finish
the entire pot that night. It turned out to be no stretch for the
small gathering—Ioan and May, Debarre, Time Is A Finger Pointing At Itself, Douglas, and End Waking himself—as they all went
back for seconds. The ranger skunk even swirled in a little extra

water once the pot was empty, using a fingerpad to wipe what stew remained down into that to make himself a thin soup to finish out of the battered mug he'd been using as a bowl for the night.

They'd each brought their own contribution for the night, as well. After dinner, A Finger Pointing pulled out a bottle of over-proof white whiskey that they passed around the circle, taking burning sips. Ioan and May brought with them a short, two-person play that they put on for the other three, full of crude jokes and self-deprecating humor. Douglas, having picked up music as a hobby since uploading, performed a trio with three instances, one on a flute, one on a mandolin, and one on a cajón.

For his part, Debarre had brought fireworks. Or *a* firework, at least. The weasel produced a double fist-sized sphere of *papier mache*, and set it atop a small cylinder right next to the fire. With End Waking watching, hawklike, he directed everyone to stand back a few feet and lit the fuse with a small punk from the fire, explaining, "I've been working on this for the last seventy years or so. It's only about fifty percent possible outside the System, but my excuse is that I never saw fireworks out there so I can do whatever the fuck I want."

The firework lifted off the cylinder it had been set on top of with surprising grace. Rather than rocketing into the air, it rose slowly, splitting in half a few inches up and rising in a tight helix, the weasel explaining that the propellant was tightly controlled to allow such, until it was hovering about three meters above the fire on a column of sparks as orange as those of the fire itself. From there, small spheres of cool-blue sparks popped free and danced around it in slow, hypnotic whorls. Finally, in a fountain of green fire, billowing into the shape of a tree, it fell back into the campfire with a hissing sigh to be consumed by the flames.

"Out-fucking-classed," A Finger Pointing grumbled. "You said 'bring something', my dear, so I brought a bottle to drink, and you all bring plays and music and fireworks."

"You will hear no complaints from me," End Waking said, grinning toothily. "Do you know how long it has been since I have had whiskey?"

She laughed and shook her head. "I will bring you a case next time."

The skunk shook his head. "I am enjoying the ability to taste something again after years without. I have missed it and that makes it special."

"Sap."

He rolled his eyes and made a rude gesture at her.

A Finger Pointing fit neatly into the pattern of a human Michelle, though over the centuries, she had opted for a form that was a little taller, a little slimmer, and bore more heavily styled hair. More chic, perhaps. She was prone to grand gestures and grand outfits in all black or all gray or all red. She had also leaned into hedonism more so than any of the other Odists Ioan had met. She ate heartily, drank more than all of them—though this mostly manifested as a ruddy glint to her cheeks and a more wicked grin than usual—and brought with her a very comfortable-looking camp chair.

Even having worked with her for nearly a decade as a playwright and under her direction as an actor for the last few years, ey continually found emself surprised by her simple desire to enjoy life, put on good plays, and be friends with everyone she could. It was a simplicity that was lacking from so many of her cocladists that ey'd had a chance to meet.

"Do you wish that you had the chance to meet them?" End Waking said, once the fire had been stoked back up to stave off the deepening darkness.

"The Artemisians?"

He nodded.

"Kind of, yeah," She said. "I was pleased to hear that bit about how important they find stories, so I would like the chance to hear some directly from them and see what they think of ours."

"And you, my dear?"

Debarre shrugged. His and End Waking's on-again-off-again relationship seemed to be back on the rise, and so the skunk and weasel shared a seat on the log, tails draped across each other's. So stoic was the Odist, though, that while this was the only outward sign of affection between the two, it came off far sweeter than Ioan would have otherwise expected, especially given his cocladist's constant touch in eir own relationship. Ey'd certainly never heard the skunk use 'my dear' with anyone else. Ey reveled in the compersion ey felt for them.

"I've never been a huge fan of sci-fi," the weasel said. "I suppose it'd be neat, but it feels really out there. I mean, I'm obviously excited, and I'd love to meet them, but it all sounds more like a fantasy than anything, so I'm not too put out."

"Ioan?" the skunk asked.

Ey shrugged after a moment's thought. "I'm lucky. I get to share all the good stuff with you all direct from a cocladist. I wouldn't turn down the chance to meet them, but I'm also happy with this."

"Why?"

Ioan frowned. "Why am I happy with just this?"

"Yes."

"I think because the part of my life spent right in the thick of it is over. I'm a different person, now. I've grown, changed. I've moved away from the Ioan who sat and watched as eir job. I'm a different me, now. I'm happy with being excited from a distance. I'm happy with the romance of it all."

May, tucked firmly against eir side, dotted her nose on eir cheek. "Different kind of nerd."

"Pretty much, yeah." Ey laughed. "Besides, Codrin said they've been bandying about the idea that none of it's real, that they've been dreaming the whole thing. I'm more curious to see that play out than actually experience meeting the Artemisians."

"It does not matter," End Waking said.

"What?"

"It does not matter whether or not it actually exists. If there is no ship named Artemis full of four races of aliens, the world which exists within Castor is still a new and interesting one. It is still a world worth exploring." The skunk shrugged. "The question of their existence beyond Castor is purely academic."

"Well, huh," ey said. "I'll have to pass that on to Co-drin#Castor, then. Perhaps it'll ease some anxieties."

End Waking nodded, then continued around the circle. "How about you, May Then My Name?"

"A part of me wishes I had the chance, but it is a small part. The rest of me is smug in my decision to remain behind preventing me from doing so. I cannot change that decision and go meet them, and that in and of itself is exciting, is it not?"

The other skunk turned his gaze on Douglas.

"I think I'm probably the outlier here, in that I was—or am—kind of crushed by the fact that I won't be able to meet them." He poked a stick he'd found at the base of the fire. "Here I am, someone who spent eight years in university studying spaceflight, someone who did all he could to specialize in the System, and I'm stuck reading second-hand accounts on a five thousand year old civilization flying through space on a system of their own. I got over my frustration at having not uploaded in time for the launches years ago, but this is bringing it all back."

"What would you do, had you the chance to meet them?" End Waking asked.

"Oh, I don't know. That's the thing. I don't have anything concrete in mind that I feel like I'm missing, it's just this envy over not having the chance. I'm sure I'd ask them a million questions about spaceflight and System shit, because that's just how I am. I want to know how they keep their vehicle in working order over so long a time. I want to know how they can receive images and sounds and video instead of just text. I want to know all sorts of things, but that's ancillary to the fact that I'm just not there."

This short speech demanded a silent acknowledgement of a few minutes, and the five sat in quiet, watching the fire or looking up to the stars and moon overhead. Douglas poked at the fire. May rested her head on Ioan's shoulder. A Finger Pointing, Debarre, and End Waking drank.

"I would like to know their forests," the skunk said at last. "And I would invite them to know mine. Do they hunt their own venison and dig their own parsnips? I do not know. If they do not, I would show them. If they do, I would want them to show me."

"Even if that meant uploading to Artemis?" Ioan asked.

"Yes."

"It doesn't sound like a pleasant place for Odists, from what May's told me."

The skunk shrugged. "That is not enough to stand in the way of my desire. Would I go mad in the midst of their forest? Very well, I would go mad."

"Is that what it feels like? Going mad?"

"I am not sure how else to put it," he said after a long silence.

"I was on a field of dandelions and grass," May said, her voice distant and dream-fogged. "And there was no echo. The world stretched out before me in empty nothingness, and there was no echo. At my back was a bar—scratched wood, stools, a foot rail, a gutter for pouring drinks—and the only way I could hear my own voice pass through the air was to huddle between those stools and face the bar."

"Words came unbidden," A Finger Pointing picked up where May left off. "And as they passed through my mind, they dripped and smeared—a painting with too much wet paint on the canvas stood on its edge. The dreaming mind did not know what to do with language that close to the surface, and so the language stained all it touched."

End Waking nodded, speaking toward the fire. "And so I screamed and I ran, and when I looked back, the bar was gone, and when I looked forward again, there it was. Had I turned?

Was the world so small? The words came unbidden, and with each one that left my mouth, a cord that tethered me to reality snapped, and I grew lighter and lighter, and I feared I would float up into the sky, into the sun."

"And through it all, time was unmoored and set adrift," May said quietly. "Sixteen hours, twenty three minutes is what they said, but I lived lifetime after lifetime beneath that sun. The light thrummed and vibrated around me, and I lived and died and lived again. I watched eternity fall away and rot at my feet."

"Or perhaps it was just an instant," A Finger Pointing said.

End Waking's words came with a finality that seemed to draw the memory to a close, though nothing about the recitation—monologue?—had felt memorized or rehearsed. "And so I went mad."

"Jesus." Douglas's whisper broke the long silence that followed. "And you're afraid that's what would happen on Artemis?"

"Not exactly that," he said. "But when presented with the fragility of eternity once more, I cannot imagine that I would remain sane. That any of us would."

"This is what we fear," May said.

"With the Artemisians and their time? I saw through your eyes," Debarre said, so quiet as to be almost a whisper. End Waking rested a paw on his knee. "I was so happy to see you, and so terrified to be there. Two and a half minutes was enough for a lifetime."

"Or memory?" Douglas added.

May nodded, tugging Ioan's arm tighter around her middle. "A madness born of eternities. Memory upon memory upon memory. Our memories, our whole subconscious, lie too close to the surface, and that barrier between the conscious and subconscious cannot bear the weight of an eternity. And so the cracks widen."

"Do you think that's what happened with Death Itself and I Do Not Know? To Michelle?" Ioan asked.

End Waking dipped his snout and drew his hood up over his head once more. Debarre looked away into the dark of the forest. A Finger Pointing took a long drink from the bottle of whiskey.

"I do not know, my dear. I will never know. It is very hard to quit when one is at the root of a clade, or even a larger subtree. Like pushing through a barrier or wading through mud. Death Itself may have been struggling to do so for a long time. I cannot imagine how difficult it must have been for Michelle. The System is not built for death."

Ey felt eir muscles tense, was helpless to stop it.

"I am sorry, Ioan. The System is not built for death, just as you are not. It wants to keep us alive, and so to end a clade is very difficult."

Ey nodded slowly, focusing on night above em, the log they sat on beneath em, the warmth of the fire before em. Ey focused on those around em—A Finger Pointing, Douglas, Debarre, End Waking, and of course eir own dear May—pinning em to a time, a place, a mood. Ey focused on the feeling of being alive and being *here*, of being present and in the world, digital or otherwise.

"How heavy must that madness be, then," May continued. "To crash through so many failsafes and allow someone who has been within the system for more than two centuries such a death? This is what we fear."

Tycho Brahe#Castor — 2346

"I would like to ask a few questions about forking versus skew," Tycho said, when a lull between the two parties ran long enough that he felt comfortable doing so.

Both the Odists and Iska turned their gaze on him, intently enough that he was caught short in his speech. Intensity from the Odists had become at least recognizable, if still not exactly comfortable, but the length of Iska's neck allowed them to push their head toward him to an alarming degree without necessarily leaning forward.

"I'll try to keep it on a scientific rather than social level," he added, somewhat diminished.

Turun Ka lifted its chin in assent. "We are amenable to this."

"Alright." He spent a moment gathering his thoughts, looking down at the brief set of notes he'd taken on his pad. "The first and largest, I suppose, is does skewing faster than what I've heard you call 'common time' lead to increased load on your system?"

Iska, having started to pick up on human mannerisms, nodded, though it was a somewhat more elaborate gesture than any of them might have made. "The faster one experiences time, the greater the load is. There is not as much need for it these days, but originally, the ability to skew up was governed by a system-

209

wide algorithm such that the more individuals that were skewed up, the lower the maximum skew was. This was balanced by those who were skewed down."

"Here on our System, prior to some technological advancements, forking was limited by a reputation market," True Name said. "I will leave the historical and sociological implications of this to the emissaries on Artemis, however, I can speak to the mechanical aspect of it."

Iska nodded. "I will compare with what I remember."

"I do not know whether any of you have explored the functionality, but forking is an act of intent. One projects the desire to fork and, when that intent is recognized by the System, the fork is created. Does that align with the mechanics of time skew?"

Iska sat still and silent for a moment, and Tycho imagined a hidden frustration within them. While they'd been nothing but cordial throughout the visit so far, they had also stated plainly that they were uncomfortable with the lack of time skew and had refused the fork they were permitted in their rest area. He imagined that they'd like nothing more than to take their time coming up with the perfect response to this question in a fraction of a second, common time, but lacked the mechanism within the System.

"That aligns with our experience. I would not have used the words 'intent' and 'project a desire' prior to hearing them. I would have said that one 'remembers' being at a set skew. One remembers being or having been at skew plus one, and then one is. One remembers having been at common time, or perhaps remembers sliding down from skew plus one to common time, and one does so." After a hesitation, they added, "But the concepts map almost exactly, so I will gladly accept 'intent' and 'project a desire' as terms."

Codrin spoke up next. "My counterpart on Artemis described in a note to me that 'common time feels like a pin in a lock clicking into place as you move faster or slower'. I am assuming that this is what you mean when you say 'one remembers having been at common time'?"

Iska bared their teeth, a gesture that the delegates had agreed must be a sort of smile. "The common time consensus sensation is provided as an aid to all consciousness-bearing entities, yes. I am told that, when one first experiences skew, it can feel, *lu*...slippery, perhaps. It can be difficult to aim for a skew and remember that exactly, so one slides toward it and may overshoot. I am nearly five thousand years old, Artemis reckoning, I have forgotten how it feels for skew to be slippery, but yes, that is why it exists."

"But since aiming for common time is so important, an aid is provided?" Tycho asked.

"Precisely, scientist Tycho Brahe."

True Name continued, "The second part of my comparison was regarding the sensation of not having the ability to fork or skew, which, as appears to be the case for both of our Systems, is no longer much of a factor. When one did not have enough reputation to fork, that intent felt less real, as though one could not possibly fork, as though it was an impossible act. What was the experience of not being able to skew any faster?"

There was another long moment of thought before the secondracer nodded. "Again, it has been a long time since I have experienced that sort of limitation, but yes. One simply could not remember skewing any faster. There is still an effective upper limit on skew, but very few consciousness-bearing entities find skew above plus eight to plus ten to be comfortable, and in practice, few go above skew plus five."

Why Ask Questions frowned. "Uncomfortable how?"

"The, *lu*...level of interaction decreases as one's skew increases. Above plus one, sound does not transmit to common time and touch is impossible. Above plus five, movement becomes difficult and one feels...*baenåt*...restrained, perhaps. Movement takes effort. The effort required to move slows one down to where positive skew is no longer effective though one may use the time to think."

The two Odists exchanged a look, and a brief glance at Codrin showed the writer looking more intently at them than at Iska.

"I would like to move on to a related question," True Name said, at which Codrin wrote something down on eir pad.

Tycho made a note to talk to em after, find out what had intrigued em about the Odists' reaction.

Iska nodded.

"Are there any corrective measures that your system can take?"

"Please clarify if you are able."

"Well, for example, the vast majority of forks are not created for individuation but to accomplish a task while the original instance—what we call the down-tree instance—carries on what they were doing before, or to increase the workforce on a task. When the fork quits, the down-tree instance has the option of integrating some or all of their memories. This can lead to inconsistencies—which we call conflicts—when memories do not align well, and one will be prevented from keeping memories from both instances. Are there instances where your system might need to take corrective action?"

The secondracer tilted their head, then set up a cone of silence so that the Artemisians could discuss their answer.

"True Name desperately wants to ask about the political ramifications of all of this," Why Ask Questions stagewhispered, elbowing Tycho in the side. "You are going to have to preempt her, Tycho, if you do not want to be trampled."

"I brought you into this world, my dear," True Name retorted. "I can and will take you back out of it."

The delegates all laughed, but Tycho readily picked up on the subtext: *you're the scientist, do your job.*

He wrote down a few more ideas for questions while they waited.

"There are very few automated corrective actions," Iska said once the cone dropped. "One might consider the increased restrictions on movement at higher relative skews. As mentioned, sound does not transmit beyond a relative skew of one, and touch on both individuals and physical objects is reduced as relative skew increases in order to reduce destructive collisions."

"That answers part of my question," Tycho said. "As I was wondering how the system dealt with the transfer of force at higher relative skews. Can this be bypassed, though?"

Iska tilted their head again, further this time. "Why would one, scientist Tycho Brahe?"

"Well, we can turn our sensoria's sensitivity up and down on an individual level, and we can increase or decrease collision sensitivity on a sim level. Like, in public sims, collision sensitivity will be conservative so that you can't bump someone too hard. I was wondering if there are similar mechanics on Artemis. Are there sims where that restriction on touch at high relative skew is relaxed?"

The secondracer's expression was what Tycho could only describe as shocked. "That could lead to physical damage to one or both objects involved in the interaction."

He frowned. "Of course, that makes sense. I only ask because that functionality is available to us."

For the first time in the conversation, Artante spoke up. "This is veering into the territory designated for those aboard Artemis, but I will try to keep it grounded in the science and mechanics of our differences. Scientist Tycho Brahe, are there situations within your system that one might wish to cause physical damage to another?"

True Name stiffened in her seat, but before she could reply, Tycho said, "Sure. There are combat sims and some forms of participatory art where risk of damage is considered part of of the experience."

"And one is often advised or required to send a fork to these, *anem?*"

"Almost to a one, yeah."

Iska had been gripping the edge of the table tightly and finally seemed to cave to emotion and set up a cone of silence. He watched as, within, they said something that looked quite angry to Artante, who nodded calmly and said something in return. There was an angry retort, and then the same response from Artante.

Both firstracers sat by impassively. They may have been talking, but there was no visible indication of such. Stolon, meanwhile, sat between the two, looking miserable.

When the cone dropped once more, Artante continued. "In a system without forking, scientist Tycho Brahe, you must understand that there is no analogue to such. A system which could intentionally allow egregious harm to its occupants is unacceptable to us."

"Oh, right," he said, frowning. The sight of True Name scribbling notes with alarming intensity distracted him, but he managed to say all the same, "My apologies, I'd not put that together until we talked through it."

Artante and Iska both bowed, though Iska's was noticeably more curt.

"We understand," they said. "We have analogous experiential and participatory art using skew, but that is not for this meeting to discuss."

A cone of silence dropped over their side of the table and Codrin turned to True Name, asking, "May I ask what you were writing?"

The skunk frowned. "Why?"

"You were very intent on it," ey said. "And I was wondering if it's something that might be relevant to the rest of us or if it was something destined for True Name#Artemis."

There was a silent pause where True Name looked first at Codrin, then at Why Ask Questions, then back again. "I had intended to send it to #Artemis, but I take your meaning. You know that Jonas and I have thoughts on an appropriate level of discomfort and danger within a society in order to maintain stability. A system that restricts violence by mechanics such as these may—and that is a very big 'may'—speak to one that falls below that acceptable threshold for us."

" 'Pain, anxiety, the need for something greater, these are all essential for survival. Without them, the world would be an impossibly dangerous place', you mean." Codrin quoted.

She laughed. "Indeed. You may thank Jonas for that one. That they may disagree with this could say a lot about them. If they have somehow moved past the need for pain and anxiety, we will have much to learn. If they object to it on moral grounds, we must be wary."

Tycho watched the exchange with mounting confusion before making note of yet another thing to ask Codrin about over break.

Codrin Bălan#Castor — 2346

True Name's ability to keep a steady, half-smiling expression was admirable. Even Why Ask Questions appeared to be only just barely keeping frustration at bay.

Having instructed the Artemisians on how to use cones of silence, there were far fewer breaks throughout the last two days, limited to one in the morning, one in the afternoon, and a longer lunch in the middle. That did not stop them from settling into private conversation every few minutes to discuss whatever answer they might give.

Ey initially found it strange that added downtime would make their party more tired rather than less, but after some consideration—and a brief talk with Sarah—ey'd come to the realization that those periods of quiet between question and answer were still spent in expectation. They were still working during those pauses. They were still in conversation, if only by way of watching and waiting, trying to guess what might have led to the need to have that private discussion. Ey could not read expressions beyond eir limited notes so far, could not speak the language well enough, and certainly could not read lips, so ey was left only with guesses and suppositions.

And through it all, True Name seemed to be trying to match the firstracers for patient expressions.

217

It wasn't until that second day's lunch that the skunk showed any breaks in that patience. She picked up a plate piled high with salad, brought it over to the table in the center of their rest area then stepped back a few paces, where she activated a cone of silence. She brought her tail around toward her front, held in both paws, and buried her face in it. Ey could only assume by the sudden way that she bent at the waist and pinned her ears back that this was done to muffle a scream or some violent obscenity.

Then, as though nothing had happened, she sat down to eat.

Lunch after that had been filled with laughter and truly terrible jokes. Sarah, it turned out, collected them, and the delegates unanimously voted hers the worst.

All throughout, though, Codrin couldn't shake the image of True Name throwing a very short, very tightly controlled tantrum. The sight of her letting loose so strong an emotion had immediately knocked em back to an interview—decades ago, now—where she'd wound em up enough that ey'd started shouting at her in her own office, then bounced em from her sim.

That, ey'd later understood, had been intentional on her part. It had been a way for her to spin her story in a very carefully crafted way. It set it to a level that sat just on the other side of the line between plausible and absurd. It had wrapped em up in a story that was just a little too much to believe, and the end result was a softening of the impact of the *History*.

She was a consummate actor. Nothing about that experience had been done with a wink and a nudge, just as nothing about this had contained any such acknowledgement that it was intentional, but ey was nothing if not primed to expect her actions to be based in manipulation. There was a non-zero chance that this tantrum had been more for the benefit of the other delegates than anything. It was a way to show that she, too, was frustrated, just as the pun-off that had followed had been a way to loosen everyone up by lampshading the absurdity of the whole venture.

And then, it was over. True Name cleared away her plate, explained that she was going to write a letter to her #Artemis instance, made a final joke about needing to do so over letters being much more up Codrin's alley, and then stepped into her room to work in silence.

"What was that about?" Sarah asked, once the skunk and Why Ask Questions had wandered off again.

"What, the thing about the letters?" Ey shrugged. "I guess it was deemed a risk setting up radio between the DMZ and–"

"No, no," she said, shaking her head. "Sorry, I mean, what was with the scream and then all the jokes?"

Ey frowned and set up another cone of silence for the two of them. "I was just thinking about that, actually. I was wondering if she really is frustrated enough to scream or if it was intentional to make her seem more normal like the rest of us mere mortals."

"I don't think it was that extreme. Maybe some part of her was trying to build camaraderie with us by doing so, but I'm wondering if it was more that she was trying to downplay the news from Artemis."

Codrin sat up straighter. "You mean the Odists struggling over there?"

She nodded. "It sounds like moving them to a unison room is helping, but they're still struggling with that...what did Codrin#Artemis call it? The omnipresence of time?"

"Yeah. Dear had talked about it some. It called the feeling of being lost as being stuck in an 'endless place of no time'."

"I was going to call that poetic, but the more I think about it, the less I think I could describe it without a whole lot of metaphors, myself." She pushed a few remaining pieces of lettuce around her plate with her fork. "I was wondering if maybe she's trying to hide how she's feeling about that by amping up other emotions. Hiding trauma with humor is not uncommon, and I'm sure she has trauma of her own."

Ey frowned. "It would make sense, yes. This morning's letter from Codrin talked a bit more about them, about how they seem to be struggling in masking more powerful emotions. 'I don't think I've ever seen an Odist well and truly furious,' ey said, which I agree with. I've seen Dear angry, and Ioan says that ey's seen May Then My Name get furious—at True Name, no less—but I've never seen any of them truly furious. 'True Name keeps getting these flashes, though, where her face will twist up in what I can only call abject fury. It'll only last a second or so, and then it's over and she's back to looking tired or in control or whatever she was before'."

"Anger is a strong emotion. It's hard to cover up something that overwhelming."

"Right. Anger and sadness or depression seem to be the two that keep cropping up. They've had to take a few breaks so far when Why Ask Questions wound up in a crying jag."

She shook her head. "I've not heard anything from my #Artemis instance, which is fine, but I wonder how she would describe it."

"Want me to ask? I was going to send off a note before we started back up again."

"Please. I was going to write something myself, but if you're already sending one, might as well tack it on there, instead."

Ey nodded and scratched out a note to emself in eir notebook. "Before I get to that, though, I have a question for you. Something before I drop the cone, I mean."

Sarah leaned forward, elbows on her knees, and ey did the same. The added secrecy of talking quieter was a difficult habit to break, and eir mind was still on the topic of lip-reading from earlier.

"#Artemis hinted at something and I'm not quite sure what to make of it. That ey's even hinting at it rather than just saying it outright is telling in and of itself, of course, but I can see why, given the context. The messages are clade-eyes-only, so others can't read them unless one of us grants permission, anyway. It's only a hint, but I think...I mean, I think maybe ey's suggesting that it's not Why Ask Questions on Artemis, but Answers Will Not Help."

The psychologist frowned down toward the floor. "What form did this hint take?"

Ey dredged up the memory of the postscript. "Ey asked Dear to check eir work. I remember that, during Secession, Why Ask Questions managed sentiment sys-side and Answers Will Not Help did the same phys-side. The hint was asking, 'Is this correct? I've only met the two of them recently, so I'm unsure how that plays out in their social interactions.' I remember that, of course, so the hint is in the question."

"Anything in subsequent letters?"

"Well, Codrin#Assist confirmed it, saying, 'Dear says that's correct. Why Ask Questions worked sys-side, Answers Will Not Help worked phys-side'. Neither #Artemis nor I have brought it up again since."

"You obviously know your communication style better than anyone else, but do you think ey's hinting at the fact that they were switched specifically for their roles? Intra- and extra-system sentiment?"

Ey nodded.

"Well, that'd be a hell of a stunt to pull." She sighed, steepling her fingers before her. "I could only really tell them apart by the way they acted, but, like you, I only met them a week or so ago. Is ey sure that it's not just due to the way the skew is impacting them?"

"I don't know, really, but given that a good chunk of the rest of the letter, as well as subsequent ones, has been about that impact and the effects it's having on the meetings, I don't doubt eir observations."

There was a moment of silence as they both digested the conversation. They still had a few minutes of time left, if ey still wanted to write eir note, so ey allowed the moment to stretch.

Finally, Sarah said, "I guess I have a few thoughts on it: the first is that Answers Will Not Help struck me as less grounded than Why Ask Questions. They're both weird, but Answers Will Not Help was always much more intense, and she sometimes got petty and cruel. The second was that maybe we could ask Tycho. We got a few days with the two of them, but he's been working with them for much longer, since they led with a bunch of science."

"Alright," ey said, scratching out another quick note to emself. "I'll figure out a way to ask if that's where the observation came from."

"Oh? As in maybe Tycho noticed that and told Codrin#Artemis?"

"Right, yeah. Maybe he picked up on it first because he's had more time with her, or maybe her reaction to the skew tipped him off. Who knows?"

"Think you'll ask in a hint, too?"

Ey nodded. "There's some subtext there that I'm not totally picking up on, and it seems best to be safer than not."

"Any guesses as to that subtext?" she asked.

"Only incomplete ones. I wonder if it's to keep Codrin#Assist from reading too much into it since ey's not experiencing any of this."

"And you're worried ey might bring it up with the Odists?"

Ey laughed, shaking eir head. "Nothing so grand. It's just hard for us to leave well enough alone. Ey'd probably start cataloging the differences between them. Well, ey probably already is, given the hint, but without the context that we're seeing here, it'll be somewhat less pointed."

"Right, that makes sense. That still seems a little flimsy for a reason to be this vague of a hint."

"Agreed," ey said, then shrugged. "Could be that ey just doesn't trust that clade-eyes-only works on Artemis. All the same, I'll hint back and see what comes of it, just to be safe."

She grinned. "Alright. Keep me up to date, I guess."

Codrin dropped the cone of silence and stretched eir arms up over eir head, "I'll see you in there in a few, then. Thanks for chatting."

Sarah stood, waved, and wandered back into the room, leaving em to brush out eir blouse and straighten the apron that rested over eir skirt before starting the note.

Codrin#Artemis

Not a whole lot to add here on my part, and I need to get back to it momentarily, so just a quick note for now. There's been some talk on biology and a bit more on astronomy. This always gets Tycho super excited, of course, so we have to space the topic out so that he and Stolon don't completely monopolize the meeting.

This morning we discussed the science of forking as it relates to time skew, but it was hard to keep the talk out of what should be your area up there.

The most pertinent thing of late has been some discussion over language and how that has changed over time based on the physiology of the races. Iska spoke some "old Nanon" for us, which was beautiful, but almost uncanny. I'd keep almost catching words, but then they'd slip away from me again. Why Ask Questions understood better, and was able to ask some questions about linguistic evolution. Most of those went over my head, but she seemed surprised at how little things had changed over that long a time span, which got us on the topic of the history and politics of language. That was cut off since that's your bailiwick up there, so I expect TN will be getting a note to that effect.

Sarah requests that her counterpart reply with her thoughts on the Odists.

223

BĂLAN CLADE-EYES-ONLY MATERIAL

I hope things with the Odists are going as smoothly as possible. It sounds really stressful, particularly with how it's affecting WAQ. You mentioned that Sarah's been keeping an eye on it, but how about Tycho? I know he can get kind of skittish. He's also been around those two longer than any of us, though, so maybe he's got some insight into it.

END BĂLAN CLADE-EYES-ONLY MATERIAL

Codrin#Assist, pass on my love. Pull Dear's tail for me.

Codrin Bălan#Artemis — 2346

Convergence T-minus 1 day, 4 hours, 7 minutes

The Artemisians had continued to fine-tune the new setup of the meeting space for the emissaries, so that the Odists' beds were no longer in the same room as their half of the table. Now, there was a small, stone-paved unison room for their half of the table, at the back of which sat a low bench for sitting and talking, as well as a pitcher and glasses of water. To the side of that, a short hallway led to the two unison bedrooms.

That True Name and Answers Will Not Help had requested separate bedrooms had felt notable to Codrin, though ey could not put eir finger on why. Perhaps one or both of them were having a hard enough time even while sleeping that it was keeping the other awake? Answers Will Not Help certainly looked as though she'd not slept since arriving.

Both Odists had taken to spending any break longer than five minutes laying down, and ey'd taken it as eir task to ensure that they were up and moving a minute or so before the meeting resumed.

One upside of this, however, was that it gave em as much latitude as ey wanted to talk with Tycho and Sarah without feeling like ey was leaving True Name and Answers Will Not Help behind.

Or, ey realized, like ey needed to hide anything from them.

"So. Day three."

Tycho groaned. "Yeah, though I feel like we've been here for at least a week by now."

"Might as well have been. The room is pinned at plus point two, so we're already given far more time than we might have on an ordinary day."

"At least it's easy to take a long, lazy break," Sarah said. "But yes. Day three, I guess. What are your thoughts, Codrin?"

Ey leaned back against the column outside the unison room, arms crossed, and looked up at the clear sky above the open courtyard. The blue was more intense than ey remembered from Earth or any of the sims ey'd been in. Ey always felt as though ey was falling up into it, whenever ey stared up like this.

"I'm tired," ey said at last. "Some of that's from just how long it feels like we've been running, and how I feel like I need to be *on* for all of that time, but part of it is our other emissaries."

"Oh?"

"Them being so...is unwell the right word?"

Sarah nodded, "Maybe, yes. Unwell. Struggling?"

"Right, yeah. Them struggling so much means that I have to be an active part of the discussions as well as focused on them. There's nothing I can do to help them, but I still feel like I need to be attuned to everyone around me."

"Is that part of your amanuensis duties?" Tycho asked.

Ey frowned, silent, as ey thought. "Perhaps. It is part of what's going on here, isn't it?"

"It is," Sarah said. "But you don't need to be a complete sponge, soaking everything up."

"I don't know that I can just turn that off."

"And that's okay. It's less about turning it off than mitigating it. Find the times where you can turn down your engagement and use those where you can. Find the things that don't require your full attention and let them go, even if only for a few seconds."

Ey smiled, feeling the tiredness in eir cheeks. "You were a

therapist, weren't you? Maybe I should steal some of your time after this is all over."

"Gladly," she said, nodding. "I've been thinking about restarting my practice, anyhow. It's been too long of just lounging around on the System."

"Certainly got a pile of work for yourself now," Tycho said. "What are your thoughts, while we're on the subject?"

"This is going to sound weird," she said after a moment's thought. "But it's way more normal than I expected. It's a strange situation, to be sure, but it's still just a meeting between people who are trying to figure each other out. They're alien, but not so far as to be completely unintelligible. It's almost prosaic."

"Think it's going well?" Codrin asked.

"As well as it can be, all things considered. We've not wound up in any thorny patches or anything."

Tycho nodded. "Agreed, though I have to admit that I'm getting kind of bored. Codrin told me I should steal some time with Stolon, and I've been doing that whenever I can, but the rest is just...boring. I want to be able to engage, but it's just all over my head, and when I do start feeling like I'm getting a hold on it, Turun Ka or True Name will nudge us back 'on topic'."

"'On topic' meaning history and politics and the like?"

He nodded. "I knew that going into this that #Castor would be having much more fun than I would."

"Well, let's see if we can find you something to focus on," Sarah said.

He tilted his head, frowning. "How, though? I can't exactly ask us to just start talking about the science side."

"Well, no, but you can keep an eye on data. Maybe look out for dates and the like and start using that with what we *do* know of the science behind everything. Start thinking about where they might have been coming from before the...uh, gravity assist? Is that it?"

His frown deepened, but he nodded.

"Start thinking about what's in that direction and how long it might have taken them to get here."

"You can probably keep track of the math involved with the time scale better than any of us, too," Codrin added. "So you can see where there might have been inflection points in history and if that might've had to do with any of their travel. If there were big societal changes, then maybe–"

Tycho held up his hand, and Codrin watched as his eyes lost focus, staring into nothing for a long few seconds, breathing rapidly in some faster time.

Ey looked to Sarah, who shrugged.

"Sorry, skewed faster," he mumbled. "You just reminded me of something, is all. There's a lot beneath the plane of the ecliptic relative to us, but only a little bit of it is close for them to have plausibly passed by it. A few of those systems are kind of interesting."

"Interesting?" ey asked.

"Like, stuff we've been keeping an eye on for possibly having life, that sort of thing."

"Maybe Artante's system?"

He shook his head. "Closer than that, I think."

Codrin stood up straight again, tugging eir blouse straight. "Are you saying you think they might've stopped by somewhere else?"

"It's a very big 'might'," he said. "They could just have been using the stars for slingshots, after all."

"But it's a possibility."

He nodded.

Sarah shook her head. "To make sure I'm following, you think they may have suspected there was life elsewhere? Do you think they might have run across other possible societies and not had them join them as a race?"

"Right. Could be they just hadn't started uploading." He hesitated, then added, "Or that they had, but didn't want to join or didn't make the cut."

Codrin rubbed eir hands over eir face, willing away the tiredness that kept threatening to come back. Like Tycho, every time ey felt like ey was getting a hold on the situation ey was stuck in, some other bit of info would be brought to light and eir grasp would slip once more.

Now here this was. Perhaps the Artemisians had run across more than just races two through four on their journey. Perhaps there had been failed convergences, not counted among the existing three and the fourth they were living through.

Tycho's comment about 'not making the cut' carried with it additional implications, as well. It implied that there was a barrier to entry that one had to pass. This, in turn, implied that there were a set of requirements for getting to join as a race. Unspoken ones.

There may very well be specific steps they had to take that had never been provided to them. Hadn't ey picked up a sense of that from the letter so long ago? 'You have asked the correct question'?

When ey shook away the rumination, ey found both Tycho and Sarah staring at em. "Sorry if I was mumbling. Tycho, hold off on actually asking about this for now, but keep thinking about it, alright? At least let me run it past True Name first."

The astronomer nodded.

"On that note, we should probably start getting ready again," Sarah said.

They broke after that, Tycho walking another lap around the courtyard and Sarah making for the pitcher of water, while Codrin went to rouse the Odists.

Ey fetched True Name first. The skunk was already awake—or perhaps had never managed to fall asleep for the nap she always talked about—and sitting up blearily in bed.

"Good afternoon, Mx. Bălan."

"Morning," ey corrected gently. "Next break will be lunch. Manage to get any sleep?"

She shook her head. "I am guessing that it is time to head back?"

Ey nodded. "I have a question about a topic Tycho brought up, first, if that's alright. If you need to wake up a bit more first, that's fine. I can ask later, but I'd at least like it on the docket."

"I do not know that I will be feeling any better later," she said, attempting a smile. "Ask me now, and if I am unable to answer, ask me again at lunch."

"Alright." Ey sat on the chair next to True Name's bed. "Sarah and I suggested that Tycho start making educated guesses about their route and if that might be reflected in historical inflection points."

The skunk frowned, but nodded for em to continue.

"He mentioned that there might have been some planets on their path that were inhabited but not welcomed as one of the races."

"Ones with life? Ones with uploads?"

Ey shrugged. "Perhaps, yes. In particular, he said that if the race had uploaded, maybe they wouldn't want to join, or wouldn't have, in his words, 'made the cut'."

The skunk stared down at her paws in her lap, the claws on her thumbs tapping gently together. "That is a good observation from our friend. What question do you have for me about it?"

"Should we ask more directly about it? I told him not to until I'd talked with you."

"Thank you. Yes, he should hold off for now. It may be best to ask about the sentiments within the society during those inflection points first. Coming at it sideways like that will allow us to phrase the question about other convergences more effectively."

Ey nodded. "If there was strife, it may not have been a good convergence, you mean."

"Precisely." The skunk wobbled to her feet, accepting Codrin's offer of a hand to steady herself. "Come. Let us see how Why Ask Questions is doing. Better, I hope."

"Given the differences between our systems, the focus on time skew versus forking, I'd like to see what some of the political and sociological differences there are that resulted from that," Codrin said, once the meeting began again.

Both Iska and True Name sat up straighter.

"This is broad-large-all-encompassing topic, recorder Codrin Bălan." Turun Ko angled its head down and to the side, a move that appeared either confused or perhaps condescending. "Please restrict-refine."

"Well, okay." Ey tapped the end of eir pen against eir lower lip, considering. "Perhaps we can begin with how common working with skew is among everyday individuals. We have our concept of dissolution strategies, based on how one approaches forking, after all."

There was a blurred conference between the Artemisians, then Iska said, "There is a spectrum of approaches to skew. Some rarely utilize it, some utilize only fast-time to complete tasks or slow-time to pass long stretches of time out of boredom or to wait for a specific event. Some, such as myself, utilize skew for enjoyment."

"These map loosely to your concept of taskers, trackers, and dispersionistas," Artante added. "We noticed similar during the third convergence, though the concept remained only within fourthrace, and died out within a century of the convergence. I was reminded of the topic by one of your early letters."

"I remember you mentioned that fourthrace had forking," True Name said, voice tightly controlled. "Was the transition from that to skew difficult for those members of fourthrace that joined?"

"For some, yes. There was one recorded instance of a member of fourthrace becoming so despondent about the lack of forking that they exited the system."

True Name and Answers Will Not Help looked at each other, letting the silence that followed speak for itself.

Codrin allowed the moment to pass before continuing.

"Thank you. For what occupations there are—I believe you also described them as 'intensive leisure activities'—is there any particular expectation regarding one's approach to skew?"

"'Expectation'?" Turun Ko asked.

"I suppose activities have their own requirements for how one utilizes skew. For instance, representative Iska doubtless relies on it quite heavily. Does knowing one's interest tell you about their skew habits? Is there pressure for one to not take up an activity due to the skew habits one has already formed?"

Iska was practically purring at this turn in the conversation. "Had one of us asked that question, I would have said 'no', but hearing it from you has made me think about it in a new way. I would have said that one simply would not think to take up that activity, but now that you say such, I think that this is the case. I am uncomfortable with not utilizing skew, yes, but for activities that are pinned to common time such as preparing food and performing music, there is an expectation that I would not be a good chef or musician, yes. Were I to pick up an interest in cooking, I would be looked on with a small amount of concern. One would say about me: 'I hope that they do not burn the food by shifting to slow-time' or 'I expect that their food will be very rushed'."

Codrin grinned as ey took down notes of the answer. "One of my romantic partners, as an instance artist, has stated that it can't understand what a life without profligate forking would look like, but has never said that it feels as though it is not able to take part in another profession. That said, there are several interests or professions that one would not expect taskers or even trackers to go into. Many would sneer at a tasker trying to go into instance artistry. Does the same apply here? Are there more interests or professions that are out of reach for those who do not use skew than for those who use skew often?"

Another, longer blurred conference followed this question, during which True Name gave em a tired smile. "Excellent questions, Mx. Bălan."

"We have decided that there has not been much thought put into this topic, but that our instinct would be to say yes, the interests which belong to those heavy users of skew are more specific and thus more likely to carry some level of prestige that might be out of reach for those who prefer to remain in common time."

Sarah sat forward, leaning on her elbows on the table. "Can you expand on 'prestige', here? Are there interests that are considered less prestigious? Do some interests reflect poorly on the individual?"

"Please confirm: do you mean social-stratification-caste?" Turun Ko said, and both Codrin and True Name rushed to write a note.

"I'd also like to know about that, yes, but let's come back to that later. In this instance, I was wondering there are interests that are seen as distasteful or silly."

"We have decided that there are not any that are seen as distasteful," Turun Ka said after another conferral with its delegates. "But there are many that are seen as frivolous. Some view contemplative or spiritual life as frivolous, particularly among secondrace, which is very old."

Codrin frowned, making a note to ask about that later. They had the concept of spirituality, and even the concept of a life lived in contemplation. It raised several other questions besides, such as why it was that the second oldest race bore the brunt of that assumption, and why it had been implied that firstrace was immune. Were religions shared between the races? Were religions time-bound? In eir 128 years of life, time had run out on countless end-of-the-world predictions.

Ey shook the rumination from eir eyes in time to hear True Name asking, "What is the population's view of the Council of Eight?"

Turun Ka rocked its head from side to side. Amusement, Codrin#Castor had written. "We are seen as almost vestigial except during convergences. What guidance we provide we do so through advisory not–"

It was interrupted by a bang as Answers Will Not Help, who had been nearly in a stupor up until this point, slammed her fists down on the table. "I must keep no veil between me and my words. I must set no stones between me and my actions!"

There was a tense moment of silence.

"Apologies," she said, rubbing her hands over her face and then yelping as a wave of skunk washed beneath them. "I cannot stop myself from speaking."

Artante nodded slowly. "Would you like to take a brief break, representative Why Ask Questions?"

"I...yes."

"We shall reconvene in five minutes common time," Turun Ka said. "We wish you the best, representative Why Ask Questions."

Sarah helped her to her feet and walked her down the hall to her room.

True Name slouched down in her seat with a wave of Michelle rolling across her form.

"Are you alright?" ey asked, patting her paw/hand.

She jolted to the side with a quiet grunt, pulling her hand back as though burned. She rolled her head to the side against the back of the chair looking steadily at em. "I will be okay, Mx. Bălan. Thank you for your concern. Please refrain from touching me when my form is shifting, though. It is quite uncomfortable."

"Apologies." Ey bowed her head. Something about the skunk's voice brooked no further questioning.

"You asked some very good questions today. I am quite happy that you decided to come along."

"It's an honor."

She rolled her head back once more to stare up at the ceiling. "Have you heard further from your counterpart back on Castor?"

"Ey mentioned that the common tongue is remarkably well-preserved for being on the system for four thousand years, and suggested that there might be political implications behind that."

"Right, yes," True Name said, closing her eyes. "Should Why Ask Questions start feeling better, perhaps we can have that discussion more in depth, but I will ask either way. Anything else?"

Codrin#Castor had clearly picked up on eir hint, and had hinted in return. There would be much to think about and ey had a return letter planned, as well as a discussion with the other three delegates. It had been a good guess on #Castor's part that Tycho had been the one to spot the subterfuge.

"No," ey said. "They wish us well."

Tycho Brahe#Castor — 2346

Tycho had spent his share of time in conferences, both phys-side and sys-side. They all came with their exciting parts and their boring parts. They all came with peaks that left him completely rapt, and valleys that were so excruciatingly dull that he had, on more than one occasion, feigned illness to step out of a talk or away from a panel discussion or a lecture.

This was different, though.

It wasn't that it didn't have its peaks and valleys, for it surely did. There were more sciences, he had been reminded several times, than astronomy. He knew it, too. There was no reason that the LVs and home System would not benefit from a knowledge share on biology or psychology, and certainly there could be much to learn about the construction of an embedded world. All that knowledge, all that history—so many centuries!—was enough to convince him of the reality of the Artemisians, or at least enough that he could drown out that niggling voice in the back of his head thinking in terms of dreams. There was more than enough to learn, so that wasn't it.

It was that, even during the boring parts, there was Stolon sitting directly across the table from him, the thirdracer looking just as antsy and restless as he felt, even though it was only the third day. He knew that he and Stolon could talk for hours about the stars, that they would if only given the chance, and yet he had to sit here and, however rightfully so, listen to Why Ask Questions grill the Artemisians on parallel evolution.

Throughout the talks, no matter the science, there lay a thread of five thousand years of history. Hundreds of years would go by, and then a sudden jump in knowledge. Biology, language, astronomy, psychology, physics; sciences hard and soft would wind up with sudden injections of knowledge throughout each of the convergences.

Except, he kept finding himself thinking. *That's not all.*

It would be of no surprise for a sudden leap of knowledge to occur every handful of decades. Some new way of looking at the world brought about by some spurt of genius, even in the functionally immortal.

What was surprising was these renaissances in *all* sciences that had happened a total of five times that he'd counted so far. Three for convergences—that made sense—but what of the other two?

This wasn't supposed to be his job. This wasn't supposed to be any of their jobs, here in the DMZ. History as a topic belonged to the emissaries sent to Artemis. He'd only started asking how long ago various tidbits of knowledge had been gained on a whim.

And so he sat and he waited until there was a time that he could speak, and even when he probably should have been paying attention, he spent much of his effort on trying to figure out how best to word his question in such a way that wouldn't get him in trouble with the Artemisians or, worse, True Name.

His cue came in the form of Why Ask Questions racking her sheets of notes into a neat pile before slouching back in her chair.

"I have a quick question about science in general, if I may," he said, preempting comments from any of the others.

True Name frowned, nodded.

"It'll come in the form of an astronomy question, but bear

with me. Can you tell me a bit more about your path from firstrace's home world to our system?"

Stolon sat up straighter, head tilting far to the side in what Tycho had decided was a sort of intense interest. "Artemis comes from firstrace system, aims for nearest stable star, performs, *lu*...gravity assists and extra maneuvers, solar sail, magnetic *irr*..." After a moment's silenced discussion with the other Artemisians, they returned with, "Magnetic field hydrogen collector—you call 'fuel scoop' maybe?—and then final adjustments to next prospective star."

"And how many times has Artemis performed this act?"

"Seven times, scientist Tycho Brahe," Turun Ko said.

"Three of which were convergences, yes?"

"*Anem, anem,* scientist Tycho Brahe," Stolon said. "I only was...*suhernachi...lu...* living-embedded for third convergence, but yes, three convergences."

"Okay," he said, pausing to compose his next sentence carefully. "As we talk about the way that we learn, I've heard of more than three jumps in scientific knowledge during the millennia that Artemis has been travelling. Do these maneuvers around systems...I don't know, make everyone curious enough to start doing a bunch of research?"

Until this point, True Name looked as though she were about to nudge Tycho to move on to the next topic, perhaps sensing that he was veering closer to history, but as he finished his question and the Artemisians set up a cone of silence for a very animated discussion, he could see nothing but intense focus on the skunk's face. Even Codrin and Why Ask Questions were furiously scribbling notes at this point.

Sarah gave him a grin and a subtle nod. It was nearly five minutes before the cone of silence around the Artemisians dropped, during which he'd received nods of approval from the rest of the delegates as well.

Looks like I asked the right thing, he thought, doing his best to tamp down the sense of pride that had begun to grow within him. They were all here for a job, and when that job is learning, there are no right questions, just on-topic ones.

"You are correct, scientist Tycho Brahe," Turun Ka said once the cone dropped. "Though it is less that curiosity intensifies during these maneuvers than there are more observations to be made when passing near a star. We learn astronomy and physics, yes, which slowly bleeds across sciences. Physics impacts Artemis's hardware, so our technicians learn from that. Our hardware impacts our experience, and so sciences surrounding individual and collective consciousness-bearing entities benefits from that."

All five of the delegates took notes as quickly as they could while the firstracer spoke. Tycho made a note to himself to ask what sorts of things they tended to learn when passing close to a star, as well as a note to ask Tycho#Artemis to bring up similar on Artemis, focusing instead on the history of their course.

True Name leaned forward enough to catch Why Ask Questions's gaze, sharing a meaningful look. Codrin frowned, scratched out another note in eir notebook.

"Leader Turun Ka," True Name said with a hint of a bow. "Thank you for your answer. Would you be amenable to a short break? I would like to sync up with our delegation."

The firstracer lifted its chin in assent and those around the table stood, exchanging bows before making their way each to their own rest area.

Once they'd made it around the corner into the common area, the skunk grinned at Tycho. "Good catch, Dr. Brahe."

"I was a little surprised, myself. That gives us a good idea of their speed and perhaps their traj–"

"Shut up, Tycho," Why Ask Questions said, laughing. "We will get to all the delicious science you could ask for soon enough. Your question went more than a little beyond that."

He frowned. "What? How?"

True Name patted him on the arm. "Do not mind her, my dear. It was a good question because it suggests to the sneaky pieces of shit among us that they might be being sneaky, themselves. Come, let us sit so I can write to True Name#Artemis."

Once they'd sat down at the common table, the skunk explained. "They have all of the time in the world over there, do they not? They can speed up and slow down whenever they want, and use that to get all of the heavy lifting of thinking and studying and lecturing done even when they are around a star, never mind when they are out between them, yes?"

He nodded. "But their observations–"

"Are limited to when they are near something interesting to observe, yes, but they can spend as long as they want with those observations, poring over their views of the star or measurements from external instruments. They are not time-bound for those. In fact, the only times that they seem to be time-bound are when it comes to interaction with other time-bound events."

"Well, sure," he hazarded. "But perhaps they turn off the ability to skew when they perform an assist or something. We didn't get the chance to ask them any more questions."

"We will, do not worry," she said, mumbling as she dashed off a few more lines on her note, handed the slip off to Codrin, then turned to face him, paws folded on the table before her. "But they are also time-bound talking with us who are not able to utilize time skew, correct?"

Tycho crossed his arms and slouched back in the chair, staring up at the ceiling. "Well, shit."

Codrin laughed. "You see then why it was a good question?"

"They didn't say anything one way or another," Sarah said. "So you could very well be right, Tycho, but you saw their silenced conversation."

"Even that could be them trying to figure out how best to tell us what they did, though," he retorted, though even he could tell his heart wasn't in it.

"All of these facts are interesting," Why Ask Questions said. "Even if that is all they did, even if they do only turn off skew for slingshots. We are sold on it no matter what. When you take the facts together as a whole, however, those of us with a sense for it can catch the scent of politics in there."

"Sneaky pieces of shit, you mean?"

True Name laughed. "Yes, those. You lack the sense, Dr. Brahe. Codrin has seen it, Ms. Genet can sense it second-hand. We need someone like you to play the role of earnest seeker-after-knowledge."

He rolled his eyes. "Or gullible dupe."

"A very smart gullible dupe," Why Ask Questions said. "It is no shame to be a gullible dupe, Tycho. You ask the things we never think to because we are too busy being sneaky pieces of shit."

"Well, I'll leave the politics to you all," he said, grinning and shaking his head. "I'm going to write my own note while we have a bit of time."

Tycho Brahe#Artemis — 2346

Convergence T-minus 1 day, 2 hours, 38 minutes

Over the last hour of common time, what tension was bound within True Name seemed to have been refocused from struggling quite so hard to maintain her form into being present and taking part. This meant that, while she was more susceptible to waves of shifting species and the occasional gasp or shudder, she grew far more intent on the task at hand, of learning from the discussions with the Artemisians.

Tycho found the ways in which her face would ghost first one way then the other fascinating and unnerving, but also the steadfastness with which she moved in the context of the meeting in spite of that admirable. While the talks had continued apace, with frequent breaks on the part of the Odists, there felt like more forward momentum thanks to this sacrifice.

Codrin had noticed the change as well, and when asked, ey had nodded in agreement. "She approaches much of her...well, I was going to say life, but it goes beyond that. She approaches much of her existence as a cost-benefit analysis of sorts. This level of control and momentum is worth the cost she's paying in comfort."

"Leader Turun Ka," True Name began as soon as the session restarted after a break. "I would like to ask how you manage sentiment here on Artemis. Are there many situations where the direction, momentum, or clarity of social change must be managed from a high level?"

Codrin, Sarah, and Tycho all frowned at this. Answers Will Not Help seemed only able to grit her teeth.

There was a blurred conversation among the Artemisians, after which their leader spoke up. "In order to ensure that we answer the correct question you are asking, do you want information on how we govern?"

The skunk nodded. "That, yes, but I am also interested in how you might control the flow of information across the system. Do you inject opinions, or restrict the transmission of opinions that the Council of Eight might feel uncomfortable being displayed openly?"

Artante's eyes darted over to Sarah, who lifted her eyebrows in a hint of a shrug.

"I will answer the question about governance first, and then we shall proceed to the second one," it said. "We, in our capacities as leaders, perform very few actions in the time between convergences. In many cases, we act simply as those one might go to for advice. Something less than advisory. Lu..."

"More of a familial role," Artante said. "Avuncular, perhaps. The Council is comprised of individuals who are exemplary in both intellectual and emotional intelligence from among their races, and any aboard Artemis may request a meeting in order to discuss solutions to difficult problems."

"And during convergences?" True Name asked.

"During convergences, we act more in the way that you suggest. We act as a filter between the recipients of the information and the converging civilization. The cases in which we might block information or shape it to our own means remain rare, but the ability to explore the ramifications of that information and prepare for possible outcomes we have found useful."

"This makes sense. Thank you, leader Turun Ka. We work along similar lines, where we have first access to information coming from Artemis—our only convergence thus far—and we are able to run simulations on possible outcomes in order to prepare for reactions."

The firstracer turned its head to the side in what Tycho supposed must be confusion. "Please expand on 'simulations', leader True Name."

"The term is overloaded, perhaps. We explore possible reactions by playing them out among members of our clade or others in an advisory role. Some instances of ourselves will play the role of the recipients of that news while others play the role of those who are receiving the information. Another, perhaps more distasteful, term for this, is 'wargaming'."

The Artemisians immediately sped up for a private meeting, and Tycho once again turned his attention to True Name's face, searching for any sign of anxiety, anything to show that she regretted having said a word that implied violence.

There was nothing there. She just looked tired. Calm, but tired.

Once they returned to common time, Turun Ka continued. "Of the four races aboard, three of them have an analogous term, though it has not made it into common usage in our shared language."

"*Tuvȧrouni* is the word for wrestling in the common tongue, but 'push-play' in the context of planning can mean 'to wargame'," Iska said. "It is not common except in the context of old *Nanon* stories."

Both Codrin and Sarah took notes throughout the description, True Name looking on in exhaustion to ensure that they got the topics down.

"Thank you, leader Turun Ka, representative Iska, for explaining. Another part of my question would be do you shape information via communications? For instance, in order to quell fears that there might be some breach in our DMZ—demilitarized zone, if you will pardon more warlike language, the air-gapped sim in which these conversations are taking place on Castor—we injected communications into the news feed in the form of carefully worded questions about the nature of the security measures, snide remarks about how thankful people were that the security was in place, or subtle propaganda."

"This is not common for us, no," Turun Ka said. "Part of this is due to the lack of centralized news and communication sources between the races."

"Is there so little communication between the races?" Sarah asked.

It was Artante that answered. "There is communication, yes, but large portions of the four races aboard stay within enclaves made up of members of their own races. All shared areas except for this complex are open to all races, and there are news sources available in there, but by virtue of infrequent access by large portions of the population, news does not spread very far."

"Not even by way of rumor?" True Name asked.

"Rumors do spread," Iska said when the Artemisians returned to common time. "Much of Artemis likely knows of the current convergence by now. We do not attempt to control the rumors."

"Not even by considering the wording of this news?" Tycho could hear the control in the skunk's voice. Was she frustrated, perhaps?

"We write-speak-disseminate clearly-precisely," Turun Ko said. "But-yet even fourthrace understands-knows that convergences occur and that they are handled-dealt-with."

True name nodded and subsided, bowing her head with blurring of her form. "*Eslosla datåt,*" she said. "Thank you all."

"No ranks of angels will answer to dreamers," Answers Will Not Help whispered when the silence drew out, then stood unsteadily, ghosted images of a tail jolting her hips first this way and then that. "No unknowable spa...spaces...my apologies. May we take a break?"

"Yes, of course," Artante said. "Please be well."

After True Name and Answers Will Not Help tottered off to

their rooms, each leaning on the other, Codrin, Sarah, and Tycho sat on a pair of beds, heads down and running in fast time in order to discuss the last segment of conversations.

"I wasn't expecting her to be that open about political machinations," Tycho said. "I'd think she'd want to keep it under wraps. If her and Jonas and their friends have been working to shape our past so much, you'd think they'd want to be a bit more subtle about that."

Sarah shrugged. "Maybe, though it could be many things. Could be that they're aiming to show the whole of us, positives and negatives, as the Artemisians don't have the context of the *History*. Perhaps she wants to show that we have a society strong enough to handle manipulation without slipping into authoritarianism. The fact that we use language so consciously is probably a sign in our favor, in the end."

"Or she could just be slipping," Tycho added.

"She's hardly winding up in word salad territory," she allowed. "But it's hard to tell how much of that was telling the truth, being a politician, or actually getting into the territory of grandeur."

"No reason it can't be both, I guess." Codrin sighed, buried eir face in eir hands, and rubbed eir face vigorously. "She might be working on some level way above our pay grades and still having a hard time keeping it together."

Tycho frowned as those fears once more floated to the surface. Something was going on in these talks that he simply didn't understand. Things were being said with so many different meanings and the subtext felt completely disconnected from the text.

"Is it always like this?" he asked.

"Is what like this?"

"Working with them. Working with any politician."

Codrin grinned. "Well, I can certainly confirm that the Odists work in ways that feel distant from what we're used to. Dear will occasionally say something that makes no sense in context, but then a week or two later, I'll realize what it actually meant, or that it was a suggestion that I'd subconsciously started following without really thinking about it."

"They're incredible at reading people," Sarah said. "At least with Dear, I can see it being sort of a positive—or at worst, playful—way of influencing. I'm not sure with True Name, and have no idea what Why Ask Questions might be doing otherwise."

Tycho looked to Codrin, who gave him a subtle shake of the head. "Me either," he said at last. "Hell, I have no idea what's going on with them either, other than what Codrin's told me. Have you heard anything else from the delegates back Castor?"

"Just a little bit about language," ey said thoughtfully. "We actually touched on it today with that bit about 'old Nanon', so I'll write em back. I'd asked em a question about the Odists and what their roles had been because I was having a hard time piecing together memories, and ey confirmed that."

"What sort of question?" Sarah asked.

Ey hesitated. "Well, I was asking about the difference between Why Ask Questions and Answers Will Not Help since we've worked with both of them. Ey confirmed that both worked on shaping sentiment, just different areas of expertise. My guess is that if...well, Why Ask Questions were feeling better, she'd have a lot to add to the conversation we had today."

Wonder how the Artemisians would react to that? Tycho thought. *True Name was honest, but not enough to bring up this little bit of trickery.*

Part III

Intensity

And so the ark was sent out into the sea of the night, making waves in the black between the stars and leaving a wake of dreams new and old behind it.

From *An Expanded Mythology of Our World* by
May Then My Name Die With Me of the Ode clade

Codrin Bălan#Artemis — 2346

The next note that came from Castor included a block of inde-cipherable text that was marked as clade-eyes-only for Turun Ka.

Codrin puzzled over this during a private minute in fast time.

Normally, clade-eyes-only or individual-eyes-only text for someone other than the recipient appeared as that header of, for instance, *Bălan Clade-Eyes-Only Material* followed by an indi-cation that such text might be there, but nothing about its con-tents, including its length or composition. For em, this usually appeared as an ellipsis in square brackets, long-standing tradi-tions of elision being what they were.

This, however, appeared to be text of the type ey'd grown used to in encrypted blocks. Letters, numbers, punctuation, all crammed into a single unbroken chunk. More, some of the char-acters appeared to be restless. They strained at their form, as though they desperately wanted to be something else, and when ey looked away and back, they were indeed that other form, and some other character nearby would be itching to change, in-stead.

Clearly, one of the delegates from Castor had instructed the Artemisians on not just how to send text back to Artemis, but how to do so in a private way. Artemis itself, however, couldn't figure out how to represent that, and perhaps that's what clade-eyes-only text might actually be in the perisystem architecture.

Ey recreated the note on a few fresh sheets of paper, eir own message on one and Turun Ka's on another, and headed back to the meeting.

"Leader Turun Ka," ey said, once they were gathered together once more. "I have received a message from your counterpart back on Castor. It is encrypted for your eyes only, though I'm not sure how well that functionality transfers between systems."

The firstracer's head remained still, leaving no clues as to its opinion of this matter, and it gracefully accepted the note that Codrin passed over. It didn't hold it up to see or bow its head to look down at it, so ey figured that as soon as it changed hands, it must have changed its form. Paper, after all, was only a symbol. Letters, words, and written language only signs.

"Thank you, recorder Codrin Bălan. The information is intact."

As ey expected, this was followed up by a blurred meeting of the Artemisian delegates in fast time.

Ey spent the time sneaking glances at True Name and Answers Will Not Help, catching Tycho and Sarah doing the same.

True Name, despite maintaining careful control of her expression, still appeared to be beyond tired. The flickers of her human form came more regularly, now, and, while her appearance as a skunk remained polite, attentive, and receptive, that human face showed only exhaustion.

Answers Will Not Help, however, was a mess.

Her form rippled between species, and with it, so too did her expression. She would veer wildly between barely constrained laughter and agony, all while tears coursed down her cheeks or left tracks in fur. She managed to keep quiet for the most part, though occasionally a snippet of poetry would escape her: here a line of the Ode, there a bit of Dickinson. She had even startled Tycho at one point by quoting something ey didn't quite recognize: "I have sown, like Tycho Brahe, that a greater man may reap..."

This wild dissociation from the world around her was made all the more unnerving by the fact that ey could tell that she was having a difficult time staying within common time.

She never veered far from it, only within a range of 0.5 to either side, but even that carried with it a sense of wrongness. They were in a unison room, something that she had specifically requested, which ey'd been told meant that she specifically *shouldn't* be able to do that. Skew simply wasn't available to em when ey reached for it.

Iska had hardly taken their eyes off her since they'd noticed as well, as though they were trying to puzzle out just how it was that this was happening.

They were only two and a half days into the conference and, while both sides had learned much about the other, ey wondered if they'd even be able to make it to a week.

Or even the end of today, ey thought. *Answers Will Not Help looks like she's about to explode.*

"Leader True Name," Turun Ka began, once the delegates had returned to common time. "While I am not able to divulge the contents of the note I have received, it has led to a discussion amongst us, and we would like to ask about your history."

"From the founding of the System?" she asked, voice tight.

"Apologies, leader True Name. We would like to know about your history. You and your cocladist."

Her shoulders sagged. "Would you like information specifically relating to our appearance here on Artemis?"

"This is a good place to begin."

The skunk looked as though she hadn't the faintest idea of where to begin, as though too many thoughts clouded her mind for her to decide.

Codrin nodded toward her, "By your leave, True Name?"

"Please, Mx. Bălan." She sounded quite relieved.

"Prior to the founding of the System two hundred thirty-one years ago, long distance communication and interaction took place over a global network. It worked much as it does here, in that there are designated locations—sims, a name which has stuck with us—and we interacted through forms such as these. The origin of our System came about shortly after a brief period of political unrest wherein some political entities released a type of virus into the implanted hardware we used to connect to the 'net. Those who came across too much information relating to this unrest had the virus triggered and were trapped in a vegetative state, locked within their minds." Ey paused and looked to True Name, who nodded. Answers Will Not Help just hugged her arms to her front, looking pale as she silently mouthed some litany ey couldn't guess. "Michelle Hadje, the root instance of the Ode clade, to which True Name and Why Ask Questions belong, was one of these individuals. The lost, they called them. Dear, my partner, is an Odist as well, and mentioned to me beforehand that a malleable sense of time sounded much like what it experienced during that period."

"You are not normally like this," Turun Ka said. A statement rather than a question. "My counterpart on Castor describes you as solely in the form you primarily occupy here, and Why Ask Questions solely in, *lu*...a human form. You are both described as calm, confident, and politically adroit."

True Name winced. "It is uncomfortable for me to be in this state. I am not up to my usual standards."

"This has led-turned-into a situation of unequality-power-dynamic," Turun Ko said, picking up where the leader had left off. "For this we express-offer concern-well-wishes-condolences."

"We are unable, at this point in the convergence, to accept other delegates, or we would offer you greater respite than we have already," Turun Ka finished.

"Thank you for your concern," the skunk said. "I understand your reasoning, and would not wish to miss these discussions. I

254

have trust in Mx. Bălan, Dr. Brahe, and Ms. Genet, however, to share our load."

Both Turun Ka and Turun Ko lifted their heads in assent, the leader adding, "As always, we will strive to make your stay as comfortable as possible."

True Name nodded her thanks.

At a glance from Artante, the Artemisians slid up to fast time for a brief conversation before returning. "We of fourthrace experienced similar prior to the creation of our embedding system. This was the result of a war, a virus targeting a nation that led large sections of the population being affected."

"Were they able to free those who were?"

"Only approximately a quarter. Some three million of my race died from various causes while...lost."

Codrin blinked, leaning back in eir chair. "Three *million?* Good Lord..."

Artante nodded. "Of those who returned, all suffered what representative Sarah Genet has called post-traumatic stress disorder. None were affected such as you, leader True Name and representative Why Ask Questions, but many also experienced chronic episodes of psychosis combined with logorrhea, glossolalia, and graphomania, if I am understanding the terms properly."

Codrin's eyes darted over to Answers Will Not Help—as, ey noticed, did the rest of the emissaries. She averted her gaze, lips still mouthing countless words. Ey hastened to catch up on the notes ey'd been taking to cover for emself.

"Did any of those affected upload? Or...embed?" True Name asked.

"Of those who did not take their own lives, all–"

"I cannot feel em!" Answers Will Not Help interrupted, nearly shouting. Tears were streaming down her face, now. "I cannot...here...b-beside whom..."

Something akin to anger or fear tore through True Name's exhaustion and she sat bolt upright, glaring down the row of emissaries to Answers Will Not Help. "Why Ask Questions, my dear, please do try to remain present," she said, voice eerily calm, soothing.

The silence at the table was absolute. All delegates on both sides held still, and Codrin suspected that all of the emissaries from Castor were holding their breath. All had experienced the laser-focused wrath of at least one of the Odists in the weeks leading up to the conference.

Answers Will Not Help hunched her shoulders, cowed. Every ounce of control she had remaining seemed to be dedicated to keeping her crying as quiet as possible.

"Leader True Name," Artante asked, voice just as soothing. "You do not need to answer, but may I ask what just happened?"

"I will not answer, representative Artante Diria," she said, voice once more slipping into exhaustion as a wave of human form washed over her features. "It is a private matter between me and my cocladist. My apologies."

The fourthracer bowed her head. "I understand. Would you like to take a break?"

"Perhaps a brief break would be nice," Sarah said, nodding. "We can collect ourselves and move onto a separate aspect of the history of the System."

True Name nodded.

"Your break-respite need not be brief-short," Turun Ko said. "We are capable-of-able-to-permitted-to skew the unison room to allow for longer rests."

"No!" This time, Answers Will Not Help did shout, voice shifting slightly as she slid this way and that away from common time. "Sorry. No, please do not—motes in the stage-lights—please do not take time from us. No, no no no, please..."

Iska's expression had steadily grown more and more alarmed throughout the proceedings. "I do not–"

"We will reconvene in fifteen minutes common time," Turun Ka said. Nothing in its voice changed from how it normally spoke, though it having spoke was enough to quell Iska to silence. "Representative Artante Diria, representative Iska, please convene to address this issue moving forward from a psychological and technical standpoint. When we return, we will indeed move on to another subject."

Iska bowed their head in assent.

Answers Will Not Help was sobbing in earnest now, stifling it as best she can with her face hidden behind the notebook she had before her but had yet to touch.

"I cannot feel em"? Feel who? Codrin thought, frowning.

Ey leaned forward again to write notes on what had just happened, but before eir pen could touch paper, True Name pulled it slowly but insistently from eir hand.

"Nothing of these happenings is to wind up in writing except that it be sent as a clade-eyes-only letter to the Odists," she said, the words softened by a shaky smile. "I would like to discuss these events with my cocladists, first."

Ey nodded numbly, accepting eir now-capped pen back.

"Now, I would like to lie down during this break. Please accompany me so that I may dictate this letter."

Ioan Bălan — 2346

Convergence T-plus 30 days, 13 hours, 47 minutes
(Castor–Lagrange transmission delay: 30 days, 14 hours, 36 minutes)

Ioan#98ae38dc arrived at the appointed coffee shop a good hour in advance. The meeting had been eir idea, but it had also been eir primary source of stress during the day prior to it.

The idea of meeting up with True Name in a neutral setting had not gone over as poorly as feared with May. She hadn't been pleased, to be sure, but given the news from Castor, she had accepted that the chance of further contact with her down-tree instance was likely anyway, and had stated that she was unwilling to engage with her further on the point so ey might as well.

So, ey had forked, given her double kisses on the cheeks along with #Tracker, and stepped away to sit and fret somewhere where ey'd not be a bother.

The coffee shop was quite comfortable, familiar from when ey'd first met Dear so many years ago. A cozy affair set in a simulacrum of a small town. Cute shops, gas lamps, brick-paved roads.

Inside, ey staked out an L-shaped couch for their meeting and sat, sipping eir way slowly through first a coffee and then a tea, figuring that eir nerves were jangly enough without the added caffeine.

True Name arrived fifteen minutes before their scheduled meeting, looking far more collected and confident, far more herself, than she had the last time ey'd seen her. She smiled brightly to em, ordered her drink, and then sat primly on the couch across from em, blinking a cone of silence into existence as she did so.

"Mx. Bălan, thank you for meeting with me. I was surprised—pleasantly so—to have received your invitation."

Ey nodded. "Thank you for accepting. I figured it might be nice to have a calmer conversation than our last one. I want to make sure that we stay on at least polite terms as...in-laws of a sort."

There was no shift in the skunk's attentive expression, nor in her posture. She simply nodded and took a few laps of her drink, wiping a dollop of whipped cream from her nose after. "I appreciate that. I understand that our dynamic is complex and that of May Then My Name and I all the more so. We will never be close, you and I, but I can accept that."

"Right, and I don't want all of our interactions to be stressful."

"If you will forgive a bit of small talk, may I ask after your partner's well-being, at least? I understand through intraclade communications that she had...that there was..."

"She wound up overflowing, yeah. She's bounced back well enough for the most part, and we've been back at work."

True Name nodded, a hint of a bow. "Thank you, Ioan. It is encouraging to hear. And you are working on a play regarding our visitors on Castor?"

"Bit by bit," ey said. "I add to it every time we get a bit of news. That was another reason I wanted to meet up."

The calm smile that the skunk had been wearing slipped down into something more businesslike. "Yes. May I ask what information you have received?"

Ioan pulled the few sheets of folded paper from eir pocket and unfolded them, skimming through the notes. "The talks have begun and sound like they're going well enough on Castor, but that True Name and Why Ask Questions on Artemis are struggling, though they've been working through it as best they can. That's the last I've heard."

Ey handed over the letters, already trimmed of clade-eyes-only and other personal information. True Name read through them quickly, nodding.

"We have heard much the same. It was a calculated risk, sending myself and Why Ask Questions rather than a Jonas or someone else less affected by this time skew that they have mentioned."

"It sounds reminiscent of what I saw of Michelle. Certainly unpleasant."

She sat in silence for a few long seconds, both paws wrapped around her wide-brimmed mug of coffee. Her face was impassive and posture unreadable. Even her eyes remained fixed on some spot over eir shoulder, unmoving. She seemed frozen.

"True Name?"

"No," she said at last, her shoulders sagging a fraction of an inch, enough to show some level of exhaustion that had previously been hidden. "It does not sound pleasant."

"End Waking put it, 'when presented with the fragility of eternity once more, I cannot imagine that I would remain sane'. None of the Odists I've talked to sound happy about this."

"We are not," she said. "Ioan, may I ask that we talk about–"

"In a moment, True Name, I promise." Ey took a deep breath, setting eir tea down on the table in front of the couch, turning to face the skunk. "Again, I don't want to leave the air clouded between us, but this is important to me, too. I'm sure you understand."

She nodded, straightening up as though steeling herself for a coming blow. "I imagine it is. Then yes, it is unpleasant. I do not think that either of my cocladists aboard Artemis are in any imminent danger, but it is bringing uncomfortable memories to the fore."

"End Waking said that, too. I have my concerns for your cocladists aboard Artemis, but I'm more worried about these uncomfortable memories cropping up across the clade."

"This is about Death Itself and I Do Not Know, is it not?" she asked, voice quiet, tightly controlled.

Ey nodded.

The skunk clutched her coffee closer to her chest, as though that might serve to shield her. It certainly felt as though she was struggling not to close herself off from the topic entirely. "We are very old, Ioan, and the implication of eternity has affected us all differently. I am beginning to think that it has less to do with memory than we had all originally suspected, but all the same, we have all begun to struggle through the centuries."

Ey nodded, but remained silent. She was speaking slowly, and did not appear to have finished.

"I did not talk with Death Itself much, and I was never able to speak with I Do Not Know. I did not know them except through observation. I am sorry– no." She shook her head, frowning. "I was going to say that I am sorry that they are no longer with us, but you know as well as I that this is not some small loss for us to be brushed away with thoughts and prayers, even for those of us who did not speak with them. Sad is not the correct term. I am anxious."

"Anxious of how this madness, as End Waking called it, might affect you and yours?"

She nodded, averting her eyes. "I am fucking terrified, Ioan. What am I to do in the face of such enormity?"

Ey blinked, taken aback. This was not how ey'd imagined the conversation would go. Ey'd pictured her providing some glib explanation for what was happening and perhaps outlining the steps that she and her close cocladists were taking to control the situation. Ey was expecting her to steer em towards confidence in her, and hopefully even to soothe eir fears about May through doing so.

This wasn't the True Name ey remembered. Were these her own cracks showing?

Ey prowled through memories of the conversations ey'd had with her over the years—several, during those first few years after launch, then the rapid decrease after the publication of the *History*—and tallied up each against the next.

"You've changed quite a bit, True Name," ey said. "I don't know what you're supposed to do, that's out of my league. All I can say is that you've changed. It looks like it takes you a lot of effort to keep the confidence that used to be so integral to your personality."

Ey watched as she bridled, subsided, and nodded. "I am not what I was."

"What changed?"

She shrugged helplessly. "If I knew, perhaps I could fix it, bring back that easy confidence."

The conversation was veering further off-script. The skunk herself was veering far afield from the one ey'd pictured in eir head. "Your counterpart on Castor sounds much the same as I remember. The True Name on Pollux has, from what I hear, wound up in a relationship and started to guide more openly over the last few years."

Looking down to where she held her mug against her front, True Name blinked rapidly, nodding.

Tears? Really? Ey frowned, searching her face and posture for any hint that this was some calculated display of emotion, then chided emself for such cynicism.

"Is it something about the Lagrange System?" ey asked, hunting for something to fix, helpless to stop emself from doing so. Some anxiety over that lack of control drove em to try and smooth out the situation *somehow*. "Is the culture that different here? Maybe something about the System itself? I'm trying to think of what might be different."

"I do not know, Ioan." She sniffed, sat up straighter, and smiled tiredly at em. "Again, if I did, perhaps there might be something that I could do to address it. I know what I am—what I have become—in comparison to my peers. While I am trying not to view that as a failing, it is...difficult."

"Something with Jonas, perhaps?"

She winced and looked away, ears pinned flat.

Ey had to resist the urge to reach out and offer her eir hand to hold for comfort as ey did so often with May. They looked so similar, even still, even after centuries of divergence, and all the more so when struggling with overwhelming emotions.

She must have caught some slight movement or hint of this on eir face or in eir posture, as she chuckled. "If I were built more like your May Then My Name, then perhaps I could more easily accept comfort, but I am not. Thank you for listening, though. I cannot talk about these things with many others."

Ey laughed, shrugging sheepishly. "Sorry, True Name. Long habit. Still, I'm happy to listen. I know that my relationship puts us in a precarious position relative to each other and there are still some aspects about our history that are...difficult to internalize, but, well–" Ey sat up straighter at a sudden memory. "Hey, have you talked with In Dreams yet? Or this Sarah Genet?"

"I have spoken with In Dreams, yes," she said, tilting her head. "Though I am not sure in what capacity you mean. She has kept me up to date on the cross-clade issues. I only know the name Sarah Genet from the communications from Castor."

"Really? I thought that they had been in contact with all of the clade they could," ey said, frowning. "But perhaps that's still in progress. Either way, you mentioned having someone to talk to, and In Dreams has suggested taking a therapeutic approach to this. She and Ms. Genet have been working on setting up a course of therapy sessions for Odists and a few of the other old clades that are struggling. Perhaps that's something that could help. May has an appointment in a few days." Ey hastened to add, "I'm still happy to listen, but I'm hardly trained in that."

The skunk laughed, and it was difficult to miss the bitter tone in her voice. "I spoke with In Dreams this morning, and had not heard this. Perhaps it is an issue of priority."

Eir frown deepened.

She made a setting-aside gesture that ey'd grown used to from May, as though the topic were unimportant, not worth discussing. "I will contact them. Thank you for suggesting that, Mx. Bălan. Even if they are unwilling to help, it is probably a good idea that I seek out therapy. Lord knows I need it."

Ey nodded, wary to continue. As the silence that followed stretched out, ey retrieved eir tea and sipped it before it grew too cold.

"Why are you happy to listen to me, Ioan?"

Ey shook emself from eir own rumination and back to the present. "I'm sorry?"

True Name smiled. "You said that you were happy to listen to me. Your partner hates me—let us not mince words: she hates me and I have grown to accept that as best I can. You are close, as partners should be, and you have as much reason to hate me as anyone, and yet you met me here—asked to meet me here, even—and say that you are happy to listen. Why?"

"Oh. Well," ey began, then stalled out. Ey raced through eir memories for a reason ey could articulate. "It was something that Codrin#Castor said. Em and Dear both, actually. Codrin passed on a letter that Codrin#Artemis sent, saying that it has been difficult emotionally to watch what ey remembers from Michelle in your cocladists. When ey mentioned the time skew to it, Dear said to be watchful around your counterpart, saying, 'remember what I said: even True Name has emotions, even she will be affected'."

The skunk sat back, looking stunned, then choked out a half-laugh-half-sob, setting her mug down on the table so that she could rub her paws firmly over her face, leaving them to cover it. "Even I have emotions. Even I!" she said between deep breaths. "I know that your cocladist and Dear meant well by this, but how damning an indictment. *Even I.*"

"I'm sorry, True Name."

She shook her head, took a moment to regain her composure, and said, "No, I suppose I do, at that. It is difficult to remember even from the inside, my dear. Thank you for reminding me, and thank you for listening."

The skunk reached out a paw toward em and, after a moment's hesitation, ey took it and gave it what ey hoped was a comforting squeeze. Ey was once more startled by the similarity of her to May: the softness of her fur, the satiny feel of her pads, those well-kept claws.

She laughed and shook her head, pulling her paw back. "How silly. I believe I stand by my assessment that comfort through physicality is not for me, but thank you all the same. That you have the capacity to comfort...well, even me does mean a lot, Mx. Bălan. I appreciate your empathy."

Ey smiled cautiously. "Worth a try, I suppose."

"Yes. Worth a try." She stood slowly and gave a hint of a bow. "I have much to think about, Mx. Bălan, and a message to send to Ms. Genet. Please spend some quality time with your partner tonight, and I hope to see you in the future."

"Of course. Until next time."

She bowed again and stepped from the sim, leaving em to sit on the couch and finish eir tea, mulling over the differences between changing and forgetting. Without forgetting, all True Name had, all they *all* had, was the ability to change, and all they could do was hope that this would be enough to keep them all sane.

Tycho Brahe#Castor — 2346

Convergence T-minus 1 day, 2 hours, 28 minutes

"This has...wait, don't leave yet, #Assist," Codrin said. "Is this really a clade-eyes-only message for both True Name *and* Turun Ka?"

Both Sarah and Tycho sat up straighter.

Ey shrugged, saying only, "It appears Codrin#Artemis has instructed the Artemisians on how to relay such in turn. I guess ey did a while back, actually, but this is the first time they've taken advantage of it. Or, well..." Ey trailed off.

"Hard to tell how much time has passed up there?" Codrin#Castor asked.

"Yeah, haven't the faintest. Anyway, I'm not sure how you want to pass it over. I figured a separate sheet would be easiest and you can decide from there. The news from #Artemis seems mostly to be about the Odists, so perhaps that's what Turun Ka is getting. True Name has her own message in here." Ey nodded over to the skunk, handing her a separate sheet

Both of the Odists, having claimed the other table in order to have their own hushed conversation quickly moved over to rejoin the other three. They all watched as ey frowned, nodded, and skimmed quickly over the letter addressed to em.

Eir frown deepened. "Thanks. Here, hold on–" Ey quickly jotted *Message received, passed on, more soon, updates from others?*

on a slip of foolscap and handed it to the other Codrin. "Send this for now, just so we're on the same page at as close to the same time as we can manage."

"Whatever that means," ey said, laughing and pocketing the slip. Ey prodded em in the shoulder and added, "Dear threatened to beat me up because of you, so thanks for that."

Codrin#Castor smirked. "Well, did it?"

"No, of course not."

"Just have to pull harder, then." Ey sighed and shook eir head. "Self-deprecating humor aside, tell them I miss them."

Ey nodded. "Of course."

"I'll see them soon enough, I guess. A few weeks, tops, though at this rate, I'm guessing only a matter of days. Tell–"

"Codrin," True Name said, nodding to the writer. "Please come with us. We have only a few minutes to sort this out before we start, and if you are correct about Turun Ka receiving similar information, I would like to plan."

Ey shrugged to Tycho and Sarah and stood to follow the two Odists to True Name's partitioned rest area. Codrin#Assist stepped from the sim and back to Castor proper.

"What do you suppose that was about?" Tycho asked, setting up a cone of silence around himself and Sarah.

"Best guess? More about how they're struggling with the time skew over there. Maybe something specific happened, and that's why everybody's gotten messages all at once."

He nodded, sighed, and rubbed over his face with a hand. For as little as was actually happening, he was incredibly tired. Conferences were always like this, felt like.

"Well, neither of us got anything, and it's not worth speculating, especially since I figure we will learn soon enough," she said. "I'll start to sound like a broken record before long, but how are you feeling about how things are going?"

"Uh, well, much the same, I guess. I'm pretty sure they're real, now," he said, laughing tiredly. "It's been interesting seeing what we know that they don't. Far less than what they've been teaching us, though."

"Oh?"

He smiled lopsidedly. "True Name cornered me when this whole thing began and quoted some poetry at me that got me in mind of keeping track of all this. Something about how we may sit humbly at each others' feet while the other shares their later sciences."

"I can never pick apart when she's being blunt or subtle."

"Well, she followed it up with, 'That is a poem about death. Please understand that there is risk here, as well' so, maybe it was a bit of both."

Sarah laughed. "Well, okay. I'll grant you that. Sounds like working with her has been kind of an adventure. You've had more experience than I."

"It hasn't been too bad, all told. She's been nothing but polite, and sometimes even nice. It's hardly been a bad time. I think the biggest block has actually been squaring what I'm experiencing with what I'd assumed about her from the *History*."

"She didn't exactly come off as kind or polite in there, no."

"Codrin mentioned something about that, about how they wanted the *History* released, but wanted to control how. Ey said that she'd acted as dramatic as she had in order to make the end result seem more sensational than realistic. "Shaping the narrative," she called it."

Sarah laughed. "Well, I'd certainly call *that* subtle."

"Right," he said, grinning. "So I guess it's kind of making me reassess how I feel about them."

"The Odists?"

"Them too, but I was thinking more the *History* and *Mythology*. Like, if they're the product of social engineering to make them sound worse than they are to achieve a goal other than what Codrin, Ioan, and May Then My Name intended, then it's probably worth me actually paying attention to how things really are. That, and how they're engineering what's going on here."

"Sure, that makes sense," Sarah said, sitting back with her hands folded in her lap. "I can pick up little bits and pieces of her and Why Ask Questions trying to nudge things this way or that, with mixed results. It's giving me a new appreciation for what Codrin does, honestly. Ey's got maybe the hardest job of us all."

Tycho nodded. "I don't envy em that. Ey told me at the beginning that I'd be doing the same, in my own way—listening and coming away from this with a more complete picture—and I think I lack the experience ey has, both the training as an amanuensis and from living with an Odist."

"They're cute together, though. Pulling Dear's tail sounds like a recipe for disaster, but I guess if you've been together for forty years or whatever, you can get away with it."

He laughed and shook his head. "Yeah, no way. Never really was my thing, so I have no idea how it all works."

"What's that?"

"Relationships. Never really got into them, so the banter is cute to watch, but just as over my head as all of the politicking."

Sarah nodded. "They're not for everyone, especially here, where you have the problem of perpetuity."

"Precisely," Tycho said. "I can't imagine being around one person or group of people for forty years and still expect to do so for a hundred more."

"To be fair, neither can I," she said, laughing.

After a suitable pause, he nudged the subject back toward the previous topic. "Has your opinion of the *History* changed at all?"

"A little, I suppose. A lot of the dramatic interactions felt like just that: drama. It's the type of thing that I'm attuned to, though, based on my work. The Odists have a flair for that, though, which I guess makes sense, given where they come from." She paused, gaze drifting off towards nothing. "I guess if my opinion has changed, it's been to understand just how deep it all goes. Not the behind the scenes stuff, that's whatever, but their control over themselves. True Name especially. Control like that is often used to cover fear and trauma."

"It kind of makes me wonder–"

Tycho was cut off from the rest of his sentence by Codrin stepping into his field of view outside the cone and waving. He dropped the silence.

"Sorry, you two. Time to head back."

"Everything alright? You look...I don't know, like you were just put through the wringer."

Ey smiled weakly, shaking eir head. "Not me, no. I'm very tired, though, and I imagine things are only going to get more stressful over the next few hours."

"Why? What–"

"I'm sorry, Tycho, I really do want to answer your questions, but we just don't have time."

Codrin Bălan#Artemis — 2346

Convergence T-minus 1 day, 2 hours, 12 minutes

During the short break, Codrin helped True Name compose her letter and, after ey sent it, simply sat with her in quiet. The skunk remained still throughout, sitting on the edge of the bed and staring down at her knees. She looked small, and some part of em wanted to sit beside her and try to comfort her, but for the emotional and social distance between them, as well as her still jittery form.

And so ey simply sat at her desk and watched her manage her breathing, keep her composure, meditate, or whatever it was that an Odist unbound did.

Finally, ey reached out to offer a hand to the skunk to help her stand. "It's time we start back, True Name."

She sighed, nodded, and waved eir hand away, standing on her own. "Thank you, Mx. Bălan. I appreciate your help."

Ey nodded, hesitated as ey composed eir question, and then asked, "I don't wish to overstep my bounds, here, and will accept no as an answer, but can you tell me what exactly it was that Why Ask Questions meant by 'I cannot feel em'?"

After a moment swaying, the skunk straightened up and brushed her paws down over her blouse, straightening some imagined crease. "You ask because of the pronoun?"

Ey nodded.

"I cannot tell you," she said. Looking steadily at em, she fixed a kind and competent expression in place. It bore a force to it, as though she was willing em to drop the subject. "And that I cannot should explain enough."

Codrin blinked, clutched eir notebook closer to eir chest, and bowed to her. "Of course, True Name. Shall we fetch Why Ask Questions?"

The other Odist was not to be found in her room. She had apparently remained where she had been sitting before, arms crossed on the edge of the table with her head resting on them. Every time there was a shift in her form, it brought a jolt or an uncomfortable squirm, and yet she did not lift her head, even when True Name knelt down beside her to speak in hushed tones.

The rest of the delegates arrived shortly after, Tycho and Stolon both looking quite happy. There was a moment's shuffling as Tycho, Sarah, and Codrin were shifted down by one so that True Name could remain sitting by her cocladist.

Even so, the meeting was slow to get started. There were a few questions asked by both sides about history, but they all felt very careful, well constructed, and circumspect. It was plagued by silences and subtle glances to where Answers Will Not Help rested her head on the table.

"From the sounds of it," Iska said. "Of the four organic species present, all began their projects of building embedding systems after a traumatic event. It seems to be a common feature of biological systems. The desire to protect oneself or one's species from trauma is a common feature of all life."

"We ran-existed in simulation space within our physical-corporeal bodies-shells. There was no difference-change from post-biological life-existence and living in embedded form," Turun Ko added. "We are unable to add-explain to the topic of biological trauma. Apologies."

True Name nodded. "We understand, recorder Turun Ko."

"If I may ask," Codrin began. "Was there a period of adjustment for firstrace after–"

"Prophets!"

Silence fell once more around the table. Answers Will Not Help pushed herself to her feet. Waves of skunk and human crashed violently across her form. She was crying harder than before. Her back arched taut and she laughed up toward the ceiling, a choked, gasping sound.

True Name, struggling to hold her own form together, reached out to tug at Answers Will Not Help's sleeve. "Please, my dear," she murmured. "Representative Why Ask Questions, please sit down. I know it is–"

"I am not her! I am not her. She is another me, who dreams when she needs an answer. I am Why Ask Questions When The Answers Will Not Help, who knows God when she dreams. Dreams! If I dream, am I no longer myself? Don't...I..."

True Name froze. Everyone froze.

"We were told–" Sarah began, before Answers Will Not Help cut her off.

"Prophets! Oh, where is Ezekiel when we need him? A meeting of prophets! *Navi* to *nevi'im!* The voice of God from the sky in a pillar of flame!" She looked around, wide-eyed, and her voice grew conspiratorial. "Or Qoheleth, a prophet of our own blood, bearing warning of memory entrancing!"

Her words came out in an unceasing torrent. She waved her hand/paw toward the Artemisians, giggling. "But instead we are Israel to *nevi'im,* a people to prophets, a people to prophets! A people with our own personal HaShem, and the only time I know my true name is when I dream, and to know one's true name is to know God. Time feels so vast that were it not for an Eternity— Fuck, I...time makes prey of remembering, I...I fear me this Circumference engross my Finity— Oh AwDae, oh AwDae. Could you ever have guessed at the depths of the death of memory?"

True Name stood quickly enough to knock her chair back

and, with a decisive wash of skunk down her form, growled, "How fucking dare–"

The rest of the delegation pressed away from her with a shout. The firstracers rose up to their full height and Iska blurred quickly to stand atop their stool, shouting, "*Iha!*"

"To his exclusion who prepare by process of Size...of..." Answers Will Not Help continued, unfazed. She was phasing in and out of common time now, despite the promise of unison. Her words jittering now fast, now slow. "I cannot feel em here. We are so far away from home. I cannot...I miss em, I miss em. I miss...was that eir prophecy? Was that why ey wrote me? Is this AwDae's words come true?"

"Stop!" True Name shouted. She swiped out at her cocladist, managing to grab a fistful of her blouse, roughly yanking her closer.

With surprising speed, Answers Will Not Help slid a foot back and struck True Name's forearm with a downward strike of her own, getting a yelp from the skunk and forcing her to let go. She stumbled back, gasping, "The flow of prophecy climbs up through the years, winter upon winter upon winter, and compels the future to do its bidding! Ey said...ey said..."

True Name bared her teeth, tackling the blurring, crumbling form of Answers Will Not Help to the ground. "Fucking stop! You cannot–"

After a moment's tussle, Answers Will Not Help sprawled flat the ground, limp and laughing, retching, crying. "For the Stupendous Vision of eir diameters—" she said, and then quit, leaving True Name to fall to the ground, weeping.

There was a shocked silence around the table, and when no one moved, Codrin slid out of eir chair to kneel by True Name's side. Her form had begun to waver once more, and, remembering the aversion to touch that came with that, ey simply knelt beside her, waiting until she calmed down.

It was Sarah who broke the silence. "What just happened?"

Codrin spoke carefully. "As mentioned, True Name and,

uh...Why Ask Questions—that is, Michelle Hadje—were among the lost, and I guess time skew is similar enough to–"

"No," the Odist said between heaving breaths, clutching at her arm where it had been struck. "She was right. That was Answers Will Not Help."

Tycho frowned, nodded. "We had guessed."

"She should not have been able to do that," Iska said, nearly growling. "She should not have been able to do any of that. No skew, no exit. What was she? Who are you?"

"Leader True Name," Turun Ko said. "Please explain 'lost' in this context."

She did not move from her spot on the floor. "You have heard about what it means to get lost, but there is no possible way that I can explain the way it has warped us. To get lost is to go mad."

Silence and stillness fell once more as all waited for True Name to continue. After a few long breaths and coarse swallows, she mastered her form once more. She knelt beside Codrin, wiping at the tear streaks on her muzzle and the dripping from her nose.

"We are incomplete. We are unwhole." Her voice was bitter, even as she worked to bring back that mask of competence. "We were broken and remain so. I do not know how it is that Answers Will Not Help was able to...to manage skew or quit. You have my most abject apologies for the trouble caused, and for the deception with–"

"Leader True Name," Turun Ka said, interrupting as politely as it had before. "There will be time to discuss this topic. That time remains in the future. For now, please take this opportunity to, *lu*...gather yourself and clean up. You may take as long as you require. When you are able, you and I shall meet in our role as leaders."

The skunk wilted, her ears splaying to the sides. "Of course, leader Turun Ka."

"Are you amenable to increasing the skew in the unison room? This will allow you to take all the time you need."

She nodded. "Yes, that would be fine. It is uncomfortable, but I can sleep through the discomfort."

"*Aën*," it said. "We shall return here in half an hour. The other participants shall meet in the central courtyard."

"I will join shortly," Iska said. "I must contact a technician, first."

They did not wait, but seemed to disappear as they shifted up to a high enough skew to travel faster than ey could perceive.

Codrin nodded to the other emissaries. "Go ahead. I'll help True Name to her room, then join up with you in a bit."

"I am sorry," True Name mumbled, barely loud enough to be heard.

"Leader True Name, please understand that you are in no way responsible. Even your deception was, as you say, wargamed. We will discuss shortly."

"Rest," Artante added. "Become whole."

As the others departed Codrin held out eir arm, letting the skunk clutch it tightly as ey helped her to stand. They swayed together at the brief sensorium twinge as the unison room was skewed up by a factor of two.

The walk down the hall was a slow and unsteady affair, and Codrin couldn't help but see every one of True Name's two and a half centuries in the way she moved. She looked as she always had, was as strong as she'd ever been, and yet each one of those long years seemed to be a weight she had to draw along behind her. She kept her grip on eir forearm throughout, however, as though the contact kept her pinned to one reality.

Ey guided her into her room and helped her to sit down on the edge of her bed, and even then, it took her a few long seconds to loosen her grip.

"You heard nothing today, Mx. Bălan," she mumbled, quiet enough that ey had to lean closer to hear. "I know what you thought you heard, but you heard nothing. Do not tell anyone.

Do not tell Ioan, and certainly do not tell any others within the Ode clade."

Ey took a half step back from the skunk. So hoarse and clouded was her voice that ey couldn't piece together her mood. "I...is that a suggestion or a threat? I'm sorry, True Name. I know how much it means, I just–"

She smiled weakly and shook her head before laying out on her side, rubbing her arm and wincing. "It is a request from me to you, Codrin, from my clade to yours. Across our two entangled clades." The smile faded as she added, "Not...a request. A plea."

Ey nodded, struck silent by the sincerity in her voice. Real, actual sincerity. It made em feel bashful. Ey bowed and started to turn back toward the door.

"Codrin?"

"Yes?"

Her voice was small. It bore fear and anxiety alongside the omnipresent exhaustion. "Can you please stay for a few minutes?"

"I, uh..." Ey swallowed dryly. "Do you need anything?"

"Just for someone to be present. I may need your help writing another note back to Castor in a bit," she said, then had to master some hidden emotion before continuing. "But right now, I just need someone to anchor me. You are very good at that."

After a moment's hesitation, ey nodded, pulling up a chair from the small table in the center of the room. Ey sat beside the skunk as she lay still on the bed, eyes closed, her breathing growing more steady, and then slowing as she drifted into sleep.

Ey watched her doze fitfully.

What was it Dear had said? That she was still a fully realized person? *She does still have emotions, they simply come from a place that we cannot access.*

Ey wasn't sure how much ey believed that now, that they came from a place ey could not access. True Name had the same emotions ey did, ey knew now, and they came from that very same well within her. She had just become so singular an entity that their expression could only be framed through one very small, very precise lens.

Hers was a control borne of anxiety, a competency borne of trauma, and this knowledge meant that ey could never unsee the core, fully realized humanity within her.

All that may be, but what do I do with it? ey thought. *And how the hell am I going to keep what I heard hidden and buried?*

Ioan Bălan — 2346

Convergence T-plus 33 days, 15 hours, 39 minutes
(Castor–Lagrange transmission delay: 30 days, 14 hours, 36 minutes)

Depression, Ioan had long known but struggled to internalize, was fundamentally different from sadness, just as it was different from May's overwhelming waves of emotions.

Ey was confronted with it now, forced to see the way the emotion—or non-emotion, as May put it—affected one on a more fundamental level than anything so simple as sadness could hope to. Those overwhelming waves, as the one she'd just recovered from, were fundamental in their own way, but far, far less existential.

It was bound by the cycle of the day, and so Ioan and May would spend their mornings strategizing their evenings, ensuring that they were able to have as pleasant a time as that ashen feeling May described would allow, to work as well as they could manage through that fog.

"We are not unfamiliar with it, Ioan," A Finger Pointing had said when, after watching Death Itself and I Do Not Know quit, May's countenance grew duller and duller, and the skunk spoke less and less. "We know depression from the embodied world, and it comes up every now and then for each of us here, too."

"Even True Name, I suppose," ey had said, describing the conversation ey'd had with her.

She had nodded. "It will pass, and we will make the shows work, my dear. Keep her company and be good to her, and you need not worry."

Some dark look must have crossed eir face at which the director had shaken her head and hugged em. "Do not worry about that, Ioan. There is no death in her, I am sure of that. I am sorry that there are no easy ways to explain it, but I promise that what I expect she is feeling is separate from what our cocladists felt."

When presented with this along with eir anxious expression, the skunk had laughed and tousled eir hair. "She is right, my dear. It feels uncomfortable at best, bad at worst, but only ever bad. I am simply a bit crashy after a little too much all at once."

So for the last few days, they'd strategized in the mornings and then done what they could in the evenings. Scenes in plays were reworked for understudies, dinner menus shifted towards comfort foods, temperatures and weather adjusted, old comfort-hobbies dredged up from the past—the skunk had been littering the house with origami figures. Ey'd even tried reading aloud to her, her with her head parked on eir chest and em with a book held above them. This had gone over well, and ey had that on the menu for later in the evening after dinner.

Today still held the first meeting with Sarah Genet, however, so ey focused on making a good breakfast, and spending a bit of time relaxing on the porch swing with May, giving her pets and quiet company.

"How are you feeling about this?" ey asked, voice muffled. May had requested a brushing of her tail, which meant a face full of fluff.

"I do not know. I am anxious. I am trying to keep up that sense of hopefulness that I had when we began planning this, but the anxiety is getting in the way."

Ey tamped down the urge to ask what the anxiety was over, knowing that the answer would likely be *I do not know* or *nothing*—rightly so, for eir own anxiety often seemed to have no basis in reality. Instead, ey asked, "Do you want me to be there with you?"

May scooted down a little on the swing, enough to get her arms around eir middle. "Please. It is just an initial meeting, I do not imagine there will be any need for privacy."

"No deep, dark secrets, then?"

There was a muffled laugh from where the skunk had planted her face against eir belly. "I do not know that I have any of those from you, my dear."

"Other than the obvious."

May stayed quiet, shifting the rest of the way so that she could lay her head on eir lap, looking off into the yard. Finally, she murmured, "We will need to talk about that at some point, Sarah and I. The pressure surrounding it is building."

This did not seem to be an open conversation, so ey nodded, settling into silence with eir partner.

Sarah arrived an hour later, a quiet knock at the door accompanying the sensorium ping of her arrival.

May had melted into a beanbag when they'd come back inside and was folding paper crane after paper crane from a bottomless stack of origami paper, so Ioan capped eir pen and slid cir project into a drawer of eir desk. The skunk studiously avoided eir gaze, the tightness of her expression showing anxiety with tears near at hand.

"Mx. Bălan?" the psychologist said, bowing. "Nice to meet you."

"And you, Ms. Genet." Ey stood aside, gesturing toward the hall. "Please, come inside."

"Just Sarah is fine." Smiling kindly to em, she nodded and stepped inside. She seemed to be taking the sight of their home in with some deeper understanding than ey could grasp. Ey wondered just how much she could tell by how clean or messy a place might be, and thanked past-Ioan for cleaning up quite well after breakfast.

The skunk had finished her crane and levered herself out

of her beanbag by the time they made it to the den. She was standing by the kitchen table, paws folded before her and ears perked up, looking polite and attentive, though Ioan could still read the exhaustion in her face.

"May Then My Name Die With Me," Sarah said, bowing once more. "A pleasure to meet you at last. Thank you for helping to organize this project."

"Please, just May Then My Name." She returned the bow, cleared her throat. "Thank you for going along with it. It will be a large one, and I– *we* appreciate all the help we can get."

They sat down around three sides of the dining table. The skunk surprised em by ensuring that ey, rather than her, sat across from the woman.

"So, there's no real agenda today other than to just get to know each other. No hard topics or anything, just chatting. Stuff like that helps me get used to how you communicate." Sarah nodded toward May. "Though I would like to know how you're feeling."

"Tired." The skunk looked down at the table where her claw-tips traced wood-grain. "Quite tired. I am not feeling myself currently, forgive me."

"That's alright. There's been an awful lot going on, from the sounds of it." Sarah shifted gears smoothly away from the topic of current events, asking instead, "I know you two are in theatre, from what you've said. What all does that entail, though? I haven't been to a play or anything since university before uploading."

May smiled weakly. "Lots of work. We share jobs from start to finish. There are more of us working as stage hands and crew than there are working as actors. Ioan even writes many of our plays."

"I guess that means you both know your way around the craft better than most, since you have to keep all of that in your heads. I'm curious, though; what all goes into the crew side? Are you also...what's the term. Stage managers? Techs?" Sarah shrugged, looking almost embarrassed at her lack of knowledge. "Lights? Sound?"

At the word 'sound', a stricken look washed over the skunk's face. She sat, rigid, in her chair for a moment before shaking her head, the movement jerky and uneven. "I...I will leave...I will leave Ioan to answer that."

Alarmed at the sudden change in her demeanor, Ioan looked between May and Sarah, the latter's face set in an expression of concern.

"May?" ey asked quietly.

"You must...you must forgive me. I have to...lay down. Or something." She swallowed several times in a row, as she always seemed to do when holding back tears.

The skunk stood and swayed, clutching at the edge of the table hard enough for claws to dent the wood.

"Of course, May Then My Name. Would you like to meet another–"

"Please discuss with Ioan," she whispered, eyes clenched shut.

Ioan forked quickly, the new instance taking May by the elbow and guiding her carefully toward the bedroom, leaving #Tracker and Sarah to sit in stunned silence, watching them leave.

There was a brief sensorium message, a few quiet words from eir fork, and ey nodded. "She panicked for a moment but is just going to disengage for a bit. She says to carry on since you and I might as well get to know each other, too. She'll reschedule for the near future."

"Alright," Sarah said, still frowning. "I know I said just chat, but I don't think I can just let that go. Can you explain what just happened?"

Ey sighed, nodded, and rubbed eir palms against eir slacks. "She will wind up getting overwhelmed by emotion sometimes, once every six months or so. It'll take her out for a few days then pass. She just got through one not too long ago—I think she contacted you the day after she got back."

"So this is another bout?"

"No, I don't think so. She's been kind of depressed over the last few days, which is different than when she overflows. She says it's not uncommon for her to 'crash' after really big events. She slows down and has a hard time enjoying things, which I suspect is common with depression. But also, little things will trigger large emotional reactions."

Sarah nodded. "That makes sense, at least. 'Trigger' is probably the right word, there. That certainly looked like a trauma response. One she was trying very hard to control, of course, but I could almost see the adrenaline rush through her."

"There's been quite a bit of trauma of late, with her cocladists quitting."

"Very much so, yes."

Ey rubbed at eir eyes. They were burning, though whether from exhaustion or eir own emotions, ey couldn't tell. "I have no clue what was the trigger there, though."

Sarah waved her hand. "She and I will talk that through, it's alright. How are you doing, though?"

"Me?" Ey frowned. Talking with a therapist had never been on the table for em through this whole endeavor, but ey was so wrapped up in it now... "I'm stressed. I'm tired and stressed and feeling like I'm just fumbling in the dark to find something that will keep May safe."

"I'd be surprised if you weren't stressed, honestly," she said. A blink, a cone of silence fell around them. "Aliens visit one of the LVs and both your clades get wrapped up in it almost immediately, and then her cocladists quit in the midst of all those overwhelming emotions. There's a lot on the table here. Do you worry she won't be safe?"

Ioan shrugged helplessly. "I trust her when she says she's not in any danger of anything like that and that she's doing her best to stay grounded, but that doesn't stop me from worrying."

"That's part of being in love, I think."

A pang of that love tugged at em. Sarah must have seen it on eir face, as she smiled sympathetically to em.

"I don't do well with loss. That's why I'm here, really. On the System, I mean," ey said, then recounted eir and May's previous conversations about the death of eir parents and how that factored into eir anxieties.

The conversation wound around from there. Ey could tell that Sarah was guiding it gently, giving careful nudges toward positive topics when the heavier ones began to loom too near, but always keeping it productive, substantive. It was, ey realized, the sort of mirror image of what ey'd seen from much of May's clade. Subtle influencing borne out of years of reading and responding to the actions, words, and expressions of another. Rather than aiming to control, however, Sarah seemed to be doing all she could to keep the control in eir hands, acting almost as a tool for em to use to examine emself, though far more human that that made it sound.

It was refreshing. Too many Odists over the last twenty years, perhaps.

"Well," Sarah said when they'd reached a lull in the conversation. "I should probably get going so that I can give you guys some space. I'll be in touch though, okay? I'll make sure to catch up with May Then My Name when she's feeling a bit better."

Ey nodded gratefully. "Thank you. This has been good for me, as well, so hopefully we can have the chance to talk again, too."

"Of course. Some of my appointments with her will involve you as well, but I'm also happy working with just you, too. Scheduling is certainly less of a constraint here on the System." She hesitated before adding, "Though for that, I may keep a separate fork for privacy's sake."

"Right, of course." Ey stood when she did, walking with her down the hall to the door. "By the way, have you been in touch with True Name? The Only Time I Know My True Name Is When I Dream?"

"Yes. She got in touch with me yesterday, and we have our own appointment scheduled. Why do you ask?"

Ey hesitated a moment, unsure of whether to divulge the fact that In Dreams seemed to have decided not to connect the two. "I'm worried about her," ey said eventually. "I just wanted to make sure she's also working with someone."

Sarah turned in the entryway, looking at em searchingly. "You know, back phys-side, I was your cocladist's partner's therapist, and we've stayed friends since uploading. They all but forced me to read the *History*. From what I could tell, your relationship with True Name did not seem to be one that included you worrying about her."

"She's changed a lot," ey said, speaking slowly as ey tried to puzzle out eir growing empathy for the other skunk — along with the fact that this was a thing that needed puzzling out. "She's been looking rough, lately, and even for someone I have a complicated relationship with, it's tough to watch."

"That I can understand. Does she look like May Then My Name? A furry?"

Ey nodded.

"That probably helps, too." She shook her head. "Anyway, I should be going for real, now. I'll be in touch to see about talking with you more soon, alright?"

"Of course," ey said, bowing. "Thanks again. I think I needed that more than I knew."

Back in their room, May and eir other instance were sitting cross-legged on the bed, the skunk trying for the dozenth time to teach em how to fold a paper crane.

Both looked up when ey entered and, though her cheeks still showed the marks of tears, ey was pleased to see May smiling.

Eir fork quit and as ey let the memories of the last hour settle into place, ey climbed into bed to take eir spot.

"I am sorry, my dear," the skunk said, leaning forward to dot her nose against eirs. "Thank you for all of your help through that, both in here and out there."

"Of course, May. Feeling better?"

She nodded, held up her paper crane, the bottom pinched between fingers, and tugged at its tail, making the wings flap. "I have been making things."

"Other than a mess, you mean?"

Ey winced and laughed as the origami bird hit em in the face.

"I will have you know that all of the messy ones are your doing, Mx. Ioan Bălan," she said primly. "Mine are perfectly neat and orderly."

Still grinning, ey ruffled a hand through her headfur, tugging affectionately at an ear. "Right, right. Just like you."

She chirped and tilted her head toward eir hand. "Did you have a good therapy session, my dear?"

Ey nodded. "I did. I wasn't expecting it, but it was helpful. Sarah says she'll be in touch to meet again soon."

"Alright. I will not apologize again, but I do still feel bad for how I acted."

"Shush, you're fine. I think she, of all people, understands a reaction like that." Ey picked up another square of paper from the stack and began trying to fold again. "But that's enough talk of that for now. If you want dinner, you have to help me get at least one of these made."

Codrin Bălan#Castor — 2346

Convergence T-minus 1 day, 2 hours, 2 minutes

"To begin with an example concept, I have noticed that your common language is very irregular and relies heavily on a small vocabulary and nominal compounding," Why Ask Questions said. "As we classify our languages into families based on several factors, including compounding, can each of the races expand on various features of their languages?"

"You speak on general terms?" Iska asked.

She nodded. "I am curious if you have noticed consistencies between the languages of the various races as they have been incorporated during the convergences."

The secondracer brushed their paws over their whiskers, a gesture that seemed somewhere between grooming and a thoughtful habit. "I will speak to old *Nanon* as it is spoken in primarily secondrace sims. You have guessed that it relies heavily on compounding. We say 'old', but the language remains similar to its modern form as it was during the first convergence. That which we used to call old *Nanon* was, *lu*...synthetic language, you may call it. Inflectional. There were eight grammatical cases and three grammatical genders–"

"Apologies for interrupting," Codrin said. "But do those genders map to the prefixes we used when addressing ourselves? *Uchles*, *achles*, and so on?"

Iska nodded. What had begun as a curiously outsized and clumsy gesture had settled into something more akin to how True Name and Dear might nod. "*Anem,* yes, recorder Codrin Bălan. They were, *lu*...you might say animate, inanimate, and conceptual. In later evolutions of the language, they began to define levels of respect, and then mark roles in society as they fell out of use in cases other than referring to individuals."

Codrin nodded, made note of this, and flipped to the next page as the discussion continued.

Ey was finding the linguistics portion of the discussion particularly fascinating. Although many of the scientific topics incorporated history, this was the most easily digestible for em. Both Why Ask Questions and Sarah had studied up on the topic intensely during the days and weeks leading up to the meetings.

It would be interesting to compare notes with Codrin#Artemis, and ey was looking forward to the merger down the line. Ey wasn't sure yet whether this was accompanied by a desire for the talks to be over, for there was also the fact that ey missed home greatly.

Ah well. Until then, ey dedicated as much of eir attention as ey could manage to keeping up on eir job as recorder. Each of the races continued in turn, describing various features and aspects of the language or languages of theirs which had made the transition through the convergences.

Each, that is, except the firstracers, who did their best to express the features of their mode of communication, apologizing for being unable to describe the languages that had existed during their biological period.

"Thank you," Why Ask Questions said. "I have a few questions on the use of metaphor and analo–"

Most of those around the table jumped as a second instance of True Name appeared at the end of the table beside the fountain, bowed, and said, "My apologies for interrupting. #Castor, please merge immediately."

After the second skunk quit, True Name #Castor frowned.

The frown deepened, then transmuted to one that bordered on panic.

"Leader True Name, please explain," Turun Ka said.

She stood, composed herself, and bowed toward the Artemisian delegates. "My apologies. That was a second instance of myself bearing news. She quit and merged back with me so that I may have her memories. It was the fastest way to receive news. I would like to call a halt to the current topic and make an announcement."

The firstracer tilted its head up in assent. Codrin scanned the rest of the delegates and found a look of concern on Iska's face, one recognizable from discussions on forking. Stolon appeared nonplussed, and Artante intensely focused.

"There has been an incident aboard Artemis with the delegation regarding one of our representatives."

Why Ask Questions sat bolt upright.

Could they have discovered the subterfuge? Codrin thought. Ey frowned and scooted eir chair back from the table a fraction of an inch, prepared to bolt.

"I will explain in full and then accept questions," the skunk was saying. "As I have mentioned, and perhaps you may have heard from your counterparts on Artemis via relayed messages, my entire clade struggles with the concept of time skew. It recalls a portion of our lives that is...indescribable. Needless to say, that became too much for Why Ask Question's counterpart, and she lost control in grand fashion and quit in the middle of proceedings."

"That should not have been possible," Iska muttered. "Apologies. Please continue, leader True Name."

The skunk hesitated, frowning. "We will discuss that aspect after this, perhaps. The reason that I wish to address this before we have a conversation is that, in the process of our party transferring to Artemis, Why Ask Question's counterpart was replaced with a separate fork of mine named Why Ask Questions When The Answers Will Not Help. She is another up-tree instance of myself, which I believed to be acceptable, but we have discussed the topic of individuation, and as both representative Why Ask Questions and Answers Will Not Help were forked from me 222 years ago, they have long since become separate individuals.

"The reasons for this deception are complicated, relating to the origins of both of the forks' creation." She clasped her paws on front of herself and bowed. "Please accept my apologies on this matter."

There was silence around the table for a few seconds, and then both parties set up separate cones of silence.

True Name sat back down and faced the rest of the delegates on her side of the table. "Apologies are due to you three as well for being kept in the dark. We had our reasons, for doing so, which I will explain during our next break."

Codrin nodded. "I'd appreciate a more solid explanation, but I guess I should also say that our instances on Artemis had guessed this, as well. Codrin#Artemis's theory was that, as Why Ask Question's role was to manage sentiment sys-side and Answers Will Not Help's was to manage phys-side."

The skunk sat back, blinked rapidly, then laughed. "Well, then."

"The best laid schemes o' skunks an' Jonases," Why Ask Questions said, giggling. "Gang aft agley."

"Well, that aside, I am unsure what to do with the remainder of the news from my position here on Castor," True Name said. "Mx. Bălan will remember some of what we struggled with from eir meeting with Michelle. My counterpart has been holding her ground against it as best as possible but I suppose it was not the case with Answers Will Not Help. With them being on Artemis, her instance here on Castor will not receive a merge."

"And now we will have to see just how fucked we are," Why Ask Questions said. "I do not imagine that they will be all that pleased with us."

"Was this an attempt to control the situation? The convergence?" Sarah asked.

True Name smiled wryly. "Your *History* was a very sensational book, Mx. Bălan, was it not? Please remember, Ms. Genet, that it is only ever our goal to guide and protect. We did what we felt was necessary to ensure the continuity and stability of the System."

She nodded, but didn't look convinced.

"The Artemisians are coming back," Tycho noted. "Should we?"

The skunk shrugged, nodded, and dropped the cone of silence.

"Thank you for your honesty in this matter, leader True Name," Turun Ka said. "We have a few questions to ask you before making our statement in turn."

She perked up at that, nodding. "By all means."

"The first question: you spoke of the reasons for the origins of these two individuals. What were their origins?"

"The System—the original one you observed at the L5 point which we call Lagrange—seceded from the political systems on Earth 221 years ago. My root instance, Michelle Hadje, was on the Council of Eight at that time. Due to the difficulties that I mentioned before, she created ten forks to pick up various interests, and then retired. I was the fork which wound up primarily in the political arena, and along with another clade not present here, I aided in the campaign for secession."

Why Ask Questions picked up from there, so smoothly that Codrin suspected that this scenario had been wargamed as thoroughly as any. "There were many aspects to that political referendum, both sys-side—that is, on the embedded side—and physside. True Name spread the work required for those aspects out over instances of her own. Answers Will Not Help and I were forked at the same time, both to encourage a positive attitude towards secession."

"Why Ask Questions focused on this task on the System,

while Answers Will Not Help focused on sentiment phys-side through the usual text channels," True Name said. "As each already had a specialization relating to two sides of a political event, we made the decision to do so here as well."

When it was clear that there wouldn't be any further explanation from the Odists, Turun Ka said, "Thank you. Second question: what was it that you hoped to gain from this strategy?"

"My goal in this case is the same as my goal during Secession and Launch—the effort that led to this vehicle—which is to maintain the stability and continuity of our existence. I do not wish to govern or control, but I do have at my disposal a set of tools to help in my aims."

There was a silent conversation between the Artemisians during which Codrin finished up the notes ey'd been taking on the conversation. True Name was being surprisingly honest about the whole endeavor. Ey was sure there were some aspects that she was withholding, but the initial announcement and answers that she'd provided thus far contained no outright lies that ey could tell.

Perhaps this too is a way of shaping their responses? Or maybe she just can't register them well enough to tell how best to lie, ey thought, then sighed. *And maybe I'm just being too cynical.*

The silent conversation among the other delegates wrapped up, and Turun Ka spoke once more. "Thank you once again for your honesty. This event is one part of the confirmation we have required, and the talks will now move on to the next stage, after a one hour common time break."

The skunk looked taken aback, nearly speechless. "Confirmation...? Can you explain–"

"Now is not the time for this discussion, leader True Name," Artante said, voice gentle but insistent enough to silence her. "We will have that discussion when the convergence progresses to the appropriate stage. For now, we offer condolences for the loss of that instance of representative Answers Will Not Help."

And with that, the Artemisian delegation stood, bowed, and returned to their rest area.

"Well, I will be damned," True Name said, then laughed.

"What just happened?" Sarah asked.

Why Ask Questions was laughing as well. She shrugged and grinned to the psychologist. "Fuck if I know. Come on. The least we can do is make some guesses over the next hour. I need a drink."

Codrin Bălan#Artemis — 2346

Convergence T-minus 1 day, 1 hour, 58 minutes

As suggested, Codrin and Sarah wound up in the courtyard.

There seemed to be no immediate recovery from the events of the past hour. There was no conversation to be had, no words that could be spoken to express so singular an event. There had been a...was it a death? Answers Will Not Help had made it less than three days into the conference, and already she was gone.

And ey had witnessed True Name...was it sharing in confidence, a request for companionship, or something else?

Ey felt dazed, unmoored from reality. Ey could feel more clearly the way that time clung to em in a way it couldn't back home, back on Castor. It was no stronger now than it had been at the beginning of the day, but, as might happen when one remembers that one is breathing, ey was suddenly and intensely aware of it.

"Codrin?"

Sarah's voice jolted em back to the present, and ey smiled tiredly to her. "Sorry. I was elsewhere. What's up?"

She laughed and waved away the comment. "It's alright. That was a whole lot all at once. I was asking how True Name was when you left her. Is she alright?"

"Yeah. She was sleeping. I don't know how much they– well, how much she has been sleeping of late, but given that she seems constantly exhausted, I'm glad she's getting at least a little."

"This does seem to be taking its toll on her. When this is all over, I'd like to sit down with you and her and learn a bit more about this." She hesitated, then added, "Or at least with you, depending on how willing she is."

Ey nodded. Ey could feel the knowledge of what ey'd learned sitting heavily in eir gut, clawing at eir insides. The Name, the pronouns, feeling the owner of the Name in the system. It wanted out, at least in some way, but there was no one other than True Name ey'd be able to share that with from now until eternity.

Swallowing down the feeling clutching at eir throat, ey said instead, "You know, when she was laying down to nap, she said something like, 'I need someone to anchor me and you are very good at that'. Come to think of it, I got a note from Codrin#Castor that Tycho said similar earlier, that he said I'm 'grounding'."

Sarah nodded readily. "You are, yes. Why do you bring it up?"

"It's not something I'd really considered about myself." Ey spoke slowly, piecing together eir thoughts as ey went. "I've been questioning my path in life moving forward. I've been very passive, very much like a recorder. I'm *good* at being an amanuensis, but I also feel like I get dragged into it more often than I choose to do so."

"Does being a grounding person help with that?"

Ey shrugged. "I suppose so. Empathy helps, because it lets me understand what's happening more readily, lets me build a more complete story. The way Tycho and True Name put it, though, sounds...I don't know, more active."

She nodded again, waiting in silence until ey was done speaking.

"Ioan's moved on to theatre, Codrin#Pollux is a librarian now, and I'm just doing the same thing I was doing almost a hundred years ago. This whole thing about being grounding combined with the need for something new just has me thinking about what to do with my life."

"It's a complex question, Codrin. Hell, even when we were limited to ninety or a hundred years, folks would talk about having midlife crises, questioning what it was that they really wanted to do, and a lot of times it came down to feeling a lack of agency. Psychologists would..." She trailed off, looking over eir shoulder. "Well, lets pick this up later. Artante and Turun Ko are on their way."

Ey turned to look, noticing the two Artemisians moving slower than expected. A moment's thought showed that ey was still running at a skew of one point two as the meeting had been, so ey dropped back down to common time.

Turun Ko dipped its head as Artante bowed, saying, "Recorder Codrin Bălan, representative Sarah Genet. Do you know where the scientists are?"

"They're probably down the hall," Codrin said, returning the bow. "Every time they sneak off, they head for an alcove there and talk as much as they can."

"We are pleased-excited to witness mutual-shared enjoyment," Turun Ko said, voice bouncing between registers in amusement.

The fourthracer laughed. "I am not surprised. Will you join us in finding them?"

Codrin led them down the hall past their rest area. The hallway continued beyond, though it ended at a flat wall that ey supposed must be an exit when the place was not in use for a convergence. To the side, though, there was an alcove, windows on the three walls looking out over a garden. It seemed perpetually sunny, and every time ey'd seen them there, the thirdracer had been sunning themself while they chatted.

"*Nahi,* recorder Codrin Bălan," Stolon said, then sat up straighter when they noticed Turun Ko, bowing from a seated position to the other delegates. "*Rehas' les.*"

Ey bowed. "Apologies for interrupting. I figured I'd get us all together as suggested."

"*Ka, ka,*" Stolon said, bobbing their head.

There was a ping against eir sense of time, a sensation of insistent pressing.

"Please?" Turun Ko said. "We will speak at synchronized skew."

Ey frowned, relaxing against the sensation and feeling eir control over time diminish. After a moment of looking uncomfortable, both Sarah and Tycho nodded as well.

There was a brief lurch as time skewed quickly up to two point five, moving far more quickly and with more surety than eir experiments up to that point.

"Thank you, recorder Codrin Bălan, representative Sarah Genet, scientist Tycho Brahe." The firstracer eased back, settling onto its haunches and tail and clasping its hands together over its front, which appeared to be the default resting state for its race.

"How do you feel the convergence is going?" Artante asked.

Tycho picked at a corner of the stone sill, shrugging. "Well enough, I suppose. I'm feeling really in over my head."

Stolon tilted their head far to the side. "In over...?"

"*Nu...nukupot...kopotla...*" he stammered. He had apparently held true to his promise to learn more of the language.

"*Iha! Ka, ka, nukupotla,* not-knowing?"

"Something like that. I don't know what's going on, and don't have much to contribute. Not much knowledge to give, I mean, when we're talking about social stuff."

"*Irr, ka,* I also." The thirdracer made a frustrated gesture with one of their hands and then shifted to drape languidly over the edge of the windowsill, hands hanging nearly down to the ground and feet kicking lazily behind them in the alcove. It was a nearly childlike move that Codrin found incredibly endearing. Something more...well, not human, but perhaps personable in this otherwise impersonal conference.

"I went into academia because– sorry, into studying as one of the only things I do in my life because that seemed to be the only way I could just do what it was that I wanted," Tycho said. "No commitments, no distractions. Just the stars and math."

Stolon stretched out long enough to grab a curly-edged leaf from one of the short bushes, picking at it between dull claws. "I also, *ka*. I am not...combination? Child? I am from before embedding. Before before, I also study. I study stars and inside planets. I also in over my head. I am knowing how convergence works, so I am here, but still I dream of stars."

"I was on my way into academia as well," Codrin said, filing the thirdracer's use of 'child' and 'combination' away for later questioning. "But I guess my chosen interests align a bit more with politics than astronomy."

"*Anem, anem.*"

Turun Ko looked to Sarah.

"Stressful," she said. "I really don't know what to make of earlier."

"I am, *lu*...sorry that your friend exits," Stolon said, and Artante nodded in agreement. "I do not know how, Iska looks into this."

Turun Ko bowed its head. "We wish to speak-discuss with you the events-proceedings from earlier."

"To begin with," Artante said, picking up the conversation. "Do you have any questions that we can answer? This may inform the discussion."

When Sarah and Tycho did not speak, ey asked, "I don't imagine there's much you'll be able to answer so soon in the talks, but leader Turun Ka mentioned that deception had been wargamed. Is this the type of thing that's expected at a convergence?"

"Yes, recorder Codrin Bălan. The possibility-probability that a new race-culture-species practices-engages-in deception is one item on a checklist of one beginning and two endings."

"Beginning? Endings?" Ey shook eir head. "Well, stepping back, what do you mean by checklist?"

"Convergences are processes. Processes may be smooth-easy or rough-difficult. It is our goal-aim to ensure smoothness-ease, as I think-suspect must be that of leader True Name."

This was the most that Turun Ko had said at once over the last few days and, despite its statuesque nature, ey was keen on drawing more out of one so aligned with eir own goals. "So you have a list of items and possibilities that might happen during a convergence and we're making our way down the list?"

"*Anem.*"

"And the beginning was first contact?"

"*Anem.*"

"I am studying convergence also. I learn your language, not so well, maybe." Stolon chattered their teeth in amusement. "Also I learn path of convergence. Items on checklist, leader Turun Ka says. We have list of steps for convergence, and each of us...*jaruvi*...see? Notice...each of us notice what you say and what you do, and we complete checklist. I study this before."

Ey frowned. Ey wanted nothing more than to write this down, to do as ey always had done and incorporate this into a story, but something about this meeting seemed to preclude that possibility. Something about it was meant only for this space.

"I see," ey said. "And that you have two endings implies that there is a goal, *anem?*"

"*Anem.*" Turun Ko lifted its snout. "You will join-converge with us as fifthrace or you will not."

There was silence within that bubble of fast-time, and ey imagined that it was em, Tycho, and Sarah struggling to process this information while the three Artemisians waited patiently for the next step in the conversation—or perhaps the next item on the checklist.

The pressure to ask the correct question weighing down eir shoulders, Codrin nonetheless stood up straighter. "Is there a correct ending?"

A smile tugged at the corner of Artante's mouth, leading to a sense of relief within em. Ey suspected that em asking that very question might have been an item on their list.

"*Unot.* The endings share equality-correctness."

"Will the decision be mutual?" Sarah asked.

"*Ka,* representative Sarah Genet. The decision-ending must be mutual-shared before the Ansible-transmission-mechanisms will be unlocked-ungated-opened on both Castor and Artemis, *anem?*"

"It has to be," Codrin said. "If one side, as a whole, did not want to join, they wouldn't turn on their Ansible for general use."

Artante nodded. "And the other, seeing that, might feel enough unease that the decision would become mutual, even if it had not started that way."

"Are we on the path towards becoming fifthrace, then?" ey asked.

After a pause, Turun Ko said, "The list does not work-function in this way, recorder Codrin Bălan. The decision-inflection-point is preceded by a cloud-tree-collection-net-pile-table-graph of interconnected actions-items-steps."

It took em a few seconds to plow through the litany of synonyms to reach the heart of the statement. "To be clear, there are a bunch of steps leading up to this decision point?"

"*Anem.*"

"Can you tell us what they are?"

"*Nu.* We cannot."

"There are some different shades of meaning to that word, recorder Turun Ko," Sarah said thoughtfully. "'Cannot' can mean that you aren't able to, or that you are unwilling to. Can you expand on that? Are you able to, I mean?"

"We cannot," it repeated, and Codrin once more caught that ghost of a smile on Artante's face.

"Either could be true, but that's not the correct conversation to have right now," ey guessed.

At this Artante laughed. "You learn quickly, recorder Codrin Bălan."

Ey smiled, shrugged. "It's my job to pay attention."

Stolon bobbed their head. "*Anem*, recorder Codrin Bălan. We find patterns and say 'yes yes' or 'no no' and do next thing. You hear, 'this is not time to have that conversation.' We say because we use checklist."

"Alright. You can just call me Codrin, by the way."

"And you can just call me Sarah."

"Tycho."

"*Ka, ka*, can call Stolon also."

"*Aën.* Thank you Codrin. We will continue to use full names during the talks, but you may call me Artante outside of them."

"I will remain-always-be Turun Ko."

There was another moment's silence as they processed and the Artemisians waited. Tycho and Stolon drifted back into quiet conversation, the secondracer plucking at another leaf or two.

There was so much to take in here, but on further examination, it all made quite a bit of sense. The Artemisians had prepared for this event as thoroughly as had the Odists and Jonases. Of course there would be things that would happen—or at least could be reasonably expected to happen—throughout the convergence. The Artemisians simply had a head start in that they had history to lean on: they'd been through at least three convergences prior to this one.

"I don't imagine there was anything like what happened with Answers Will Not Help in your steps," ey said, finally.

"*Nu.* There are analogous-similar topics. Psychosis and time-sickness have been seen-observed in the past. This is why quitting-exiting-death are prevented-illegal in the conference and rest areas. That representative Answers Will Not Help quit-exited-died is upsetting-distressing-concerning. Representative Iska has undertaken the task of exploring-examining the event."

"Right. I'm sure True Name and Turun Ka are discussing this, too."

Artante shook her head. "They are having a different discussion. It is not the time for them to have the conversation of steps and checklists."

Sarah frowned. "Should we tell her about this discussion?"

After a hesitation, the fourtracer replied, "There are steps on the checklist for if you do and if you do not."

Sounds like a no, then, Codrin thought, working to maintain a neutral expression. For all their talk about staying away from manipulation and subtlety, there sure seemed to be plenty going. It was as Tycho said: they seemed to be working on some higher level, less comprehensible to em as a mere mortal. Ey supposed five thousand years of flying around through space would change how one engages with the world no matter what.

"And how about you two?" ey said.

Turun Ko tilted its head far to the side. "*Lubaenåtam?*"

"Do you two have steps of your own? Desired outcomes?"

"You ask an interesting question," Artante said, sounding thoughtful. "I want what's best, and with each passing conversation between delegations, the meaning of 'what's best' shifts. I'm sorry that I can't put it more clearly than that, though I can assure you that I consider us to be together in this: what's best for the Artemisians will also be what's best for you."

"And you, Turun Ko?"

It straightened up, joints and synthetic flesh shifting smoothly in a well-articulated dance, as though it was running through some internal checklist to correct its posture. "I want-desire stories. There is no combination of steps-items on our list that will not result-in-lead-to stories, so I will not be disappointed. I have received-learned many already, and I am content-happy-satisfied-fulfilled and will remain-continue-to-be so even if you become-turn-into the most exceptionallystupendously boring-droll numbskulls-sadsacks-dipshits in the visible-observable universe."

Codrin and Sarah both stared at the firstracer before laughing, joined by Artante. Even the fourthracer seemed taken aback by the sudden injection of humor.

"I guess we have proven interesting, if nothing else," Sarah said.

"*Anem*," Turun Ko confirmed, and the single word came out nearly a song.

Conversation waned. Silence. Comfortable. Warm. The six of them seemed content to bask and watch the shadows of leaves play on the wall. Ey was tired, ey realized. Dreadfully exhausted. The warmth of the sun, even standing up, seemed to be doing its best to lull em to sleep. Stolon also seemed to be enjoying it quite a bit, stretching languidly, speaking lazily.

"I am not worrying." They poked a torn bit of the leaf into their mouth and chewed thoughtfully before spitting it out with a choking sound. "*Natarla...*"

Laughing, Tycho said, "Not so tasty?"

"*Nu, nu*," Stolon said, chattering their teeth again.

Codrin shook emself to wakefulness, rubbing at eir face with a hand. "Why aren't you worried?"

The thirdracer shrugged, tail flipping about in a wide arc as they rolled over onto their back, flexible enough to drape over the windowsill and sun their belly that way. "Convergence is convergence. Is to be happy and safe, *anem?* Is for leaders and representatives. Scientist, am not worrying. Stars are not lying. Artemis is not lying. Physics is not lying. If you do not join Artemis, will, *lu*...think about? Will think about you, but good to be happy and safe, and science is not lying."

Throughout Stolon's short speech, Tycho sat up straighter, his grin growing wider. "Yeah, I like that. Science is not lying. It can't, really, can it? Politics can lie, and maybe that's why I hate it so much."

"*Ka, ka.*"

"And I'd think about you too, if things go that direction. I honestly didn't really think about that being on the table until after the conference started and we began actually interacting with each other, and now I have to admit that I'm really hoping it *does* work out. For us joining, I mean. I like it here."

The two scientists seemed to have fallen back into their own world, leaving the others to stand by and watch.

"Two of a kind," ey heard Sarah murmur, and ey nodded, grinning along with her.

"Is home, *anem.* I am liking it, but I am also only living here."

Tycho nodded, "I'm only on Castor and Pollux, yeah."

"Is Pollux same?"

"Yeah, they started out identical, but they've diverged over time." He frowned, shrugged. "I bet Tycho#Pollux is feeling awful now, missing all of this."

"No Tycho on Lagrange construct?"

"Nope, I invested fully. Did you leave an instance of yourself back on your original system?"

"*Lu*...yes, but they exited after convergence and distance grew. Friends say that Stolon got sad, spent all of time thinking about Artemis." They lifted their snout to peer up at him. "Tycho will join if possible, *anem?*"

Codrin also looked to Tycho. The astronomer was already grinning widely. It was far more positive emotion than ey'd seen on his face to date, and ey couldn't imagine any other answer than what came next.

"*Anem!* Of course I will."

Ioan Bălan — 2346

Convergence T-plus 72 days, 23 hours, 48 minutes
(Lagrange–Pollux transmission delay: 30 days, 14 hours, 41 minutes)

Ioan,

I must admit, I'm really not sure what to say about all of this. Thank you for waiting until you have a substantial amount to send to me, at least. Dear threw a little tantrum about this "We have received messages over the last few days" bit, but I appreciate having an initial digest to work with so that I'm not left a fretting mess (as you say you were) by the simple news that, oh look, aliens! I threatened to bundle it up in blankets until it was immobile for a few hours, though, and it calmed down. I may do so anyway.

Four races! Five thousand years! One language! Have you learned any of that, yourself? And yet maybe it's all a dream! Truly fascinating. As you can imagine, Dear latched onto that quite quickly.

How is May Then My Name taking it? You mention True Name, but have you heard from any other Odists? Any other friends? If Lagrange is anything like Pollux, people are talking about little else.

The news broke over here much as it sounds as though it did on Lagrange: with tightly controlled excitement. There is no doubt that the powers that be continue their work across all three Systems, but it's always fascinating to see. The amount of bafflement was outweighed by the amount of excitement. The excitement also outweighed the amount of fear. Everyone's eager for every scrap of news that they can get.

How much of the delay in sending word to us was due to True Name and her friends? I imagine she had words about the first message, at least, but a whole week's worth of messages feels like a good deal must have been going on.

No matter, though. We're all eagerly awaiting every little snippet that we can get from you. I know that you won't get this for another, what, 30? 31? And that a month from when you sent it! I know you won't get it for a while, is what I'm saying, but please know that you're free to pass on information directly from here on out! We'll be learning plenty from the news we're allowed to see over here, anyway, so any juicy tidbits in addition to that will be greatly appreciated.

I am continually confronted with the ways in which we have diverged. May Then My Name and Dear#Castor mentioned how upset they were by the idea of time manipulation, but my Dear...well, it did not seem pleased with the idea, but its reaction was not nearly so visceral. It simply got a sour look on its face and said *"I do not like the idea of a place where I cannot fork. Can you imagine a place so boring?"*

BĂLAN CLADE-EYES-ONLY MATERIAL

The last few years have seen a drastic reduction in the amount of times that Dear has overflowed. I don't know if ey's been passing on every instance from Castor, or if you have been passing on every letter in turn, but it sounds like the same is true of Dear#Castor as well, for which I'm thankful.

I'm sorry to hear about May Then My Name, though. Discussion of 'cracks showing' always seems to crop up whenever one of our loved ones goes through a rough period such as this, and your news spurred a conversation between the three of us plus Serene, and despite the relative quiescence of Dear's symptoms, such as they are, we have noticed an uptick of oddities in Odists over here, as well. Not just Odists, of course, but a few of the older clades. Hell, a Jonas even went haywire a few weeks back.

Still, I'm happy to hear that everyone's tallies are lining up well: far fewer old clades over here are experiencing such symptoms than feared after the publication of *Perils*, for which just about everyone is happy. No one wants to deal with an impending burden of insanity on one's two hundredth birthday, so to hear that it's only a fraction and that maybe there's something that can be done (or so we hear; has there been news of psychotherapy as a treatment over there? I've been hearing whispers) has kept the population at large from freaking out. I imagine you have it worse, though, given the relative skew towards dispersionistas on the LVs; I bet early taskers are freaking out.

Either way, Ioan, I am concerned for you and your partner. Our lives are informed by trauma, and the trauma that we hold in particular leads to a sort of conservatism that is particularly focused on our loved ones. I know that you want nothing more than to see May Then My Name continue to thrive, and I know that seeing her struggle is incredibly painful as it touches on the roots of those very same traumas. I know that the two of you will make it through alright, but, as this is in the clade-eyes-only section, do remember to keep yourself safe. You have Douglas. You have Debarre and End Waking (are they back together? Please say yes). You have A Finger Pointing. You have so many delightful friends I've yet to even meet and some I'll never have the chance to. When you need, nudge May Then My Name to her support network and lean on your own.

IOAN BĂLAN INDIVIDUAL-EYES-ONLY MATERIAL

The following is in strict confidence with you and you alone, Ioan. I've received permission to share from all parties involved.

I don't know how much of Codrin#Castor and my messages between each other that you've read, or if that would even have helped, but watching the slow individuation of a loved one is an experience unique even from watching oneself individuate. The Dear I am in love with feels much like the Dear I fell in love with decades ago, and yet slowly the Dear on Castor begins to feel like a stranger to me.

Dear#Castor sounds so much more conservative—in its approach to life, of course, rather than that of the division of the Odists—than what I've grown used to. The prairie remains the same. The house remains the same. Codrin#Castor's struggles with agency and directedness in life feel as unfamiliar to me as you have mentioned. You have taken control of your life as I have taken control of my own, each in our own way. To put this on the Odists feels at once unfair, unfortunate, and totally accurate. May Then My Name has changed you in so many irreversible ways, just as Dear changed me so many years ago. Changed you, too, for when we merged and then diverged, you were no longer the same Ioan that remained behind. You were the type of Ioan who could fall in love with May Then My Name in the first place.

So when Dear gave up the prairie and dragged Serene over to build out our little world into something grander, a place more well-rounded than just flat plains, we were both ready because, hey, this was Dear, right? So we built out our little world of plains and hills, forests and lakes. And then that spur-of-the-moment shift redirected our lives in unforeseen ways. With the acceptance of variety, Serene moved in to continue her work, and then her elliptical orbit passed through our lives for a while before she drifted away again.

Despite lingering taboo, I am not ashamed of having wound up, for that one short year, in a relationship with two members of the same clade. None of us are; not even Dear and Serene, they promise us. It's not shame that keeps me from telling those on Castor about this. It is the completely alien way that those who feel as though they ought to *be* us interact with the world that leads to such. I feel as though I am unable to tell Codrin#Castor about what happened because to do so feels like explaining the alien to someone who really, truly, in all ways ought to know. Ey ought to be able to feel the same things that I feel, correct? Ey ought to also love Serene, oughtn't ey? Ey must, for ey is me, is ey not?

And yet ey is not. I cannot bring up our relationship with Serene because Codrin#Castor—that is, specifically *me*#Castor— does not have the same thoughts around intraclade romantic relationships that I do, and by virtue of the direction that the Odists steered us (or, as feels more accurate, crashed with us headlong and heedless) into this future, we are now completely different in that way.

The Dear that I live with has, in comparison to Dear#Castor, relaxed and moved on to an approach to life that is far more laid back. As a result, we *all* have, me included.

Also, as an internal postscript, I should note that the three of us are all still deeply in love with Serene and she with us, so please do not misconstrue the past tense above, but good Lord. Two foxes in the same house? Never again.

This is the end of the private content of the letter. Please redact this in its entirety should you pass my thoughts on to Castor (though of course you may talk about it with May Then My Name; she'll understand the sensitive nature of the topic).

END IOAN BĂLAN INDIVIDUAL-EYES-ONLY MATERIAL

END BĂLAN CLADE-EYES-ONLY MATERIAL

I am settling in quite well at the university and they are as excited as I am to receive the inevitable dump of information that comes from Artemis. It is a librarian's dream. I have seen quite the bump in my reputation, oddly enough, just by having my co-cladist's name attached to the project over on Castor. No complaints, but honestly, what is a librarian to do with reputation?

Pass on our love to May Then My Name and tell her that we are all incredibly happy to hear that there is no more news of broken noses in this letter.

Codrin#Castor, know that you've got us backing you as well. The world lies before you and is not nearly so black and white as it might seem. Search for those shades of gray that allow you to take a step forward.

It's been more than twenty years (or forty, if you count splitting from you, Ioan), and it still feels incredibly weird talking myself up, doesn't it? If nothing else, take it from yourself that it's possible.

Cheers,

Codrin#Pollux

Codrin,

Wonderful as always to hear from you. This will, of course, reach you long after the point where I could answer any pertinent questions about Artemis that I have not already done so by forwarding on what I've learned, myself. The amount of updates quickly got to the point where it didn't feel worth it to try and summarize them at all, so you're getting them all. Besides, you can summarize as well as I.

Dramatic, isn't it? Convergence! I just sent you a letter earlier today about the latest from Tycho on Artemis, so I don't have too much to add, really.

I'm curious about how things are working out over there with True Name and the leadership. We haven't heard anything yet from Castor about how she's doing over there, but it's always good to get a fuller picture of how things are going when they are, yet again, involved in something enormous.

Hell, on that note, how is the sentiment overall? There's been a lot of chatter; on the night of the announcement, we had to cancel a performance due to how excited everyone was. A Finger Pointing was quick to capitalize this, and went on a tear of digging up every single production that she could find about aliens to start scheduling. When she found a relative paucity of such, she started digging into sci-fi, going all the way back to

R.U.R. I have, surprising no one, been contracted to write one for the occasion, and I've been doing so with what information that I have.

(Also, to your question: yes, End Waking and Debarre have settled back into dating. I do wish you'd gotten a chance to meet End Waking. He is a delight to be around in his own coarse, woodsy way.)

I'll pass on the snippets of secondrace language that I've received so far. Codrin promises that the grammar and dictionary will be forthcoming (probably in the next few days, if I'm calculating the transmission times right, but says that True Name has suggested that any large messages from Artemis be sent after a thorough evaluation. I can't tell if that means an evaluation of their contents or an evaluation of any hidden intent on the part of the Artemisians.

BĂLAN CLADE-EYES-ONLY MATERIAL

CODRIN BĂLAN#POLLUX INDIVIDUAL-EYES-ONLY MATERIAL

This is in confidence.

It was interesting hearing the story of your triad (is it still a triad? I was unable to parse to what extent Serene may still be a part of your little polycule, though it does sound as though there is a healthier distance between you all now) in your words. Serene actually contacted us a few months back to pass on the story, herself, also in confidence. She made us promise to keep it to ourselves, even from you. I pinged her with the fact that your letter contained this information to make sure that I could confirm this with you, and she said yes.

I found the whole story as she told it to be terribly fascinating. There was a brief twinge of surprise at the idea of an intra-clade relationship, but it was not the first that I've heard of since Launch. They're hardly common back here, but neither are they unheard of as individuation increases and taboos lessen. Still, this is the closest that we've been to one. No friends, even, just right into our own clades.

It sparked a long, drawn out discussion between May, Douglas and I, actually. Less, I think, because there was any chance of that between the three of us than because Douglas is hungry for essentially every bit of information about the clade that he can get his hands on—though, May being May, she would leap at the chance to get closer to him, but the most he is comfortable with from anyone is friendship and physical affection (he will pet May for hours if she'll let him—and she always does).

On my end, I was mostly interested in May's thoughts on the matter as, except for a drunken (very drunken) night with A Finger Pointing, the two of us together have at most friendly relationships with any other Odist. We've not talked about that night with anyone else, either, and hardly even with each other. When I brought it up, both May and A Finger Pointing laughed at me and told me to "get the fuck over it" because apparently that's just how theatre nerds are.

However, when I asked May about it directly, she confided in me (and again, the anxious part of me compels me to note that I have permission to share this) that nearly seven decades back, she was nudged toward another Odist (one from the first stanza, though she did not specify which) by True Name, and a fork of her remained in a relationship with them for some time. Perhaps they are still together. May does not know. When pressed as to how this worked, she said that the instance who began that relationship was "no longer me". I did not ask further.

Either way, it's something of a relief to be able to talk about this openly (or, well 'openly') with you. Keeping a secret about one's own cocladist from them is uncomfortable.

That digression aside, I take well your meaning about the divergence of Castor and Pollux. I see the divergence in you two, and while it has mostly just been an interesting point to consider at times, occasionally it becomes very pertinent very quickly. I have often admired the ways in which you moved beyond the Bălans of old. It's nice to see proof that we can truly own our lives—which is not to say that I don't feel that about myself, but in comparison with #Castor's current malaise, it comes in stark contrast.

I don't know how Dear would take a nudge from you, and it certainly isn't my place, but I do plan on helping Codrin over there however I can. I've been discussing this with May as well, and we are brainstorming suggestions for new paths for em. I don't think that ey could manage hopping right into life in academia as you have, both because of the differences in the university between the two LVs as well as the differences in your histories over the last few decades.

I also want to discuss this with May as well, though I will await your permission. I do not think that she is at as much risk of conservatism as it sounds like Dear#Castor is, but there have been several conversations between us now regarding the directions that the clade that I'll speak to in normal clade-eyes-only, as I plan on sharing these messages with #Castor.

I'll keep you up to date either way.

END CODRIN BĂLAN#POLLUX INDIVIDUAL-EYES-ONLY MATERIAL

While I'm sure that another Odist has already passed on this information, you should know that two Odists have quit recently, May One Day Death Itself Not Die and I Do Not Know, I Do Not Know, leaving behind no forks. The Ode is now ninety-seven.

May and In Dreams were there at the end, and this has led to an increased sense of urgency when it comes to the clade approaching their affliction. To that end, several Odists are working with a psychologist recommended from folks on Castor (the Sarah Genet mentioned in the messages I've been forwarding) to discuss paths forward.

These events took place during May's aforementioned overflowing spell, which led to it being prolonged to nearly a week. She has made it through, and my nose remains intact despite getting tackled, as usual. She has recovered well despite some lingering depression, but this, in combination with some of the news from Castor which you also will have received before this, has me more worried for her than usual. She may be a little terror, but she is my little terror.

All of them seem to be dealing with this in their own way. May and Dear overflow in their own ways, End Waking's desire for solitude will override his relationship with Debarre for a time, and now this over on the Death Itself stanza.

Can you do me a favor when you get a chance, and let me know how True Name#Pollux is doing in this respect in particular? Doesn't need to be anything too in-depth, but, well, she is a part of this as always, and clearly there is something going on with her here.

END BĂLAN CLADE-EYES-ONLY MATERIAL

Pass on my love. I miss you and yours.
Ioan Bălan

Codrin Bălan#Castor — 2346

Convergence T-minus 0 days, 2 hours, 53 minutes

Despite the burst of excitement, the talks remained surprisingly banal. Even when the topic of the Odists' deception and the troubles that True Name#Artemis still suffered on Artemis arose, the talks still felt like a political summit. The conference was still a conference, with its cloth-covered table and shitty pens, its uncomfortable chairs and weary participants.

Ey counted emself among the weariest of them all. Tycho was still in his stride, and Sarah was keeping up well enough, though she remained fairly quiet throughout, focusing on watching rather than speaking or taking notes. Why Ask Questions had proceeded as though the news had never happened, continuing on in her litany of questions around biology and linguistics. In fact, the only one more tired seemed to be True Name.

There was a tension around the skunk's eyes, a tightness to the cheeks that ever so slightly drew her lips back. Even when she smiled, her expression remained fixed and rigid.

It made sense, after all. Acting in the capacity of leader was more than just overseeing the talks, it meant wrangling every conversation, and still managing to keep up her own side of it. Beyond even that, the skunk had been drawn into several conversations alone with Turun Ka over the final hours of the third day. Ey hadn't expected the conference to include anyone but the entirety of both the parties, so ey wasn't quite sure what to make of this, but none of the other Artemisians seemed unnerved by the leaders stepping aside in half-hour increments to hold what appeared to be—at least from True Name's expressions—in-depth conversations about very serious topics.

Sleep brought little relief.

The beds were comfortable, but empty. There was no wind against glass, no crickets stilled to silence with the passing of some imagined bat. There was no fox to curl around, no soft sounds of breathing.

Ey plowed through two cups of (thankfully quite good) coffee on the morning of the fourth day, and brought a third with em to the conference table.

The talks were slow to resume. There were a few halting attempts at starting up conversations about astrochemistry, but neither Tycho nor Stolon were well-versed on it enough to have the conversation without additional research first.

Why had they divided the subjects between the locations? ey wondered for the dozenth time. *I'm sure that every one of us wants nothing more than to ask about the history of their trip, just as I'm sure that there are topics surrounding science that those on Artemis would love to ask about.*

It seemed such a strange limitation to put on talks such as these. Why divide them by subject when the participants were identical? Were there deeper reasons beneath this? Was there a logic to having the discussions of science on Castor as opposed to on Artemis? Was it so that the less-advanced Castor would still benefit from the science and Artemis from culture if the talks went pear-shaped?

Questions such as these littered the verso pages of eir notebook, the recto pages reserved for notes about the topic at hand. Ey'd sent dozens of those questions over to Artemis already; it certainly didn't seem as though this was the place to ask them.

Answers had been sparse. The responses had invariably been "it is not the time for that conversation". At least the most recent note from Codrin#Artemis—running at nearly three pages—had explained the use of that sentence, as well as so much else. Checklists and goals, indeed.

It had also contained a more detailed account of Answers Will Not Help's breakdown and quitting, as well as the extended interactions with True Name that Codrin#Artemis had been having.

"I hate to do this to you," ey had written, individual-eyes only. "But I simply cannot overstate just how dramatic and anxiety-inducing the whole event was, and I mean this in the most literal way possible. There are things that I cannot tell you. I cannot put them into words, and I certainly cannot set them to paper. It is overwhelming. The import is crushing. I feel like I'm going to burst and there's nothing I can do or say about it, and the only reason I'm describing it like this is that I *can't* be the only one who knows this, even if only at one layer removed. You will remember soon enough, I think, but until then, I just need to offload some of the pressure."

Ey had no idea what to do with this information, other than to accept a share in that load.

With questions running thin and the table plagued by awkward silences, it was almost a relief when Turun Ka requested that it and True Name discuss sentiment shaping surrounding the arrival of Artemis, leaving the others to have a conversation of their own or not as they wished. There was no explicit communication suggesting such, but it seemed implied whenever this happened that Codrin and Turun Ko would be left 'in charge' of their respective delegations, if there was such a thing.

The skunk and firstracer stood and walked to the far side of the fountain where True Name could sit on the rim and Turun Ka could settle onto its haunches before her. They set up a cone of silence, and once more begin discussing what seemed to go beyond simply the fallout of deception.

After a few more minutes of silence. Why Ask Questions stood, said that she was going to take the opportunity to get another glass of water, and wandered off without another word.

That seemed to be signal enough, despite the deputization of the recorders, for everyone to take a break. Tycho and Stolon paired off immediately, already chatting about albedo or some other topic ey could not guess. Iska excused themself and returned to their rest area.

Codrin closed eir notebook, finished eir coffee, and scrubbed at eir face with eir hands.

"Alright," ey said. "Would it be alright if I ask you an off-the-record question, recorder Turun Ko?"

"*Ka,* you may. I may want-need to defer-delay response."

"Of course, that's fine. Why are we divided like this?"

"Please explain-expand, recorder Codrin Bălan."

"Why only talk science here on Castor and leave history and society to the talks on Artemis?"

"It is not the time to have that conversation."

Codrin did eir best to restrain a sigh. "But it *is* a conversation? There is a reason for it?"

"*Anem.*"

"If I ask you—you as Turun Ko, not in your capacity as recorder, or even you, Artante Diria—questions about the topics that are being covered on Artemis, would you be able to answer?"

"*Ka,*" they both said at once. Artante picked up after that, "We might defer, as is our habit, but it would be impossible for the formal discussion to be the only context in which we communicate. Even if it were, there are layers to communication that go beyond words. We are learning some of each others' non-verbal communication, *anem?*"

Ey nodded. "*Anem.* My counterpart on Artemis has written me regarding a sort of checklist that you are following when it comes to the convergence. Is this true?"

Artante sat up straighter, sharing a meaningful glance with

Turun Ko. "Yes, recorder Codrin Bălan. There are steps that we have noticed in convergences in the past and, in order to be prepared, we maintain a list of these that we look for throughout the process."

"And to confirm, the possible outcomes are us joining you as fifthrace or not?"

Sarah leaned forward onto her elbows, watching the conversation with an intense curiosity.

"*Anem.* We will converge-join-together or we will not," Turun Ko said.

"I'm guessing that asking what items are on the checklist isn't really on the docket," ey hazarded.

Artante nodded.

"That's alright," ey said. "I'm sure True Name and the others in charge on our end had their own checklist that they're keeping up with."

"If you have wargamed, as you have said, then almost certainly."

Ey mulled over eir next question for a moment, considering as many ramifications as ey could, given the knowledge of this checklist. Finally, ey asked, "Are convergences only named such if a race joins you on Artemis?"

There was a brief flicker of some emotion ey couldn't decode on Artante's face. It was almost a smile, almost pride, almost contentment, but it was quickly replaced by the polite expression she seemed to wear at all other times. "It is not the time to have that conversation. We will soon, I suspect."

"It seems pretty easy to read between the lines on that answer," Sarah said gently. "Though I don't suppose it can be helped."

Artante spread her hands over the table, palms up. "As I said before, it would be impossible for the formal discussion to be the only context in which we communicate."

"Text and metatext," Codrin mumbled, and with that, an idea dropped, fully-formed, onto em. Ey could feel the weight of it land on eir shoulders, the import of it digging into eir back like claws. Ey sat up straighter. "With the understanding that there are correct times for conversations, may I *give* you information for you to access at those times?"

The fourthracer looked to Turun Ko, who raised its chin in assent. "You may, recorder Codrin Bălan."

Ey nodded, hoping against hope that ey even had the ACLs to do as ey'd planned. Ey knew that ey could create as much paper as ey wanted, though ey wasn't sure whether ey'd be able to create paper with text already on it. Ey knew that ey could create notepads, but had yet to try creating a notebook, as ey hadn't finished the current one yet.

Nothing for it but to try.

A desire to create a hardbound book was rejected, but the desire to create a soft-cover book seemed to be available to em. Text was a bit more difficult to guess at without testing, so ey brushed eir hand across the table, projecting the intent for a sheet of paper with the word 'TEST' written across the top.

Success.

"Alright. One moment, please."

Ey rifled through eir exos until ey found the correct ones and, with a single wave of intent, dumped their contents along with the desire for a softbound book into reality, lifting, one at a time, two books from the surface of the table. They were far from fancy, but their utility was all that mattered.

"This is the first volume of *An Expanded History of Our World*, a text containing a succinct description of the series of events that led from the creation of our System to the launch of Castor and Pollux." Ey handed the book over to Turun Ko, then handed the other to Artante, saying, "And this is *An Expanded Mythology of Our World*, which contains many of the same stories as the *History* as told through the framework of myth and legend. Together, they make up *On the Origin of Our World*."

The silence around the table was profound. Both Artemisians looked at the books they held, as if still internalizing the import of what they'd been handed. Sarah looked startled, even anxious.

"What is the nature-disposition of this document?" Turun Ko asked at last.

"It's a narrative of the overall history of our System from a social and political perspective. The first volume is a summary constructed from interviews conducted with those who uploaded in the very first days of the System's existence all the way up to those who had uploaded the year before it was written."

"Codrin," Sarah said quietly. "Are you sure that's such a good idea?"

Artante looked between them, picking up on the anxiety. "May I ask as to the import beyond its contents?"

"It...doesn't exactly paint the prettiest picture of some aspects of the System," Sarah said, audibly hunting for a diplomatic way to phrase it. "It led to a reevaluation of the...political nature of our lives."

Ey tensed, realising the import of what Sarah was getting at. While there were countless reminders as to the books impact on the Ode clade, it had always seemed an unintentional side-effect of what was otherwise a text that strove to be above all else an accurate historical document. It was bound up in those who had lived those lives, those who had been influenced by the Odists.

Ey'd meant to provide it strictly in that historical sense, but realized that, in the context of her deception, the discussion of True Name and her friends guiding the trajectory of society within them might color the talks moving forward.

No, ey thought. *This goes beyond the Odists and all their schemes.*

"It's important," ey said decisively. Sitting up straighter, ey drew on all the gumption ey could. "It shows more than just the political lives we've led, including the behind-the-scenes guidance that True Name has engaged in from the origins of the System two hundred thirty years ago. This is as important as anything else when it comes to understanding us as a species."

Sarah's frown deepened. "Which is why I question the wisdom of providing it at this point."

"We're at an impasse, I think," ey countered. "We haven't had a single meaningful conversation as part of the talks since news of what happened on Artemis arrived. It feels like we're waiting on some cue, like we're expected to do something."

Artante was nodding, though whether in confirmation or agreement, ey couldn't tell.

"This feels like a dangerous way to force the conversation to move forward."

Ey shrugged, holding onto that courage and sense of right action. "They deserve to know more than just the synopses and sugar-coated aspects of our society. The thing with Answers Will Not Help is something she and True Name dreamt up, but not representative of us as a whole. We're more complex as a species than just her, or than even the five of us."

Flipping through the pages at the rate of about one per second, Turun Ko said, "A conversation will happen-occur when leaders Turun Ka and True Name return shortly-momentarily. Please wait. Their conversation-discussion is artificial-superficial, intended to give-provide delegates other than leadership options to change-shape outcomes."

Ey stared at the firstracer. "You mean–"

"A step in the process of convergence is assessing the willingness of non-leaders to act other than their leaders might or even against the stated structure of the discussions in order to forward what they believe the good common to all races," Artante said. "It allows us to assess the strength of individuality and self-sacrifice for the betterment of all."

"Opportunities were provided," Turun Ko said simply.

That feeling of being in way over eir head that ey had felt so often during the writing of the *History* hit em full force once more and, stunned to silence, ey leaned back in eir chair, looking between the Artemisians and Sarah.

"So," the psychologist began. "Is this a good step?"

"Please wait," Turun Ko repeated, then lifted its head and glanced over toward Turun Ka.

This must've been a signal of some sort, as the other firstracer held up a hand to stop the conversation it was having with True Name, gesturing her back to the table.

The skunk was halfway through the act of pulling out her chair before she noticed the books that the other Artemisians held, the titles in bold on their covers. Her gaze whipped toward Codrin so quickly and with such fiery intensity that ey shied away from her. "Codrin, what–"

"Leader True Name," Turun Ka said, interrupting her gently, but with enough authority that she stopped immediately. "This is the penultimate item on the checklist of convergence that we were just discussing. All that remains is the point of decision."

Ey watched as the skunk's eyes widened, gaze darting between em, Turun Ka, and the book in Turun Ko's hands, now about half-finished. She sat down heavily on the chair and sagged against the back. "Well, fuck me."

Tycho Brahe#Artemis — 2346

Convergence T-minus 0 days, 0 hours, 18 minutes

Tycho awoke with the idea fully formed within himself.

So sudden was the realization that his immediate instinct was to shove it to the back of his mind and do his level best to forget about it. He didn't want to admit it to True Name, to Sarah or Stolon, and even Codrin, grounding as ey was, seemed to be too real to discuss it with.

He barely even wanted to admit it to himself. Didn't want to name it, put words to it.

So he resigned himself to sitting through the meeting, trying not to look too uncomfortable as the lump of an idea sat within his gut, making itself known every time he moved, every time he thought.

He was thankful that him having been relatively quiet to date meant that him staying quiet now was not out of the ordinary.

During the first break of the morning, he retreated to the rest area rather than meeting with Stolon, requesting some distance to organize his thoughts.

He skewed mildly positive and lay on his bed for a while, letting the quiet of the room in so that he could finally admit the idea for full consideration.

The path leading up to it had been laid long before, he realized. It had been laid when he first learned about the concept of convergence. Perhaps it was at the time of his first ineffable idea more than three weeks back, when he first granted consent to four alien races to board the LV.

Or perhaps even before that. Perhaps it was something integral to him, something about what made him *him.* Some fundamental unhappiness with his life as it was. Not just the inability to see the stars, not just the feeling of being trapped, or whatever it was that had required the self-actualization of changing his name so many years ago.

I am not who I used to be, he had thought at the time. *I am no longer the me who uploaded. I am the me who had grown to recognize his own limitations. I am Tycho Brahe.*

That didn't apply here; he was who he'd always been. This decision had been with him from birth.

He left his bed, left the rest area and returned to the meeting, with no more answers than he'd entered with, only more confusion.

When he returned to the table, Codrin was standing anxiously by as Turun Ka read through a sheet of paper that, he assumed, ey had just handed it. A questioning glance at em gained only a minuscule shrug. Ey didn't know either.

He collapsed limply into his chair once more and waited for the other delegates to arrive. True Name looked somewhat refreshed from the previous day, though still exhausted, and Sarah looked as anxious as Codrin, though he could hardly guess why.

Stolon, at best guess, simply looked bored and antsy. They kept glancing at him questioningly, and he gave his best smile in return, hoping that it'd at least reassure them a little bit.

"The talks progress. Does anyone have any topics for this next segment of the discussions?" Turun Ka asked.

"I do," Sarah said. "How do you deal with restlessness?"

332

"Can you describe what you mean, representative Sarah Genet?"

"Yes. When one grows bored and unhappy with their current situation, yet with no clear idea of where to go next, it can lead to a feeling of restlessness. I mean this primarily in an existential way, rather than a practical one. Desiring getting away from scarcity to plenty is not what I'd call restlessness, but a desire to change one's surroundings because one knows the current ones too well, for example, is. Boredom and ennui are other terms."

He tentatively tried labeling the idea that coiled within him with 'restlessness' and found that it fit all too well. It expanded, rose, pressed against his chest from the inside. He tried, unsuccessfully, to swallow it down. It was quickly becoming too much. Too big. Too strong to keep within him.

"We are well aware of this feeling," Artante was saying. "After millennia, one gets bored easily, and there's–"

"I want to stay here," he interrupted, surprising even himself. "Even if we don't become fifthrace or anything. I want to stay here. I want to stay on Artemis."

Stunned silence fell around the table. Even he felt some of that shock. The words were out of his mouth before he'd even had the chance to check them for truth, and yet they bore as much truth as any mathematical theorem that he knew. They were *true.* They were *correct.* They were *anemla.*

"I also want for us to be fifthrace, I mean," he added, voice quieter. "I want this convergence to wind up with that ending of the two. I want to join you, and I want *us* to join you."

"Tycho," True Name said, voice low. "I understand that the talks are long, but I think there is time yet for that decision."

"Maybe," he said, shrugging. "But if I didn't say so, I was going to burst."

Another silence. It felt uncomfortable on their side of the table, and yet the Artemisians had already spun up to fast time, some quite high skew.

"Sorry," he mumbled.

True Name shrugged. "You are allowed to express your desires. I am simply concerned that this was not the best time for it."

"I understand."

They waited in uncomfortable silence.

"I don't know that I'll join personally," Codrin said after the Artemisians spun down but before they answered. "But I want that outcome, too. It's been dogging me all morning. I think Tycho just got to it before me."

"You want your race to be fifthrace even if you don't join?" Artante asked.

Ey nodded. "I'm surprised at how much I like it here. I could see myself living here, even. Just that joining would mean leaving behind at least one, and probably both, of my partners. Dear is an Odist, and would likely experience what True Name and Answers Will Not Help are—or did. I'm not sure that I could stomach that. Still, it's incredibly alluring, and speaks to the romantic in me. A meeting of species and cultures from light years apart, and little old us having the chance to be a part of that."

Artante looked toward Sarah expectantly.

"I find it fascinating here. I find this whole process of convergence fascinating, and I would find the process of integration even more so. I think that's why I brought up restlessness. One of Codrin's partners said, shortly after we first made contact, *'When I hear about Artemisians and emissaries, I feel every minute of that eternity. I feel every molecule of that universe. You ask how I feel, and I would say that I feel small. Insignificant, even. How much of that eternity must they have been traveling?'* My response at the time was to toast to that, 'To eternity and the weight of the universe'. I'd still give that toast now." She shrugged, looking a little sheepish at her small speech. "So yes, I want that too, and I'd send a fork to join."

"Leader True Name?"

The skunk sat in silence, her head bowed and her eyes

closed. If it weren't for the way her ears twitched this way and that as though tallying some internal checklist of her own, he might've suspected that she'd nodded off.

"I must confess that I may have forgotten what it is like to want a thing," she said at last. "I do not know what it is that I want. I cannot stay here, as is plainly evident, but I do not know what I want."

Codrin nodded. "May I quote from the *History?*"

She sighed, nodded.

"Both you and Jonas mentioned the concepts of stability and continuity during several interviews. We summarized it as, "Beyond all else, the driving factors behind Launch—and, indeed, Secession—were those of stability and continuity of the System. That life should continue, that we should continue to thrive, was the goal of those working on both projects from start to finish." Do you still want that? Becoming fifthrace as a stable and continuous society feels analogous, *anem?*"

The longer ey spoke, the more True Name seemed to perk up. By the end of eir recitation, she was sitting up straight and had a smile on her muzzle. It was slight, true, and still tired, but it was an honest smile.

"I do, yes. Thank you, Codrin. Then yes, I want that outcome as well." To the Artemisians, she said, "We began the project of Launch as a way to divest. We wanted to ensure the continuity of our species and the Systems that we live on—Castor, Pollux, and Lagrange. We want to explore, of course, and we want to change and grow and all that comes with life, but we also want to keep living. I can think of no better opportunity for divestment than tagging along on a millennia-long journey through the galaxy."

Tycho laughed, nodded. "And hey, think of the sights we'll get to see along the way."

"For certain definitions of see, yes." She smiled and shrugged. "Thank you for spurring this discussion, my dear. I do not want to take too much time away from the conference, though, leader Turun Ka. I apologize if we need to get back to the topic at hand."

After the round of answers, there was a long, blurred meeting, and then the Artemisians stood as one, each bowing as their race had when they first entered.

Tycho stood as well, and, after a moment's hesitation, so too did the rest of the table. He didn't know why they were standing and bowing, but it seemed to be what the moment demanded.

Something had happened, just then. Something of import. He had no clue as to what it had been. Neither did he understand how, he realized, but he knew that it was something decisive. Something, perhaps, momentous.

"Leader True Name, as leader of this delegation and member of the Council of Eight," Turun Ka said, voice bearing the weight of ritual. "I would like to formally welcome you aboard Artemis as fifthrace."

True Name stared at it, agog.

Turun Ko picked up from there, its speech suddenly free of doublings-back and duplicated words. "Recorder Codrin Bălan, as recorder of this delegation, I welcome you as a member of fifthrace aboard Artemis. The final step on our checklist was simply a desire to join."

Stolon continued, proceeding down the line. They were bouncing on their feet, teeth chattering, clearly quite excited. "*Ka, ka.* Scientist Tycho Brahe, I am welcoming you as member of fifthrace aboard Artemis. We will dream of stars together."

Tycho's eyes burned as he stood, rigid, and listened to the series of formal declarations. All of the delegates looked overwhelmed, shocked.

"I am not able to speak to representative Why Ask– Answers Will Not Help," Iska said. "So I will speak to all. I welcome you as members of fifthrace aboard Artemis. We, as a society, look forward to learning of your arts."

Artante was crying. Hell, *he* was crying.

"Representative Sarah Genet," she said through the tears. "I welcome you as a member of fifthrace aboard Artemis. You asked us if we dream, and we do. We look forward to dreaming together."

Silence followed the series of formal greetings, broken only by the sound of himself and Artante working to regain their composure.

"I must admit, leader Turun Ka," True Name said, voice hoarse. "I was not expecting this. I had been working under the assumption that we still had several steps to go on your checklist. This feels sudden."

"*This* is the reason for us holding two separate talks in separate locations about separate topics," it said with a hint of a bow. "Working in parallel with different parameters increases the opportunities for forward momentum. The message that I received from Castor via recorder Codrin Bălan mentioned the penultimate step had been reached, that of acting individually for the betterment of all without the blessing of leadership. With that news, we expected that the decision point would be reached today. The opportunities for happiness and safety were created. There will be further talks as long as we are within range, and even after as we join with one another, all of which will simply be between us as species with shared goals rather than delegates."

She and nodded, that faint smile returning. "A sensible approach."

"We have only small time together, *anem?* We must create speed, *anem?*" Stolon said.

"Yes. Well considered. I thank you for your openness."

Turun Ka lifted its snout. "We have passed the point where conversations must wait. All topics are open and more representatives from all races may attend. First, however, recorder Codrin Bălan," Turun Ka said, drawing a sheet of paper from the air before it. "Please send this announcement to Castor by the usual mechanism without encryption, after you have all authenticated the message with a personal detail to ensure that this is viewed as a mutual decision. Please send those signatures encrypted."

True Name accepted the sheet, read through, thought for a moment, then scribbled a short note on the bottom. She handed the sheet to Codrin, who did similar.

When it arrived before him, Tycho skimmed through the letter: "Both parties...agreed...fifthrace...welcome..." followed by a few blocks of unsettled text that he supposed must be the eyes-only signatures of the Artemisians and the other two emissaries before him.

What could he possibly write that would ensure that Tycho#Castor knew the letter was verifiable? He looked around at the other emissaries, thought back through the last few weeks, and wrote: "Remember what you told Codrin during eir interview: imagine sitting at home, knowing that you could have flung yourself off into space, out among the dangers and excitement, and choosing instead that boring safety? Well, here we are."

He passed the note on to Sarah, who affixed her signature and handed it back to Codrin. Ey held it briefly, looking to be deep in thought, then nodded. "It has been sent, leader Turun Ka."

"Tycho," True Name said, loud enough for all to hear. "Do you remember the poem I quoted to you the night of first contact?"

He nodded.

"The final two lines of the fourth stanza are the most commonly quoted: Though my soul may set in darkness, it will rise in perfect light; I have loved–"

"I have loved the stars too fondly to be fearful of the night," he finished, grinning. "That was the last thing I said before uploading. It'll be the last thing I'll say before I leave Castor."

Part IV

Integration

"How far, how far, how far away?" became the refrain of the sailors. "How far away are these campfires of the others? They must be impossibly far. They must be bound in impossible night, for we have seen the sun neither rise nor set, nor have we seen their campfires dim or fade, nor have we seen them blaze into new light."

And yet they sailed on in their ark of dreams, calling out into the vast blackness that had long since enveloped even them. And in their ark, they lived the lives they wished. They lived out their dreams in eternal bliss or eternal pain or eternal strife or eternal love, for their dreams were their own and they were not bound to any law of the ark nor any whim of any other.

From *An Expanded Mythology of our World* by
May Then My Name Die With Me of the Ode clade

Tycho Brahe — 2346

The process of leaving the talks was one of emotion bound up in the stress of merging. As unpracticed as he was at forking, the process of quitting and reconciling memories was just as foreign to him. Ordinarily it would have taken an hour for Tycho#Castor to sort through the memories from Tycho#Artemis and then another two for Tycho#Tasker to sort through the memories from #Artemis for a few weeks' divergence.

These were not ordinary times.

The better part of eight hours later, he was singular once more, back in his field, back atop his hill, finally able to sit and think and dream without having the pressing weight of memories pinning him in place. He could lay on his back and look up at the sky—no longer just his sky—and think about all that had transpired and all that was yet to come.

At least for a little while.

He didn't know why the arrival ping did not wake him from his daydreaming, but the gunshot sound of a champagne cork popping was more than enough to get him to jolt upright.

"Sorry, Tycho," True Name said, laughing. "That was far louder than intended. I did not mean to startle you."

He frowned, shook his head. "It's okay. I wasn't expecting you, though," he said, holding out one of the red-filtered flashlights that were permanently lodged in his pockets.

The skunk accepted the light and knelt on the grass beside him, holding it between sharp-looking teeth as she poured two glasses of champagne.

Well, 'glasses'; they were shaped more like wide-brimmed, stemmed bowls than anything, somewhat awkward to hold, but then he remembered similar from the dinner party three weeks ago—so many years ago, it felt like—when the skunk and her cocladist, Dear, had lapped at their wine.

He shared a secret smile with himself as he accepted his coupe glass of champagne.

She removed the light from between her teeth and clicked it off again, touching the rim of her glass to Tycho's before taking a lapping sip. "To the end of that fucking mess."

He laughed as much as he felt was required to be polite and then took his own sip. *Why is she here?* he thought, racing through a list of the day's actions, hunting for anything that might lead to a visit. He was, he realized, still wary of her, despite the memories of her struggling, of her confusion, her tears. Despite all her small kindnesses.

After all, hadn't she chided them on the *History* being a 'very sensational book'?

The silence drew out. He looked up at the stars and thought about just how much bigger the universe felt now. *I feel every minute of that eternity,* Dear had said back at that same dinner. *I feel every molecule of that universe.*

And he did, now. He felt it all as something more real than it had ever felt before. The math now stood side by side with awe in a way that it had only ever eclipsed before.

"Do you know how old I am, Tycho Brahe?" True Name said into that silence. "I am 222 years old, a fork of an individual who is...who would be 259 years old."

He waited in silence. There seemed to be more to come, so he enjoyed his champagne meanwhile. It was quite good.

"I have learned many habits, and I have dropped countless

others. Perhaps that growth is our protection from unceasing memory. We may retain our memories of concrete events, of who we must have been, but I am no longer the True Name of 2124. Even remembering her feels like remembering an old friend. I remember her perfectly, and yet I do not remember how to be earnest. I do not remember how to simply celebrate. I do not know how to simply *be*."

Silence fell again while they both looked up to the sky. Nothing needed to be said right away, he figured. Something Codrin had said, though he didn't remember when: *silences come with their own rhythms and will break when it's time.*

Once he heard the clink of champagne bottle against glass again, True Name pouring herself some more, he said, keeping his voice as kind as he could, "Why are you telling me this? Why are you here?"

She laughed, set the bottle aside and shifted from her kneeling position to more of a lounge, hips canted to the side with her tail draped down the gentle slope of the hill. "I do not know, Tycho. I do not remember how to celebrate, but I still want to try, I guess. Fifthrace! I could never have imagined." After another few laps at her champagne, she sighed and added, "Sarah has gone with Codrin to Dear's, and I am not welcome there. Answers Will Not Help and Why Ask Questions are in conversation with another me. Jonas is...Jonas. Another me is talking with him and Turun Ka."

"So you came to me, of all people."

He was startled away from looking at the sky by the sound of a sniffle from the skunk.

"I'm sorry, True Name. That was–"

"No, you are right, Tycho. I know what I am and how I became that," she said, voice thick. "But I am feeling every one of my 259 years tonight. I just wanted to be with someone. Just...be, you know? Exist with someone without having some sort of agenda other than to celebrate something big."

"But you don't know how?"

"I do not know how, yes."

After a moment, he raised his glass, and the stars glinting off the rim clued the skunk in enough to once again clink hers with it. "Champagne under the stars is a good start, I guess."

She laughed. "That it is, my dear."

"I can't speak to your thoughts on not knowing how to be. I don't think I'm any better at it, honestly. Sarah would probably be your best bet."

"I will be meeting with her soon, yes. We have much to talk about."

"About the convergence?"

She shrugged, a subtle shifting of shadow. "That too, yes, but also, news from the three Systems has been distressing. Much of the clade will be seeking...well, therapy."

He frowned up to the sky, unable to think of anything to say to that that would not sound rude or patronizing.

"Our cracks are showing," the skunk continued in a far-away voice. "Growth is colliding with eternal memory, and the cracks are showing."

He nodded, unsure of whether or not she could even see the gesture.

"Turns out getting invited on a thousand year voyage with a bunch of aliens induces a whole lot of growth *really fast*," she said, voice brightening. "So I will be dealing with that. But come, if I share any more of my weaknesses, I will lose all of my hard-won respect. How do you feel about how things went?"

With that bit of humor, the walls were back up. The perfect self-deprecating comment brought back that tightly controlled voice. He felt a sudden sense of...honor, perhaps? He felt lucky that he'd been able to see some more vulnerable side of her, and he quelled the voice within him shouting that that was all a stage play for his benefit. Even she was allowed vulnerability.

"I'm not totally sure, yet," he admitted. "There was so much that I needed to deal with when I merged that it took me all day to do so, and I'm still trying to make sense of it all."

A slight rustle beside him indicated a nod from the skunk. "No kidding. You have seen how easily we fork and merge, so it might be telling that it took me nearly thirty minutes to even manage the merge from True Name#Artemis."

He winced. "I was wondering how that'd go."

"Rough," she said after a moment. "As soon as I got back to Castor, I immediately felt better, but no less tired. My memories of my time aboard Artemis are only just barely coherent. They are fractured and scattered. I could tell a clear story of our time there from start to finish, but much beyond that eludes me still."

Tycho set aside his empty glass and stretched out on the grass, laying on his back once more, arms crossed beneath his head. "I was worried about that, yeah. I can't speak to the ease of merging, but I'm glad you made it through all the same."

He could hear the grin in her voice as she said, "I am pleased to hear that. The distance between 'we are coworkers and should act as such while at work' and 'I do not actually like you but have to tolerate you' is rather small, and I could not tell which it was with you."

"I like you," he said, laughing at her easy humor. "You're a little terrifying, but I respect you."

"Doubly pleased, then."

"How do you feel things went?"

"As well as they could have," she said, the answer coming readily. "The talks were peaceful, the instances of mutual incomprehension minimal, and the outcome amenable to both sides."

"I think I hear a 'but' coming."

He could see the shadow of her nod. "Yes. But also, there are some aspects of them that I personally do not understand, and that is uncomfortable to me. They say that they do not manage sentiment or use much in the way of subtlety, they say they do not steer, and I believe them in that this is usually the case for them, but I disagree with the assessment that their checklist was a matter of preparation. They had goals coming into this convergence, and while I am pleased that they largely aligned with ours, I am unnerved by the fact that they either do not understand the ways in which they steer or, more likely, refuse to admit such. The two failed convergences they only ever talked around show this quite well. You have heard our thoughts on the utility of social pain in maintaining defense mechanisms, after all."

"Are you frustrated, perhaps?"

There was a moment's pause as the skunk shifted to lay down beside him. "I suppose. Frustrated, a bit sad."

"Sad?"

"Do you remember what the Bălans wrote about me and Jonas in regards to the Launch project?"

"That your aim was for stability and continuity."

"Yes. There is a self-serving aspect to this, as there must always be." She sighed, and he heard her shrug against the mossy ground. "The Artemisians and I share a goal of continued existence. I am pleased that we as a whole have been invited to share in that. I would call that a success."

"But you won't be able to join them, *anem*?"

She laughed. "Practicing?"

"I guess," he admitted. "I want to get used to the language."

"A good idea. But yes, *anem*. I will not be able to join them. I will not share in that particular form of immortality. I could join for the individual continuity, but not the individual stability."

"It didn't look like a pleasant time for you."

"It was not, no. I doubt that any Odist will join them."

A slow silence played, then, as they both looked up to the guesses at stars. The mention of information exchange that was to follow the convergence left him with a hope that some aspect of their library of technical know-how would allow a modification of the sim to lead to actual visual input from the telescopes to show, since the Artemisians could apparently access audiovisual data from within their system just fine.

"How are you feeling, my dear?"

He spoke dreamily, feeling far off, far away from this hilltop, from True Name and all her subtle unhappiness. "I'm on the cusp of something big. I don't know what it is yet, and I don't know why I know it, but I'm on the very edge of it."

"Looking forward to sending an instance along with them?"

"Yeah, I think that's a good bit of it. I'm finally looking forward to something. I'm finally eager, rather than just anxious."

She laughed, not unkindly. "I am happy for you, Dr. Brahe."

"Thank you."

The skunk sighed, and he was pleased to hear more contentment than frustration in the sound. "What do you think now? Are they real, or are we dreaming them?"

"I don't think it matters," he said after a long pause.

"No?"

"No. Even if they're a dream, I'll join them. Even if this was all a dream, I'm happy to have been a part of it."

"And have you any further thoughts on uploading as the stage of civilization most likely to breach the Great Filter?" She sounded earnest, almost excited. It made him happy to hear, made him excited in turn. "I must confess that the thought has been lingering in the back of my mind since our last conversation here. Old sci-fi dreams dog me still."

"Oh, definitely feeling like I'm stuck in some crazy science fiction novel," he said. "Uploading, furries, launch vehicles, and now aliens? At this point, why not? It makes as much sense as any of this."

She chuckled. "Well said, my dear."

When next she spoke, True Name sounded almost as dreamy as he had, her voice holding the subtle cadence of a recitation. "Calmest coldness was the error which has crept into our life; But your spirit is untainted, I can dedicate you still To the service of our science: you will further it? You will!"

He spent a moment searching the perisystem architecture

for the poem True Name had been quoting from since he first met her, the one with the lines that he knew he would speak before he left, but was not yet ready to.

That is a poem about death, she had said, all those weeks—and yet so few!—ago, and as he prowled through the lines, he could see how it was that she had interpreted it, how she had seen in the words the danger of being left incomplete in one's goals, of the risk of not being able to see something through to the end.

He was nothing if not a scientist, though, and although her reading, as one who dreamed in her own ways, was as accurate as his, he knew he had his own understanding of leaving a work unfinished so that others could pick it up. That was his dream, the dream of so many calm, cold scientists before him. It was a different take on the same dream, perhaps; where True Name might see regret in that error of calmest coldness, he saw only the comforting truth of his later science.

Or perhaps that coldness was her own, and for that he could not fault her regret, only wish her the best in finding future warmth, only further his service to his science.

Codrin Bălan#Castor — 2346

While it wouldn't have been totally true to call the celebration at Codrin's return 'wild', it was certainly rambunctious in its own delightfully Dear way, with dozens of foxes scattering around the patio in a flurry of forking. Plenty of hugging and chatting and laughing and smiling.

Ey'd been startled, in that half-doubled, roundabout way that an up-tree instance might feel, when ey merged down to find that True Name and Jonas had requested that Codrin#Assist stay at their compound rather than returning home except for an hour around dinner. The fox's excitement made more sense, knowing that.

At least ey'd had the chance to pull the fox's tail.

Once it calmed down enough to do so, Dear dragged Codrin into the dining room, gesturing eagerly for Sarah to follow with. Their partner had a small spread already laid out for them.

They spent the next hour recounting, carefully, the events of the talks. Codrin had requested that Sarah not discuss the Odists' reaction to skew until ey'd had the chance to do so one-on-one with Dear. They spoke instead in general terms, discussing the Artemisians themselves, the topics that had come up during the talks, and the final announcement that they'd be welcomed aboard as fifthrace.

"What is the practical result of this decision?"

"Well, the technical details are a bit beyond me," Sarah said. "But the Artemisians and our own engineers are talking about how to let the DMZ grow in size to some maximum capacity—maybe a third of what Castor has to offer. As many of them as want to join us within those limitations will be able to join us here. They will allow as many of us who wish to join them to do so, as well."

"We'll also be exchanging our shared libraries of information," Codrin added. "I think that transmission effort has already begun, actually. We're getting an enormous dump of information from four societies, and then we'll upload all of ours to them. It's going to be a field day for librarians, I bet."

"Think you'll join?" eir partner asked.

Ey shrugged. "I'm not sure, actually. It sounds fun, but I'm not sure I'm the same Bălan who wanted to be a librarian all those years ago."

"Codrin#Pollux has headed in that direction, though," Dear said.

"I know. I just don't know if the same is something I'd like to do. I've got some thoughts on directions I might head instead, though. I've been talking with Sarah about it, and will tackle it deliberately."

The fox nodded. *"Of course, my love. I would be surprised if you were anything but deliberate."*

Ey laughed and bumped eir shoulder against its own. "Of course."

"This is all so delightfully exciting, is it not? I was worried at first that the drama would be too much. Aliens! Political summits in space! Imagine." The fox giggled. *"And it was dramatic, I suppose, but it has settled down into merely exciting. Aliens, yes, but boundless new knowledge. Political summits in space, yes, but also a mingling of societies that we could not possibly comprehend."*

Sarah laughed and raised her glass. "To the proper amount of excitement."

Dear hoisted its own glass as thought it was an ale-filled tankard. *"Precisely, my dear!"*

Codrin smiled, sipping eir wine as ey watched. *Proper amount of excitement, indeed.*

After Sarah left, the triad sat around the table, saying nothing, simply processing this new future that lay before them. It felt almost too large for Codrin to comprehend. Something new. Something enormous. Something that felt somehow larger than the launches. Those, at least, had the advantage of being something that ey could predict, a frame of reference. Society continued much as it had before, after all, hadn't it? They had decamped from Lagrange for the LVs and everything looked exactly the same, minus only the few friends who had not done so.

This, though, held so many unknowns.

It was exciting, and that it was exciting to em bore excitement of its own. Something new, yes, but something different. Ey felt before em a vast landscape ey'd never explored. While the prairie always contained unknown spaces, it could not hold a candle to the future that lay before them.

Only one anxiety remained, then.

"Dear, can you come for a walk with me?"

The fennec sat up straighter. *"Of course, my dear. Now?"*

Eir other partner lifted their gaze from where they'd been staring at the table, zoning out. "Just you two?"

Ey nodded. "Please. There's some news about the Odists. About True Name, in a way."

Their expression grew sour and they waved them away. "Don't upset it too much, then. I've got plans for breakfast for dinner, and I won't have any moping over waffles."

Dear rolled its eyes. *"I will endeavor to be my normal, terrible self by then, yes."*

Codrin laughed. "We'll end on a good note."

They stood and walked out into the prairie, Codrin brushing eir fingertips across the tops of eir cairns as they walked. They made it past three before ey was able to open up.

"You were right to warn me about True Name and Answers Will Not Help."

Dear tilted its head. *"I thought Why Ask Questions was the emissary."*

Ey shook eir head. "They pulled some nonsense. Why Ask Questions was the delegate here on Castor, but they swapped in Answers Will Not Help for those who went to Artemis."

"Because of course they did."

"I'd call it cheeky, but it was more distressing than anything." Ey sighed. "They really didn't do well with the time skew at all. When we first got there, Answers Will Not Help collapsed, and True Name was only just barely holding it together. Even when we were in a unison room—places where time skew was locked into...uh, consensus, I guess—they kept...well, they looked like Michelle. Alternating forms, exhausted, distracted."

The fox splayed its ears, nodding. *"I did not know how they would act, but I am not surprised that those memories would come home to roost. I am sorry for them. I am sorry that you had to experience that so directly. Did it negatively impact the discussion?"*

Ey thought back over the memories ey had been left with from Codrin#Artemis, frowning. "Not necessarily, though we didn't learn as much as we had hoped, I think. Things just went poorly on their end. Very poorly."

Dear waited em out.

"Answers Will Not Help lost it. She quit."

" 'Lost it'?"

"She slowly got less coherent over time, but towards the end, she snapped and started hollering about prophets and quoting poetry. Bits of the Ode, bits of, I think, Emily Dickinson."

It frowned. *"And then she quit?"*

"Yes."

Eir answer must have been hesitant enough that Dear had picked up on the complications that lay behind that single word.

It pulled Codrin to a stop. *"My love, there is something you are not telling me."*

Codrin didn't look at the fox, choosing instead to stare out into the vast emptiness of the prairie. "There is, yeah. I don't know how to tell you without...I don't know. Without causing you grief."

The fox squeezed eir hand in its paw. *"If it causes me grief, then so be it, Codrin. These things happen. It sounds as though it will not be your fault, anyway. Do not worry about me."*

Ey nodded.

"Codrin?"

"In the middle of yelling about prophets, she said that she 'could not feel em'. She said the Name several times."

The grip on eir hand went slack, and when ey turned to face the fennec, its eyes had gone glassy, whiskers and ears both drooping.

"True Name tackled her to the ground, trying to shut her up. They struggled. Fought until Answers Will Not Help quit." Ey took a shaky breath. "So, now three others outside the clade know the Name. I don't think Sarah or Tycho know that they do, but I do."

Silence. Stillness from Dear.

"I'm sorry, Dear."

The silence continued.

"Do you want me to do as you did? Try and forget it?"

The fox let out a breath in a coarse gust, and ey realized that it had been holding it the whole time.

"Dear?"

"It is the end of an era, then, is it not?" it said, words enunciated carefully.

"I don't know." Ey squeezed its paw in eir hand, though no returning squeeze answered. "I don't know what to do. I can try to forget–"

"There is a pain — so utter — It swallows substance up — Then covers the Abyss with Trance — So Memory can step around — across

— upon it...Did she quote that one?"

Ey shook eir head.

"There is no forgetting, my dear. You bear it within you."

"All the same, I could–"

The fox's laugh surprised em. It was breathy, hyperventilating, but sounded almost relieved. *"No, Codrin. You do not need to. The poem continues: — As One within a Swoon — Goes safely — where an open eye — Would drop Him — Bone by Bone —"*

Ey was too anxious to puzzle out the opacity of the language. "I'm going to need some help disentangling that, Dear."

"There are very few times that memory can hope to be selective. When one is drunk, perhaps. Drunk on wine, drunk on love, drunk on pain. Perhaps when one is drunk on a life lived too long, as I am. It is the end of an era, and perhaps we are all becoming inebriated by too long a life. Do not forget it, Codrin. Do not do as I have done. It is stupid, is it not? Look at me. I am in all ways drunk on time."

Codrin smiled cautiously.

"Do not tell me, of course! I do not know what that would do to me, after all that I have done to myself. And certainly do not tell any other Odist. I do not want assassins visiting us in the night to shut you up," it said, laughing in earnest now. *"But also do not worry about your new knowledge. It is high time that we unclench our collective anus and let that shit go."*

Ey laughed as well. "Right, right. True Name suggested not telling any other Odists, too."

"Did she tell you to keep it from Ioan?"

Ey nodded.

"Ignore that. Do not tell em the name directly, but do send a clade-eyes-only message to em saying that you know. Tell em to pass it on to Codrin#Pollux, as well."

"Why?"

"So that you need not be the only Bălan carrying this burden. After all, we are in love, are we not?" It grinned, finally squeezing eir hand in return. *"We are in love and Ioan and May Then My Name are in love. We are bound together."*

"Aren't you worried we'd hold that over your head if we got mad or something?"

It shook its head. *"If you did, then we would not be in love, would we? I will write May Then My Name and the other Dear, as well, and tell them my thoughts."*

"Well, so long as you're sure that neither of them will snap and start hunting Bǎlans."

"The same applies to us, my dear," it said. *"If they snap, then they were not truly in love, but they will not. I have faith."*

"It sounds like you want to test all of our relationships."

"It is not a test. It is a game." It giggled. *"Come, my dear, this will be fun! The other two Odists will think so, as well, I promise."*

"A game, huh?" Ey let go of the fox's paw to poke it in the side a few times, hunting for ticklish spots. "You're so weird."

"A game! A game!" It laughed helplessly, then darted away from em, cavorting through the grass. *"A game! And you are it! Catch me if you can, you fucking nerd!"*

Codrin laughed and chased Dear around the prairie for a bit, the fox occasionally forking off to dart in some new direction, only to be followed by a new fork of the writer, until the prairie was littered with forks of them both. Each time one of em would tap one of it, both would quit until only two remained. They raced each other back to the house, nearly bowling over their partner at the door.

"Holy shit, you two," they said, laughing. "What the hell did you talk about out there?"

"When Memory is full," it shouted, dancing in circles around them. *"Put on the perfect Lid!"*

They rolled their eyes. "Uh huh, sure."

"Can we have eggs as well? And bacon? Bacon and waffles with syrup is a true delight."

"Sure, why not. Want some hash browns, too? Might as well go all out."

Codrin leaned in to kiss them on the cheek, still working on catching eir breath. "Yes. Definitely hash browns."

Tycho Brahe — 2346

Convergence T-plus 4 days, 20 hours, 18 minutes

"Who's idea was this?" Tycho asked, staring, unbelieving, at the heat-haze shimmer before him.

True Name grinned proudly. "A cocladist of mine came up with this. I would not recommend walking past the barrier. It is dreadfully hot beyond there, even for a desert creature such as her."

He shook his head, looking once more from the ground to the sky. They stood on a well trimmed lawn at the edge of a forest, the shade provided by lingering oaks and birches delightfully cool amid the just-shy-of-too-warm day. The grass continued right up to a shimmering barrier of heat, where it quickly failed, a no-man's-land of scrub lasting only a few feet before it fell away into sand. Deep desert stretched out as far as he could see before him. Rolling dunes, painfully blue skies, mirages dancing along the horizon.

So extreme was the temperature differential in so small a space that the barrier between the two, that shimmer of heat-haze, appeared to be a very literal wall extending as far as he could see in either direction, though after a few dozen yards, the forest crept right up to the barrier once more, impossibly dense, impassible.

And there, right in the middle of the clearing, sitting flush against the wall of heat, sat a low tollbooth. There was a glass-walled cubicle, large enough for one person to sit on a stool, huddling beneath a canopy, a small A/C unit gasping and rattling atop it. A red and white striped gate blocked a concrete sidewalk leading directly into the desert.

The whole affair was dusty and tired, as though it had weathered a hundred sandstorms and would doubtless weather a hundred more, though it would never be truly clean again.

To the side of the tollbooth, straddling the border, a squat, flat building sat, fronted by a sign declaring it to be 'Customs — Please Use Other Door'. From the roof, an aged radio tower reached toward the sky: a narrow pyramid of angle-iron painted in that same red and white. A light flashed sleepily at the top.

"You guys are really weird, you know that, right?"

True Name gave a flourish of a bow, laughing. "Of course, my dear. You will go through customs soon, but until then, please follow me."

The skunk led him up to the gate beside the tollbooth—a peek inside showed the hazy form of an older gentleman dozing within, chin resting on his chest. The gate lifted automatically, and when they walked through, there was the briefest rush of heat, the haze of the barrier washing over them like a waterfall, enough to dazzle the eyes so that they arrived at the courtyard he knew so well by now as though through a dream.

The space had been subtly re-structured, repurposed from a conference space to a small, comfortable plaza. The cloistered walk remained, as did the fountain, but the plaza itself had been made much larger, the trees spaced further apart, and comfortable seating of diverse shape spread throughout.

"This will be the entryway that those arriving to the DMZ will see," True Name said. "It is intended to be an area where the newly arrived can orient themselves, but also one that will be pleasant for those who have visited before. We are working with a few sim architects from Artemis to introduce a few mixed aspects of greenery and architecture to make it feel familiar to all five races."

"Are we going to keep calling it the DMZ?"

She shook her head. "That would not be a good look, no. We have a short list of names that we are in the process of work-shopping. The current top of the list is simply Convergence, though 'Gemini' and simply 'the shared space' are also in the list."

He shook his head. "Gemini doesn't fit. Tyndareus, if you want to stick with the Castor and Pollux names, but that'd make more sense for Lagrange. I like Convergence best."

"Convergence it is, then," the skunk said, chuckling and ges-turing him toward a shaded bench. "Beyond this area, how-ever, there is not much else. We have a smaller version of our compound already ported over, and I am pleased that you have agreed to let us bring your field over."

Tycho sat on the bench and leaned back against it, looking out into the plaza. "Nothing else, though?"

"Not yet. The border will open officially later today to mem-bers of both Castor and Artemis. The passage into Convergence from Castor will be rate-limited throughout this process. We will ensure that this area does not beggar the rest of the Sys-tem for capacity, as we were informed during the conference that the Artemisians all take up a bit more space than we do, as should probably be expected by five-thousand year old con-sciousnesses. Still, we are not hurting for space."

"Yeah, though thankfully they're not carrying around an entire five millennia of memory."

"Very true," she said. She gestured to the space before them, willing a small table into being, along with two glasses of iced tea, one of which she took for herself.

He took his own glass and sipped. It was quite good.

"Are you excited to join them, then?"

He sat in silence, drinking his tea and looking at nothing in particular from the dappled shade. Too many thoughts crowded his head, none of them worth thinking, and once again, an idea sat within his gut, demanding to be spoken. He savored it intentionally, rather than shying away from it as he had the last one. The feeling of these decisions was becoming familiar. *Trust your gut* indeed.

"Tycho?"

"I'm going to invest fully."

True Name blinked several times as she processed the statement, then grinned wide. "I would call that excited, yes. I am very happy for you."

"I don't know where the decision came from," he said, speaking slowly. "I *am* excited, yeah, but this just sort of came to me fully formed, like I'd made the decision before even thinking about it."

"It need not make sense. I am in no way surprised that you have made that decision, whether it was conscious or not. We will miss you, Dr. Brahe."

He smiled to the skunk and nodded. "Thanks. I'll miss you too. I'll miss all of Castor."

"No, you will not."

The phrase came at him like a blow to the stomach, and it was his turn to sit in silence.

"I think you will miss some people here. A handful of coworkers. What few friends you have admitted to having. Me, perhaps, as you say. But you will not miss Castor."

"Well, huh."

She shrugged. "This is why I am happy for you, my dear. You do not seem content with the life you wound up with. It is okay to want to leave unhappiness behind."

He nodded. "I suppose it is. Even then, I think most of my coworkers and friends are coming along with. Sarah will be there. Dr. Verda will be there. It sounds like even Codrin will join us for a time."

"I was surprised to learn that, as well," True Name said, leaning back against the bench with her tail canted to the side. "Ey has come to eir own decision, though. It makes sense for one such as em to send along a fork."

"Right. I'm sorry that you and Why Ask Questions or Answers Will Not Help will not be joining us. It'd be nice to have the emissaries together there."

"We will visit once more before Artemis leaves effective Ansible range, but no, we will not stay."

"Well, as I said, I'll miss you."

She bowed her head in acknowledgement, ears splayed.

"And you'll get to meet your fair share of Artemisians here, as well."

She nodded, smiling once more. "I will, yes. We will still have plenty to do, even if we do not remain aboard Artemis. We will visit there, and it sounds like some of them will visit here and not remain. Codrin has talked Dear into giving one of its performances in Convergence so that Iska may see, though they will not remain here."

"Oh? Did it say whether it would try to see one of their performances aboard Artemis?"

"It was undecided, last I heard."

"And the other delegates?"

True Name looked thoughtful. "I have not spoken with them since they left. My guess is that Turun Ka and Stolon will join. I know that Iska will not. I do not know about Turun Ko, but I would say that there is a good chance of it and Artante joining."

"Stolon said they would join, yeah," he said. "They want to make sure that they get to see more of the galaxy, and will happily spread themself out to do so. We'll still remain in contact with Artemis for years after the Ansible connection closes."

"You will not be able to see the galaxy from here, if you do not remain. Are you okay with that?"

"Yeah," he said after a long pause. "I think I am."

They sat in quiet, then, finishing their drinks and then watching the ice melt in the mellow warmth of the day.

Ioan Bălan — 2346

Convergence T-plus 39 days, 3 hours, 23 minutes
(transmission delay: 30 days, 14 hours, 36 minutes)

Ioan and May both awoke to messages. May, however, was the first to read hers, having gotten up before her partner, so when Ioan stumbled out of bed toward coffee, the skunk was already sitting at the table, her note before her and eirs still in its clade-eyes-only envelope, waiting for em.

"As soon as you are a real person, my dear, I need you to read this and tell me what is happening."

Ey frowned, nodded, and diverted from the coffee pot to splash water on eir face to wake emself up faster. Something about the skunk's attitude suggested something stressful was afoot. Stressful or exciting. Ey couldn't tell which.

Once ey sat down with eir coffee, ey opened eir letter and began to read.

May giggled. "What the fuck does that expression mean?"

Realizing that ey was frowning, squinting and chewing on eir cheek all at the same time, ey forced emself to relax. "Uh...this is weird. Does yours have something to do with it?"

"Yes. It is from Dear, who says that Codrin sent you a letter containing a game."

"A game?" Ey frowned, started at the top of eir letter and read straight through to the bottom. "How is this a game? Codrin says...but, well. What does Dear say, exactly?"

"My dear May Then My Name," she read aloud. "Ioan will be receiving a letter concurrent with this that will bear both the end of an era and the beginning of a game between our two clades. The rules are as follows. First: remember that you love em, that ey loves you. Second: remember who you were, who you are, and imagine what you can become. Third: let go. Fourth: have fun. Fifth: pass this on to Dear#Pollux concurrently with Ioan passing on Codrin's letter."

Eir frown deepened.

"Fucking foxes, I swear to God," May said, laughing. "Now, I am assuming that those rules apply to you, too. Remember that I love you and that you love me. Remember who you were, who you are, and imagine what you can be. Let go, have fun, and tell me what the fuck your letter says already."

Ey did eir best to square Dear's 'game' with the text of the letter ey'd received. There were so many ways this could go sideways. *Let go, hmm?* ey thought. *I guess there's nothing for it. Let go and try to have fun is about all that one can do in this situation.*

"Alright," ey said, holding up the letter to read aloud. "Ioan, I hope you are well. We have finished our talks with the Artemisians in grand fashion. They have invited us to become their 'fifthrace', meaning that as many of us as would like are able to join them on Artemis, and the DMZ will be expanded to allow a portion of them to join us. There is so much more that I can say here, and will say in future letters, but this one comes with a specific purpose."

"God, even when you talk to each other, you are nerds."

Ey forced a laugh, shaking eir head. "May Then My Name will be receiving a note from Dear about a game. I'm not entirely sure I understand it, but it promises me it's an Odist thing. When I think too hard about it, I get anxious all over again, but Dear keeps telling me to 'let go and have fun', so I suppose all I can say to you is the same...

"Uh, May," ey said after a moment's pause. "This is making

me really anxious, too. I promise I'm trying to follow Dear's rules and Codrin's suggestion."

The skunk's smile fell. "Well, please get it over with, then, and we can judge Dear on what it considers a game soon."

"Alright," ey said. "During the talks on Artemis, the time skew got to be too much for who we thought was Why Ask Questions and she lost it. It turns out that, through some design of True Name's, they swapped in Why Ask Questions When The Answers Will Not Help for the emissaries to Artemis rather than sending Why Ask Questions.

"Anyway, she snapped. She quoted several lines of the Ode as well as several lines of Emily Dickinson, talked about how she, quote, 'could not feel em', and then she said the Name aloud. True Name got–"

"*What?!*" May pushed her way up out of her seat and began pacing. "She did what?"

Ioan realized eir hands were shaking too much to continue reading the paper like that, so ey set it down on the table. "Ey goes on to describe what happened, but does not include the Name itself. Ey continues: While I now know it, I'm following Dear's suggestion to keep it to myself lest I piss off a bunch of other Odists. It described it as...well, ey continues, but you look like you're going to explode. Do you want me to stop?"

May's pacing had picked up in intensity and she had started compulsively brushing her paws over her whiskers and cheeks, up over her ears. Ey couldn't read her expression.

"Ioan, listen," she said. "Wait, no. Remember where you first took me for a hike? Bring me there again. Quick."

Ey frowned, stood, snatched up the letter, and took her paw in eir hand before stepping out to Arrowhead Lake, the wooded, mountainous sim ey had taken her several times over the years.

"You don't think someone's watching us, do you?" ey said, looking around at the placid water, the deer trail, the forest.

"No, but...well, better safe, yes?"

Eir frown deepened.

"Okay." She looked to be forcing herself to stand still, now, and her grip on eir hand only tightened. "I see what Dear is trying to do, and it is really, really smart. Please do not be anxious. At least, not of me."

Ey looked down at the letter ey still held in eir hand. "Well–"

"No, disregard the letter, Ioan." She laughed and added, "Or at least disregard it for now. There is info in there, I am sure, but the message is in the dynamic. Dear is an asshole, but a clever one. It has ensured that it doesn't re-learn the Name and that you never learn it for yourself, all while making sure that it becomes an in-joke between our two clades. It has removed culpability from the Bălan clade and given both itself and me an out, should someone like True Name come asking. She can come hounding you for information like she did after that first letter and all she would find is a clever little way for lovers to poke fun at each other. Let me guess, Codrin said something about how it feels like this is something a Bălan could hold over an Odist."

Ey blinked, lifted the letter, and read aloud, "I do worry that this is the type of thing a Bălan could hold over the head of an Odist, but–"

The skunk smiled, lifted eir hand, and licked the back of it affectionately. "You two are so predictable. But yes. I do not think we need to worry about that. You did not learn the Name, and Codrin#Pollux will not learn it, but it is enough that Codrin#Castor will not be crushed by the knowledge. It is a delightful strategy. Dear has suggested a move that will preempt most every compunction the conservatives might have. It even used your concerns over power dynamics as part of it. I bet it told Codrin to leave that bit in. It always was good at chess."

"But ey still knows–"

"Who the fuck cares about the Name?" she said, swinging eir arms playfully as she held onto eir hands. "It is a stupid hook. It is a way to make us seem more mysterious than we really are. What began as a way of protecting our friend's identity during a shaky political period turned into a way to control how we were perceived. It is our own personal MacGuffin."

"Wait, what? Really?"

"Yes, really. Obviously, I do not want to share it. Dear does not want to share it. We are still serious about not wanting to share it. Serious enough for one of the conservatives to assassinate one of our own, even. This is a dynamic that has arisen over time, though. The Name itself does not matter anymore. The bearer of it has been lost to time, and any reason to keep it confidential is lost along with em, but it became a hook, and then it became an identity."

" 'Em'?"

She winked.

Ey shook eir head numbly. "You're all completely nuts."

"Yes, well, tough shit. We have rules to follow, remember? I love you dearly, and I know you love me. I remember who I was. I was built for a purpose, and then I was a tool of True Name's. That is no longer who I am, though, is it? I have changed, and I can imagine who I will become. I can let go of this anxiety around names enough to understand what Dear is doing. And hell, it really is fun. You are stuck with me, Ioan Bălan."

"Yes, yes. Stuck with the world's most annoying skunk." Ey lifted eir arm up, nudging May to twirl, balletic, beneath it. "I don't totally understand, but I trust you on this. You can play your game all you want, but can we head back now? I left my coffee behind and you have therapy in a little bit."

Codrin Bălan — 2346

Convergence T-plus 10 days, 15 hours, 42 minutes

The decision to send a fork along to Artemis had gone over better than ey had expected. Eir partners had initially bridled at the idea of em—or at least an instance of em—moving on without them, but when ey explained that that fork would miss them dreadfully and could also quit at any time in case ey began to miss eir family too much, they relaxed.

"While I do not wish to see you test whether or not you will be able to get over missing us," Dear had said. *"I recognize the impulse to explore and advance one's own knowledge."*

"Oh, I don't know," eir other partner had responded. "I wish that Codrin the best of luck. Perhaps it will become a case of em picking another name and growing a new identity."

At that, Dear had clapped its paws. *"Yes! Yes, I can see that. Were that to be the case, my love, what name would you choose?"*

Ey had laughed and shrugged. "I don't know yet, but I think you may be right that this is an inflection point similar to the one from forty years back."

And so here ey was, up early one morning before both of eir partners—Dear had grumbled sleepily at em when ey slipped away—standing beside a cairn with a mug of coffee, thinking about changes and a future alone.

Codrin Bălan — 2346

I can quit when I want, if I need, ey thought. *If it gets to be too much, I need answer to no one and can quit when I want. That will be proof enough of my love.*

There were several weeks still within Ansible range, but something about this morning felt like now was the time for big decisions, for big changes. A dream, perhaps? Ey didn't remember eir dreams, but perhaps it was one of those ones that lingered beneath the subconscious, making itself known only through the acts one takes throughout the day.

Ey nodded decisively and dumped out the dregs of eir coffee, waving the mug away so that ey could walk without littering the prairie with dishes.

One step away from the cairn, ey forked, and a new Codrin fell into lockstep beside em. Each step after that, each footfall that hit the earth, eir new instance began to change, forking nearly in place to bring each change to reality as the two of em made their way to the next cairn out into the prairie.

Eir hair grew straighter, only some slight waviness remaining.

Ey lost a few centimeters in height.

Ey gained a curve to the hips.

Ey traded in eir pronoun, and she continued on in her contemplative walk with her down-tree instance.

A dozen steps before they reached the next cairn, they were joined on one side by a failing in the land, a meandering streambed—dry now, more of a wash, perhaps—that had not been there before the arrival of the Artemisians, nor even, ey suspected, before ey'd made this decision. Neither stopped to stare, overshadowed as it was by pending goodbyes, but Codrin thought back to that letter from Ioan so many years back, of dandelions in eir yard, of May telling em about the subtlety of the System, of Dear saying that perhaps this sim that Serene had designed might react to the dreaming of its inhabitants.

How long until a ravine forms? A canyon? ey thought. *How long until the rains carve away the land? How long until willows take root* and huddle around the wash until the water no longer dries up, but becomes a creek? A river?

There were so many changes bound up inside em—inside them both—and now, whatever subtlety the system bore had caught on and began to reflect some part of em. Something new. Something big.

Her skin grew smoother, softer, fairer as they walked; her cheeks grew fuller.

She adopted the Romanian skirt, *fotele*, and blouse ey'd worn to the talks as her own.

And with that last footfall, she chose a name.

All throughout, Codrin walked and thought. Ey thought about what lay in the future. Ey thought about the agency ey still held. Ey thought about the words ey'd heard about being anchoring, about being grounding. Ey thought about that crossing point ey'd visited with Sarah, about the plaza that lay beyond. Ey thought about foxes and love and home and eir own anchors.

By the time they made it to the next cairn and stopped once more, Codrin had made eir own decision, eir own changes, though none showed on eir form. Both of them stood, watching as the sun slowly crept up from below the horizon.

"Have you decided on a name?" ey asked.

"Sorina."

Ey smiled, nodding toward the sliver of sun peeking above the horizon. "Fitting."

"Well, not just the dawn," she said. "But I'll be leaving our sun behind in more ways than one. I'll be leaving *this* sun behind."

Codrin sighed. "That you will."

They shared in the silence, though they had to look away from the sun before long, instead scanning the far-running prairie. Codrin did eir best to drop thoughts of leaving Castor behind. Better, ey thought to focus on the fact that ey was staying, to rush individuation as much as ey could so that the weight of eir decision wouldn't rest on the both of them nearly so heavily. That had been the point of all of the changes, hadn't it? That had been the reason why ey hadn't chosen the name first, *anem?*

"Will you miss this place?"

"Yeah," she said, voice quiet and small. "I don't know how their ACL patterns around sim construction work. I won't port the whole sim—not the house, that'd hurt too much—but I may bring along a snatch of prairie. Enough to build a few cairns."

"And do you have an idea how long you might stick around over there?"

She shook her head, and ey could tell that she was on the verge of tears. They both were. Ey took her hand in eirs and gave it a comforting squeeze, though for her comfort or eirs, ey didn't know.

There was a sleepy ping against eir sensorium and ey looked back at the house. "Dear's awake."

Sorina kept looking out into the prairie, out away from the house.

"Do you want to come back and say goodbye?"

"I don't know, Codrin," she said, voice hoarse. "I really don't know if I can."

Ey nodded. "I think they'll understand."

"Yeah, I do, too." She finally turned to face em, smiling through her tears. "Do you think you'll even tell them you did this?"

"I don't know." Ey laughed and squeezed eir hand, tighter this time. "I don't know that I have that much sneakiness within me."

"I bet you could manage. You already have one secret to keep."

Ey sighed, nodded. "I suppose I do. Why don't you head out? I'll decide on the way back whether I'll tell them or not."

"Rushing me away?"

Shaking eir head firmly, ey wiped eir eyes against eir tunic sleeve. "If you stick around, I'm going to keep thinking about it and not let you go. Individuation will happen as it will, but I'd prefer sooner than later for your sake, if nothing else."

Sorina surprised em by hugging em tightly. Ey got eir own arms around her in turn, marveling at the fact that it was already a surprise. Perhaps she'd already changed more than ey'd thought. Or perhaps ey had. She felt like a new person, completely unlike emself, or even Ioan from whom they'd both derived.

Go, ey thought to emself. *Go and be someone new. Go and be whole. Don't let your grief define you, at least not forever.*

They stood in the prairie, holding each other as they cried their goodbyes.

She eventually leaned away, pressed an awkward kiss to eir cheek and said, "Pass that on for me."

Ey laughed and let go of her. "Will do."

"Pull Dear's tail, too."

"Naturally."

She bent down, plucked a stone from atop the cairn, one of the ones that marked directions explored and said, "For luck."

Then she stepped out of the sim. Stepped away from Codrin and home. Eir home, but no longer hers.

There was another, slightly more anxious ping against eir sensorium, to which ey responded with one of acknowledgement and began to trudge back to the house, trying to tamp down that sense of loss. Ey let eir eyes follow that new wash, tried to replace more complex feelings with wonder.

"Goodness, my love, are you alright?" Dear said, frowning at the sight of eir tear-slick face.

"Yeah, I'm sorry, fox." Ey pulled it in for a hug, passing on the kiss to the cheek as ey'd promised.

"Who was that you were talking with out there?"

Ey laughed and shook eir head. "And here I thought I was being sneaky. That was the fork heading to Artemis."

"Ey did not want to come in?" the fox asked, taken aback.

"She," ey said. "She didn't think she could and still leave."

There was a moment of quiet as Dear digested this. It finally nodded. *"I understand."*

Ey gave Dear a kiss of eir own and leaned back from the hug, waving another mug into existence so that ey could get a cup of coffee. "If I talk about this any more, I'm going to cry all over again. I'll tell you more about her later, alright?"

It sniffled, nodded. *"Alright, my love. I would like that. Can you at least tell me her name before we move on, though?"*

"Sorina. It has to do with the sun. She said she was leaving ours beyond," ey said, nodding out at the morning.

Dear laid its ears flat and stepped back a half pace, growling. *"Mx. Codrin Bălan, you are the worst."*

"What?"

"You cannot say things like that to a hopeless romantic! You will destroy them! They will collapse into a swoon. They will drown in their own tears. It is frankly irresponsible. Now, if you will excuse me, I am going to take a shower and cry my fucking eyes out for a bit."

Ey rolled eir eyes, leaning over to tug at the fox's tail before heading to the kitchen. "Welcome to the club. Go get your shower, though. Cry all you need, but no drowning, please."

It grumbled and stumbled off to the bathroom, setting up a cone of silence as it went.

"What was that about?" eir partner said from the bedroom door, looking somewhere between groggy and worried.

"Sent a fork to Artemis, made Dear cry. The usual. I'll tell you all about it later. Coffee?"

After breakfast, with both Codrin and Dear looking more collected, ey ushered eir partners to the couch, moving to stand before them.

"Are you going to give us a presentation?" Dear asked.

"Yeah, basically."

"Carry on, then, professor Bălan."

Ey took a deep breath, collected emself, and said what ey'd been practicing since ey'd started back to the house. "I have a proposition, and I suspect it'll be easy enough for you two to decide on, but I've been thinking about how this all started and my complaints about feeling dragged along on adventures rather than taking part actively. I want to do something. *Actually* do something."

Both eir partners sat up straighter, suddenly more invested than before.

Ey grinned to them. "Let's move to Convergence."

Dear blinked and laughed. *"Codrin, you are such a fucking nerd."*

"You mean the whole sim?"

"Of course. All that work on those cairns? Of course it's coming with. I want to show them the prairie." Dear leapt up to wrap its skinny arms around eir middle and ey shrugged as best ey could in the midst of a hug. "I want to show them what our home looks like. I want to see Stolon sun themself out in the grass. I want you both to meet Turun Ko."

Eir partner laughed. "Well, hey, I'm game."

"Will we move as forks, or invest entirely?"

"Don't care."

The fox leaned back and smirked up at em. *"Really? You do not care?"*

"Nope, don't care. I don't care if we fork and diverge. I don't care if the rest of Castor never sees us ever again. I don't even care if it's all a dream or the LV failing or whatever." Ey straightened up and nodded decisively. "That's my decision. I invite either of you to talk me out of it, but I warn you, it'll be tough."

"No, no," Dear said, leaning up to lick at eir cheek. *"We are both game. Let us pack up and move house. Or not! Let us abandon this place to rot and create a new house, a new prairie, new cairns. Littering! Can you imagine?"*

Ey laughed and poked at the fox's side, hunting once more for ticklish spots. "Who's the nerd now?"

"Any other surprises for us, Codrin? First Sorina, now this."

"One more, actually."

"Be still my heart!" Dear said, dancing away from the hug to twirl around em, forking to do so several times over.

"I asked Sarah to help me write up the events into another book, but while we do that, she's going to teach me more about therapy and what goes into listening more deliberately one-on-one. Not a huge career change, but a good one, I hope."

"Really? A therapist? You are not going to be a librarian with all this new knowledge?"

"Nah, leave that to the other Codrin. Leave it to the university." Ey laughed as the fox kept cavorting. "I'll take some classes, talk with Sarah, and see where it goes. Everyone kept talking about how grounding I was, and I liked that. I like just being with people and listening to them."

"You *are* grounding, Codrin," eir partner said. "It'll be a good move for you."

Ey grinned, caught the original Dear in the middle of a spin, and hauled the fox onto the couch with em.

"Do you have any other surprises up your sleeves? If you do, I shall simply have to growl and froth like a rabid beast."

"No, I promise that's it for now."

"Lame."

"Shush, Dear. What are our next steps, Codrin?"

Ey shrugged. "Ask about and see what goes into moving an entire sim into Convergence. Talk with Sarah. Start compiling notes. Ensure Sorina's settling in okay."

They nodded.

"And probably throw a party. Smaller than for Launch, just friends, but there simply must be champagne."

Ioan Bălan — 2346

Convergence T-plus 50 days, 8 hours, 16 minutes
(transmission delay: 30 days, 14 hours, 37 minutes)

While Ioan could not say that the changes in May since the therapy had started in earnest were dramatic, they were immediate. Just subtle changes in the way she talked, for the most part. Ey suspected that many of them would fade over time, but for now, ey was curious to watch the ways in which she would occasionally catch herself up short, reevaluate what she was in the process of saying, and then continue more carefully. Ey was also pleased to see her journaling, as the skunk was not one for sitting down and writing, preferring to keep everything in her head unless she absolutely needed to.

She was not a 'new May' or anything so grand, but it was a sign to em that she was working hard at what she'd set her mind to, and while ey hadn't doubted that she would, it was still heartening to see, just as it had been nice to see the depression slowly lift as promised.

Today, though, was a day for picnics. This was, ey was assured, a universal fact.

Once spring began to tickle at the nose and before the oppressive heat began to drift lazily in over the lilacs and dandelions, this was the time for those who are in love to drag a thick blanket out to Arrowhead Lake, park atop that rock by the water, and share sandwiches and fizzy drinks. This was the time for stretching out in the sun, laying back on the blanket, beside each other, hand in paw, sharing in small silences and comfortable conversation.

"What do you think of Codrin's grand gesture, my dear?"

"Mm? Moving to the DMZ? Convergence, or whatever they're calling it?"

The skunk nodded, turning her head to the side to poke her nose against eir cheek. "I am also curious as to your thoughts on Convergence, but tell me about Codrin, first, as a Bălan."

Ey laughed. "Well, alright. I think it was a pretty good one, all told. It was very...em. Bringing them together to make a formal announcement of 'we're moving to convergence' is an incredibly Bălan thing to do. Still, I'm glad ey was able to manage, and I think they'll do well there. Ey certainly seems to have enjoyed eir time with the Artemisians, so I'm glad ey's going to do more than just visit with them across a border."

"Really? Ey gave an actual announcement?" May giggled, giving eir hand a squeeze in her paw. "You are such fucking nerds."

"That's nerdy even for me, I think."

"Would it have been nerdy for the Ioan of twenty years ago? Or forty?"

"Forty?" Ey frowned up to the sky. "Good question. I don't think so. That Ioan was nerdier then than even Codrin is now."

"Makes me think that Codrin#Pollux was right about em," she said. "Ey had changed the least out of the three of you. Not that it was a bad thing, except in that it led to eir crisis of identity over the last few weeks."

"The whole of Castor seems to have been the most conservative of the three Systems. Codrin, Dear, and even True Name hadn't changed much at all from what they were like closer to Launch."

The silence that followed started out tense, then eased into something more deliberate, though ey couldn't put to words how ey could tell.

Eventually, May said, "Yes, it does seem that way. How is True Name, anyway? You have spoken to her more recently than I have."

Ey turned eir head to look at the skunk, who was looking up to the sky, a far-away look of concentration on her face.

"You really want to know?"

She glanced out of the corner of her eye at em, smiling faintly. "In my own way, yes. I am striving to see the humanity in her, even if I know that I may never be fond of her again."

Ey nodded. "To be honest, pretty awful. Much of the clade has dropped all relation to her. In Dreams didn't tell her about the therapy thing at all, so I had to tell her about it and suggest she contact Sarah directly. Plus, from what I can guess, she and Jonas aren't getting along nearly so well anymore. I wouldn't be surprised if she drops out of the whole guidance business entirely—or is pushed out by Jonas—in the next few years, though they seem to have the response to the convergence pretty well in check." Ey sighed and added, "I kind of made her cry."

The smile that May had picked up quickly disappeared and by the time ey finished, she was actively frowning. "It was not my intention to have her left behind. She needs this as much as the rest of us do."

"I know, May, it's not on you."

"I am trying to internalize that, Ioan. My empathy remains, even if the emotion behind it has transmuted. Empathy *and* sympathy, as I am sorry that In Dreams left her behind. I can still feel for her, even if I do resent her." After a pause, she added, almost to herself, "I do not like that I hate her, but I am helpless before that feeling."

Ioan leaned over enough to give her a kiss to the cheek. "You're a good person, May."

She surprised em by turning her head to give the very tip of eir nose a rather wet lick. "I am an utter nightmare and you know it, my dear."

"You can be both," ey said, laughing. "Even skunks can contain multitudes."

She beamed proudly.

"Different subject. Did Dear tell you about the other part of Codrin's decision? About Sorina?"

"It did, yes. What did Codrin have to say about her?"

"Eir letter read like someone struggling not to cry. Ey sounded crushed," ey said. "From the sounds of it, they were together only ten minutes and ey still felt like ey lost a good friend."

"That, and knowing some version of emself would never see her partners again. I think there needs to be a new word for the empathy one has for someone who is oneself and yet not," May said, nodding. "It is the same feeling I have for True Name. Ey is not leaving eir partners behind, and yet ey feels that empathy with Sorina, who is. I am not struggling with the same problems that True Name is, and yet I am not so different from her that I cannot share in some of that understanding."

"I'll have to start digging through etymologies for a good one."

"I swear to God, Ioan, you are a parody of yourself. Every time I think you cannot get nerdier, you one-up yourself."

Ey laughed. "Love you too, May."

After a luxuriously long stretch, the skunk rolled onto her front, resting her cheek on folded arms. This seemed like a good idea, given the ache starting in eir back from laying on a rock for too long, so ey followed suit, and they both settled into quiet, enjoying the sun on their backs and the sound of small waves breaking over pebbles below, of the stream not too far in the distance.

Ey could feel the doziness of a nice picnic and warm sun beckoning em to nap, but ey knew that ey'd wake up a pile of aches and pains if ey slept like this.

"Tell me a story, May."

"Mm?" The skunk sounded sleepy as well. "Okay. How true would you like it?"

"As true as you'd like," ey said. "Do you have another myth you could share?"

"When the second people met the first," she said after a long pause. "They found them strange and otherworldly. The way they thought, the way they lived their lives, all of it was strange to them. When the first people looked out on the world, they saw something different than what they themselves did. They saw more, perhaps, or perhaps they saw it more vividly. None could say.

"The second people did not know their own origins, and so they invented story after story to explain where they came from, and through countless years, first one story would take root and flourish, and all would believe that they had come from dust with the breath of life blown into them by a distant God, and then that story would fade and they would all believe that random chance and unchecked chaos brought together the right elements in the right way, the right conditions crushing them into the very beginnings of life."

Ioan watched as the skunk spoke. Ey was never sure how much of her stories were made up on the spot, were composed from existing ideas, or had been long rehearsed. All the same, it was entrancing watching her speak, that far-away look in her eyes as though she were seeing the story rather than the mountains or the lake.

"When the second people met the first, their stories collapsed around them like castles made in sand, as they realized that they were not the first, that they were not alone, or original, or unique, for did the first people not exist long before them? Did they not look out on younger skies?

"The second people watched the first, and when they talked to them, they only talked around the topic of origins, for surely the first people knew where they came from, and even if they did not, perhaps they knew where the second people had come from and could offer them hope in the face of death and surety in the face of uncertainty. And yet, what a sensitive topic that must be! How embarrassing to not know one's origins."

"Did they?" Ioan asked after May's story drifted into silence.

"When one of the second people finally screwed up the courage to ask one of the first people, 'Where do you come from? Where do we come from? What is our origin, our root?' they answered, 'We were hoping you could tell us'."

Ey laughed and ruffled a hand between May's ears before petting the fur back into order once more.

"Do you really suppose the Artemisians will look to us for answers?"

The skunk grinned, dotting her nose to eirs. "I do not see how they could not, my dear. Is that not what exploration is? Do we not both dream?"

Tycho Brahe — 2346

Convergence T-plus 49 days, 5 hours, 57 minutes

"I don't own a suit, and while I could have picked one up, it seemed like too much work for the occasion," Tycho said once the clock struck eight and he'd stood from his seat at the head of the table. "So the usual jeans and flannel it is."

Those gathered laughed.

They'd claimed a portion of the plaza for his last dinner, setting up a long table not too dissimilar from that which they'd sat at for the conference. He stood at one end, and at the other True Name sat, smiling and watching him rise for his speech. To his right sat Codrin and eir two partners, both of whom had spent much of the evening conversing with each other and the few scientists who sat to his left and the Artemisians beyond. He'd not missed the fact that they seemed to be ignoring the other three Odists as best they could other than to accept praise for the food they'd cooked for the occasion.

Those scientists included Dr. Verda and several of his other colleagues who had served as on-duty astronomer for Castor throughout the long years.

Beyond them, to either side of the table, sat a gaggle of Artemisians. Both Turun Ka and Turun Ko were there, despite not partaking in the meal. Stolon and Iska sat across from them and had both tried the various dishes to greater or lesser success. Artante Diria sat next to them across from Sarah Genet, and they had spent much of the meal talking with the quiet earnestness of those who shared a profession.

Beyond them, Sovanna sat across from Answers Will Not Help—a move that surely must have been intentional—and beside Jonas. Across from Jonas, Why Ask Questions sat beside the final guest, True Name.

The dinner had been his idea, and the speech True Name's. He'd balked at it originally, but in the end, she'd won out, convincing him that if he was headed to a place where he could forget, making his last moments on Castor memorable should be a priority.

Luckily, for all his nerves, he'd always done well at giving talks at conferences, and the two and a half glasses of wine he'd already had certainly helped.

"When it was suggested that I give a little speech before I go, I was at a loss for what to talk about. I mean, I guess I could talk about the stars or something, but I've bored enough of you to death already with that, and Stolon and I will have time enough on Artemis."

The thirdracer chattered their teeth, looking pleased.

"It wasn't until I realized that this would be something of a eulogy that I started getting ideas on what to talk about. I talked with Dear about it and it laughed and told me about some thoughts that it had around Launch. I didn't know any of them then, but apparently it and its partners had a Death Day party, and that's kind of what this is, isn't it? I'm dying to many of you, only to haunt you from beyond the grave with vague pronouncements about the heavens for a little while.

"Once I started thinking of it that way, I was able to come up with some better words for tonight, some of which I'll blame True Name for."

The skunk raised her glass to him.

"When we first heard from the Artemisians, True Name met me at my sim and quoted a snippet of poetry by Sarah Williams:

Reach me down my Tycho Brahe,—I would know him when we meet, When I share my later science, sitting humbly at his feet; He may know the law of all things, yet be ignorant of how We are working to completion, working on from then till now.

"See, Tycho Brahe is a name I picked for myself twenty years ago when Codrin interviewed me for the *History*. Brahe was an astronomer born eight centuries ago this year. A lot of his science was bunk, but that's what the poem says, isn't it? He may know the law of all things, but we're the ones with the later science.

"That stanza was quoted to me as a way of suggesting that we will learn from the later science of the Artemisians, and perhaps we'll have something to teach them as well, but also, as True Name noted, it's a poem about death, telling the final words of an astronomer to his pupil."

The mood had settled into somber, present, and while most eyes were dry, he could tell there was still sadness in there.

"I won't quote the whole thing, since it's quite long, but there's a few bits that I'd like to share with you before I leave.

"*There has been a something wanting in my nature until now; I can dimly comprehend it,—that I might have been more kind, Might have cherished you more wisely, as the one I leave behind.*

"Perhaps I should have cherished you all more while I was here. I really don't know. It's not in my nature to cherish people, for better or worse, but maybe I should have cherished my time here on Castor, or even back on Lagrange, more than I did. It was still home, wasn't it? I lived here. I loved what I did. *What, for us,* Williams writes. *Are all distractions of men's fellowship and smiles? What, for us, the goddess Pleasure, with her meretricious wiles?* Pleasure came second, and the fallout of that is that I was fundamentally unhappy, and thus perhaps unable to cherish.

"That's not to say that I won't miss you all. Some of you are up on Artemis already, and some more may join in these last few days before the Ansible shuts down, but no matter what, I *will* miss you all.

"It's just that, as the poem says, *I have sown, like Tycho Brahe, that a greater man may reap; But if none should do my reaping, 'twill disturb me in my sleep.* I'm headed off to newer places, to learn the later sciences at the feet of those who have been traveling for so long. I've done my work, though I've left it incomplete. Many of you will have much to work on to complete it. You must!

"In fact, I think the only thing I'm leaving behind that is well and truly finished to my liking is my sim, and even then, it sounds like perisystem engineers are working on getting visual transmission piped in."

There were some smiles around the table, but no laughter. All were focused entirely on him, and he had to force down a wave of embarrassment at his speech.

"I only have one more snippet of poetry to leave you with, something engraved on the astronomy building on campus, back phys-side. It will be my goodbye. It was the last thing I said on Earth, it'll be the last thing I say on Castor, and trust me when I say that those words made me dizzy the first time I thought of them. 'Last thing I say on Castor'. I'll cease being here. I'll cease being among a place that is all—or, now, a majority—my own species. I'll cease being on anything made around our own dear Sun.

"I could draw out such a goodbye, but I won't. Not more than I already have. You'll have your memories, won't you?"

He lifted his half-full glass of wine to the sky and, even as the other members of the dinner began to lift theirs, downed it in two coarse swallows. "*Though my soul may set in darkness, it will rise in perfect light. I have loved the stars too fondly to be fearful of the night.*"

Perhaps they toasted to him. Perhaps they said goodbye to him, calling out. Perhaps some of them did cry, as he knew he would if he stayed any longer.

He didn't know.

Before he could look, before he could listen, he set his glass down, turned on his heel and walked straight into the customs building, temporarily off-limits for tonight's event. His event.

Within, there was a small pedestal—one among thousands—that bore a plaque he'd read countless times by now: *Place your hand on the pedestal below and hold it there for ten seconds. This is a **transfer process** of the current instance, so please be sure to leave a fork behind.*

He did not leave a fork behind. He simply closed his eyes, put his hand on the pedestal, and waited, counting heartbeats.

There it was. There was the discontinuity.

There was that slippery feeling to time. There was that change in atmosphere, that change in pressure, that change in ACLs. There was that change in the way the very fabric of the world was woven.

There, too, was Stolon standing just outside the gazebo that served as the arrival point from Castor. Stolon and Sorina and Iska and Turun Ka and Turun Ko and Artante; they were all there, his own small welcoming committee. Beside them stood the rest of what had become the Council of Ten, of which he was now a part. Representatives of all those aboard Artemis.

And beyond them, crowds and crowds of others, milling around the plaza. Firstracers through fourthracers, and hundreds of humans—no, fifthracers, now—all of whom must still be learning their way around, being shown the ropes by the volunteer guides.

He stepped out into the cool night, and, as he had slowly grown used to, let Stolon butt their head against his arm in a friendly greeting. He couldn't do the same, given the height difference, so he'd taken to bumping a fist against the thirdracer's shoulder in response.

"*Nahi,* Tycho."

"*Nahi,* Stolon," he said, taking a deep breath of the now-familiar air.

"It is done, *anem?* It is finished?"

He nodded and smiled. An earnest smile. A true smile.

He'd finally done it. He'd finally done *something.* This future was his. Even if it was all just a dream, it was *his* dream. His dream of stars to make of it what he would.

We will dream of stars, Stolon had said, and he knew they would.

Epilogue

And still, they dream.

From *An Expanded Mythology of Our World* by
May Then My Name Die With Me of the Ode clade

AwDae — 2114

The world had long since begun to blur, to sag. It had shifted from some known sense of realism to something unknown, some watercolor painting with too much medium, or perhaps an impressionist's pastels, smearing the boundaries between one thing and the next.

It was not as though ey could not see well, for if ey dedicated enough energy to the act of seeing, the act of looking, then everything was as in-focus as it had always been.

Rather, it was a sense, a sensation, a way of moving through the world that implied that *this is how it must be.* The utilitarian furniture. Eir sparse apartment in the S-R Bloc with its grimy wallpaper and mountainous views. Eir tea cup and kettle. Eir dreams. All of it was slowly losing coherence, and ey could not tell whether it was a natural process or something new brought on by all of the therapies and the two exploratory surgeries.

They had poked around in eir brain, had they not? They had dug through eir mind. They had explored eir dreams. They had delved through memory and found the choicest bits. They had plumbed the depths of eir creativity.

Ey did not know what they did. They would explain, and perhaps ey would understand, perhaps ey would not. It did not matter, none of it mattered.

All that mattered was the promise. All that mattered were the occasional glimpses into some subtle mirror that only ey experienced. All that mattered was a new thing.

AwDae—for that is what ey requested they call em moving forward—had been flown from London to Belize. From Belize to Ontario. From Ontario to Addis Ababa. From Addis Ababa to Beijing. From Beijing to Vladivostok. From Vladivostok to Yakutsk, and from there, finally, ey was driven North, North, North, and then West.

Ey did not know where ey was and, ey was promised, the hope was that no one else would either. There would be a confusing trail of visas, flight records, and brief conversations spotted here and there until ey was elsewhere, until ey was nowhere. A nowhere safe enough to stay. A nowhere ey was allowed to send one final message to Sasha, whom ey loved above all else.

The briefing, once ey had reached the compound, had lasted days.

The System engineers—so vague a name as to keep discussions impossible to trace—had been toiling for nearly a year on achieving the dream of countless futurists. They had been looking into what would be involved in moving a mind to some newer reality. Some reality built of the minds that inhabited it.

It had begun as a way to spread humanity through the 'net, and when their ethicists had warned them that inhabiting a place so ridden with terror and danger would be cruel, they had narrowed their goal to this new world. A mirror world of all the meaning ey could dream of and more.

They had been trying for nearly a year to build such. Avenues: many.

Perhaps they could read, over time, EEGs, EKGs, PETs, CATs, MRIs, however many scans they could manage, stream them in real time into a computer prepared to take them and turn them into a new person, or maybe the same person but different, running within a simulated room.

No luck. They were not enough of a person. Missing was proprioception. Missing was sanity. Missing was enough of a mind to be called a personality.

Perhaps they could map the neurons in a body and set them to running in concert, studying and building and creating and dreaming until it would become a person entire. They began on cadavers, and then on one unlucky living soul destined for death by choice and countless sheaves of paperwork

This was too much, too much. There was no way to simply emulate process after process in any reasonable fashion. When they did manage it, it was a simulation of a perfectly working body. It was not a mind. It was not a Person. They had written papers on it, gotten them published, and then moved on to explore new tacks.

Perhaps they could combine the two. Perhaps they could build a map of a system and also mesh it with scans. Perhaps, perhaps...

And yet while this creation of theirs was close to a person, it fell short as it crashed ceaselessly into strange loop after strange loop. There was no world in which they could place it wherein it could live happily.

No luck, no luck.

And here is where the lost came in. Here is where they were able to take a core dump and investigate it for the ever-changing, ever-evolving state of a delved-in personality and, on finding it, push it into being. The core itself wasn't enough—Sasha's core, ey had been told—and so they repeated this process with another of the lost yearning for death.

Presentation after presentation ey watched through watercolor-smeared vision, through surreal touch and surreal hearing.

Ey could feel that death creeping, even before ey had taken all eir flights. Ey could feel the way it stole minutes from em, borrowed hours and never gave them back, draped languidly over days and made them inaccessible.

Eir promise, eir promise...

Eir promise to emself. Eir promise to Sasha. Eir promise to Carter. Eir promise in quiet whispers over the still warm but unalive body of Prisca. *I decided against it,* ey told emself, awaiting dreams. *Truly decided: I made a conscious decision to stick around, remember?*

But the pet lost the scientists had begun with, they were madder than em, and ey was too mad to see in anything but smeared paint spelling out the language of the mad, to see in language that dripped from eir tongue in studied ink, to see in language that fell in sooty tears from eir eyes.

Their pet lost ran better than any other of their simulations before. There had been a glimmer there. A few milliseconds before the crash. A few milliseconds of life. There had been a swelling in the System. Bits and bytes and countless drives worth of data swelling and growing and they could tell that a burst of creativity had been blown into the memory of the computer—if computer it was—that was destined to be this new world.

And then, truly free, the mind had ceased to exist. It had craved death too much, and in one final act of destruction, a creation in its own right, it plowed through all of that creativity and deleted it. It wiped the computers and, through some unknown manner, reached back down the line to the machines used to create the emulation, and corrupted all of their data and scans and neural maps in turn.

Perhaps, perhaps...

You are it, they promised. You are next in line. You are the one who can do it. We have faith. We believe. More, we desire nothing else for you, for we are dreamers. Success and political advantage were in the realm of politicians, were in the realm of managers like Prakash. That was their arena. Ours is the arena of hope, of triumph, of wishing the best for you, and our success will be one of pure pride, pure joy.

This will hurt, they promised. This will hurt and you will die, they said. You will die as we map every synapse within your brain as fast as we possibly can. We will map them as your body dies, tearing through your brain at the speed of n thoughts per

x, where n is some sufficiently large number and x some unimaginably small unit of time.

It will hurt, and you will die, and you will be awake to experience it, and we will do all that we can to ensure that hope remains within you, as it flares within us.

And so ey waited and ey dreamed and, when Prakash visited the compound, ey walked with him and spoke in poetry, wrote odes to the end of death and let them drip down eir chin, staining eir clothes and hands black with an ink that ate the light hungrily, gorged on it.

Ey knew that ey was quickly losing the ability to make sense, to speak in anything beyond those too-heady words, the ones that tumbled around inside of eir mind, doing their best to crush meaning.

And so they upped the time-table, and so today was the day, and so ey followed them to a clean room and let emself be sterilized, and so ey dressed in a sterile gown and a sterile mask, and so ey lay on the table with eir head face down in a donut-shaped pillow, just as ey had when receiving eir implants some forever ago.

They pierced eir spine with a needle that brought with it a final transformation into a world painted with words.

They cut through skin.

They cut through bone.

And then something new happened, though ey knew it not: ey fell asleep. Not anaesthesia, a true sleep. A real sleep. Real rest. Ey fell into a dream, an endless dream of foxes and skunks and prairies and mountains and shores and words and some purer love.

And then that dream unrolled before em, clear as day, clearer than any painting, clearer even than the waking world. Silver of the finest quality spread around the inside of eir being and what was left of em reflected that world back in on itself, and memory became the plate-glass atop it, protecting it, binding it to circuitry and computronium. All because of eir promise, eir promise...

And, though ey knew it not, ey died.

And, though the scientists knew it not, ey gave everything ey had, everything ey was, all of eir memories, all of eir hopes and dreams, all of eir desire and anxiety, all of who ey was, to this final act of creation, and felt, with each new meter-kilometer-megameter-gigameter of silver and plate-glass ey laid into being, ey gave of emself, gave thought, gave dream, gave up what it meant to be alive, what it meant to be a mind, what it meant to be a person, and knew only what it meant to be a world.

And, though ey knew it not, for knowing is not a thing a world can do, days passed and the world persisted beyond eir death. Weeks passed and another mind was added. Another. Another still. Champagne corks were popped, managers and politicians celebrated, scientists cheered.

Sasha cried, Debarre cried, Carter cried.

And, though ey knew it not, more came, and those who came earliest spoke of a presence they could not name, first to each other and then, when the text line was provided, to the world outside. A presence that loved loved loved what it had done and what it had become and refused refused refused to let it go, to let it stop. A self-sustaining System that was not built for death.

And, though ey knew it not, it was decided by managers and politicians to try and remove this presence, to make the world a blank slate, for ey was not supposed to be there, was not supposed to have been there, never never never. But it stolidly refused and, against the demands of those managers and politicians, the scientists nurtured it instead, whispered into its ear their sweet nothings in lines of code and helped it grow into the world that it was to become.

And thus grew the System, a world that was not built for death.

And thus grew a new world, ready to someday secede, ready to someday divest, ready to accept a humanity beyond humanity, ready to welcome those from beyond the stars. It was a world ready to accept however many subtle schemes. It was a world ready to accept truths and lies and all the gray areas that lay between. It was a world for skunks and foxes and Romanian historians, a world for dandelions and lilacs and fields and prairies and mountains and forests and cafes, a world for penance and pride, for so many tears and so, so much love.

And thus died the Name.

And thus grew a new world.

Acknowledgements

Thanks, as always, to the polycule, who has been endlessly supportive, as well as to Sandy, Kergiby, Fuzz, Nenekiri, Rugger, and many others who helped with reading and keeping me sane along the way.

Thanks also to my patrons:

$10+ Fuzz Wolf; Mx. Juniper System; Kit Redgrave; Orrery; Petrov Neutrino; R. Reed; Sandy; Sariya Melody

$5 Junkie Dawg; Lhexa; Lorxus, an actual fox on the internet; Merry Cearley; ramshackle

$1 Alicia Goranson; Ayla Ounce; Donna Karr (thanks, mom); Katt, sky-guided vulpine friend; Peter Hayes; raxraxraxraxrax; Ruari ORourke; Yana Winters